Acknowledgements

Thank you to Dad, Mum, and my extended family, especially Tim Wilson, for all your support. To my wonderful friends, especially Christina Jones for your beautiful cover quote and Fee Roberts for being the first person to buy each of my books and telling everyone about them. Thank you to the wonderful team at Accent Press, especially my brilliant editor, Cat Camacho, and Stephanie Williams, Beth Jones and Hazel Cushion. Thank you to the Jersey Writers, Novel Racers and Romantic Novelists' Association and to all my other supportive writer friends, especially Liz Fenwick, Karen Clarke, Kirsty Greenwood, Jennifer Joyce, Jane Risdon and Gilli Allan. Thanks to Tess Jackson and Andrea Harrison for letting me talk endlessly about my books; to Kate Troy Goddard and Rachael Troy for being there with chocolate when I needed it and Jason and Chris Troy for letting me brainstorm ideas with them. To Courtney McCann and Lorenzo Marcotullio for their wonderful feedback – keep it coming.

A very special thanks to my lovely Max who was always with me while I wrote my first two books in this series and above all, a big thank you to my lovely husband Rob and my children, James and Saskia, who have had to put up with me spending huge amounts of time staring into space and to whom I dedicate this book, with much love.

Chapter One

'I hope you're phoning to tell me you've arrived safely?' Olly asked, his tone willing her to confirm that she had.

'Yes.' She blew her nose once again, wondering why she always felt the need to phone him every time she became too miserable. 'Nothing awful has happened since you dropped me off at the airport this morning and I haven't changed my mind about being here, if that's what you're worried about.'

'Good. Now stop snivelling and go and search for an Italian bloke to take your mind off Jeremy.' He was silent for a moment. 'Look, I know you think all your dreams for the future have disappeared,' he added gently. 'But you'll make more.'

Paige supposed he was right, but it was difficult to imagine her life without Jeremy in it. 'You never really liked him much, did you?'

Olly cleared his throat. 'I just never pictured you as a trophy wife; you're far too ambitious for that. Anyway, he was too flamboyant, always having to drive expensive cars and wearing bespoke suits.'

'I suppose so,' she thought back to her plans for her wedding. 'He was only saying the other day how well his morning suit was coming along for our wedding. I still can't quite believe it's not going to happen.'

'Yes, well one of these days you'll be grateful for him calling it off. Not every man is full of his own self-importance with a need to show everyone how successful he is. Look at me for, instance.' He laughed. 'Go on, get out there and find someone new.'

'Surely you don't seriously expect me to be interested

1

in anyone after everything that's happened?' She slumped down on the balcony chair conveniently placed under the ivy-covered pergola, grateful for its shade from the midday Italian heat. 'I suppose his family must be delighted he's replaced me with someone more to their taste socially.'

'Don't be such a drip,' he said. 'So what if they are? You couldn't stand his snooty mother; she was always comparing you to posh exes of his. Anyone would think that idiot was worth keeping. Now get off your bum, put on a pair of your more colourful sandals, then go and explore Sorrento.'

'Fine, but if I can't find something to wear that doesn't make my bottom look the size of a Shetland pony, I'm not going.' Paige glanced at the yellow shift dress she'd just dropped onto the bed and wished she hadn't bothered packing it.

'You'll be back in Jersey soon enough, moaning about wasting your trip. If nothing else, you can get inspiration for your next set of designs.'

'You've been talking to my sister, haven't you?'

'How can you tell?'

'You don't know anything about women's shoes and I've never heard you say the word sandal before,' she laughed.

'Clem's worried about you. I had to stop her from racing round to Jeremy's house and giving him hell for jilting you.'

Paige chewed her lip guiltily. She should turn to Clem before Olly, but worried about upsetting her sister further and anyway, Olly had been her best friend for so long that she was used to confiding in him. She thought back to how strange it had seemed when her sister and Olly first began dating. She was used to them being together now though and hated to think that her distress at being jilted might make them feel awkward for being so happy and in love. Her one-person honeymoon had been the only good thing to come out of this wedding mess. She still couldn't believe she'd had the nerve to come alone to Sorrento. 'I need time to think.'

'A break-up is always hard and it's only been a week since everything happened. You'll be fine, though, I just know it. Once you've had time to recover from the shock, I bet you'll come back here and be ready to focus on your shop again.'

He was probably right, but it was still a little difficult accepting that Jeremy had changed his mind about their marriage and she hadn't seen it coming. Then again, at least now she understood why he'd been acting so strangely recently. So much for pre-wedding nerves.

'Paige, are you still there?'

Had Jeremy turned to Gretchen because she'd spent all her time thinking about future designs for her shoes, like he'd said?

'Stop dwelling on that jerk,' Olly shouted, interrupting her thoughts.

'Ol, you're the perfect best friend and always ready to listen to me.' She couldn't help smiling, he knew her so well and she hated the thought that her situation was causing upset for those closest to her.

'Probably because you don't often moan about things,' he laughed, his voice sounding tinny down her antiquated phone. 'When you get back we can spend time working on the new website designs. I've had a few new ideas that should perk it up a bit.'

'Good. I know the one I have now isn't nearly stylish enough for the image I want to project.' She brushed a fly off her ankle.

'Never mind that now. You go and make the most of that incredible place.'

'I thought I'd have a look at the shoe shops here and see how their designs compare with mine.'

'You see?' Olly laughed. 'You must be feeling a little

better, because you're thinking about your shoes. Right, I'll put some ideas together while you go and mooch around Sorrento.'

'Thanks Ol,' she said glancing towards the window and staring at the rays of white gold light filtering through the metal shutters.

'Good, now get out. I don't want you back in that room of yours until it's time for you to go to bed.'

'OK, I'm going, but I won't enjoy myself,' she teased before replacing the receiver onto the eighties-style phone.

Paige picked up her red clutch bag, slipped on the matching shoes she had designed to complement it, and set off toward the confines of the old town. Treading carefully along one of the narrow roads, she breathed in the scent of oregano from the spice-filled air. This was more like it. She walked down the steps from the back garden of the hotel, at times holding on to the handrail especially where they tilted away from the cliff face. She stopped and concentrating on not looking down, stared across at the spectacular view across the sea to the other side of the Bay of Naples.

She gripped on tightly, watching her every step and breathed a sigh of relief as she reached the small supermarket at the beginning of the main thoroughfare. She was a little surprised to see so many designer shops dotted along on both sides of the road. Forgetting her nerve-wracking walk down there, she paid particular interest to the shoe shops and thought about the rumours her father had shared with her before her fateful meal with Jeremy.

What if her dad was right about De Greys? It had cost her a great deal to rent a concession in Jersey's largest department store, and she didn't think she would be able to afford to open another shop so soon after moving to King Street.

Paige stepped into the road. Catching her heel on the

edge of the pavement, she tripped, just as a car she hadn't noticed before skidded towards her. Closing her eyes she waited for the impact of the car bonnet, but hands seemed to come from nowhere, catching her under her arms, pulling her out of the way. She didn't understand what her rescuer was saying to her in the confusion, but managed to regain her footing with his help.

'Grazie,' she said smoothing down her skirt and taking her bag when he picked it up and handed it to her.

She went to say something else, but the immaculate hero smiled briefly, said something, and pointed to indicate that he had somewhere to go. Then he was gone among the crowd of pedestrians passing her by. Paige didn't want to know if anyone else had seen her reckless attempt to cross the road, so stopped to gaze at the closest window display while she gathered her senses. It dawned on her that none of the shoes in this particular shop had designs as quirky as her own. She could see the prices were similar to those that she charged and the shoes were beautifully made. Paige walked in.

'Buongiorno.' She gave them her friendliest smile and, trying to remember the sentence she'd looked up in her Italian for Idiots book, said, 'Um, vorrei consentono alcune scarpe.'

The shopkeeper and his wife laughed. Paige cleared her throat, that wasn't the reaction she'd hoped for. Wishing she'd had the sense to bring the book with her, she tried to recall how to say the phrase correctly.

'I think you probably mean, vorrei comprare delle scarpe.' A girl Paige assumed must be about fifteen said from the other side of the shop, her amusement obvious on her pretty face.

'What does that mean?' Paige asked.

'I want to buy some shoes.'

'Actually, I wanted to talk to you about maybe selling some of my shoes.' Paige laughed. 'What did I say then?'

The girl repeated what Paige had said to her parents and then turned her attention back to her. 'You said you would allow some shoes.'

Paige pulled an apologetic face at the older couple and shook her head. 'Ahh.'

She explained that she was a shoe designer and was looking for outlets in Sorrento to stock her pieces. 'I have pictures of some of my stock,' she said locating the photos on her phone and showing them.

They looked at the phone screen for a minute and then the girl looked down at Paige's feet. 'These are yours?'

Paige nodded. 'Would you like to have a look?'

The girl nodded, waiting while Paige stepped out of them and handed them to her. She gave one to the man and they both studied them attentively. 'I love this tiny 'P',' she said, pointing it out to her father. 'It is a pretty shape.'

Paige looked at the nouveau-shaped letter that she incorporated onto the back of each of her heels. 'Thank you. I have them on all my designs. Try the shoes on, they're really comfortable, despite having fairly high heels.'

The girl kicked off her flip-flops and slipped her tanned feet into the shoes, immediately growing four inches in height. 'Bellissima,' she cooed.

By the time Paige left the shop, four inches shorter in the shop assistant's worn flip flops, she knew that even if the shopkeepers never contacted her again, or ordered any of her stock, at least the young girl had a fabulous pair of shoes to show off to her friends, as well as leaflets advertising her website. Maybe word of mouth would secure a few extra sales?

It was amazing how well people could communicate when neither spoke much of the other's language, she mused as she walked along the road to find the famous gelato parlour where Gina insisted Sophia Loren had sampled the world-famous ice cream. She pushed her small notepad into her bag and tucked it under her arm. She'd taken the first step to making contacts in Italy and now she was going to treat herself. This might not be the honeymoon she'd been expecting, Paige decided, but at least the day had been eventful and she had something she could laugh about with Olly when she spoke to him later on the phone.

She arrived back at the hotel a little footsore, but happy. Maybe it had been a good idea to come on this trip, after all. She kicked off the flip flops and sat on the edge of the bed to rub her feet. She needed to make a few notes about improving those shoes. Her mission had always been to design shoes that made a statement, while being comfortable for the wearer, and the ones she had worn to go into the town were not as good as she could make them.

Paige resisted the urge to phone Olly and tell him about her successful afternoon in the town, instead she left her room and walked through to the front of the hotel, determined to find one of the two terraces depicted on the hotel website. Paige sought out a cushioned chair on the higher one and stared at the spectacular view across the bay of Naples.

'Wow,' she whispered, marvelling at Vesuvius rising up from the turquoise sea in the distance.

'Would madam care to order something?'

Paige relaxed back into the chair. 'A glass of rosé, please,' she said to the waiter.

She decided she deserved a bit of pampering and would have bought a bottle of champagne, but she couldn't bear to waste it and wouldn't have drunk the entire bottle by herself.

She was going to have to get used to being a singleton again. If only she hadn't needed Clem to look after the shop for her, she would have loved to share this fantastic place with her sister. The whole reason they had planned the wedding to happen this week was because Clem could get away from university to attend and then look after her concession at De Greys while they were on honeymoon. She sighed. She wasn't going to think about Jeremy, or the wedding right now. Paige closed her eyes for a moment, concentrating on the shops she'd visited that afternoon.

The waiter soon came back and placed her glass and a small carafe down on the table in front of her. She watched him pour the pink liquid into the glass. 'Thank you,' she said, signing the chit. Paige took a sip, it was delicious. She swallowed, relishing the coolness as it slipped down her throat.

Standing up to take yet another photo of the view, Paige smiled at the thought of Olly's dislike of looking at other people's endless holiday pictures. She sat back down, inadvertently knocked her handbag off the metal table and onto the tiles. She grabbed the chair, trying not to overbalance, and reached out to retrieve her bag, but her left foot shot forward on the slippery surface, sending her shoe flying toward the geranium-filled window boxes at the edge of the balcony. 'Argh.'

'Here, let me get those for you,' said someone with an English accent from behind her right shoulder. Paige twisted round, squinting into the setting sun to see the owner of the melodious voice that seemed vaguely familiar. 'Celebrating alone?' he asked, with a hint of barely disguised amusement, she noted.

He retrieved her shoe and she slipped it back on her foot. 'Yes, in a way, I am,' she said, wondering if she knew him. 'Celebrating, that is,' she raised her eyebrows and shrugged. 'And, in fact, alone.'

'Are you OK after your mishap in the town earlier today?'

'Pardon?' She frowned. Had he seen her trip?

He smiled and indicated a seat on the other side of the table. 'May I join you?' He raked a hand through his well-cut, almost black hair, and looked a little less self-assured than he sounded.

'I'm not sure I'd be the best company right now,' she said, not wishing to offend him. She shielded her eyes from the glare of the sun. Then it dawned on her where she'd seen him before. 'You're the one who caught me when I fell over. I thought you were Italian.'

He smiled and held out his hand. 'Sebastian Fielding.'

She stared at the well-tailored sleeve in front of her, as her eyes slowly recovered from staring up at the sun. 'Thank you, Sebastian. Please, sit down.'

His mouth lifted in the barest imitation of a smile. 'If you'd rather I left you alone to enjoy some peace, please tell me. I won't be offended.'

'No, it's fine.' It wasn't this guy's fault she was anti-men at the moment. She had forgotten not all of them were scheming pigs. 'I'm sorry. I'm not normally this unfriendly,' she said, wishing to make amends for her unnecessary rudeness. She watched him pull back the chair next to her and sit down. It occurred to her that his piercing blue eyes, coupled with his intoxicating aftershave could do an awful lot of persuading to an unsuspecting female. Not that she thought for a moment she could be so susceptible.

'I travel a lot,' he said, his clipped English accent not matching his Roman good looks, 'but it's always more enjoyable to have a conversation with someone rather than drinking alone, don't you think?'

Paige nodded.

'Would you like another drink?' He indicated her near empty glass.

'Yes please.'

He ordered and then looked out over the terrace wall. 'It doesn't matter how many times I visit Sorrento, I never tire of this view.'

'It's my first time here,' Paige admitted, wondering what he was doing here by himself.

They sat in silence for a minute or two. The waiter returned with their drinks and Paige held up her glass and smiled. 'Thank you,' she said before taking a sip.

'For what?'

'For this,' she said, holding up her glass. 'and for catching me this afternoon.'

'My pleasure. Are you here on holiday?'

'I'm on honeymoon alone, because my fiancé has decided in his infinite wisdom that he now prefers my best friend. I'm Paige Bingham, by the way,' she said, aware she hadn't actually introduced herself yet.

'Ah,' Sebastian widened his eyes. 'Not too sure what to say to that scenario.'

'Nothing much you can say really.' She wished she had not been quite so quick to open up about her private woes. 'Anyway, I'm putting all that unpleasantness behind me.' She stared down at her glass. 'Or that's the plan, anyway. Here's to a new beginning.'

'Yes, and it would be hard to find anywhere more atmospheric than Sorrento in which to start again.' He touched her glass lightly with his own. 'I'm here on business,' he said. 'As my meetings today have been a little better than I'd expected, I was wondering if you'd like to share a bottle of champagne with me?'

Should she, Paige wondered, suspecting her feeling of intoxication was due more to his presence than the alcohol she'd consumed so far. She thought back to Olly's insistence that she get out and enjoy herself and surely having a few drinks with Sebastian would be a good way to start? 'I don't see why not.'

Chapter Two

Sebastian caught the attention of the waiter. 'A bottle of the Laurent Perrier Rosé, please,' he said, turning and smiling at the woman in front of him. He must have been even more wound up about his earlier meeting not to have noticed how pretty she was when he'd caught her in the town. 'What an unexpected pleasure meeting you today.'

Paige looked down at her feet before looking him directly in the eyes once again. She was so lovely, but Sebastian didn't think she had an inkling as to how alluring she was. She seemed to be struggling for something to say and the sadness in her green eyes made him want to cheer her up. 'How long are you staying in Sorrento?'

'Two weeks,' she replied. 'You?'

'About the same.' He'd have to remember to send Linda an email as soon as he had a moment to try and clear some time in his diary. Now he'd met this intriguing girl, he was determined to get to know her a little before they went their separate ways.

'Are you here alone, too?'

He nodded. 'I am, but I've pretty much wrapped up everything I needed to do here.' Maybe this was what his secretary had meant when she suggested taking time off work and relaxing. He'd never seen the point of it before this evening.

'You could enjoy a bit of a holiday.'

'I don't take many holidays,' Sebastian admitted. 'To be honest, I can't remember the last time I travelled for pleasure.'

'So this is all work then?'

He shrugged. 'Initially, yes, but I've almost concluded my meetings here. I can now take the next ten days or so to enjoy some of the sights this place is famous for.'

'Everyone should find time for themselves. Don't you agree?'

'I do.' Hell, she was lovely. He couldn't take his eyes of her beautiful face as she smiled at him warily. How could anyone jilt this alluring creature? 'Is that what you're doing?'

Paige laughed. 'Only because my bossy friend insisted I should. I usually spend most of my time either working or thinking about it.'

'Then I'm glad your friend persuaded you to come.'

Paige nodded. 'So am I.'

'As it's your first time here, will you let me introduce you to the best that Sorrento and Naples has to offer?'

She took a sip of her drink and peered over the rim at him. 'Are you sure?'

Sebastian couldn't hold back a laugh. 'It will be fun for me to have someone to show around, and I'd hate you to return home having missed the best sights.'

She visibly relaxed. 'In that case, I'd love to join you.'

'Great. Shall we start by eating dinner out here this evening and you can tell me all about the places you had in mind to visit?' He would have loved to take her to the old town for a meal, but hadn't missed seeing her grimace and rub her feet earlier when she'd thought he wasn't looking. He would simply have to wait until tomorrow.

'Yes, I'd like that,' she said after a little hesitation.

'Should we meet down here at, say, seven thirty?'

'Perfect,' she said, a little awkwardly, before walking over to the stairs.

He watched her climb up to the first floor. 'My key, please,' he said to the receptionist, as he retrieved his

12

mobile and quickly emailed his secretary, asking her to call him as soon as she was free. It was late, but she never seemed to mind him contacting her.

The phone rang almost immediately. 'Linda, thanks for calling me back. How is everything coming along?'

'Your lawyer called to confirm that the due diligence for the buy-out is almost complete. There are only a few financial queries left to input on to your spreadsheet, but I'm waiting for those to be sent from the FD of the company. He's assured your lawyer we'll have them by start of play tomorrow.'

'Fine; as soon as you've collated all the information, forward it to me and I'll have a look. Copy in Sir Edmund to keep him in the loop and give him the chance to put forward his comments, should he have any. We don't want any excuses for a delay on this.' He waited for the receptionist to hand over his key and nodded his thanks to her. 'What's my work schedule for the next ten days?' he asked, making for the lift.

'The usual weekly meetings.' He could hear her tapping away at her keyboard. 'You have a few calls lined up, and you wanted me to set up a meeting with the President of the Chamber of Commerce in Jersey in the next few weeks. However, he's away at a conference, so I haven't been able to finalize anything with his PA yet.'

'Perfect. I'd like you to clear everything from my diary for the next week and a half. Apart from the conference calls, I'll conduct those from here.'

Linda didn't reply for a moment. 'Will you book the meeting rooms with the hotel?'

'Yes, I'll do that when I get to my room. Clear everything else though and book the Jersey meetings. The latest I want these to be held is three weeks from now.'

He'd been working on this takeover for months and once the due diligence had been completed and everything was in order, then he would have to set up a temporary office in Jersey. He would have to work hard to implement his way of running the place with the staff. He knew from experience that this was when the battles would begin. Finances he could deal with, it was people's emotions that caused delays and unforeseen difficulties.

Seb sighed. He didn't mind people standing up for what they believed in, it was their right after all, but each time he conducted a takeover there always seemed to be people who thought they knew better. He wondered if he would ever work on a business where the employees realized that their concessions had declined to such an extent that the only chance of survival was to do things his way.

Linda interrupted his thoughts. 'I'll change your flights back from Italy to the UK and email the itinerary across to you.'

'Great. I think that's it. I'll give Sir Edmund a call tomorrow. If he asks to speak to me, you can tell him I've taken a short break.'

'He'll be relieved. Your uncle always says you work too hard.' He could tell by the tone of her voice that she was pleased he was taking a little time off work.

Sebastian laughed. 'That's rich coming from my uncle, the original workaholic.'

They followed the maître d' to their table. 'You look lovely,' Seb said as soon as they were seated. 'Did you have a relaxing couple of hours?'

'Yes, thank you.'

He waited for the waiter to hand them both a menu. 'Do you have a preference for wine?'

Paige shrugged. 'Not really. I'm happy to go with what you decide.'

Seb looked up at the waiter. 'A bottle of your 2003 Pio Cesare Barbaresco, please.'

'I don't think I've tried that before,' Paige said, looking a little unsure.

'If you don't enjoy it, we can choose another.' He watched her for a moment. 'You mentioned you wanted to visit Pompeii and I was wondering if you'd like to go there tomorrow.'

'I'd love to,' she said smiling. 'Is it far from here?'

Seb shook his head. 'Only about a half hour drive. I have a car here, so it won't be a problem.'

'Have you been to Italy many times?'

'A few, but each time I come here, I discover sights I'd missed the time before.'

'I can't wait. I mustn't forget to take my camera. Olly will be expecting to see photos of everywhere I visit.'

Seb wasn't surprised there was a man in her life somewhere. They gave their order.

'Do you have family here?' asked Paige.

Sebastian laughed and shook his head. 'No, my mother's family originate from Northern Italy.' She seemed satisfied that her suspicions were correct. 'What were your reasons for choosing Sorrento?'

Paige thought for a moment. 'It always looked so romantic in photos and I thought it was,' she looked away from him, 'well, the perfect place for a honeymoon.'

'Sorry, that was tactless of me.' Sebastian winced. 'I should have realised it was an insensitive question.'

'No, not at all. I don't even know why I reacted like that. I suppose, it's because I still can't quite believe that only a week ago I thought I was getting married. It was so unexpected.'

'I can see why you needed to get away then.' He studied her pained expression, angry with her ex-fiancé on her behalf.

Paige smiled at him. 'You look so serious. Please don't concern yourself with my dramas, I'll be fine. I'm tougher than I probably seem.' She looked out across the bay.

Sebastian rubbed his chin. 'Then it's up to me to make sure you have the perfect holiday. The first thing we're going to do is forget your ex ever existed. He obviously doesn't deserve you.'

Paige glanced up and stared at him. Her gaze made his stomach clench with desire. 'Thank you. You're very kind.'

'I wouldn't be too impressed with my actions, watching you experience these incredible sights for the first time is a great incentive.'

'I suspect you'd be just as sweet if I was an ugly old lady.'

'Really? Are you sure of that?' Sebastian narrowed his eyes but couldn't refrain from smiling.

Paige laughed. 'Maybe not, but you've made me feel much better, so I'm grateful.'

'Don't be. My motives are entirely selfish,' he admitted. 'Let's eat. We need to keep our strength up if we're going to see all the attractions I intend showing you.'

'What are those?' asked Paige the following day, stopping to stand on one of the large stones and gazing down the ancient street to the side of her.

'They're ruts from the wheels of the Pompeians' carts. Incredible to think we're able to see these centuries after everything was buried.'

'Yes,' she whispered. Pompeii was far more impressive than she'd hoped and being there with Sebastian, who was making everything so much fun, made it even better. It was a little unnerving to feel this comfortable with someone she hadn't known twenty-four hours earlier.

He took her hand securely in his, leading her across the rest of the stepping stones and down a narrow street. Jeremy had rarely held her hand, so it was an unfamiliar sensation, but she couldn't help thinking how natural it felt to have her hand in his.

'This courtyard looks as if the family have only left

minutes ago,' he said shaking his head slowly. 'It's hard to imagine they relaxed here so long ago.'

Paige touched the crimson wall. 'The colours are still so vivid.' She pulled gently on his hand with her free hand so that he stopped. Sebastian turned to face her and let go of her hand. 'Thank you,' she said. 'I really needed this.'

'It's been a pleasure.' He looked serious for a moment. 'I've enjoyed it too.' He bent his head down slightly, stopping, as if he'd realised what he was about to do. He turned to focus on the painted wall in front of them. 'Actually, I should be the one thanking you.' He smiled at her.

'Whatever for?'

'For reminding me there's more to life than work.' He began walking again. 'Come along, there's a lot more I have to show you, and I know this great little café where they do delicious iced coffees.'

Paige trailed behind him enjoying her view of his tight bottom in his faded jeans.

Sebastian looked over his shoulder at her and grinned. 'Are you not paying attention to my tour?'

Paige grimaced, aware that she'd been caught out. 'Yes,' she fibbed, taking in how perfectly his white T-shirt showed off his taut back. She was going to have to be careful to guard her feelings against this man. What the hell was she thinking, only yesterday she was upset about Jeremy. She studied Sebastian silently once more. If only she'd known him before now, maybe she wouldn't have wasted so much emotion on her ex.

Sebastian stopped abruptly, and Paige slammed into his hard body. 'Ouch.' She rubbed her nose.

'Are you OK?' he turned and taking her face in his hands inspected the damage, concern obvious on his face. 'Does it hurt much?'

'Does your back?' She tried to sound light-hearted to hide her embarrassment and wiped the tears away from her streaming eyes.

He shook his head. 'No, I'm fine. Come here,' he said, his voice tender. He pulled her into a hug. 'You're so refreshing to be around.'

Paige frowned, wincing in pain. 'I am?' She wasn't sure that was the impression she was trying to give him. She would have rather he thought her sophisticated.

'There's nothing wrong with that, surely?'

'Are you laughing at me?'

Sebastian pulled a scared face. 'I wouldn't dream of it.'

She slapped his arm. 'Stop teasing me.'

'I'm sorry,' he said putting his arm around her shoulders and leading her down the road once more. 'How about that coffee? Maybe we could have some cake too?'

She tilted her head. 'It sounds tempting.'

He took her across the road to the café, and after she'd pointed out the cake she wanted to try, Sebastian ordered their coffees and led her to two seats at a table outside where they could watch the visitors coming and going from the entrance to the Pompeii site.

'I don't know how you drink that stuff,' she said, pointing at his double espresso. 'A latte is strong enough for me.' She took a sip of her drink. 'So tell me, what exactly do you do for a living?'

Sebastian shrugged. 'I work for my godfather. He has various interests, which is why I travel so much.'

'And he has business over here, too?'

'He does.'

'Which is why you're here now?' She took a sip from her drink, just as a thought occurred to her. Breathing in sharply, the latte went down her throat the wrong way. She cleared her throat.

Sebastian patted her on the back. 'Hey, are you all right? I seem to be causing you more pain than anything else today and that really wasn't my intention.'

Paige nodded. She tried her best to catch her breath,

18

drinking a little more to clear her throat. She noticed he was watching her. 'What?'

'You look thoughtful. What's the matter?'

She gazed at him trying to reason with herself. How well did she know this man? Would she have been so quick to accept his invitation to dinner, and now to Pompeii, if he hadn't been so incredibly handsome? There was something about him, a power he exuded but seemed unaware of.

'What?' He frowned.

She looked around to check that no one was in earshot and then leant in closer to him. 'You're not in the mafia, are you?'

'Excuse me?'

She could see he was trying not to laugh at her. 'You heard me.'

'Why would you think that?' he whispered, the amusement in his voice obvious. 'Do I look like I'm a member of the mafia?'

'You do, actually,' she said thinking of the gangster films Jeremy enjoyed so much.

Sebastian gazed across at the ruins thoughtfully. 'Is this because I mentioned working for my godfather?'

Paige, not trusting herself to speak, nodded.

He lowered his head a little. 'No, I'm not.' Paige looked up at him, not looking convinced by his assurance. 'Really, I'm not. The only business my godfather,' he lowered his voice and smiled, 'who is also my uncle, has over here is with property. I needed to sign some paperwork on his behalf, that's all. Nothing dodgy about it, I can assure you.'

She felt a little awkward. She was sure he was being honest, and now she'd probably gone and ruined their day by accusing him of taking part in criminal activities. 'Look at that,' she said, desperate to change the subject. She pointed at a small church perched on the edge of the hill that had been cut away to reveal the ruins tens of feet beneath. 'How odd must it be to live up there and look down on all this? It's like a huge graveyard really, isn't it?'

Sebastian looked in the direction of her focus and then back at her. 'It's all right, you haven't insulted me, if that's what you're worried about.'

She turned to him, his tanned face untainted by sarcasm, or annoyance, and she believed him. 'Sorry, but I had to ask.'

He smiled at her, kindness exuding from his dark eyes. 'I know, and it's fine.'

Paige smiled. 'Phew, that's a relief. I thought for a moment there that you'd resigned as my tour guide.'

'Not a chance.' He raised his cup. 'Here's to our Italian tour continuing for as long as possible.'

'I'll drink to that.' She took a drink from her coffee cup, and looked at him out of the corner of her eyes. 'Are you busy tomorrow, or will you be able to show me more of the sights?'

'I have an early conference call to make, but my diary is pretty clear. Maybe we should have a quieter day. We can investigate the small shops in the old town and then have lunch down in Marina Piccolo.'

'I like the thought of eating there.' She wondered if he was making the time to take her to all these places, and felt a little guilty that the notion pleased her. She was supposed to be devastated by being jilted. Surely she couldn't recover from Jeremy's actions so quickly? Then again, the shock of him jilting her had subsided a little, and now all she could muster was a deep anger towards him for being able to lie so convincingly to her.

'I've got a busy day after tomorrow, but then things should ease off. I thought maybe I could buy tickets for us to take the ferry across to Capri.'

'I've always wanted to visit Capri. I hear the views are

awesome, especially from the old town palazzo.' She tried to hold back from giving away too much of the excitement she was feeling. 'Maybe we can have lunch up there, my treat as a thank you for you showing me around.'

He laughed. 'You don't have to do that.'

She narrowed her eyes, determined not to let him pay for everything. He'd already insisted on paying for last night's meal and the tickets for the ruins of Pompeii. 'No, it's my turn to pay for something. You bought these, don't forget.' She motioned towards the coffees, and the plates displaying their impressive slices of cake that the waitress was placing on their small metal table.

'Fine, but then I'll want to arrange for us to take a taxi for a tour to see the Blue Grotto.'

She nodded. 'Sounds perfect.'

Chapter Three

Paige ate her breakfast and stared silently out of the dining room window overlooking the mist-covered roofs of the ancient town by the Bay of Naples. She didn't know if it was being away from her recent disappointments, or simply the time she'd been spending with Sebastian, but whatever it was she felt sure that inside she was beginning to heal.

She watched a cruise liner drop anchor off the Marina Piccolo, imagining the excited passengers setting off to explore the tiny cobbled streets, and wondered if the cruise her parents had booked on the Queen Victoria would be docking here. Dad would love this, she thought. She spotted a clock in a coffee shop, and remembered she was taking a boat with Sebastian to Capri in an hour's time. She would have to hurry, if she wasn't going to be late to meet him.

'Good morning,' he said, standing up to greet her as she hurried into the reception area.

'I'm not late, am I?'

'No. The ferry goes back and forth several times throughout the day. It's only in the evening when we have to keep an eye on the time; otherwise we'll be stuck there until the following day.'

Paige straightened her top. She'd decided to wear linen trousers and a baggy blue top to keep cool. 'It's hot today,' she said, plonking her floppy straw hat on her head.

'Loving the hat,' he said.

'It's not too much, is it?'

He led her outside. 'You're a hard woman to

compliment,' he said. 'I wouldn't say I liked your hat if I didn't.'

'Don't you ever lie?'

He shook his head. 'Not if I can help it.' He motioned for her to walk ahead, when the pavement became too narrow for them to walk side by side.

'Never?'

Sebastian shook his head. 'Why the surprise, do you lie?'

'No, of course not, but in my experience, men find lying infinitely easier than women do.'

'That's a matter of opinion,' he said smiling at her.

Paige shrugged. 'OK, so maybe not you, but I definitely know some who find it easier to lie than tell the truth.'

'They sound despicable,' he laughed.

'They are,' she agreed, pushing a picture of Jeremy from her mind.

Paige insisted on standing at the back of the boat on the way to Capri.

Sebastian stood next to her, leaning against the edge of the railings and stared out at sharp rocks emerging from the Aegean Sea ahead. 'I think you're going to love it there.'

Paige breathed in deeply, relishing the salty air. 'I can't wait. What are we going to do first?'

'You'll have to wait and see.'

As their boat drew closer to the island, she could see varying sizes of white homes clinging to the side of the steep hills rising sharply from the sea. 'It's magnificent.'

'It is.' Seb said.

She turned to smile at him, wondering for a moment if he'd meant the island, or her. She hoped it was the latter. She'd woken with butterflies in her stomach at the thought of seeing him this morning, and hated to think of this idyll ending. He had the personality and looks that could break hearts, and she was going to have to be wary and not allow herself to get carried away with the magic of being here with Sebastian. It was far too soon after being jilted, especially as she knew she could no longer trust her instincts when it came to men.

They waited for the ferry to dock and Sebastian took her hand to help her off the boat and onto the dockside. 'Where would you like to go to first?' Paige asked, pushing aside her concerns, impatient to start exploring the island.

'We're going with him.' Sebastian pointed over at a red fifties drophead Cadillac. 'He's taking us in his taxi to the Grotta Azzurra, the Blue Grotto. I thought you'd like to see that first.'

'Yes, please.'

The taxi driver welcomed Sebastian by shaking his hand and giving him a brief hug. 'Signor Fielding, is good to see you again. And this must be your beautiful Signora.' He opened the door for them, and waited for them to get settled.

Paige sighed. This was like a dream. She settled back against the warm red leather interior, and looked across the wide back seat at Sebastian.

He leant an elbow on the ridge of his open window. 'You approve?' He smiled.

She nodded. 'I do.' She rested a hand on his leg. 'You ready to leave?' Their driver squinted in the bright sunlight in the rear view mirror at Sebastian, who nodded.

Paige was relieved that the car moved off instantly, the force of the acceleration momentarily pushing both their heads backwards. Sebastian laughed, and her awkwardness forgotten, Paige did too.

The taxi slowed down once again and the driver settled into a gentle speed. The vehicle purred around the coast. Paige gasped at the first of the sheer drops on her side of the car. 'I never realised Capri was so enchanting.'

'You haven't seen anything yet,' he said, leaning his head back and closing his eyes for a moment.

She focused on her surroundings. Who knew if she'd ever be lucky enough to visit this magnificent place again? She glanced at Sebastian, surreptitiously grateful to be kept busy, so her troubles back at home in Jersey didn't sting quite so much.

The driver pointed out properties where famous people had lived as they drove by. She wasn't sure who Gracie Fields was, but seemed to recall her father mentioning the name. She must tell him about this place. As they rounded a sharp bend, the dramatic cliff side came into view, and Paige couldn't help comparing it to the north coast on a hot summer day in Jersey. How many times had she and Jeremy walked along the cliff paths when they were first seeing each other, she wondered. They even had a spot where he'd dreamt of building their perfect home. Not that they could have ever afforded to do so, but it had been fun to make plans, however improbable. She closed her eyes for a few seconds. Maybe, just maybe he had done her a favour? Olly had never overly liked him, despite being polite whenever the two had been in the same room together.

'Are you OK?' Sebastian asked, snapping her out of her daydream.

Paige forced a smile. 'Yes, of course.'

He thought for a moment before speaking. 'It's just that sometimes, these high roads can be a little unnerving to people who have a problem with heights.'

Paige shook her head. 'No, it's magnificent. I was just thinking, that's all.' She pushed away the thought that she should be sharing this ride with her husband, but rather than upset her as that thought probably should have done, she couldn't help feeling happy to be spending today with Sebastian. The realisation made her a little uneasy. How could she be so fickle? She was positive she'd been in love with Jeremy just over a week ago. Was she still in some sort of shock since discovering he'd been sleeping with her friend? She wasn't sure, but it made her question how she could have ever truly loved him enough to get married, if this was how she felt right now.

'If you need someone to talk to, I'm a good listener.' He shrugged. 'Most of the time.'

Paige laughed. 'No, it's fine. Thank you though.'

She focused on the view as the car descended the steep hill. The turquoise blue of the sea was enticing and made her long to kick off her shoes and cool her feet in the sparkling ocean, but more than anything she wanted to forget Jeremy existed, at least for today.

The car wove its way down the narrow roads until they reached a beach and stopped. 'Thank you,' said Sebastian as he stepped out of the car. 'Will you collect us in about an hour please?'

'Si, enjoy the grotto.'

'This way,' Sebastian winked at her. 'I think you'll like it here.'

He took her to a small boat and helped her climb in. Paige sat in the middle and waited for Sebastian to step past so that he could sit behind her. 'I'll never forget the first time I visited this special place.'

Paige couldn't hide her excitement. 'I've never visited a grotto before. Well, apart from Santa's one at the garden centre near my parents' home, of course.'

Sebastian laughed. The sound was deep and made her smile. 'I hope you won't mind not finding any elves or fairies in this one?'

'What? No Santa either?'

He narrowed his eyes and shook his head. 'Nope, sorry.'

'I'm not sure if I want to bother going there then.' She rested her hands on her hips.

Sebastian took her by the arm and laughed. 'Too bad.

27

This fine gentleman is the pilot who'll be taking us there whether you like it or not. Eh, Giorgio?'

'Si, Signor Fielding, the grotto it is unique and very blue.'

Paige widened her eyes and pulled a face at Sebastian. 'It seems that I have very little say in the matter.'

The boat was almost touching the cliff, but still Paige couldn't see an entrance. 'How will we get in?' she asked hoping she wouldn't have to get wet.

'Like this,' he indicated the chain attached to the side of the cliff. She watched as the pilot stood up and grabbed hold of it. 'Now, um, lie back against me,' said Sebastian, gently pulling her back against his lap.

Paige automatically stiffened at the unfamiliar closeness with this man she hardly knew and pushed her sunglasses up on top of her head.

'It's so you don't hit your head on the way in.'

She lay back down against him, trying not to think about where her shoulders were and gasped as the boat shot forward under the low stone arch. 'Wow,' she said, her voice echoing in the cavernous space and forgetting about Sebastian as she sat up. The coolness of the interior after the heat of the sun outside was welcome on her skin. She stared at the sharpness of the rock all around them as visitors in nearby boats spoke to each other in awed, hushed tones.

Leaning to one side, Paige looked down at the bright blue water all around them. She had never seen a colour like it, it was as if someone had dyed it. 'The water really is a perfect blue. How do they do that?'

'Apparently it's the reflection of the water from the sand about twenty metres below us. Sensational, isn't it?'

'It's incredible.' Giorgio began to sing and Paige couldn't remember when she'd last been in such a magical place.

'I'm glad you like it,' Sebastian said over her shoulder.

She could feel his warm breath against her neck and it made her shiver.

'It is a bit cooler in here,' he said mistaking her reaction.

'It's fine.' She was relieved he'd misunderstood. 'I don't think I've ever seen anything quite so incredible. Thank you for bringing me here.'

Later, as the taxi took them once again up the steep winding roads to the old town where Sebastian had said he'd booked a table for them in the piazza, Paige thought about how perfect this place would have been for a honeymoon.

'I thought you'd enjoy eating under the umbrellas,' Sebastian said when the taxi stopped. He took her hand as she stepped out onto the pavement. 'I enjoy people-watching.'

Paige nodded. 'That sounds lovely, but I'd like to pay for our meal.'

'No. I invited you.'

Paige stopped walking, so he had to turn to face her. 'So far you've paid for the ferry, taxi ride, and the boat to the grotto, and if you don't agree to me paying for our meal, then I'll eat by myself.'

Sebastian frowned. 'But ...'

Paige held up her hand and shook her head. 'I'm serious. It's my turn to pay for something.'

He shrugged. 'It seems I have no choice, if I wish to eat with you.'

Paige smiled. 'Good. So where are we heading?'

'We have to walk from here,' he said, 'but I think you'll be impressed by the shops, they have an impressive array of them, especially for such a small community.'

She pulled her sunglasses down from her head and covered her eyes against the white-washed walls along the street, so startlingly bright in the sunshine as they made their way towards the town. 'This has been a perfect day so far, thank you.'

'My pleasure, I've enjoyed it.'

Relishing the warmth of the sunshine, Paige was relieved not to have missed out on these experiences and could only imagine how perfect it would be to visit here with someone you loved.

'Tell me a little about your business,' Sebastian said, interrupting her thoughts. 'I know you're a shoe designer with your own shop, but what are your plans for the future?'

Happy to be distracted, Paige said, 'At the moment I source all my stock from suppliers in Spain because their leather is great quality. My shop is really just a small concession in a larger store. One day I hope to be able to lease, or even buy my own property and set up on my own.'

'When do you see yourself doing that?' he asked looking down at the pavement.

Paige frowned. 'Not for a few years yet, I've only been going for two years so far. I'm getting quite a reputation for my designs though, which is fantastic. Although, even though I have a great relationship with my suppliers, it's still expensive sourcing the materials. I think it's important to only accept the highest quality accessories for my designs, which means it's going to take me a little longer than I'd first anticipated raising enough money to completely branch out into my own shop.'

'Was it always your ambition to design your own shoe collection?'

It made a change being able to speak to someone who seemed interested in her work. 'Yes, ever since I can remember. I was always sneaking upstairs to walk around in my mother's shoes.' She touched a small scar on her lip. 'Sometimes I came off worse for my obsession.' She raised an eyebrow and laughed.

Sebastian smiled. 'It adds to your appeal.'

Paige hoped she wasn't blushing. It had been a while since she'd received compliments from Jeremy. It dawned on her that maybe this should have been a bit of a clue that his affections for her were waning. 'What about you? Do you get along well with your uncle?'

Sebastian nodded. 'He's a good man, but can be a little misunderstood. He's always been highly ambitious, which can make him too intense at times, but it's also resulted in him being very successful. When my father died, he promised my mother he'd take me under his wing and when I left university he gave me a job.'

'He did as he promised then?'

Sebastian smiled. 'For the most part, yes. Look,' he said, pointing up at the Dior sign behind her. 'I told you there were great shops here.'

She didn't miss his change of subject and couldn't believe that such a small island could have so many designer shops. They walked past Chanel, Ferragamo, and Louis Vuitton. 'I notice there aren't any discount stores on this street,' she said.

'Not up here,' said Sebastian. 'Would you like to buy a few things?'

Paige shook her head. She didn't like to admit that she probably couldn't afford anything from any of these places.

'Will you let me buy something for you?' he asked, looking awkward for the first time since they'd met.

'No,' she said, smiling to soften her refusal. 'Thank you though. Let's eat, I'm famished.'

Sebastian looked a little disappointed by her refusal, but nodded. 'Of course. Would you mind though if I quickly show you around that little studio over there?' He pointed across the road. 'It's run by a friend of mine and he'd be offended if I came here and didn't pop in to see him.'

'I'd love to go in.' Paige said honestly, stepping in

front of him as he held open the front door of the small shop. She glanced over at the brightly coloured impressionist painting taking up most of the window space, before walking inside the cool air-conditioned room. At first she thought the room was unoccupied, until a tanned man she assumed must be around her age stood up from behind the stone counter and smiled at her. He opened his mouth to speak, but before he uttered a word he spotted Sebastian following her inside and smiled widely, opening his arms.

Paige moved to let Sebastian greet his friend. The men hugged and she could see he obviously held Sebastian in high regard.

'Sebastian Fielding, so you've finally come back to visit me?'

Sebastian nodded. 'I said I would, but I was hoping not to have left it for so long.'

'Your uncle?'

Sebastian nodded. 'He's well, thank you.'

'Good. Please give him my best wishes and tell him I'm proving you right.'

Paige wasn't sure what was going on, but could tell the two of them were very happy to see each other again. She moved away to give them some time alone and enjoy the amazing paintings on display around the small studio.

'Which do you like best?' Sebastian's friend asked her a few minutes later.

She studied the paintings. It was a hard decision to make, they were all so beautiful. She spotted the label hanging from the back of one and wished she had a few hundred euros to spare to be able to buy one to take home to her cottage.

'Assuming you like any of them,' he teased.

'Paige, please let me introduce you to a good friend of mine, Carlo Rosselli.'

Paige smiled and shook Carlo's proffered hand. 'It's

good to meet you. Did you do all these paintings?'

'I am. What do you think of them?'

Paige raised her eyebrows in surprise, relieved she wouldn't have to pretend. 'I love them, they're stunning.'

Carlo looked up at Sebastian, and winked. 'You have a woman of good taste, Sebastian.'

'Oh, we're just friends.' Paige said hurriedly. Sebastian was great company and very handsome, but she didn't want his friend getting the wrong idea.

'Yes,' Sebastian added. 'We're staying at the same hotel and I offered to show Paige some of the sights in the area.'

Carlo's smile disappeared, but Paige couldn't tell if he was teasing her, or not, because there was a definite sparkle of mischievousness in his dark eyes. 'Excuse me, I don't wish to make you feel uncomfortable.' He stepped back and stood next to a small, but exquisite painting depicting a colourful water scene. 'My paintings, you still haven't said what you particularly like about them.'

'Carlo, stop pushing for compliments,' Sebastian said. 'Would you like to join us for lunch in the piazza?'

'I would, but I have a commission I'm running behind with. It's for a birthday present, so I have to finish it on time. Maybe another day, if you're coming back before your return to England?'

'Not this time,' Sebastian said, his voice filled with regret. 'I will be here soon though and we can catch up over lunch then.'

Happy with this suggestion, Carlo hugged Sebastian and kissed Paige on both cheeks before showing them to the door. 'Thank you both for coming here. I hope to see you again sometime, Paige.'

'That would be lovely.' She smiled at him and took one last look around his colourful studio. 'I might even come back to buy one of these from you some day.'

They walked the few paces to the restaurant and were

soon shown to a table in the packed piazza and Paige couldn't take her eyes off the obvious wealth all around her. Where were the locals? Everyone here had the best of everything, or so it seemed. 'Where do all these people come from?'

'Some of them would have come by ferry, like we did.'

She indicated the expensively clad group of people sitting at the next table to them. 'I don't think many of them came across on the ferry,' she whispered.

'Probably not. I think they more than likely have their own cruisers. This place comes alive at night when the tourists and ferries leave; it's when the parties begin.'

'Sounds like fun.' She would love to experience an evening here at some point, she decided. She took off her hat and waved it in front of her face for a few seconds, before placing it on the table. It was hot and she was glad of the shade. She was slowly getting to know more about her new friend and it had been wonderful to discover Carlo's artwork and meet a friend of Sebastian's. 'Thank you for introducing me to Carlo and his intricate artwork,' she said. 'I love discovering painters, and one day I'm going to treat myself to as many originals as I can afford.'

Sebastian smiled. 'He is very good. My uncle is an avid supporter of talent that he believes has a future.'

'And was it you who put him in touch with Carlo?'

Sebastian nodded. 'He needed someone to back his ambitions for his own studio and despite his initial reticence, my uncle eventually helped Carlo.'

She didn't like to ask why his uncle had needed persuasion. 'I was excited to discover the work of an impressionist artist when I visited Wales a couple of years ago. He's so good and I have to admit that I did buy one of his smallest paintings. I couldn't help myself.'

'If you give me the link to his website, I'll check out his work online.' He typed in the website name into his Blackberry as she gave him the artist's name.

'He's got an excellent website,' she said. 'The paintings are displayed in a much more user-friendly way than most sites. Olly's suggested I update the basic website I've currently got for my shoes and handbags. He believes I'm missing a trick because the site isn't as professional as it could be.'

'I agree with him,' Sebastian said. 'It's another outlet without having to pay rent, and you can take orders and maybe show designs before they're actually released. Teasers, as it were.'

Paige raised her eyebrows. 'You seem to know a lot about retail.'

'A little.'

'What exactly do you do for a living?' Paige pierced some of the lemon sole on her plate and put it in her mouth, relishing the delicate flavour.

'All sorts really. My uncle has 11K status in Jersey.'

Paige had heard about wealthy island immigrants, but hadn't yet met one. 'Does that mean he can only visit the mainland for ninety days at the most each year then?'

Sebastian nodded. 'It does. And you'd imagine most people would be thrilled to live in Jersey, but he finds it restricting. He loves England and resents not being able to live there all the time.'

Paige adored the island where she had been born and always lived, but decided she would hate having to be told where to live. 'Would it be too dreadful for him to go back then?'

'It would mean they'd tax him on his worldwide assets going back to the seventies when he moved to Jersey, so yes, it would.'

'Poor thing,' Paige chewed her lower lip. 'I've never imagined I'd feel sorry for someone really wealthy like him before now.'

'It could be worse,' Sebastian said, raising his eyebrows and not looking to Paige as if he had much

35

sympathy at all. 'I spend most of my time either in the office he has in London keeping an eye on everything, or working from my office at home.'

'But you travel to Jersey a lot by the sounds of it?'

Sebastian nodded. 'It's where the head office is, and where the company board meetings are held.'

She didn't like repeating her question, but her curiosity was too strong to stop. 'You still haven't said what it is you actually do.'

Sebastian seemed to consider her question for a moment. 'I mainly take over failing businesses and find a way to make them work. It usually takes big changes though and the hardest part is discarding anything, or anyone, that's surplus to the companies' requirements.'

'It sounds unpleasant.'

He pursed his lips. 'Not exactly, but when you're making people redundant and having to sort the wheat from the chaff, as it were, things can get a little heated and personal. It has its good side.' He held his hands palms upward. 'And its less savoury side, but most of the time it's very satisfying clawing a success out of something that seems to have flat-lined.'

'Impressive.'

'Not really, it is hard work though.'

After finishing their meal, Sebastian suggested they go for a walk to help their food digest. 'I'm glad you've enjoyed yourself today, Paige. I was hoping you'd like Capri as much as I do.'

She wasn't sure why he would be so pleased, but assumed that he must be one of those people who enjoyed introducing the places he loved to those who had yet to encounter them. 'It's glorious here, I'm so happy I've taken the time to visit. Let's go this way and see what we can discover.'

She relished the peace of the long winding roads as they meandered in between elaborate private homes partially hidden by their white-walled gardens, sheltered by pine and lemon trees against the sun. Paige pointed down to the sea. 'We're higher than I thought.'

Sebastian raised his eyebrows. 'Stunning though, don't you think?' He checked his watch. 'Damn, we'd better get to the funicular if we want to catch the last ferry back to Sorrento.

'The what?' she asked, not enjoying the change of mood, and his new sense of urgency.

'I'll explain as we walk. I think we have about twenty minutes and I'm not certain we're going to make it,' he took hold of her hand. 'We'd better hurry.'

He groaned when they reached the back of the queue as the crowds jostled impatiently to get on board. 'Too late,' he said, watching the carriage starting to move down into the mountain.

Paige followed Sebastian to the viewing platform. 'No wonder they were in such a rush,' she said, seeing the holidaymakers hurriedly stepping onto the last ferry. Then, aware that she wasn't as disappointed as she probably should have been, added, 'We'll never make it, will we?'

''Fraid not.' Sebastian turned to her. 'Don't look so worried.'

She didn't like to admit that the prospect of an evening in Capri didn't bother her, especially as he looked so concerned.

'We'll ask at the nearest hotel for a couple of rooms and I can book us in for the night,' Sebastian said. 'We can go back to Sorrento tomorrow morning.'

Having tried three hotels, only to discover that all were fully booked, Paige's earlier nonchalance was slipping. She was beginning to dread having to sleep outside somewhere.

'It's mid-season,' Sebastian said, reporting back to her about his latest attempt to find somewhere. 'But the girl on reception is phoning her brother. He owns a small guesthouse at the other side of the old town and she thinks he may be able to put us up for one night.'

Paige waited while Sebastian returned to the reception. She could hear him chatting away in Italian to the pretty receptionist, and couldn't help thinking how melodious his deep voice sounded as he spoke the lilting language.

He waved her over. 'They only have one room.'

'Only one?' Paige didn't like the idea of having to share a room with any man right now, even one who looked like Sebastian.

'Just the one, but don't worry, I can sleep on Carlo's sofa and we can meet up again in the morning. Shall I say we'll take it, or do you want to keep looking for something elsewhere?'

Paige shrugged. 'That's fine, if you don't mind?' She turned to the receptionist. 'Do you have Wi-Fi?' She didn't want Olly trying to contact her back in Sorrento and panicking if he didn't find her.

The Wi-Fi sorted, the receptionist gave Paige her key and instructions to find her way to the guest house.

'I'll go and speak to Carlo and give you a chance to check your emails,' Sebastian said. 'Maybe we could go for something to eat a little later?'

'Perfect.' Paige said. 'I'll meet you out the front in one hour.' She left through the large glass doors at the back of the reception and followed the pathway until she came across a couple of tiny buildings. Checking the number on her large key, she unlocked her room and entered the plain, white-washed room and sat on the bed. She longed for a cool shower, so quickly discarded her clothes and stepped into the en-suite bathroom.

Feeling much better, Paige dried herself off and dressed. Running her hands through her hair, she applied a little lip gloss and returned to the reception to use the old computer on a makeshift desk in the corner of the room. After sending Olly a quick message telling him she'd contact him the following day, and satisfied that she'd done all she could to ensure he didn't panic, Paige went outside and sat down on a weathered bench. Leaning back and closing her eyes, she let her mind wander as she soaked up the sunrays.

'All OK?' Sebastian said, making her jump. 'Sorry, I didn't mean to give you a fright.'

She stood up and smiled. 'Did you speak to Carlo?'

'Yes, he's excited that I'll be staying with him tonight. He insists we open a few bottles of his favourite wine and spend the night catching up. I was wondering if you'd like to join us?'

'Maybe for one or two, but I wouldn't want to get in the way and ruin Carlo's plans. He obviously doesn't get to see you very often and must be looking forward to having you to himself.'

Sebastian shook his head and began walking. 'He's a great guy, but I know he's going to want to cover old ground that I'd rather not discuss just yet.'

Paige couldn't imagine what he meant, but didn't push for him to elaborate. 'I'm sure it'll be fun,' she said, always enjoying catching up with her friends when she hadn't seen them for a while.

'It's going to be heavy,' he arched an eyebrow. 'There are quite a few years to cover. I can see a long evening ahead of me.

Paige accompanied Sebastian to Carlo's studio. He was already locking the front door. She noticed him quickly covering his disappointment to see her arriving with Sebastian.

'I'm only going to join you for a bite to eat and one drink, then I'll leave you guys to your evening,' she said.

'No, you must stay,' Carlo said, politely.

Paige shook her head. 'No, I'm tired and you two don't want a relative stranger listening while you chat.'

'Really, we'd love you to stay with us,' Sebastian

stepped in between her and Carlo, linking arms with them.

Paige laughed and suspected he meant what he was saying, but shook her head.

Carlo was funny and she could see that the two men had a close bond. The meal, in a secluded restaurant in one of the small backstreets, had been delicious. Paige waited for the musician to finish playing his mandolin and for everyone to finish applauding. 'Right,' she said, taking her napkin from her lap and placing it on the table before picking up her handbag. 'I think I'm going to head off now.'

Sebastian and Carlo immediately stood up. 'Already?' Sebastian asked, looking unimpressed by her imminent departure.

'Yes.' She went to shake Carlo's hand. He took hold of her elbow, leant forward, and kissed her on both cheeks. 'It was lovely meeting you and seeing your wonderful paintings,' she said, a little taken aback by his embrace.

'I'll walk you to the hotel,' Sebastian said.

'I'm fine. You stay and enjoy your evening and we can meet tomorrow morning.'

'I wouldn't hear of you going back alone.' He turned to Carlo. 'I won't be long,' he said, before accompanying her out onto the street.

'Really, Sebastian,' she said, not used to someone wanting to look after her. 'I'm perfectly happy walking back alone, and I promise I won't get lost.'

He narrowed his eyes. She could see he wasn't happy with her insistence. After a brief hesitation, he sighed. 'If you're sure you'd rather go alone.'

'I am.' She smiled, not wanting him to feel bad. 'Go back inside. I'll meet you at the piazza at nine o'clock for breakfast, then we can catch the ferry back to Sorrento.'

Paige stood on tiptoes, kissing him on both cheeks as she had done with Carlo. 'Good night,' she said, before walking away.

Chapter Four

He sat back in his chair and stretching his legs out to the side of the small wooden table, crossed them at the ankles and breathed in the warm sea air. It was hard to believe their trip to Capri had happened almost two weeks ago. He had extended his break for as long as he could, but his uncle was now insisting that he return to work. Today would be their last spent together. Why did the days seem to be rushing by so fast, he wondered. He spotted Paige hurrying down the unlevelled pavement and noticing she almost lost her footing, went to get up to see if she was OK. She righted herself by grabbing hold of a paint-flaked windowsill, glancing around to see if anyone was looking. Not wishing to add to her embarrassment, Sebastian sat down once again and concentrated on a fisherman repairing nets with his gnarled but surprisingly deft hands.

'Well, that's the last time I run in heels,' she giggled.

Sebastian glanced up and stood to greet her. Her pretty face was flushed, and he couldn't help thinking how exquisite she looked all flustered while trying to appear calm. 'Good morning, I hope you slept well?'

She smiled, and smoothed her hair down with one hand. 'I must look a wreck. I woke up later than I'd hoped and had to rush to get here.' He motioned for her to take the seat opposite him. 'I'm supposed to be relaxing on holiday, but I'll be going home with black circles under my eyes after all our late nights.'

'Nonsense.' He motioned towards the fisherman. 'I bet he would disagree with you, too.'

She glanced at the old man and smiled. 'Probably.'

'It's been fun though.'

'It has, but I'm going to have to take a break from drinking wine when I get back,' she said. 'I've had much more than I'm used to on this trip.'

They stared at each other silently for a moment. 'I was wondering what your plans were for today?' he asked, pushing aside any thoughts of how few hours they had left together. He was going to miss her and wanted to make the most of being with her while he still could.

She took off her light jacket and placed it over the arm of the chair. 'I'm not sure yet. You're leaving later on, aren't you?' He nodded. 'Where will you be flying to?'

'Rome first, and then Gatwick,' he replied, not relishing the thought of leaving her. 'I'm going to my home in London for a few days to sort some things out. You?'

'The same, then on to Jersey. That's the only problem living on an island; I have to take an extra flight whenever I go anywhere.'

'That's what my godfather always says.' He smiled at her and, realising that they would soon be able to see each other again, added, 'I'll be there in about three weeks.'

She raised her eyebrows. 'Really? Will you be coming to Jersey for work?'

Her enthusiasm at this news, however subtle, made leaving her a little easier. 'Yes,' he said. 'I have the unenviable task of working on a takeover.'

'It must be difficult having to break the news to the people that you'll no longer need.'

He sighed. 'Yes, I'm afraid it will.' He wasn't looking forward to his next project at all. He waved the waiter over to order coffees. As he watched the teenager ask Paige if she wanted something to eat and then walk away when she declined, his euphoria on seeing her again gradually began to be replaced by a sense of foreboding. He had spent all

42

his time relishing getting to know her, but it dawned on him that Jersey was a small island and the shopping area in town only held one or two larger stores. His gut tightened in dread.

'It sounds grim,' she grimaced.

He struggled to hide his growing concern. 'It isn't any fun, that's true, but someone has to do it.'

'You hear about so many companies closing down and people being made redundant at the moment. I always feel sad whenever I read about it happening in the local gazette.'

'I know what you mean, but it's also not easy being the one to make the decision to shut a place down.' He cleared his throat. 'Where did you say your business was based?'

'It's a small concession in De Greys, King Street. Do you know it?'

He closed his eyes briefly as it dawned on him why her name seemed familiar. Why did she have to be Paige Bingham, one of the names on the list of tenants he'd fleetingly glanced through with the endless files of due diligence.'

'Are you OK?' she asked, frowning.

He shook his head and forced a smile. 'I'm fine. Nothing a good breakfast won't fix,' he lied. 'I know you're probably not that hungry, but why don't we make the most of being here in this charismatic little port and eat something with our coffees?'

Paige's mouth pulled back into a wide smile. 'OK, I'll have scrambled egg on toast.'

'I'll just go and give in our order,' he said needing a moment to gather his thoughts. He stood up and made for the kiosk. Why did her shop have to be one in De Greys, he wondered, resting his hands on the serving hatch.

He gave the boy his order and walked back slowly to join her. He needed to tell her the truth, especially now that she was going to be caught up in his next project. If

43

only she hadn't been so hurt by her fiancé's cruelty when they'd first met, then he probably wouldn't have been so careful with their topics of conversation. This might have come up before now and he could have told her then. He hadn't even attempted to kiss her yet; he'd certainly wanted to. This changed everything though, he thought miserably. He might not have known her long, but he doubted she'd be happy to discover his intentions for De Greys. She'd been let down too recently for him to chance ruining this holiday by telling her. Now was definitely not the right time, although he wasn't sure when it would be.

He forced a smile and returning to join her, sat back down. 'What would you like us to do today?' He took her hand in his. 'It's your last day here and I want to make sure you enjoy every moment.'

'I don't want to think about it,' she said miserably. 'It's gone far too quickly.'

'I know.' He stroked the back of her wrist with his thumb. 'We haven't discussed what happens next either, have we?' He wanted her to feel about him the way he unexpectedly did about her. Maybe, if he gave her time to get to know him a bit better before admitting his true business in Jersey, she might give him the benefit of the doubt. It wasn't much, he decided, but it was all he could hope for now he'd realized who she was.

Her eyes widened, but he could see she was anticipating him elaborating on his comment. 'What do you mean?'

'I want to see you again,' he admitted. When she didn't react, he added, 'I thought if you wanted to, we could visit somewhere extra special, like Positano. Maybe have a long, lazy lunch together.'

'Sounds perfect,' she said thoughtfully. 'It's going to be strange going home to the same routine, but without having been married. It's not what I'd imagined at all.'

'Life does tend to throw the odd curveball at us when

we least expect it to, doesn't it?' he said, thinking about his own wedding bombshell when Lucinda, his then-fiancée, had left him without warning.

She narrowed her eyes. 'You seem a little pre-occupied.'

He shrugged. 'I think that, like you, coming here has been a welcome change from the usual whirlwind of work and flying from place to place. I came here for a few meetings and planned to leave after seeing Carlo, but I've switched off, for once. I hadn't expected to have a proper holiday.'

Paige smiled, and for the first time he noticed she had a dimple in her right cheek, it added to her fresh-faced prettiness and he couldn't help smiling back at her. 'You've made all the difference to this trip for me, Seb, and I'm grateful.' She studied her fingers for a moment before addressing him again. 'Do you believe that certain people come into your life at exactly the time you need them?'

He hadn't thought about it before, but she looked so intense waiting for him to answer that he chose his words carefully. 'I know I've met you when I needed a reminder to take time to enjoy my surroundings rather than have my head in reports all day.'

She contemplated his words, and nodded. 'Good. I'm glad I've given something back to you.'

It wasn't how he'd hope she'd remember him, but he liked her too much to chance offending her. If she saw him as a friend, then he would have to keep his attraction to her under wraps for the time-being. 'I hope you won't mind me calling on you when I come to Jersey?' he asked. Maybe, he thought hopefully, he might have thought of a way to approach the problem of what to do about her concession in De Greys by then.

'Why not?' she said, smiling at him.

Chapter Five

Why not indeed, she thought as she helped her mother manoeuvre into her father's Jaguar a few weeks later. Paige stepped into the back of the car. Her mother would be shocked if she knew how that lunch together and a romantic evening overlooking the moonlit bay had led to Paige daring to admit, if only to herself, that she was actually relieved her wedding had been called off.

Sebastian might not have even kissed her yet, but they'd spent an incredible couple of weeks in each other's company and she couldn't help missing him. An unforgettable holiday spent with a handsome stranger. Her very own *Brief Encounter*, almost. The thought made her feel deliciously mischievous.

She took a peek at his last text on her phone. 'Looking forward to seeing you soon.' Paige stroked the inexpensive coral pendant Sebastian had insisted on buying her as a souvenir on the last day of their trip. She couldn't wait to meet up with him. Sending the occasional text or email was one thing, but actually seeing him in the flesh after a few weeks apart was making her a little anxious. What if he didn't feel the same way about her as she suspected she did about him?

'I hope you're not on your Blackberry,' her mother moaned. 'You're always fiddling about with that thing.'

'I was only checking if I had any messages, Mum,' said Paige, quickly dropping it into her bag.

'Do slow down, George,' Marion shouted, her shrill voice slamming through Paige's thoughts as her father

47

swung his Jag round the narrow roads down to the restaurant at The Encore Hotel. 'This is a twenty mile per hour speed limit along here.'

'Not until the next bend it isn't. Tell you what Marion, you worry about Paige's phone and let me get us to our meal before they begin serving the next sitting.' He squinted at Paige through the rear view mirror. 'What's all that pinging noise? I hope you're not sending messages to that chap your mother said you were carousing about with in Italy?'

'I wasn't carousing about with anyone, whatever that means,' laughed Paige.

'George, just concentrate on your driving and stop nagging. She's a big girl, and more than capable of looking after herself. We're going to be late if we're not careful, and I'd like to try and get to the restaurant in one piece.'

'You two are the reason we're bloody late. What the hell do you women find to do anyhow?'

Paige wished she'd been able to meet up with Sebastian before she had to take her parents to the anniversary lunch she'd booked for them, but supposed he couldn't help being stuck in meetings. That was what he was visiting Jersey for, after all.

'I had, but Paige was dithering as usual.' Her mother checked her lipstick in the mirror on the back of the sun visor.

'Thanks, Mum.' Paige leant forward between the two front seats. 'Let's not worry about being too late; it's only the three of us anyway. Clem would have loved to join us, but it's very expensive flying back from Brighton just for one lunch.'

'Of course, it is,' her father said, probably relieved he hadn't been asked to pay for his younger daughter's flights once again. 'We'll have a splendid lunch.'

'Yes.' Her mother reached her arm back between the

48

front seats, patting Paige awkwardly on her knee. 'It was very generous of you to arrange this surprise for us, darling.'

'I'm happy to do it,' Paige said.

'After all,' continued her mother. 'It can't be easy for you.'

'Marion,' the warning in her father's tone was unmistakable.

Paige sighed. 'It's OK, I haven't forgotten it's Jeremy and Gretchen's wedding today. I'm fine though, honestly, Mum. You mustn't worry about me.'

'They arranged everything bloody quickly, if you ask me.'

'We didn't, George.'

He ignored her. 'Just think, it could be worse,' her father added, pulling into a parking space and turning off the ignition.

'I can't see how,' her mother groaned.

He got out of the car and walked round to open the front passenger door, stopping as Paige stepped out from the back seat. He took her by the shoulders. 'It could have been you marrying that idiot.'

Paige gave an involuntary shiver at the reminder. She leant forward and kissed her father on his ruddy cheek. 'Thanks.'

He hugged her. 'Frankly, my darling, as far as I'm concerned, you've had a lucky escape.'

'I can't help agreeing with you,' she admitted.

Sebastian still couldn't believe that she had a shop in De Greys. Then again, he remembered, St Helier was a small town and didn't have large shopping malls like the towns he was used to in England. The odds of this happening on an island where De Greys was one of only two larger stores housing small franchises were stacked against him. He should have been honest with her, but after the time

49

they'd spent together in Sorrento, he wanted to figure out a way to make things right before she discovered exactly who he was. He couldn't help worrying that the longer he took to tell her, the worse her reaction might be.

He turned the pages of the board information pack in front of him, unable to concentrate on what his accountant was saying. He was not going to lose this woman. He'd already fallen in love with her, and if she discovered he'd known about her predicament and not mentioned anything, he was almost certain she would never forgive him. He needed to think. And fast.

He realized the other board members were waiting for him to speak. He focused for a second, and pointed out an anomaly he'd picked up the previous evening when giving the report a final once over. Distracted by this new information, the other attendees of the meeting began talking at once, giving him the chance to think about Paige. Knowing she was nearby had been a continuous distraction, and he couldn't wait for an opportunity to see her and discover whether or not he'd imagined their deep connection in Sorrento.

His phone vibrated. He picked it up from the table in front of him, hurriedly checking it. Paige. 'Just arrived at The Encore.'

She was here. He waited for his financial director to finish speaking and pointedly checked his watch. 'It's 1 p.m. and the hotel staff are probably waiting to bring in the sandwiches, I suggest we take a short break for lunch.'

The others in the room nodded their agreement. 'I'll see you all back here in a few minutes. Linda, please give the hotel manager a call.'

'Xav Wilson?' she asked, picking up the phone.

'Yes, that's him. Let him know we're ready for refreshments.'

He'd just left the room intending to speak to Paige in the bar, when he spotted her walking across the reception area towards the ladies room. Quickening his step, he soon reached her and tapped her on the shoulder. She swung round, looking as pleased to see him as he was to be with her again. 'Seb.'

He relished the look of joy on her face it confirmed his hopes that she did have feelings for him. 'Hello. Did your parents like their surprise anniversary lunch?'

She nodded. 'Mum loves it here. She panicked about what she was going to wear, of course, but was thrilled that I'd booked for us to eat here today. How was your morning?'

'This place is out of town, so it's perfect for private meetings. Sir Edmund was easily persuaded to come here. You look stunning, by the way.'

'Thank you.'

She seemed a little shy. Paige went to say something else, but he'd waited far too long already to kiss her. Pulling her closer to him, he tilted his head down, but before their lips touched someone coughed behind him. 'Yes. What is it?' he asked trying to mask his frustration. 'Ah, Xav,' he said, when he spotted who had spoken. 'Sorry, I didn't mean to snap.'

'No, I'm sorry, Mr. Fielding,' Xav said, looking awkward at interrupting their intimacy. 'Luncheon has been served, and I've been asked to let you know that they're waiting for your return.'

'Thank you. Please tell them I'm on my way.' When Xav had left and they were alone once again, he pulled an apologetic face. 'I'm going to have to go.'

'It can't be helped,' she said smiling up at him.

He stared at her making a mental note of every glorious detail. After the last few weeks, it was hard to believe she was finally in the same room as him. 'I'm sorry I haven't finished with these meetings yet, everything was delayed after a few hiccups this morning. I doubt I'll be able to catch up with you before you leave here today now.'

'Don't worry,' she said, her voice quiet. 'I won't get much of a chance to leave the table once my mum starts talking anyway.'

He couldn't help smiling at her. Despite wanting more than anything to stay, he couldn't delay the meeting any further. 'I'll give you a call later, if that's OK? We can arrange something then.'

Was that disappointment on her face, or could it be his guilt making him question her feelings? He cursed his busy itinerary.

Having reapplied her lipstick, Paige hurried back to her table. At the end of the meal, she swallowed the last spoonful of crème brulée and leant back in her chair. 'That was delicious.'

'It was, darling. Thank you for treating us today, it was a generous gift and much appreciated.' Her mother took a large sip of her Pinot Grigio. 'George, stop mumbling to yourself.'

'What?'

Her mother narrowed her eyes, giving Paige a pointed look. 'Don't you have something to say to your daughter?'

'Yes, I do, as a matter of fact.' He frowned. Paige wasn't sure she wanted to hear what he was about to say. 'How do you know Sebastian Fielding?' he asked, taking her by surprise. He wasn't smiling, she noted.

'How do you know I was talking to him?' She tried to recollect what she and Sebastian had said to each other.

'I passed the ladies a few moments ago and couldn't believe it when I saw you both by the entrance. How long have you known him? In fact, why didn't you tell me you knew him when I told you about the suspected takeover of De Greys?'

'Sorry?' Paige struggled to work out what he meant.

'You appear to know him rather well.'

Paige had no idea what her father was talking about,

but could see he expected an answer. 'It's fine, you've no need to be concerned. We met briefly in Sorrento.' She thought for a moment. 'I didn't know you knew his name.'

'He's well known; Sir Edmund Blake's right-hand man.' He glanced around, as if to check no one was listening to what he was about to say. Then, leaning forward, he lowered his voice and added, 'I've been chatting with a chum from my Chamber of Commerce days, and he's certain they're going to make a bid for your shop.'

'My shop?' Paige asked, incredulous that her father should think anyone would want such a tiny enterprise.

'For pity's sake, I don't mean Heaven in Heels,' he sighed. 'He reckons they're about to make a move to buy the company that owns De Greys.'

Paige let this piece of unwelcome information filter through to her brain, certain that Seb would have told her if he was going to do anything connected with her business. The implication that the man who had treated her so thoughtfully on holiday, who had almost kissed her earlier, could be arranging a takeover of not only her business, but the place where many of her friends worked, was too incomprehensible to process. How could he keep something like that from her? She swallowed the bile rising in her throat and took a few sips of water.

'You seem bloody upset about someone you only just met.' George narrowed his eyes.

'I'm worried about my concession. Surely if they buy the store, then they'll probably want to make changes,' she said remembering Sebastian's words about businesses being surplus to requirements. 'I could never afford to find another place situated so well in the town as De Greys. Are you certain that they're buying the place?' Paige couldn't believe this was happening, just when her life seemed to be getting back on track so perfectly.

'Almost one hundred per cent. My informant has his

fingers on the pulse in Jersey's financial world, and bugger all gets past him. I doubt he's wrong about this.' He patted her hand. 'Are you all right? I don't think it's anything too awful for you to concern yourself with, although that Fielding chap hasn't earned his reputation by being soft-hearted.'

'Sebastian Fielding,' she whispered trying to take in her father's unwelcome revelation.

'Yes, one and the same. You want to watch yourself with him. They say he hasn't got a conscience, and you've had enough to deal with recently without becoming involved with him.' He studied her for a moment. 'You look rather pale, maybe it's time we made a move and went home.' Without waiting for Paige to answer, he waved discreetly to her mother. 'Marion, I think it's time we left.'

'No,' argued Paige, desperate to hear more and not wanting them to leave early on her account. 'This is my treat to you and Mum.'

'And it's a thoughtful one too, sweetheart, but you look tired. You're always working so hard. It's supposed to be your day off and I don't want you overdoing things, especially with the uncertainty about your shop.' He looked over at her mother. 'Marion, come along.'

She took a deep breath and stood up to follow her parents down the pathway to their parked car. As she passed a window Paige was attracted by a movement, and glancing inside caught Sebastian's attention. He nodded, but Paige turned away. How could he have spent so much time with her without telling her what he was about to do?

Paige hardly heard the conversation between her parents during the short journey down the back lanes towards Bonne Nuit Bay, where her cottage nestled among towering pine trees so common in Jersey. She replayed her conversations with Sebastian in her head. Surely he would have said something if he'd known about Heaven in Heels being in De Greys?

'You sure you're all right?' her father asked, as she closed the rear car door behind her.

'Positive. I'm just a little tired; it's been a busy week at the shop.' She gave him a reassuring smile. 'Now you drive home carefully.' She waved at them as they drove off, glad to be home again, and alone with her thoughts.

As soon as she closed her front door, Paige leant against it, finally able to allow her tears to flow. She wanted to curl up into a ball and, what? What did she want? She went to the kitchen and ripped off a square of kitchen towelling, blowing her nose. Sebastian, that's what.

'Sod him,' she cried, running up to her room and discarding her restricting outfit before dragging on her most comfortable pair of tracksuit bottoms and a sweatshirt. Her life was one long disappointment after another. She thought Jeremy dumping her had been upsetting. She realised with a start that this was far more painful. She realized for the first time that what she'd felt for her ex hadn't been true love, and perhaps she had found something closer to it in Sorrento with Sebastian.

She went downstairs and poured herself a glass of rosé. She desperately wanted to speak to Sebastian and insist he dismiss her father's information as rubbish. Yet her father was rarely wrong about anything, and she knew instinctively that he was right. There'd been gossip about De Greys floundering for months, but she hadn't taken it too seriously.

It was hard to relate Sebastian to the man her father described earlier. She had to trust his instincts on this, which could only mean that whether she liked it or not, Seb had the power to ruin everything she'd worked for. Could he do such a thing to her? If he was buying De Greys, then he must have done his homework and be aware that the store had held the prime position in the only high street on the island for over one hundred years.

'Hell.' She took a large sip from her wine glass and slumped down in her favourite armchair. She couldn't see how he could ever realistically fit in to her life anyway; he didn't live here and travelled a lot for work. She wasn't sure she'd like such a distant relationship.

She'd told him where her concession was, so he already knew he was about to make decisions about her fledgling business. She hated the fact that he wasn't the man she'd thought him to be. Paige took a gulp of her wine to force down the lump constricting her throat. This changed everything between them.

The phone rang a few times during the evening, but Paige didn't pick up. She read Sebastian's text telling her he would get in contact with her the following day.

Her impatience taking over, she dialled his number. 'Sebastian,' she said, before he had a chance to speak. 'Is it true you're about to buy De Greys?'

'Paige –'

'Well? Is it true?' She clenched her teeth desperate to shout at him, or for him to deny it and prove her father's information wrong. How could she be so wrong about another man? What was wrong with her?

'Yes,' he said simply. She couldn't miss the change in his usual tone. 'I was going to speak to you about it. Could we possibly meet up now?'

'No,' she snapped. 'but I do want to know if you already knew where my concession was when I told you about it being in De Greys that morning we had breakfast in Marina Grande?'

His pause confirmed her suspicions. 'Your name did seem vaguely familiar, but it was only that morning that I understood why.'

'And you didn't think you should explain everything when you had the chance then?'

He sighed. 'I'm so sorry. It was our last day together, I

didn't want to spoil it. Please let me come and explain everything to you now.'

'I said no.' She took a deep breath.

'I'm so sorry.'

Paige ended the call, not wishing to hear what else he had to say. She wasn't going to give anyone the chance to deceive her again; she'd learned her lesson too thoroughly with Jeremy.

Chapter Six

The following morning, she still hadn't come to terms with what she'd discovered about Sebastian, but put on a brave face to welcome her customers. She managed to sell three pairs of her most expensive designs to the vivacious younger wife of one of the island's wealthiest men. Paige knew the woman would be meeting friends for lunch, where hopefully she would tell them she had bought the boots from Heaven in Heels. The thought helped lighten her mood on what would otherwise have been a miserable morning.

'Why didn't you answer your phone yesterday?' Olly ran up to her, panting after running down the stairs from his office two floors above Paige's concession where he worked as an IT consultant. He dropped his sandwiches onto her counter and handed her a cappuccino. 'I rang at least twice during the day.'

'Don't sulk, Olly.' Paige noticed his unshaven face. 'Sometimes I need my own space, and yesterday happened to be one of those times.'

'Lunch with the parents went badly then, I take it?' He glanced around the small space. Paige quickly snatched her notepad and pen away from him before he started doodling all over her rough sketch of the latest idea she had been working on before his arrival.

'Yes, but not in the way you mean,' she said, taking a pair of navy boots and arranging it neatly on the shelf. He sat down on the stool behind the counter.

'So, what happened?' He bit into his sandwich, eyes

wide as he waited for her to answer.

'I'll tell you later, it's a long story.'

Olly pulled a face. 'Why not tell me now?'

'Because I don't want to, anyone could be passing.' She could tell she had fired his interest far more than she was intending to, and tapped the side of her nose with her finger. 'Later, I promise.'

'Sounds juicy.' He raised an eyebrow, and put his hands together pleading for her to continue.

'No, not really,' she said, refusing to be persuaded. 'Anyway, shouldn't you be fixing computers or something useful? After all, it is what you're paid to do.'

'Spoilsport,' he frowned. 'I'm wasted in IT. Messing about with screens and wires loses its attraction very quickly, you know.' He glanced at his new Tag Heuer watch. 'Sod it. I hate it when I only get a couple of minutes for lunch. I'd better get off. Can I call on you tonight? Or will you need your space then too?'

'Don't be sarcastic. The sooner you move out of your parents' place and get your own flat the better,' she laughed, unable to feel cross with him for long. 'Then you won't be next door to spot whether I'm at home, or not.

'You know I've only just finished paying off my uni debts. Anyway, I'm saving for a deposit to buy one of the new waterfront flats.'

'You'll need to stop treating yourself to expensive watches then.' She shook her head. 'Come round whenever you like, though give me a chance to have at least one cup of tea before descending on me.'

'No worries, sweetcakes,' he said, using the name she hated so much. He grabbed the remainder of his lunch, and left.

She stepped back to assess the spacing between the boots and shoes in front of her.

'Sweetcakes?' said a deep voice she recognized instantly.

Paige swung round. 'I don't have anything to say to you,' she said wishing he'd go and leave her to simmer in peace.

Seb stood, unsmiling, with one hand in his pocket. 'I tried to call you a couple of times again last night.'

She could see he wanted to speak to her, but there was nothing he had to say that she wanted to hear. 'I don't think we have anything left to talk about, do you?' She busied herself putting the empty boxes behind the counter into the storeroom. She came back out to face him once more.

He frowned. 'If you let me explain, then you might not be so concerned about what's going to happen here.'

Was it her imagination, or did he look guilty just then? 'Really? I doubt that very much,' she held her arms wide to encompass her shop. 'You know how I feel about this place, or at least you should do after I went on about it in Italy.' She spotted a customer coming her way before she could say anything further.

'Who told you?' he asked, taking a step towards her, stopping when she moved away from him. 'We hadn't even met when I took on this project.'

'No,' She smiled at the customer, wishing Sebastian would leave her in peace to simmer quietly. 'But you did know that Heaven in Heels was here when we were still in Italy. You had plenty of time to explain everything then.' She waited for him to answer, determined not to allow him the satisfaction of seeing her disappointment in him.

The customer held up a boot. 'Could I try this in a five, please?'

Paige nodded. 'Of course.' She walked towards her storeroom and Sebastian followed.

'Paige, please let me explain,' he whispered.

'No, Sebastian.' She almost spat his name. 'I'm busy at the moment, and I'd like you to leave.' She turned her back on him and looked for the correct boots.

He bent his head down from behind her; he was so close she could feel his breath on her cheek.

'I would have told you last night if you'd answered and given me the chance to do so,' he said quietly, before leaving.

She grabbed two different colours of the same design and returned to her customer. She took the boots out of their boxes and, forcing a smile, handed one pair over. Paige breathed a sigh of relief, as, only half listening to what the woman was saying, she heard his footsteps receding down the Victorian arcade that ran the length of the grand store. Paige was grateful for the clever design that allowed her concession a chance to make the most of pedestrians taking the short cut from Queen Street on the main thoroughfare to the cafes and restaurants at the back of De Greys.

It hadn't occurred to her until now exactly how unsettling it was going to be having Sebastian in such close proximity. It certainly wasn't going to be easy trying to run her concession in the same premises where he now appeared to be based, at least for the foreseeable future.

She could hardly avoid him, especially if he chose to seek her out again. Running her shop single-handedly, with just the occasional help from her sister, meant the only time she was away from the place was on buying trips. So, she mused, she would undoubtedly be seeing a lot of him. Then again, if his project involved her losing her place in the store she wouldn't be here to see him at all.

'Why did he have to come here?' she grumbled, carrying a pair of boots to her client.

'Did you say something?' the older woman asked.

'Sorry, I was mumbling.' Paige replaced the pair of discarded boots back into their tissue paper.

'Man trouble, I presume?' The woman lifted her Dior sunglasses, giving Paige a knowing look.

She nodded. 'Nothing I can't sort out,' she fibbed, wishing she felt as confident as she sounded.

'If you take my advice, dear girl, you'll steer well clear of the pretty ones, they're always the most trouble.' The woman took out her purse, and selected a credit card. 'By husband number four, I finally worked out where I was going wrong.'

Paige laughed. 'I'll try and remember, though I haven't found husband number one yet.' She found it odd that the image she'd held for so long of Jeremy being by her side was fading rapidly.

'You soon will do, I'm sure of that.' She pressed in her PIN number with a perfectly manicured scarlet fingernail. 'That divine specimen talking to you as I arrived was the epitome of the type I'm warning you about, handsome, and definitely more trouble than he's worth. Take my word for it.'

'Don't worry, I will,' Paige assured her with as much conviction as she could muster. 'Thank you,' she said, handing the woman her credit card and a large cream bag with her brand's simple black logo across the side. Paige decided she would have to find a way to keep some sort of distance between her and Sebastian.

'Why can't anything interesting ever happen to me?' Olly moaned, once Paige finished describing the previous day to him. 'And how do you think you'll manage to stay away from this Sebastian character, if he's going to be based at De Greys?'

Paige refilled Olly's empty glass with some of her favourite Merlot. 'I haven't figured that out yet. I think I'll have to deal with each occasion it arises. I do know it's not going to be easy though,' she said closing her eyes.

Olly shook his head. 'Only you could fall for the bloke who'll be deciding all our futures.'

Despite the heat of the evening, and the lit cathedral

candles flickering away in the grate next to her settee, she couldn't help feeling a little chilled. 'I know. Isn't it just my shitty luck?'

'Yup,' he sighed. 'Mind you, there must be a part of you that finds it a little exciting not knowing when he'll next appear in front of you.' He raised an eyebrow. 'I've heard some of the other concessionaires gossiping about him. I gather he's some sort of A-lister in the looks department. They seem to think his arrival is going to liven up the place no end. Bastard.'

'Not for me it won't,' she said, giving him a playful punch on his bony shoulder.

'Ouch. I'm assuming that hurt more than you intended it to.' He rubbed the pain away. 'To make up for your spitefulness, I think you should offer to feed me tonight.'

'Too bad,' she said giving him a brief hug to make amends for being so rough. 'I'm not in the mood for cooking.'

'Don't be such a misery. How bad can it be?' He shrugged. 'You never know, you might end up getting together with him.'

'Stop it, Olly,' she said, miserable at the thought of such an improbability. 'It's not funny. He was such a gentleman in Italy and I really enjoyed his company. How can I even consider being with someone who'll probably be the reason I lose everything I've worked so hard to build up?'

'It's a shame though. You were glowing when you returned from your trip,' Olly said pulling a sad face. 'I don't think I've seen you look so relaxed since we went on holiday to the Greek Islands with our housemates from uni after graduation.'

'I can't be with someone who could do that to my friends, or to me. I do have morals you know.'

'You do. But don't let them hold you back from being happy, Paige.'

Chapter Seven

Sebastian waited for his electric gates to open. He would have preferred to remain in Jersey and resolve his differences with Paige, but couldn't put off the meetings he had scheduled on the mainland. Conference calls were fine to a certain extent, but he knew he needed a couple of days in the London office, however inconvenient they may be to his personal life.

He shook his head at the memory of the morning in Capri that had begun so positively. 'Why her?' he groaned driving into his double garage and parking the car.

The lights in the flagged hallway immediately lit up, it was a silent welcome of sorts. Sebastian smiled when he spotted Mrs Hutton's note on the black marble worktop in the kitchen. Putting down his briefcase, he shrugged off his jacket before reading it.

'Lasagne – 4 mins in the microwave. Please eat it. No takeaways! Harley taken to vet's today for annual booster. Sulking in den. Will be in 9 a.m. tomorrow. Mrs H.'

He whistled for Harley, and crouching down didn't have long to wait for the Labrador to come bounding through to greet him. 'Hello, boy,' he said ruffling the golden fur on the old dog's head. 'Has Mrs H been taking you to horrible places again?'

The dog did a figure of eight round Sebastian several times, his tail whipping his owner's calves as he passed. 'It's good to see you too,' Sebastian laughed. No matter how often he travelled, he always hated saying goodbye to Harley. 'I suppose I'd better eat this food too. She'll be checking the bin as soon as she gets here tomorrow.' He stroked the dog's ears. Harley followed him to the microwave and stared up at him, waiting for more attention. 'I'm glad you're pleased to see me. It's good to see a friendly face.'

He opened the briefcase and took out several spreadsheets from a buff folder. Whether he liked it or not, his expertise lay in restructuring failing businesses. Despite his attraction to Paige, he had a duty of care to his shareholders to ensure he made the right decisions. He needed to work through the task list in front of him and get on with implementing the changes at the store. If it was going to survive for the next hundred years, then Sebastian knew he'd have to make some hard choices. He hoped Paige's beloved Heaven in Heels wasn't going to be one of those casualties, but if it was, then he was going to have to deal with her in a professional manner.

'Easier said than done,' he said, patting Harley's head. At least the tenants and employees of the firm had received the statement advising them that the takeover had taken place. Now he needed to give them all a little time for the news to sink in. He'd call a meeting and allow them to voice their concerns on his return to the island. He wasn't looking forward to it.

Paige didn't see Sebastian for the next two days, and despite her best intentions, couldn't help feeling a little disappointed.

'The gossip was right, for once.' Olly sat on the chair behind her counter doodling on her notepad.

'Stop that,' she took the pencil away from him. 'So it seems. What are we going to do if we lose our jobs?'

'No idea,' he moved to let her have the stool. 'It shouldn't be too hard for me to find something, there's always work for IT guys. You're the one with the real problem, especially if you have to move your business.'

Paige sighed. 'I was only just starting to make a little money, and now this has to happen.'

'You don't know if you are going to have to go yet. Don't panic too soon.'

Olly was right to an extent, but if she did have to move, then Paige wanted to be ready and not panicking at the last minute. It was going to be hard enough, without having to deal with her attraction to Sebastian.

A constant stream of customers flowed through the shop for most of the afternoon, keeping her busy and filling her till with receipts.

'This is mainly thanks to your brilliant incentive, Ol,' she said as she cashed up at the end of the day.

'It was your birthday present from me and Clem. In fact,' he added thoughtfully, 'It was the first joint present we bought anyone as a couple.'

Paige was relieved that her sister and Olly falling for each other all those months ago hadn't turned out to be as strange as she'd feared it would be. 'I know, and it was a generous one. I still feel bad that you wouldn't let me at least cover some of the cost.'

'It was nothing. I'd spotted flyers from one of the other shops in the *Jersey Gazette* and thought it could work well for you too.

'It's made a great difference to my takings since they came out.' Paige waved one in the air. 'They're so striking, and I really appreciate it.'

'It wasn't as expensive as you probably think.' Olly studied the copies of Paige's designs on the front of one of the flyers. 'I persuaded an old school friend to print them off. He owed me a favour or two and only charged me the cost of producing them.'

'Yes, but I'm glad you eventually gave in and let me pay for them to be inserted in the evening paper.'

Olly pulled a face. 'You're a determined madam when you want to be. Forty thousand or so newspapers delivered every night, each with a flyer offering a 10% discount on any purchase for the following two weeks. If it works then it's worth every penny.'

'You're so clever,' said Paige. 'Look how my shelves are clearing. I owe you big time for this.'

He pulled a serious face. 'I know you do.' He laughed. 'Of course you don't, it's nothing.'

'How can you say that? I don't think you realise how much I needed those extra sales.'

'You deserve it. You work hard and I want you to succeed.' He gazed down at the floor for a moment, his usual exuberance forgotten.

'What's the matter?' Paige asked.

'I phoned Clem last night to say I was planning to go and visit her next weekend at her uni in Brighton, and she finished with me.'

Paige gasped, stunned at this unexpected bombshell. 'Why? I thought you two were so happy together?'

'Me too,' he said, his voice cracking with emotion. 'I thought everything was going brilliantly between us,' he said. 'I didn't see it coming at all.'

'Olly, I'm so sorry.'

He stared at her for a moment. 'I can see by the look of surprise on your face that she hasn't said anything to you.'

Paige shook her head, relieved to be able to answer him truthfully. 'No, nothing.'

'Will you ask her for me, when you next speak to her? She refused to tell me anything. She said it was nothing to do with me, so I can only assume she's met someone else.'

Paige doubted it. The last she'd heard from Clem, she'd gone on about how much in love she was with Olly. She gave him a hug, not sure what to say next.

'Hey, don't fret. I'm fine,' he said, obviously lying. He pushed his long fingers through his sun-bleached hair. 'How about we go out tonight to cheer ourselves up? We could celebrate your successful campaign and treat ourselves to a slap up meal at The Anchorage?'

'Oh, I don't know,' she said, thinking about the long soak in the bath she had been looking forward to. Then seeing his face and remembering how much he'd supported her, felt selfish and decided it was the least she could do for him. 'Oh, go on then, why not? You'd better get back to your desk before you're missed now though. Why don't you give me a knock at about seven tonight? We'll go on down to St Aubin then.'

Olly's face broke into a smile. 'Great. I love going out with you, although you seem to indulge yourself rarely these days.' He held his hand up when she went to argue. 'No, don't speak. I'll go. I'd hate to give you a chance to think of a reason to change your mind.'

The Anchorage was packed. Paige followed Olly, and waited as one friend greeted him after another, continually stopping him to have a quick chat. She noticed that most of them were beautiful and female, and had noticed Olly. Paige had been his friend for enough years to know he was too much in love with her sister to be interested in finding someone to replace her in his affections. She was relieved when eventually they reached the bar.

Having greeted him with obvious delight, the waitress showed the pair to their table. Paige sat back and gazed out of the vast window overlooking the tranquillity of the boat-filled harbour, where silvery ribbons reflected from the lowering sun making tiny waves on the gently moving tide.

'I always thought the masts of the moored yachts were haunted bells, when I was small and heard them clanging together,' Paige admitted absent-mindedly as she studied the menu.

'Not the brightest of sparks then?'

'Sorry?'

'You and the masts,' he laughed. 'Bless. I bet you still believe in fairies too?'

'Of course I don't,' she said, unable to stop giggling. 'Now stop teasing me and choose what you're having.'

'I'm going to try the watercress soup and mushroom risotto,' he announced, slamming shut the leather bound menu with relish.

'What happened to my carnivorous neighbour?' she teased, her brow creased in a confused frown. 'You always have rare steak. And, it always looks disgusting.'

'That's where you're wrong. Since Tuesday morning, I've been a born again vegetarian.'

'You're kidding?' She frowned, baffled by his unexpected announcement. 'You, not eat meat? Are you serious?' It was hard to know if he was joking.

'Why? What's wrong with that?'

'Olly, you're the most enthusiastic meat eater I've ever come across.'

'Not any more.' He motioned for her to come closer to him. 'I don't know who he is, but there's a well-dressed guy watching me with great intensity from over by the bar.' Paige went to look over her shoulder. 'No. Don't do that.' He grabbed her arm and pulled her back round. 'He'll know we're talking about him.'

'Olly,' she groaned, desperate to take a look. 'Don't you recognize him at all?'

'No.' He peered over the top of his glass past her. 'At least, I don't think so. Come to think of it, he does look vaguely familiar. I wonder where I've seen him before.'

Paige tried to peek out of the corner of her eyes, but the mysterious man was too far behind for her to be able to. 'Let me have a look.'

'Not yet, he'll see we've been talking about him, and if it turns out I should know him, I'll look a bit of a fool.' Olly picked up the menu, opening it, and holding it up in front of him as a screen. 'Maybe he's someone off the television?'

Paige waited for as long as she could manage. 'That's

70

it, I've waited long enough. I'm going to the loo, and you can't stop me.' She had only taken several steps from her seat, when she stole a peek at the focus of Olly's avid attention.

'Sebastian?' Her eyes widened in shock, as he stepped forward, giving her just enough time to save herself from slamming straight into him.

Chapter Eight

'Are you still determined not to give me a chance to explain, Paige?'

'I think it's all pretty clear-cut,' she said.

Sebastian could see she was flustered and caught off guard. 'I see.' He looked down at her, hating how much things had deteriorated between them. She was having fun with the guy she'd been sitting with, so maybe she wasn't as interested in him as he would have liked. 'You could have told me at The Encore that I had the wrong idea about us. I would have understood,' he lied. 'I've already apologized for not telling you about my involvement in this project.'

She shook her head. 'That's the trouble, though, Sebastian. To you it's a project, but this is my livelihood we're talking about. The place I've dreamed of selling my designs since I was a teenager, and it's also where several of my friends work. What about them?'

Glancing over her shoulder Seb recognized her dinner partner as the same man he'd spotted her leaving the shop with a few days before. Sebastian couldn't miss his obvious interest in their conversation, or the way he quickly looked away when he caught Sebastian looking at him.

'You could always change your mind,' she joked.

'I can't do that. I'm contracted to carry out the changes. This isn't easy for anyone, Paige, and strange as it may seem to you, I don't enjoy having to make decisions that change people's lives in ways they don't want. Whatever you may think of me, I do try to help everyone as much as

I can.'

She didn't seem to know what to say next. Why was she so uneasy, he wondered? He knew it was difficult between them, but surely they'd be able to find some way to deal with their differences of opinion? 'Paige?'

'I'm still shocked that didn't tell me what your next job was, Sebastian. I'd like to find a way to forget that, but I can't.'

'I understand you're hurt, but we'll find a way round this.' He ignored her look of surprise. 'Why don't we arrange to meet somewhere where we can talk this through?' he said, wishing he didn't want her so badly and that he could simply agree with her and let her go. 'However difficult it is between us, we have to deal with this issue, especially now we'll be working under the same roof for the foreseeable future.'

'Fine.' Paige sighed, after a moment's deliberation.

Sebastian smiled, relieved she had agreed. He almost expected her not to, and it gave him a little hope.

Paige held up her hand. 'I would like to ask you to try and find a way for my shop to stay at De Greys, because I can't afford to move, but I won't ask you for any special privileges.'

Irritation flooded through him. 'You know I couldn't make that promise, even if I wanted to.'

'That's something, I suppose.' She glared at him.

He took a deep breath. 'What, that I've just told you I can't help you?'

'No, that you have the morals to do the right thing, even if it doesn't suit me.'

She really didn't like him very much if she thought that little of him, he decided. 'Just give me a chance to find a solution to this mess. I know you don't believe me, but I'll do all I can to help you through this.' It was an untenable situation, but one he was determined to solve. If only she'd trust him, he thought, although going by her set expression he doubted she was going to give him the chance to prove himself to her.

She looked up at him, a searching look in her emerald green eyes. 'I suppose so,' she murmured.

What did she suppose? 'You'll give me a chance?' Sebastian usually found it easier to persuade people do as he asked. She was proving to be more stubborn than most.

'What do you want me to say?' she asked, eyes narrowing. 'That all is forgiven?'

He raised an eyebrow and smiled. 'It would be preferable to us fighting.'

She leant in closer to him, a steely glint in her eyes. 'I'm not ready to forgive, or forget. I don't like deception, Sebastian.'

He stifled a groan. Why was this woman so difficult? 'It wasn't intentional. I was going to tell you.'

'When?'

'Soon.'

'Really? Are you so sure?'

'Yes, of course.' He glared at the group of people standing next to him, their curious gazes obviously attracted by his raised voice. They immediately looked the other way. Turning his focus back to Paige, he lowered his voice. 'Can we continue this outside?'

'No, I'm with a friend, and I think I've spent long enough listening to you.'

He clenched his teeth together working the muscle in his jaw. Taking a steadying breath, he closed his eyes for a second. Sebastian knew Paige well enough to be aware that she wasn't going to take any half-cocked excuses. He was going to have his work cut out for him if he wanted to carry out his job properly, and somehow keep her happy. 'Fine. Will you let me come to your house, so we can talk this through?'

'No.'

Why was she being so infuriating? Didn't she realize

they were going to have to see each other regularly at De Greys? 'Whether you like it, or not, you're going to have dealings with me over the next few months. So, the sooner we find a solution, the easier it's going to be for us both.'

Paige stepped from one foot to the other. He couldn't tell if she was considering his suggestion, or if she was simply bored and impatient to get away from him. 'I'm sorry, I don't really see how we can get past this.'

He checked over her shoulder and saw her companion once again pretending not to look at them.

'Come to my house for dinner,' he suggested. 'We can talk everything through without being overheard.' He knew the brunette next to him at the bar was listening intently to their conversation, and by the look of distain Paige was giving her, she'd noticed too.

'There's always someone you know, wherever you go in Jersey,' Paige said pointedly.

Unable to help himself, Sebastian smiled. 'Tomorrow night. I can pick you up if you like?'

'I don't think that's a good idea.'

'You can't ignore this, Paige.' He shook his head, knowing that he had no intention of giving up as easily as she obviously seemed to want him to. He indicated over to Olly. 'I think your friend is about to implode with curiosity.'

'Probably,' she said pulling a face at Olly.

He envied her familiarity with the man.

'Olly works at De Greys too, he's in IT, so you'll no doubt come across him at some point.'

'I really am sorry about this,' he said.

'Me, too.' She looked up at him and Sebastian could tell that his deception had hurt her. She was still reeling from her ex-fiancé letting her down and was too proud to forgive him lightly. He wasn't used to giving up on something and in this case someone, he wanted. He needed to work out a way to get her back. The problem was how.

Chapter Nine

Paige turned on her heel and made for the sanctity of the bathroom, slamming the cubicle door and locking it. She knew instinctively that Olly would have watched the interchange between them with interest. Secretly, she would have loved nothing better than to be able to spend time with Sebastian once again. Paige sighed. Why was life so sodding unfair?

'You little minx,' Olly said, as soon as she returned to the table. 'I've remembered who he is now. He's our new boss, isn't he?'

'He is,' she cringed, hoping no one could overhear what Olly had said.

'Those girls were right at De Greys, he looks like some sort of fifties film star. I notice you left that bit out of the conversation, when you came back from your trip and told me all about this mysterious man.' He leaned forward and narrowed his eyes. 'I wonder what else you failed to mention.'

Paige waved him away. 'Nothing.'

Olly stared at her, his eyes searching her face for clues. 'Somehow, I don't believe you.'

'Stop it. He's just a man, Olly, nothing special,' she fibbed.

'Only a man, she says to a mere mortal. How can the likes of me compete when someone like him is sauntering around the place?'

'There's nothing wrong with you. You're completely different from each other, that's all.'

'That, my friend, is plainly obvious.' He picked up a

warm bread roll and tore off a chunk, coating it with Jersey butter before popping it into his mouth.

'Stop moaning.' She giggled unable to stay defensive for long. 'You know you're irresistible to most of the opposite sex.' She was glad she had made the effort to come out for the evening. Olly always managed to cheer her up.

He sighed. 'So you say, although unfortunately your sister seems particularly immune to my charms.'

'She isn't usually,' Paige said. 'I tried to call Clem before, but she wasn't answering her phone to me either.'

'She's so perfect for me,' he said, a forlorn expression on his face. 'I can't imagine not being with her.'

Paige knew that if she didn't want to spend the evening with a depressed man, she would have to change the subject, and quickly. 'Will it help if I change the subject and tell you what I was discussing with Sebastian?'

'Maybe,' he said, a smile lighting up his face.

'Fine, if it means you'll stop you sitting here droning on about my sister, I'll tell you.'

Cheering up immediately, he listened avidly to every word she said.

The following evening Paige kept her mind off Sebastian by going through ideas that Olly had put together to improve her Heaven in Heels website.

'Right, look at what I've done so far.' Olly nudged her and began moving the mouse across the screen on her laptop. It seemed to go from one page to the next, showing her links from the home page through photos of her designs.

'Here you can have copies of your sketches. I thought you could add one a week as a teaser for the prospective buyers to look at. It'll need to be updated regularly, and I thought you could send out a newsletter, or people could subscribe by email for any updates, say, one day sales, ten per cent gift vouchers, that sort of thing. Keep reminding clients you're out there.'

Paige nodded. 'It looks amazing, Ol, thanks so much.'

He pushed the mouse over towards her. 'Have a go. You'll need to check through the links and pages to find your way round. The more you use it, the more I'm hoping it'll inspire you with ideas on ways to build the site with different options to gain the most sales.'

Paige began clicking through the pages. 'It's brilliant.'

'It's not finished yet. Think of the better online stores you've used, and the aspects of those sites that you like best.'

'I don't really shop online that much.' She laughed at his shocked expression. 'I don't have time to faff about on the internet, unlike you.'

'Yes you do, you just choose to spend your time with your nose in sketch pads. Now you need to do a little research, you have to give me more input.'

'I will,' she said, fascinated to see her stock displayed so cleverly on her laptop.

'You play with that, and I'll have a look at my spag bol.' Olly walked out to the kitchen. 'Wine?'

'Yes please,' she shouted, clicking through several links to see one of her designs from the front, side, as well as the description of the materials described in one box and smaller tick boxes for the sizes and colours. 'There should be some in the wine rack, I stocked up yesterday.'

Olly returned with two glasses of Merlot. 'Here,' he handed one to her. 'You'll have to get used to uploading new designs when they arrive in the shop too. There's no point promoting this new website, if you're not going to keep the stock current.'

She smiled at him. 'You're a star.'

'That other one was so basic, I'm relieved hardly anyone ever found it.' He shook his head. 'Right, let's stuff our faces.'

Paige sat down at the small oak table and unfolded her napkin. 'This looks delicious; I could never have rustled-up something so tasty in so little time.'

'You couldn't manage this if you had all the time in the world,' he teased, stabbing a few spirals of fresh fusilli with a fork and holding it by her mouth. 'Anyway, you're getting too thin. I've suspected you've not been bothering with meals at night, and I know you don't eat much during the day.'

'It doesn't seem much of a point, when you're only cooking for one.'

Olly shrugged. 'I suppose so. Anyway, my ma feeds me every night and it's satisfying to be allowed to take over someone's kitchen once in a while.'

'You can take over mine whenever you like, if this is what you concoct.'

'I might take you up on that. Now, eat.'

Paige took a mouthful. 'Delicious. I owe you one.'

He raised his eyebrows. 'You owe me lots, but helping me get back with your sister will be all the payback I need.'

Paige felt her mood dip. 'You know I'd do anything to sort you two out, don't you?'

Olly smiled. 'I know. But enough sympathy, or I'll start feeling sorry for myself again. You know you're going to have to deal with Mr Perfect. For some reason, he doesn't seem to be the sort of bloke that takes rejection lying down.' He winked at her. 'I don't think he's going to back off as easily as you seem to think.' He motioned towards the leftover spaghetti. 'More?'

Paige shook her head. 'No thanks, this is perfect.' She agreed with Olly. Sebastian hadn't reached where he was in life by doing as he was told. However, she was still too annoyed to have to deal with him right now. She was going to keep him at arm's length for the time being.

Paige was wiping up the dishes, when Olly turned to

her. 'Who's that?'

'Sorry?' She'd been miles away.

'I heard a car, but it's not one I recognize. Your father isn't coming round tonight, is he?'

Paige shook her head. 'He never mentioned anything, but that doesn't mean much. He's always escaping here when Mum has a rant about something.' She finished drying the plate and placed it in the overhead cupboard, then drying her hands walked to the front door. 'Sebastian,' she said, taken aback to discover him standing on her doorstep.

'I was worried that my welcome might be less friendly.'

She dropped the tea towel, irritated for being so clumsy. 'What are you doing here?'

He bent down to pick up the discarded material, and held it out for her. 'We need to talk.'

'I said I didn't want to see you.'

'You said you didn't want to come to my house for a meal.'

Paige folded her arms in front of her chest vaguely aware that she must be looking her very worst. 'So, you thought you'd come here?'

'Correct.'

'You're determined, aren't you?'

'I am.'

'Paige, where have you put the...?' Olly shouted, as he left the kitchen and stepped into the hallway. 'Oh.'

'I don't think you two have met yet?' Paige stepped back giving Sebastian an opportunity to walk into the cottage.

He held out his hand towards Olly. 'Sebastian Fielding. You must be the nosy neighbour?'

Paige noticed the twinkle in his eye, and could have slapped him. Was he trying to be as infuriating as possible?

81

'Thanks, Paige,' Olly said, narrowing his eyes at her before shaking the proffered hand in front of him. 'The name's Olly, and I work in the IT department at De Greys.'

'So I gather.'

'I'll leave you both to it,' Olly said, moving round Sebastian. 'Call me later, if you like,' he whispered loudly.

'Will do, and thanks again for dinner.'

'No worries.'

She watched Olly leave, ignoring the sly wink he gave her as he did so and closed the door behind him. She took a breath and turned to face Sebastian. The look on his tanned face made her stomach flip over treacherously.

'Your hair suits you like that,' he said. 'I don't think I've seen it up before.'

Paige automatically reached up and touched the ponytail at the back of her head. She took the proffered bottle of Fleurie from his hand, flinching slightly as her fingers grazed his.

She glanced into his eyes unable to miss the haunted look in them, before realising that he was saying something. 'Sorry, I was miles away,' she said, leading him through to the living room. 'Take a seat.' She was confident that even if she didn't look well groomed her only reception room was at its best, the quivering flames of the cream cathedral candles illuminating the stone inglenook to perfection. She might not want to face him right now, but Sebastian intended speaking to her, and at least this was in the privacy of her own cottage.

'You have an incredible home,' Sebastian said, bending slightly to view the array of family photos in mismatched silver frames on Paige's polished mahogany table. 'It seems to have captured your essence somehow.'

'I'm very happy here,' she admitted.

'I can understand why,' he said, looking, Paige thought, as if he belonged there. The thought threw her a little, and saddened her.

'Take a seat, I'll open this. I have a feeling we're going to need it.'

Sebastian sat against the worn fabric of the sofa, one muscled arm draped casually across the back of it.

She walked into the kitchen and grabbed the two wine glasses she'd only just finished drying. Then swallowed the lump forming in her throat at the thought of the lost future, she wouldn't be able to enjoy with him. Returning to the living room she passed him a glass. She hesitated, unable to decide where to sit, as there wasn't much choice. Her mind raced, she'd planned this moment many times over the last few days, but unable to remember what she had been going to say, she played for time by taking a long drink from her glass.

He touched her arm gently. 'I just want to clear the air and set matters straight between us. If we have to work closely with each other, I thought it best if we resolved any issues we may have now.'

Paige nodded. She was relieved he'd been so direct, making it less awkward between them. 'Easy to say,' she refused to look at him. 'You're the one with the power to decide my future.'

He shifted on the seat and turned towards her. 'I wish I'd known who you were,' he said. 'I think it's obvious that I'm fond of you, Paige. My time in Italy with you was magical and I'd hoped we could build on what we'd had there.'

Paige chewed on her lower lip, hating the way everything had turned out, and knowing she felt the same way. 'Yes, me too,' she admitted miserably. 'but that was before you lied to me.'

'I didn't lie.'

'You withheld the truth.' She could hear her voice quavering and took a calming breath. 'In my book that's just as bad.'

'What would you rather I'd done? Tell you that morning in Sorrento and ruin the rest of our time together?'

She stood up abruptly, spilling her wine over her sofa and cursing under her breath. 'Yes.'

Sebastian looked utterly miserable. 'I'm sorry I didn't now. I thought you were still too upset about your fiancé, and I didn't want us to fall out unnecessarily.'

'Well now we have.' Paige put down her wine glass and glared at him. 'Surely that should have been the time you explained exactly what was going to happen at De Greys.'

'It was confidential. I couldn't discuss the takeover with anyone.'

'And you can now?'

'I'm not,' Sebastian stood up towering over her. 'I haven't told you any more than any of the other tenants will know.'

'Oh.' She wasn't sure what to say to that admission, but before he could say anything further his mobile rang.

He pulled his phone out of his pocket, and checked the screen, frowning. 'I'm going to have to take this call. I won't be a moment.'

She watched him walk slowly out of the room, silently listening to whoever was talking to him. She didn't know how, but she was desperate for him to find a way for them to get back to how they'd been in Italy. She missed his company, and knew it was only her pride that was holding her back from accepting his explanation. Pride and the determination not to allow another untrustworthy man free access to her heart.

'Paige,' Sebastian came back into the room, interrupting her thoughts. 'I'm going to have to leave.' He rubbed a hand over his chin.

'Why? What's happened?'

'De Greys is on fire.'

Chapter Ten

'What did you say?' Paige couldn't believe what she'd just heard.

'Apparently there was a suspected break-in earlier this evening. It sounds like they've caused a lot of damage,' he said, the strain of the call showing across his face.

'My shop?' She barely managed to ask, but knew she had to find out.

'Probably.' He pushed his hand into his pocket and pulled out his car keys. 'I'll call you as soon as I know what's going on.'

'I'm coming with you,' Paige said, hardly able to take in what was going on. How could her shop be on fire? 'Is anyone hurt?'

'They didn't say. Why don't you wait here? It'll probably be chaotic at De Greys tonight and I don't even know if they'll let me go near the place.'

'I'm not going to sit here not knowing what's happening.' She tried her hardest to sound calm.

He touched her lightly on the arm. 'I'd better go. I'll call you as soon as I can.' He hesitated before making for the door as if to say something else, but then left hurriedly.

Not daring to drive after a few glasses of wine Paige was contemplating what to do next when the front door banged open against the hall wall.

Olly charged in. 'I saw him leave,' he said, striding along the hallway towards the kitchen. 'What happened?' Paige opened her mouth to speak. 'He looked furious when he raced out of here.' She could hear Olly come into the living room. 'There you are,' he said. 'Hey, are you crying? What happened?' Olly pulled her into his arms. 'Did that bastard do something to you?'

'No, of course not,' she said, gently pushing him away and explained about the fire. 'I have to get to the shop,' she said tearfully. 'I need to check if my stock is OK.'

'Fine, if you insist. But I'm driving; you're in no fit state to.' When she went to argue with him, he added. 'I barely touched my drink. Come on, let's go.'

Paige wished he'd slow down. She might need to get to De Greys as soon as possible, but they'd have more chance of doing so if he drove a little slower.

'Bloody hell,' she breathed in disbelief as he stopped the car down the street from the shop entrance. 'Look what they've done.' Paige tripped out of the car, grabbing the door to stop her falling before pushing past the crowd of onlookers. Her route to the front door was stopped by a tape barrier pulled tightly across the front of the ornate building and looped between four lampposts.

Paige looked up at a light wisp of smoke escaping through a panelled window. Three fire engines, their blue lights still flashing, were parked outside on the pedestrian paving. Firefighters strode purposefully into the building, their breathing apparatus strapped to their backs. More people assembled, craning their necks, and watching the scene unfolding. She could hear some exchanging theories about the damage inside, others speculating the cause. Paige couldn't believe there were bystanders taking photos and filming with their mobiles.

'Why are there so many people standing out here like ghouls?' she shouted to Olly. 'I don't recognise any of them from the shop. Why are they here?'

Olly stood protectively behind her, rubbing her arms. 'People can't help being fascinated by drama. It's just news to them.'

Paige pushed her way to the nearest policeman.

'Excuse me, I have a shop in there and I need to get inside.'

He shook his head and held up a hand to stop her moving any closer. 'I'm afraid you'll have to wait until we're sure this structure is safe. I suggest you come back tomorrow, or contact whoever's in charge of the premises. I very much doubt this place will be open for business for a while yet.'

'You don't understand,' Paige argued. 'I have to go …'

'No. You don't understand,' he said, his pockmarked cheeks reddening. 'No one is going in there until I get the nod that it's in order for them to do so. Now, why don't you do as I've already suggested and go home?'

'Hang on a minute.' She took a step closer to him, only for Olly to pull her backwards and away from the shop. 'Olly, stop it!' she shouted, trying unsuccessfully to shrug him off.

'Paige, give up. There's nothing you can do tonight.' He held on to her ignoring her protests as he pulled her away. 'You're only upsetting yourself staying here. Come home, and calm down.' Letting go of her, he hugged her tightly. 'Take it easy,' he said into her ear. 'You've had a nasty shock and whether you like it or not, I'm taking you home.'

As Paige opened her mouth to retaliate, she glimpsed Sebastian striding out of the front door, smudges of soot blackening his face beneath his yellow hard hat. He appeared to glance at her, as Olly stopped speaking and began leading her away.

She would have liked to speak to Sebastian, but by the look on his face he was not in any mood for talking.

Sebastian watched in silence as Olly led her away. Didn't that guy ever leave her alone? He looked around to see if the store manager had arrived, then unable to spot him, went back inside. The fire was out and even he could tell there'd been no structural damage to the building. The small shops inside were another matter. He knew that Paige would want to know the state of her own space. He walked down through the arcade towards her doorway.

He didn't intend lying to her about the extent of the damage. From now on whatever her reaction would be Sebastian decided that the truth would always have to be his priority. Lies were just a way of putting off the inevitable truth, he reasoned striding past the blackened pillars towards her shop.

There in front of him, virtually untouched, was her pride and joy. The thought of her spending time designing each pair of shoes and boots she'd then displayed so thoughtfully made him proud of her. Beautiful, as well as talented, he mused, saddened to know that even though her contents appeared untouched by the fire, smoke could do as much damage ensuring her valuable stock would probably have to be discarded. He hoped her insurance policy was good. She was probably going to need to make a big claim.

Sebastian knew enterprises such as Paige's could rarely afford setbacks as expensive as this one would potentially be. He walked over to the nearest shelf and lifted a green leather boot, holding it to his face to smell the suede. He groaned as a definite odour of smoke instantly wafted up his nostrils. He put the boot back down again, hearing two of the security guards being questioned by one of the firemen.

'You're sure,' the fireman repeated.

'It looked like a body. No idea who it could be though.'

Sebastian hurried over to them and introduced himself. 'I need to know everyone is accounted for before I leave.' He waited and when the fireman didn't reply, added. 'I know the layout of this store, surely that will save you time looking around.'

The fireman shrugged. 'Fine, let's get a move on.'

Without waiting for him to change his mind, Sebastian took the stairs two at a time, finally reaching the fifth floor storeroom to find what did indeed look like an inert body on the floor over by the window. 'Shit.'

The head store man was already there. Noticing Sebastian approaching he held up his hand. 'It's OK, it's a mannequin.'

Relief coursed through Sebastian. He hadn't noticed he'd been tensing most of his muscles until the relief of this statement allowed him to relax. 'Thank God.'

'Too right,' said the fireman coming up behind him. 'It makes the investigation a lot easier when there aren't any casualties.'

Sebastian sighed. 'Right, I'll leave you to it. I don't suppose the store's going to be opening again in a hurry?'

The taller fireman shook his head. 'You can tell your tenants not to expect to be able to return to this building, at least for a few days. We'll let you know when they can come and check their stock, then it'll be a while after that before work can be carried out to clean up the mess.'

'Thank you,' Sebastian said, pulling his mobile from his jacket pocket. The first person he wanted to speak to was Paige. He knew by the look on her face earlier that she was in a terrible state, and didn't want to keep her in suspense for a moment longer than necessary.

As he moved through the parting crowds towards his parked car, Sebastian visualised Paige's shop. It broke his heart to think that she could be put into financial difficulties thanks to some vandal. She didn't deserve this. He understood how hard she'd worked to be able to start up her own business, with no backing from anyone else, and nothing but hard work and a determination to push her forward. She was going to need that tenacity even more so now.

It had all seemed so easy in Sorrento, and it saddened him to think that their reunion hadn't gone according plan.

In fact nothing had since his arrival in Jersey.

'Paige,' he said as soon as her answer phone message had finished. 'It's Sebastian.' Leaving a message for her, he arrived at his car. Of course, he realised, she was probably being comforted by Olly. What was all that about? He seemed very attentive for a friend. He terminated the call with more vigour than was necessary on the touch screen. So much for their evening together.

Sebastian stepped into his Mercedes and started the engine. He had a lot of planning to get through before tomorrow. He may as well get started now. He liked to be organised and, if nothing else, it would keep his mind busy and stop him from thinking. He hadn't realised how deeply Paige had affected him. Sebastian sighed. He shouldn't have fallen for her, not with the decisions he was going to have to face in the immediate future.

'Do you think my insurance policy is going to cover all the damage to the stock?' Paige asked Olly as they drove home. She couldn't afford to be out of pocket, and began to feel sick at the thought of what she could have lost in the fire. Those shoes were a culmination of years of hard work, designing, sourcing materials, and concentrating on intricate details.

'I'm sure you'll be properly covered,' he soothed. 'You went through the estimates with a fine tooth comb before making your final choice.'

As Paige stepped into the warmth of her narrow hallway, she immediately noticed the flashing light on her answer phone machine. Pressing 'Play', she felt her stomach flutter as she listened to a message from Sebastian.

'Paige, I noticed you came to De Grey's,' he said, his voice huskier than usual, which she assumed must be due to the smoky atmosphere he had just been in. There was a slight pause before he continued. 'The centre will definitely be closed for the rest of the week. Give me a call if you want to inspect your stock at some point, but I doubt you'll be able to go in there for at least another two days. There's a lot of clearing up to do, which can only be started once the police have completed their investigations.' There was another pause. 'Try not to worry too much.'

Paige threw her coat onto the arm of the sofa, while Olly poured her a glass of wine from the bottle Sebastian had brought earlier in the evening. Unable to believe so much had happened in such a short time, she stood next to Olly as they listened in silence to Sebastian's message once again.

'This is horrible, especially when you spent so much money on those flyers for me. What a waste.'

'It's Sod's Law.' He passed her the glass. 'Why would anyone start a fire deliberately? Morons.' He glanced over at the worktop. 'I'm starving. Shall we have something to eat?'

Paige shook her head. She didn't have the stomach for food right now. 'I don't want anything,' she said, going into the lounge and slumping in her armchair.

Olly shrugged. 'Can I make a sandwich then?'

'Of course you can. Help yourself to whatever you can find in the fridge.'

'Sure you don't want one?' he shouted from the kitchen.

'No, thanks.' Paige took a sip from her glass. All she could think of was having her shop back to how it had been when she'd closed up earlier that afternoon.

Olly returned with a plate of toast covered with bolognese sauce. He switched on the television on his way to sit down. His phone bleeped. Taking it out of his trouser pocket, he read the message, raising his eyebrows as he did so. 'Apparently, when the guys from the fire department first arrived at the scene, they thought they'd found a dead body in one of the larger storerooms.'

Paige shivered. 'Someone died? That's horrible. Do they know who it is?'

Olly waved his hand at her. 'Calm down. I said they thought that was the case. It turned out to be an old mannequin.' He laughed, looking as relieved as she felt. 'I remember the blokes in there used one as a coat rack in the winter.'

'Don't frighten me like that, you dope.'

'You have to see the funny side,' he said pulling a silly face at her.

She didn't smile. 'It's been a strange day all round. Don't let's talk about it any more.'

'I've just thought,' he said, stabbing his fork into a mouthful of food. 'That mannequin could have been me.'

Paige frowned, unable to see how. 'Seriously?'

He nodded. 'I've been working late for weeks, only finishing on time for the past few days.'

'Olly, stop, or I'm going to have nightmares.' She grimaced at the thought. 'Anyway, you would have escaped from the building, everyone else did, and let's be honest, you've never bothered to work that late.'

'I have actually. My workload has increased massively since this bloody takeover. Mr Perfect has wanted reports on everything. I know he's trying to find a way to cut costs, but I have spreadsheets coming out of my ears. I walked in on the secretaries moaning about it, the other day.' He grabbed the remote control. 'Let's keep the news on, see if we can find out anything else.'

There was nothing new to report. All the newsreader did was to reiterate that the shop would be closed to clients, as well as staff, for the rest of the week until a structural survey had been carried out and tests performed.

Paige tried to concentrate on making a mental note of her stock, but her mind kept wandering back to the haunted look on Sebastian's face. She'd begun to imagine them spending time together ever since those carefree days in Sorrento, and even tonight, with his face flecked with soot, she couldn't help thinking how attracted to him she was. Paige sighed, taken aback at how soon she'd managed to get over Jeremy.

'What's wrong?' Olly mumbled, placing his empty plate on the table in front of him and rolling over onto his side on Paige's sagging sofa.

'I'm fine,,' she said, picking up his plate and grabbing him by the arm. 'I'm just tired and I think it's time you went home.' He opened his mouth to argue. 'You live next-door, it's not like you have a commute, now go.'

'Fine,' he said groaning as he stood up. 'See you in the morning.'

She phoned Sebastian on his mobile as early as she dared the next morning, unable to stop the feeling of frustration when her call was sent straight to voicemail. Clearing her throat, she said, 'This is Paige. Thank you for letting me know about the shop. You're bound to be busy over the next few days, so I'll call you soon to arrange a convenient time for me to inspect my stock.'

Olly knocked on the front door and walked in to the kitchen just as Paige was opening a pack of bacon. 'Your timing is incredible,' she said laughing. 'I won't bother asking if you want breakfast.'

She made them both a bacon sandwich and strong mug of tea and carried hers through to the living room. Pulling open the curtains and French doors to let fresh air in to the room, she sat down and smiled at him. 'You look like you had a bit more to drink when you got home last night.'

'I feel rough,' he groaned, holding his head in his hands. He took a sip of the tea. 'This should sort me out a bit though, thanks.'

Paige turned on the television. 'The news will be on in a minute. Maybe there'll an update?' She was hoping to find out more information, but knew she'd have to physically go to her shop to understand the full extent of the damage to her stock.

'You're not going to try and go in today?' he asked, munching on his food. Paige shook her head. 'Me neither, not much point I suspect.'

There was only a repeat of the previous night's information on the news with a short extra confirming that staff should not to go in for the rest of the week.

'Great,' Olly said. 'You don't need to tell me twice.'

'Maybe there'll be more in the *Jersey Gazette* later?'

'But that won't be out in the shops until at least two o'clock this afternoon, I can't wait until then.' Olly gulped down the last of his tea. 'I'm going home to shower, and make a few phone calls. Someone must know something.'

'You're just nosy and want to know any gory details.' Paige dreaded the thought that anyone could have been hurt. 'Call me later.'

'Will do.' He patted the top of her head.

He reached the front door and opened it, but before stepping outside turned to her. 'Don't let this situation upset you too much.'

Paige went over to her desk and pulled out a lever arch file. It was time to sort through her outstanding invoices. At least she'd always made it her policy to remove her takings from the shop every night. She knelt down and pulled back a corner of the lounge carpet to the side of her desk. Opening the small floor safe underneath, she took out the cloth bags containing her cash. Paige placed it onto her desk, and began sorting the notes. She bagged up the change in small plastic bags, ready to take it all to the bank later in the morning.

She knew it was going to be difficult to estimate her losses. It depended on how long the shop would be closed, and even though she was going to be able to make a claim for any damaged stock, the cost of restocking her designs lay mainly in the wait for them to be made to order. She would have to be very careful, at least until she knew where she stood financially.

She hoped Sebastian would phone her soon, to let her know when she could go and inspect the damage. It would only be then that she would have an idea what she was dealing with. However dreadful matters were, the bank would still expect her to keep paying for her house, the lease on her shop, her bills.

The phone rang. 'It was Frank.' Olly announced breathlessly, without waiting for her to say hello.

'Frank who?' Paige shook her head to clear her thoughts.

'He was one of the messengers.' When she didn't speak, he added. 'The older one, with the broken nose.'

'He started the fire?' Paige asked, pushing the blue moneybag into her briefcase.

'No, he's the one who spotted it and called the emergency services.'

'He must have been terrified.'

'I suppose so, but more to the point, what the hell was he doing there so late at night? He's a part-time messenger and contracted to finish before three. Why would he be there at seven in the evening?'

Paige tried to come up with a logical answer, but failed. 'No idea, strange though.'

'He doesn't have any family, bit of a loner by all accounts,' Olly continued, sounding excited by the unexpected drama.

'Where did you find all this information?' Paige always teased Olly, when he couldn't help being nosy, but this time he had surpassed himself.

'One of the other messengers told me. Couldn't wait to spread the word,' he said gleefully. 'They called him into the station to question him about Frank's usual duties, and the times he carried them out. Maybe they suspect him of starting the fire. I can't wait to find out more.'

'Hey, this isn't an episode of *Bergerac*, you know,' she teased, relieved he had something else to think about other than his relationship with her younger sister. 'This is real.'

'Sorry, I forgot. I can't help getting carried away. It's interesting though, don't you think?'

'Not really. Someone could have deliberately set this fire without knowing if anyone was in the building. Whoever did this has caused difficulties for a lot of people.'

It disturbed her that something suspicious had been going on in the very department store where she worked. She knew without doubt there must be more to this story than they were aware.

She made her excuses. 'Why don't you go and carry on your investigations,' she suggested, checking her watch knowing she should be getting on with things. 'I'm going to phone the insurance brokers and find out exactly where I stand.'

She wasn't looking forward to hearing bad news, but couldn't bear not knowing how serious her situation might be. Paige picked up the phone and keyed in the number.

Chapter Eleven

Arriving home after doing her banking, Paige sent off an email to her suppliers with several sketches and notes for the designs, and an explanation about the fire. She asked them if they could give her the earliest possible date for delivery of the new shoes, and took out her stock list, cross referencing it against her sales.

All she needed to know now was exactly how much of her stock had been affected by the fire. Not wishing to fret unnecessarily about it, she then set out a spreadsheet ready for the day that she could go into her store and check off each item she was unable to salvage. If nothing else, she would be prepared for the inevitable meeting she knew she'd have to endure with the insurance assessor.

Paige ended the call and sat back in her chair. At least she now knew she would be reimbursed for most of her damaged stock. She just had to hope that she would receive the insurance payment soon so that she could pay for the replacement stock her suppliers would be making for her.

With nothing left to do, she vacuumed her cottage to keep from fretting further. She was struggling to cram the vacuum cleaner back into a narrow broom cupboard, when she heard a knock at the door. 'Come in,' she shouted, wondering why Olly was back again so soon. 'What's happened now?'

'I've jacked in uni,' Clem announced.

Paige swung round, slamming her fingers in the cupboard door as her bottom bumped it, pushing it shut.

'Bugger.' She put her fingers into her mouth and sucked gently to ease the pain. 'What are you doing here?'

'Nice welcome, sis,' Clem said. 'Can I borrow some cash to pay the taxi driver? I didn't have enough.'

Paige nodded towards her red handbag on the sideboard. Hurrying over to the tap, she turned it on and held her purple-tipped fingers under the running cold water. 'Ooh, that hurt.' She listened as Clem closed the front door and returned to join her.

'Well?' Clem said, standing just inside the kitchen doorway. 'Are you going to give me a hug, or what?'

Paige turned off the tap, and without thinking did as her sister asked. 'Come here then,' she said, concern coursing through her. 'Why would you pack in your studies now?'

Clem didn't answer. Paige could see by the look on her face that she was in some sort of trouble. 'Does this have anything to do with you finishing with Olly?'

'No,' she said defensively, taking a seat on one of the high stools by Paige's short breakfast bar.

'What is it then?'

'It's nothing really.' She shrugged, reminding Paige of a naughty schoolgirl trying to avoid getting a telling off. 'I'd just had enough and wanted to come home.'

'Fine.' Paige didn't believe her, but filled the kettle and switched it on. 'So, why are you here and not at home with Mum and Dad?'

Clem pushed a lose strand of her auburn bob behind her ear. 'They're not back from their cruise until tomorrow, and anyway, I was hoping I could move in with you for a bit. Help you out at the shop when you go on buying trips, that sort of thing.'

'For how long?' she asked, adding. 'And when were you thinking of going back to uni? You can't miss too much of the term, you'll never catch up again.' Paige felt a sneaking suspicion creep slowly through her brain.

'That's just it,' Clem smiled, hands on her hips. 'I'm

not going back.' She held up a hand when Paige went to say something. 'And I'm not in the mood to talk about it at the moment, if you don't mind.'

'Open the door.' Olly shouted up at her window. Paige groaned. She had enough to contend with without getting mixed up in Olly's dramas with Clem. Paige pretended she couldn't hear him, hoping he'd get bored and leave her alone. No such luck. 'Bugger off, Olly,' she shouted her voice croaky with sleep.

'I'm not going anywhere, so you may as well let me in.'

Paige groaned. Her head hurt, probably, she presumed from so much thinking and tension. 'Can't this wait?' she asked, opening the window and flinching at the bright light outside as memories of the night before filtered through to her. She and Clem had sat up talking for a couple of hours, until Paige relented, agreeing that she could move in on the understanding Clem phoned their parents as soon as they'd settled back in after their trip.

'No,' Olly argued. 'I need to speak to you. Let me in.' He glanced over his shoulder in the direction of his parents' house. 'Unless you want my mother coming to find out what's going on?'

'All right, I'm coming.' She dragged on her dressing gown, pushed her feet into her slippers, and ambled downstairs to let him in.

'What do you want?' she asked, pulling open the front door, hoping not to wake Clem. She didn't want her sister to make an appearance just yet. She wasn't ready to be caught in the middle of any row Clem and Olly were bound to have.

'Blimey, is that a birds' nest on your head?' Olly teased. 'And why were you still asleep this late?'

She put her hands up to her head. Paige sighed. 'What time is it?'

'It's almost ten, so you can stop giving me the evils and offer me a coffee.'

'What?' She felt sick, and supposed it must be the lack of food. 'If you insist on being here, go and make yourself useful in the kitchen. Then you can tell me why you woke me up.'

'Your mother couldn't get through to you on your landline, and your mobile's turned off,' he said, filling the kettle from the tap and pressing it on.

Paige nodded. 'I needed a little peace,' she fibbed.

'She said something about the fire at De Greys. They've been catching up by reading the gazettes their neighbour kept for them when they were away. They were upset you didn't tell them about your predicament, and that they had to read about it.' He pulled a scared face. 'She also mentioned Clemmie but I've no idea what she has to do with it, and your mother wouldn't elaborate when I asked her. They should be here by noon.'

Paige rubbed her eyes. 'I was hoping to have a bit more time before they found out about everything. Why do they have to come racing round here?'

'They love you,' he said. 'I thought I'd come and rouse you from your pit, give you a chance to smarten yourself up and look remotely human for when they get here. You know what your mother's like about these things. If she sees you looking like this, she'll assume the worst, and I'm sure the last thing you need right now is to have your parents involving themselves in everything.'

'True,' she said, imagining how her mother would have ranted on to Olly when he had answered his phone. 'You're right, of course. Sorry for growling at you.'

'No problem, I'm used to your grouchiness in the morning. You always took ages to come to life when we were at uni and you obviously haven't improved since then.'

He took her by the shoulders, turning her towards the

staircase. 'Now, I suggest you make the most of this achingly slow kettle and get your butt up to the bathroom and take a shower. Be prepared, as they say.'

Paige frowned. 'What?'

He shook his head in defeat. 'Just hurry up and get dressed.'

She finished drying her hair, dragging it into some semblance of a ponytail, just as her parents' Jaguar pulled in to the driveway, giving her enough time to run downstairs to greet them. Paige couldn't understand how Clem managed to sleep through all the noise in the house.

'Mum, Dad, come in,' Paige called, more cheerily than she felt, as she waited for them by the front door. She noticed her mother's frown and knew she was going to have her work cut out, if she was to convince them Clem would be fine. It was obviously the real reason they were at her house. She doubted their visit had much to do with the fire.

'Where is she? I've barely unpacked. I haven't even started the washing machine. Well?' her mother asked, shaking her head, stopping instantly the moment she noticed Olly. 'Oliver, you're here,' she declared, looking a little taken aback when he stepped out from the kitchen in front of her.

'You phoned him, remember?' Paige smiled at Olly apologetically.

'Did we? I'm still recovering from my trip.' She sighed heavily.

'Marion, we've flown in from Southampton. You don't have jetlag after a half-hour flight.'

'George,' she said glaring at him, narrowing her heavily made-up eyes. 'I'm exhausted from our cruise. I haven't had a chance to acclimatize back into the swing of things yet,' she said before marching down the hallway towards the living room without waiting for him to retaliate.

George focused his attention on Paige. 'I'm sure you can understand why we felt the need to come here.' He glanced down the corridor at her mother's receding back and gave Paige a quick hug. 'Are your phones not working?'

'Sorry, I turned them off.' She pulled her Blackberry out of her handbag and quickly switched it back on. 'There.'

Paige prayed they didn't say anything about Clem before she could speak to Olly and let him know what was going on. First though, she needed to get him to leave so she could deal with her parents. She would explain everything to him soon. It was not something she was particularly looking forward to.

'Go through. I'll make us all a coffee and then we can have a chat.'

Olly touched her lightly on the shoulder. 'Would you rather I stayed?' he whispered from behind.

Hell, no, she thought. 'No thanks. I'll catch up with you later.' She looked in the direction of the lounge where she could hear her mother's voice getting louder by the second. 'Thanks for waking me up.'

'No problem. I'll leave you to do your thing.'

'Thanks, Ol,' she said, unable to stop feeling guilty.

Deciding to begin with telling her parents about the fire, she explained that as soon as she received a call from Sebastian, she'd go and survey the damage to her stock and take it from there. She couldn't miss the meaningful tilt of her mother's head to her father when she mentioned Sebastian's name, but chose to ignore it. Dealing with the fire incident and Clem's unexpected return was enough for one day.

'I've gone through all my paperwork and thankfully, as I had a sale on, my new stock is either still in storage, or hasn't yet arrived on the island.'

'So it could have been far worse?' her father asked,

pointedly looking in her mother's direction.

'Yes, much worse,' Paige assured him.

'I hope you took on board everything I've said about that Fielding character?'

Paige nodded.

He didn't look convinced. 'I know many of you youngsters aspire to the celebrity lifestyle,' he patted her shoulder. 'I don't mean you, of course, but you're not used to the sort of life he has with all those paparazzi nutters hanging about on his doorstep to get pictures of him whenever he sets foot outside.'

'Really?' She had no idea Sebastian had to put up with such an intrusion into his life.

'Oh there was some big thing about his marriage, or engagement, a few years back.'

It was the first she'd heard of Sebastian being famous in any way.

Her father shook his head. 'OK, so he's not one of these footballer types, but he's a well-known entrepreneur and his reputation is increasing by the year. You don't need to be involved with those sorts of issues.'

She smiled, and shook her head. 'I'm fine; you don't have to worry about me.'

He stared at her in silence and seemed to be making up his mind whether or not to believe her. 'Fine,' he said satisfied with her assurances. 'Don't forget that he'll be far more experienced in the cut-throat ways of the world than you are.'

God, this was getting a bit much. 'I'm not a teenager. Please stop fretting about me.'

He pushed his hands in his pockets and stood by her mother's chair. 'OK. Now we're convinced you're bearing up, I think we should have a word with your sister, if she's still here.'

'Yes, where is she?' her mother asked, animated once more. 'I have a few things to say to her before I leave.

George,' she said waving at him. 'Make sure you speak to Clementine.'

Paige pulled a face at her father. Did she think Dad was some sort of tyrant they were frightened of, Paige wondered. He might bellow occasionally, but they all knew he was a softie underneath all that bluster.

'Go on, you'd better bring her down,' he said.

She ran up the stairs to fetch Clem, knocking on the door, before opening it a fraction. 'Hi,' she said, a little taken aback to find Clem sitting, freshly showed and dressed in jeans and a T-shirt. 'You OK?'

She nodded. 'I was just building myself up to face Mum.' She looked up at Paige. 'I heard Olly earlier. You haven't told him anything, have you?'

'Not yet,' Paige was relieved to admit. 'But you do know I can't keep this from him for long. He's my closest friend, and living next door he's bound to see you at some point.'

'I know.'

Paige couldn't help feeling sorry for her and knew her sister hadn't told her the real reason for her return to the island. Clem had always wanted to go to university and study History. Even when she and Olly had got together, no matter how devastated she'd been to leave him behind, she still never considered giving up her degree. Paige studied her for a moment.

'I'll leave you in peace,' Paige said, as her sister entered the lounge to greet their parents.

'Don't feel you have to,' Clem said, attempting a smile that didn't quite make her it to her eyes. 'I have nothing to say.'

'But your degree,' Marion cried, one hand to her throat as if someone had just threatened to harm her. 'All that studying wasted. Not to mention the fees. If only we could get student loans in Jersey for further education like they do on the mainland,' she said. 'I'd rather have time to pay

104

off a loan than have to struggle to find the fees at the beginning of each year.' She shook her head. 'We've already paid this year's fees.'

'Marion,' their father glared at her. 'Never mind the fees. I'm sure Clementine has her reasons for this decision.' He turned to focus his attention on his youngest daughter. 'And as soon as she's had time to think things through, she'll be returning to England to carry on with her studies.'

'But, Dad,' Clem said, before being interrupted.

He held up his hand. 'No. Enough now.' He shook his head. 'I'll speak to you in a few days; see if you've come to your senses by then.'

Both girls knew better than to argue with their father when he was in this mood.

'Marion.' He held out his hand to help their mother stand. 'Come along, let's go.'

'We're going to lunch at Samsons,' she said, trying to distract him like she always did when she felt he'd gone on long enough. 'I think I'll try the scallops.'

'You always have the scallops, Mum,' Paige said, glad not to have to listen to more advice from her father. She gave her mother a peck on her cheek. 'You go and enjoy yourselves.'

'Thank God that's over with,' Clem said, falling back into the large armchair, when Paige returned to the lounge having seen their parents out.

Paige was about to agree when she heard her phone bleep from inside her handbag. Saved by the phone, she thought, and went to check the message.

'I can meet you at 9 2moro @ yr shop, Seb.' Her heart skipped as she read it. He could have phoned her, she thought, conveniently forgetting that she was the one who had unplugged her landline and switched off her mobile.

'I can go in to the shop at nine tomorrow morning to check everything out,' she relayed to Clem. 'I'd better go

105

next-door and let Olly know, otherwise he'll be over here to find out.'

Before she had time to knock at his front door, Olly pulled it open with a flourish. 'Has anyone contacted you yet?' she asked, as he poked his head out.

'Just now,' Olly held up his latest phone. 'I was just about to come and tell you. I suppose we've all received the same message.'

Paige looked at his screen. It seemed like they had, she thought miserably. That said it all.

'Mine's from my manager,' he added, as if reading her mind. 'I was hoping for more time off, but I suppose they need the computers up and running as soon as possible.'

'They'll need you to make sure the cash registers are working too.' Paige felt a little cheered Seb hadn't been the one to contact every member of staff, after all. Then feeling foolish for being so immature, she added. 'Why don't you call for me in the morning? We can go in together to see the state of the place.'

'But I thought I'd come back with you to your cottage now,' he said, looking confused.

'Not today, Ol.' She moved back from his doorstep.

'Is everything OK?'

Paige smiled in what she hoped was a reassuring way. 'Fine, really. I just need some time out, that's all.'

Chapter Twelve

'It's not as bad as I thought.' Paige glanced around her shoe display and at the shelves at the back of her shop.

Sebastian could hear the relief in her voice as he walked up to the partition at the beginning of her concession.

'It all looks fine to me,' agreed Olly. 'I'm pleased for you. At least now you won't have to take out another loan to pay for new stock.'

Sebastian stepped past a pillar. He saw Olly pull back the sleeve of his sweatshirt and checked his watch. 'I'd better get up to the office before he notices I'm missing and has me shot.'

'Fine, see you later. Oh, and don't forget to find me before going home. I don't want to have to walk back.'

'Um, hi,' Olly said awkwardly, spotting Sebastian standing there.

'Hi,' Sebastian said, irritated by Olly's comment about him and envious of the closeness between Paige and this man. He stood back to let Olly leave. 'They may not look as if they've been affected, but I think you'll find some of them will be smoke-damaged.'

'I didn't see you there,' Paige said.

'You'll need to smell them,' Sebastian continued, ignoring her obvious contempt for him.

Paige frowned. 'Smell them?'

'There was a lot of smoke in the building, although more at the front rather than back this way, but you don't want to sell anything to your customers and have it returned later as soiled goods, do you?'

She stepped forward, and picking up a purple leather boot with skyscraper heels and tiny chains across the ankle, she breathed in deeply. Sebastian couldn't imagine anyone being able to balance on such thin heels, let alone walk in them. She seemed unsure and sniffed again.

'Mmm, there's only a slight smell. Thankfully, it's only the stock on display that's been badly affected. The rest are locked away, in tissue paper and boxes, so they've been spared. I think I'll take the ones that have been affected home to air for a few days. Hopefully, then they'll be all right.' She turned to face him. 'How's the rest of the building?'

'Not as bad as we first thought,' he said, surprised she was engaging in conversation with him. He watched her full mouth as she spoke for a moment before realizing he hadn't heard a word of what she was saying. Sebastian shook his head. 'Sorry, what was that?'

'Don't worry,' Paige said, sarcasm filling her voice. 'It wasn't anything important.'

Sebastian stepped closer to her and went to take her hand. Paige moved away from him. 'Paige, I know what you must think of me.'

She narrowed her eyes. 'If you did, I'm sure you wouldn't waste your time talking to me.'

'You don't have any intention of forgiving me for what I've done, do you?'

Paige shook her head. 'Not yet. Can I ask when I'm likely to discover, let me see,' she said holding a finger up against the side of her jaw. 'Oh yes, whether I'm surplus to requirements, or not?'

'Are you serious?'

'Don't you recall telling me in Sorrento how you have to categorise the concessions and decide which you'll keep and those that are surplus to the company's requirements?'

He couldn't make up his mind if he wanted to shake

her, or kiss her. 'I've a feeling it won't matter what I say to you. I think you've already made up your mind about me. However, if you need any help removing stock from the store, let me know.'

'Thank you,' she snapped. 'But I'll be fine.'

'I'll leave you to it then,' he said, trying not to smile as he watched her silently before turning and walking away.

With her father's words ringing in her ears, Paige knew she was right not to ask for Sebastian's help. Olly stayed behind after work to help her move her stock in his car, making her feel even guiltier about keeping her sister's presence from him. Back at the cottage, she took each pair of boots and shoes from their boxes and lined them up in her small conservatory, covering the whole floor space with them.

Paige opened the two windows. 'Hopefully they'll get enough of an airing this way.'

'I couldn't smell anything to begin with,' Olly said, passing her the last pair of black leather shoes. 'Luckily, your shop is well away from the worst of the damage. The clothes shops from the first floor are in a right mess. They're going to have to dump all their stock. The insurance claim is going to be massive.'

'Is there any news on the bloke who reported the fire?' She knitted her fine eyebrows together in confusion, wondering where her sister had gone, or if she was keeping out of the way in her room.

'What, Frank Bellows? Nope, they still can't get him to say what he was doing there so late at night. He insists he didn't see anything suspicious. I was wondering if it was some sort of protest against the company takeover that probably went wrong. He's been there for years, after all, and won't take kindly to any changes.'

Paige sat down. 'Poor man.' She shook the thought from her head. 'I'm glad I'll be off to Spain next week, and away from all this chaos.'

'Buying again so soon?'

She nodded. 'I emailed off the latest designs to my supplier. Can you believe it's three months since I last went? You know how I have to time my trips to coincide with the university holidays,' she added without thinking.

Olly visibly brightened. 'Does that mean Clemmie will soon be back from uni to look after everything?'

'Um, yes,' Paige said, wishing he would stop looking so hopeful. Then, unable to keep it from him any longer, she took a deep breath. 'In fact, she's already here.' There. She had done it. There was no going back now. Clem might want to kill her, but right now she didn't care. The startled look on Olly's face made her want to give him a hug.

'Already?' His thick blond eyebrows knitted together in a frown. 'Why didn't you tell me before?'

Paige chewed her lower lip trying to think up a plausible answer. 'Because she asked me not to,' she admitted, relieved to be telling her friend the truth. 'Clem's insisting she's not going back, which is why my parents came over to the house the other morning.'

'I thought it a little dramatic for them to race over because of the fire. I mean it's not like you were hurt,' he added thoughtfully. 'So, has she mentioned me at all?'

''Fraid not.' Paige shook her head, furious with her sister for treating someone as decent as Olly in such a shabby way.

'She hasn't said anything to you? What, nothing?'

'Sorry.' She stroked his arm gently, wishing she could take away some of his hurt. 'Don't worry, I'm sure she will do when she's ready.'

'Yes, but when will that be? I still don't have a clue why she dumped me. One minute everything was great between us, and the next.' He slammed his fist down on the counter top, causing the merchandise to shudder.

110

'Sorry.'

'It's fine. I can understand how frustrating this must be for you, but I've no idea what happened either.'

'I want to be angry with her, but I can't help feeling something is wrong. I'm worried for her. This is so out of character.' He raked both hands through his messy hair.

Paige thought so too, but didn't like to add to his concern. 'Let's not get all worked up. Clem just needs a little time and at least we know where she is while she's doing it.'

He seemed to accept this. 'True, I just hope she doesn't take too long, I'm going mad waiting, and it'll be worse now I know she's right next door. Somehow it was easier when I thought she was away.'

Great, thought Paige, not the effect she was hoping to have. She was also worried about Clem's reasons for finishing with Olly. They seemed so perfectly matched and had obviously been very happy the last time she'd seen them together. Something was very wrong, and she needed to discover what it could be in order to be able to help her sister in any way.

Paige was relieved when the day she was leaving for Spain finally arrived. Inviting her sister to the shop to go through everything, she told her that she could have two of the six smoke-damaged pairs.

'Two pairs?' Clem shrieked with excitement, grabbing the emerald green thigh-high boots and putting them on. 'I've had a passion for these since you first showed me the sketches.'

'You'd be having a third pair, if they weren't too small for you,' Paige said, thinking how well the colour suited Clem's skin tone. 'They look gorgeous with your long legs. You're so lucky.'

'Why, because of the boots, or my legs?' Clem said, smiling for the first time since she had returned from university.

'Because of your legs.' Paige pulled a face. 'Stop showing off, you know how I hate my short ones.'

'They're hardly short, just shorter than mine.' Clem took off the boots and tried on the other pair Paige had given her. 'These are gorgeous. Thanks, Sis.'

'My pleasure,' Paige said, determining it was now time to broach the subject of Olly. 'Clem,' she said, tidying up the boots scattered on her lounge floor.

'How's Olly?' Clem asked interrupting her as she studied her reflection in the full-length mirror. 'Is he still working upstairs at De Greys?'

'He is.' Paige nodded. 'Why, were you thinking of having a chat with him?'

Clem groaned. 'I don't want to, but I know I owe him some sort of explanation.'

Me too, thought Paige. 'He's confused about why you finished with him. And I can't say I blame him.'

'I know. I promise I'll talk to him soon,' she said, frowning. 'Not yet though.'

'Please make it soon. It's putting me in a very awkward position.'

'I will,' she said. 'Does he know I'll be working here while you're in Spain?'

Paige nodded. 'So, unless he avoids you, you're bound to bump into him at some point.'

'Great,' Clem said, sounding anything but happy at the thought.

Paige chewed her lower lip. 'Maybe I should postpone this trip for a few weeks?'

'No, you won't.' Clem shook her head. 'And don't look at me like that, I'll be fine. You go and have a productive trip. Bring back some fab footwear.'

Paige didn't like leaving her sister in this frame of mind, especially as she still had no idea what was wrong. She had no choice though. She needed to sort out her designs for the forthcoming season. 'I'll see you on Saturday morning. Try to behave while I'm away.'

'Yes,' Clem said, giving her a hug. 'I have the keys right here and memorized the security codes. I know what I'm doing. Now bugger off.'

Chapter Thirteen

Paige couldn't believe it was already early June and the last night of her trip. Her feet ached from walking around the large warehouses where she'd been taken to inspect the leather her supplier was proposing to use in her next designs. She turned on her mobile to check for any messages from Olly. She had phoned Clem each day and been relieved to hear that as far as they were concerned, the shop was selling everything at a speedy rate.

'I think it has something to do with the ghoulishness in the customers.' Clem told her. 'Every last one of them asks about the fire and is trying to find out any gossip about what happened.'

'I don't mind what reason they have for coming in to the shop,' Paige said. 'As long as they buy something while they're there.'

'Just you make sure we have enough stock,' Clem laughed. 'We're starting to run a bit low, and there isn't too much left in the storeroom to bring out to replace everything I'm selling.'

Paige was sure her supplier would send her order on time. He always did, she thought with relief as she swiped the tip of her finger across the screen to open her phone and retrieve her messages. The first was from Sebastian.

'Dinner? Will collect you, Sat @ 8. Seb.'

Paige's heart immediately thumped a little faster. Then thinking how confident he must be that she would accept his invitation, she couldn't help feeling a little annoyed. She sat and thought for a moment. She was going to have to get used to having him around at De Greys, so maybe it wasn't such a bad idea to go out with him and at least talk? She pressed her keypad, 'OK, where?' she typed.

Her phone bleeped almost immediately, making her jump. 'Wherever u like.'

Paige had no idea where to suggest. 'Will leave it up 2 u. C u Sat. P.'

'Saturday it is.'

Paige pushed her reservations about Seb to the back of her mind. She was determined to enjoy herself, justifying their meal out together by telling herself that if nothing else, maybe one prospective client might approach her to ask where she had bought her footwear. Paige pushed the thought that she was kidding herself out of her mind, as soon as it popped in there.

'It's been great,' Clem assured her. Paige noticed as Clem placed her case behind the counter that her sister was still wearing her green boots with aplomb.

'I've bought your perfume,' Paige said, handing her sister a box of Jo Malone's Pomegranate Noir.

'Thanks, Sis.' Clem took the black-edged box from Paige, gave her a hug, and put it into her bag.

Paige took out the small brown envelope holding her sister's wages for the week and handed it to her. 'Clem, this is also for you. Why don't you pack up and go home. I'll stay here and close up the shop.'

'I will, but only if you're sure. Aren't you shattered after your flights home?'

'Not really. I'm used to travelling. Anyway I won't be long,' she said, looking forward to spending a little time in her shop.

'Great thanks. I don't need telling twice.' Clem pulled on her jacket. 'It's been exhausting this week. I don't know how you keep this up month in and month out.'

'Necessity.' Paige said, smiling as she took her place

behind the counter and began clicking the mouse to start working through her sales list.

Satisfied with her checks, she locked up the shop, but could not shake off the feeling that something was amiss.

'Olly,' she murmured. Always impatient to fill her in on any gossip she may have missed, he never failed to contact her as soon as she returned from a trip. She sent him a message asking him to come and see her. Five minutes later, and she still had not heard from him.

Paige decided to make her way home without him. He always let her know if he wanted a lift anyway, so maybe he was simply staying away from the shop to avoid Clem. Despite her best intentions, she knew it was completely out of character for him. She pushed her worries about Olly to the back of her mind, although it would be comforting to have a quick chat with him before going out and know he was OK. Olly must have his reasons for keeping away. She checked her watch and gasped. She needed to start getting ready for her date with Sebastian.

Not knowing where he was taking her was a bit of a clothes problem. What should she wear? She didn't want to put on jeans, and appear as if she hadn't bothered, or a dress and look like she had taken this offer of dinner too seriously.

'Bugger,' she grumbled, throwing down a red cotton dress. 'Why can't I ever find anything decent to wear?'

Paige ran a bath. Now, that should calm me down, she thought, watching mandarin and basil fragranced bubbles cover the surface of the water. Pinning up her dark hair, she stepped in and lay back.

'You look lovely,' said Sebastian as he watched her open her front door.

'Thank you.' Paige said, glad she had decided to wear a pair of tailored navy trousers and a red silk top she had originally bought to wear on her honeymoon. She stepped outside, locking the door behind her. 'So, where have you decided to take me?'

'I've booked a table at the Pink Pots, unless you'd rather try somewhere else?'

'No, I like the sound of the Pink Pots,' Paige said, as he sat down next to her and started the engine. 'I've not been there before, but I've heard great things about the food and the atmosphere.'

'It's run by a friend of mine. Well, she's more of a business partner. She's spent years running restaurants for other people, and decided to make a go of her own place. I'm sure she'll do well. She deserves to.'

'I think it's good when friends can support each other's ventures,' she said.

He couldn't mistake that jibe and didn't blame her for it. 'Have you ever thought of branching out and leasing an entire shop, rather than limit your sales to an area in a department store?' He slowed down to let another car pass by in the narrow lane, and glanced at her as he waited for her to answer.

Paige looked confused. 'I'd love to, but I still need to build up some collateral first.'

'They're your own designs, aren't they?'

'They are,' she said, looking flattered that he would know this about her. 'I've been commissioning Spanish contacts to make my drawings into the shoes and boots I've been selling for the past two years, but I still can't help feeling a bit of a fraud, as if I'm only impersonating a designer.'

'You're no fraud, Paige,' he said, admiring her honesty. 'I'm not a connoisseur of women's shoes, but they look great to me. You appear to do a roaring trade, so they must be what the customers are after.'

'Thank you. They're beginning to sell well. You're right, I'd love my own shop someday, but it'll have to wait a bit longer, especially now I've had this set back.'

118

'It doesn't have to be a negative change, you know.'

'I agree, but I wouldn't be able to afford a larger shop than the space I'm renting now.' She relaxed further into her seat and looked away from him out of the side window.

She obviously didn't intend to continue discussing the possibility of her moving from De Greys. Maybe now wasn't the time to push the subject. After all, he mused, it wasn't as if he'd decided if she would have to move yet. Maybe he'd be able to find a way for Heaven in Heels to stay in the store, and then all this anxiety on both sides would have been for nothing.

He took her hand in his. 'Paige,' he said, wanting things to be better between them.

'No, Sebastian.' She pulled away. 'Don't say anything. We both know we can't carry on like we did in Italy.' She glanced back at him the sadness in her green eyes unmistakeable.

'I don't see why it has to be like this,' he said keeping his voice level, even though he wanted to shout at her in frustration 'And I'm sorry you feel so adamant.'

'I believe you're a good man at heart,' she said. 'And maybe, if our circumstances had been different, we could have been able to carry on seeing each other.'

'Be a couple?' He sighed heavily at the thought of never being with her again.

'Yes, but I think that after tonight, it would be best if we had a clean break from each other. It's probably the best way forward for both of us.'

'Maybe that's the case for you, but I don't happen to agree.' He tried to hide his frustration.

'Can you think of another way to resolve our differences then?'

Sebastian pulled into the restaurant car park next to the beach, and brought the car to a halt. 'It's not in my nature to give up on something I believe in,' he said to her as he turned off the ignition and unclasped his seat belt. 'I will find a way to make this work for us both.'

Paige waited for him to open her door. 'I can't see how,' she said as he took her hand and helped her outside. The smell of the hot sand in the warm summer air was soothing.

'You're here,' shouted Sara. He could never get over how such a petite woman could have such a loud voice. 'What do you think?' she asked, her hands outstretched.

'If you want me to comment on the doll-sized dress you're barely wearing, I'm not going to.' He laughed.

'Spoilsport. You're looking as dashing as ever.' She gave Sebastian a peck on the cheek before holding out her hand towards Paige. 'Hi, I'm Sara. I hope you'll have a wonderful evening at The Pink Pots, even though you're with this reprobate.'

'I'm sure we will,' Paige said.

Sebastian leaned his head closer to Paige. 'She's joking,' he whispered.

'I'm not.' Sara winked at Paige. 'I've reserved our best table for you.'

'I expect nothing less.' Seb placed a hand on Paige's back, ushering her through a granite archway.

'This is amazing,' Paige said, staring at the driftwood framed paintings and windowsills topped with oddly shaped shells, as they walked past. 'Are they yours?'

'Some of them are. All the furniture, flooring and decorations are made from reclaimed wood,' Sara explained, showing them through the busy room to a window side table, close to a roaring fire. 'We have so many young artists living over here and I like to support them, as I've been supported.' She smiled at Sebastian. 'Thank you, again.'

'Stop it.' He wished she didn't feel the need to be so grateful all the time. 'You know I wouldn't back you if I didn't think you'd be successful.'

'He's not lying either.' Sara widened her eyes at Paige.

'I can believe that,' she said, sitting down opposite him.

Sara handed them each a menu and walked away. 'It's wonderful here, don't you think?' Sebastian asked, determined to warm the atmosphere between them both.

Paige nodded. She seemed entranced by the orange and golden sunset lighting up the entire bay through the picture window next to her. 'I love it when those rocks are lit up by the moon.'

'I thought you'd enjoy this view.' Seb agreed. 'I'm so often too busy to notice the natural beauty we have around us in Jersey.'

Sara reappeared before Paige replied, and placed two champagne glasses on the table in front of her guests and an ice bucket perched on steel legs next to Seb.

'We didn't order this,' he said glancing at the chilled bottle of Laurent Perrier Rosé.

'No, I know, but it's your first visit here, and without you, I wouldn't be doing what I love most,' Sara insisted, opening the bottle with expertise. 'It's the least I can do.'

'Sara, really, it's not necessary,' he said, patting one of Sara's hands.

'Yes, it is.' She stared at him for a moment. He wished she didn't feel quite so grateful towards him all the time.

He noticed Paige tense. Sara must have too, because a moment later, Sara smiled at him. 'Hey, don't think you'll be getting this treatment every time you deign to visit The Pink Pots.' She tilted her head to one side. 'It is great seeing you here though.' She paused for a second or two. 'Any ideas what you two fancy eating tonight?'

He could see Paige staring thoughtfully at Sara and didn't want her to get the wrong idea about their relationship. Sara had once made a drunken pass at him, but they'd laughed it off the following day and managed to remain close. Paige seemed to be sizing her up.

As soon as Sara had taken their order and left them

alone, Sebastian poured them both a glass of champagne. 'It's not quite the same ambiance as in Positano, but pleasant nonetheless.'

Paige picked up her glass. 'To success,' she said before taking a drink.

Sebastian watched her trying not to catch his eye. 'To resolutions.'

Paige glanced up at him. 'Resolutions?'

'Whether you believe me or not, I'm going to find a way to resolve this matter, Paige. I'm not in the habit of letting problems get the better of me, and I don't intend giving up on what we had in Italy as easily as you seem to think I will.'

Paige pulled a face; so he did feel a connection to her in Italy then? She was relieved not to have imagined it. 'Not even when things have deteriorated as badly as they have between us?'

'You're here with me now, that's a start.' When she didn't argue, Sebastian concentrated on keeping the conversation light throughout the rest of their meal. He asked her about her buying trip to Spain and told her about Harley, admitting how much he missed the dog every time he had to leave him behind at his home in London. 'He always gives me such doleful glances whenever he spots my overnight bag,' he said shaking his head at the thought.

'Can't you bring him over here?' she asked resting her chin on her cupped hand.

Sebastian took a drink of his cappuccino. 'I'd love to, but he needs to be where I'm the most settled and right now that's London. I'm constantly flying back and forth, but over there he's well taken care of by my housekeeper, Mrs Hutton. She adores him and takes him for his daily walk when I'm not there; feeds him, that sort of thing.'

'Is he alone much?' Paige frowned.

'No, never. Mrs H has an apartment at the house where she stays when I'm away. The rest of the time she goes back to her place about a mile away. . I've asked her to move in permanently, but she shared her home with her husband for decades before he died, and although she's happy to stay at my place, she says she's not ready to sell up just yet.'

'She sounds dedicated,' Paige said, looking over his shoulder in the direction of Sara's laughing voice.

'She is.' Sebastian smiled at the thought of his trusted housekeeper. 'I wanted to bring you here to talk things through,' he said. 'But as soon as we arrived, I realised it was a bad choice.'

'Why? The meal was excellent,' she said, a little too quickly. 'I've had an amazing evening.'

He shook his head. 'Me too, but I only meant that I forgot it would be a little too cosy in here for us to be able to speak freely without someone listening.'

'You don't like discussing business in public, do you?' Paige said interrupting his thoughts.

'Not really. I think it should be kept between those it affects.'

'I hope you enjoyed your meal,' Sara said, arriving at their table.

'Perfection.' He glanced at the bill and gave her his credit card. 'You look very busy tonight too.'

'Yes,' she looked around the room. 'we have been, but then again, the chef is excellent. Thank you again for finding him for me.'

Sebastian didn't miss Paige stiffening at the reference to his helping Sara. 'It was nothing. That's what partners are supposed to do for each other. I'll speak to you soon, Sara.' Sebastian stood up and pulled out Paige's chair for her. 'Shall we take a stroll on the beach?' he asked, aware that Paige looked very thoughtful. 'I don't think it's too chilly out tonight.'

'Good idea.' Paige smiled at Sara. 'I could do with walking off some of this delicious food, I've eaten far too much of it.'

Sara nodded. 'I'm glad you enjoyed it,' she said. 'It was good to meet you, Paige.'

'You, too,' Paige said.

Chapter Fourteen

'Yes, and thank you,' Paige added, accidentally glancing down at Sebastian's perfectly flat stomach as she walked through the front door.

They went down the granite steps to the beach. Paige marvelled at how the reflection from the full moon splashed shards of silver onto the damp sand in front of them as the waves lapped lazily near their feet along the shoreline.

'Finally,' Sebastian said, his voice shattering the stillness of the evening. 'We can talk without anyone trying to listen in to our conversation.'

Paige noticed he was looking out across the channel and not at her. 'It was busy in there,' she said, wishing they could simply enjoy the moment and forget their differences for once, despite this being her justification for coming out with him in the first place.

'We have unfinished business, and I don't mean at De Greys,' he said, as if reading her thoughts.

'I know,' she said, a deep sadness enveloping her. 'But however much you try and keep those parts of our lives separate, it can't realistically happen.'

'But that's ridiculous.' He took hold of her hands and pulled her close to him, so that although she couldn't quite make out the details of his face, she could feel him watching her. 'Surely you're not going to insist we don't see each other because of my job?'

Paige hesitated. 'It's not just what you do, it's your lifestyle,' she whispered, feeling his breath on her face, and a familiar tightening in her chest.

'Would you say that if I was a road sweeper, or a teacher?'

'Of course not, but I wouldn't have to worry about my personal life being written about in the newspapers if I went out with someone from those professions, would I?'

'Ah, I see.'

Paige could have cried with frustration. Why did he have to be who he was? 'And because they wouldn't have the power to ruin my business with a single signature on a piece of paper,' she said honestly.

'What?'

'I presume it will be you signing the notices the tenants will receive?'

Sebastian let go of her hands and kicked the damp sand with the tip of his shoe. 'Paige, you have to listen to me.'

She noticed he didn't deny it and held the front of her jacket closed against the cool, salty air. 'I would happily listen, if there was anything you could say to change things, but you still haven't let me know if I'm going to be one of the tenants who'll be asked to leave De Greys.'

He began walking along the water's edge.

Paige ran a couple of steps to catch up with him. 'I need to make some sort of plan, if you are going to give me notice, and it's stressing me out not knowing.'

Sebastian stopped abruptly. 'I'm so sorry. I do know how you feel, but I honestly can't tell you anything until the list has been finalised. It would be unfair of me to do that. I probably won't know for certain until that point if you will have to move.'

So, she was part of a list, a meaningless group of names to be deleted from Sir Edmund's empire. Paige swallowed a lump in her throat. How could he see her in this way? How could he think for one second that she and her designs were separate entities?

'Let's enjoy being here together now,' he said, taking

hold of her by the shoulders and turning her to face him once more. Paige tried to shrug him off, unable to look at him. 'Paige,' he said. 'You know I'd never let you leave, if I thought it would ruin everything you've worked so hard to build up.'

'How would you help me?' she asked, unsure how he could possible come up with an ideal alternative for her. 'There isn't a way round this.'

'There's always a solution,' he said. 'For example, we could go into partnership.'

Paige knew her mouth had dropped open. She closed it, and composed herself before answering. 'Us, go into partnership together?'

'Why not? You've seen first-hand how well it works between me and Sara.'

'No,' she snapped. Then seeing the look of shock on his face realized she'd been rude and concentrated on softening her voice when she continued. 'I'm sure it works well between you two, but it's not for me.'

'Then, let me help you financially with the lease,' he said. 'Help you find a new shop of your own.'

'No.'

Sebastian touched her shoulder lightly. 'Everything we're saying now is hypothetical. You don't have to make any rash decisions. Think about it.'

'No, you don't understand,' she said. 'You can't throw your money around to impress me.'

'I'm not trying to impress you, I'm trying to help you.'

'I don't want your help. I was doing perfectly well before you became involved with De Greys and all this happened.'

'There are other ways to move forward, Paige.'

'You tell me you'd never do anything to harm my business.'

'I won't,' he raked his hand through his hair.

'But you are. Why don't you understand that?' She

turned and began walking away.

He caught up with her seconds later. 'I've promised I'll take care of you and I will.'

'You don't have to look after me, I'm a grown woman. I'll find my own way to make things work.' Paige didn't miss the hurt look on his face, but it made her feel in control once more to show him she wasn't going to be manipulated by him.

'You're cold.' He took off his linen jacket and draping it across her shoulders, put his arm around her and started walking. 'Maybe it's time I took you home?'

'Yes, I think you could be right,' she said, her conflicting emotions exhausting her.

Driving her home, Sebastian made small talk all the way back, and parked the car outside her cottage. She put her hand on his to stop him getting out of the car. 'I can see myself in,' she assured him, as gently as she could manage. 'Thanks for this evening. I've had an interesting time.' She stepped out of the car and walked to her front door.

'I don't feel like we've sorted anything out between us,' he said. 'I had hoped to do so.'

Paige didn't answer. She knew he was watching her from the car, as she unlocked her front door, but when she turned to wave goodbye, he was already reversing out onto the road, looking away from her as he did so.

She closed the door, leaning back against it for a moment. She knew she had acted in the only way she could. Maybe he didn't understand her motives, she thought miserably, but as much as she would like to trust him, she had learnt the hard way from Jeremy's actions that the only person you can truly trust is yourself.

Determined to push any further disturbing thoughts about Sebastian to the back of her mind, she pulled her phone out of her bag to check if Olly had left any messages for her. Still nothing. She couldn't help feeling slightly panicky at the discovery. 'Strange,' she said. He never went two days without any contact.

Chapter Fifteen

The following morning, finding Olly's mobile still turned off, Paige ran upstairs to Clem's room. She pulled back the curtains and sunrays streamed across the room. 'Have you seen Olly at all?'

'No,' Clem winced and pulled the duvet over her face. 'Why?'

'I haven't heard from him since I came back.'

Clem groaned. 'So?'

'So, that's unusual, and I'm getting worried.' Paige dragged the duvet down to unveil her sister's head. 'You look awful; late night last night?'

'I wish,' Clem said, peeling open her eyes and grimacing at the light. She focused as best she could on her sister. 'You don't think anything has happened to him, do you?'

'No,' Paige said, determined not to get too concerned. 'But this is out of character.' She sat down on the side of her sister's bed. 'He was devastated when you finished with him. You're going to have to speak to him soon and put him out of his misery. He doesn't deserve to be messed about like this.'

'I know, but it would make things easier if you and he weren't such close friends.'

Paige sighed. 'True, but you're still going to have to speak to him.' She drew back the curtains and opened the window.

'Do you have to do that?'

Paige ignored her sister. 'Why did you finish with him?

You still haven't told me yet.'

Clem turned face down into the pillow. 'Not now, please,' she said, her voice muffled.

'Fine.' Paige said knowing when she was beaten. 'But make it soon.' She went to her room. Pushing her feet into faded pink pumps, she walked next door to his mother's house and rang the bell.

The door was answered almost immediately. 'Hello, dear, if you're looking for Oliver, I'm afraid he's staying with friends.'

Paige could not remember him telling her about any plans to go away. 'I'm glad everything is all right,' she said smiling at his mother, not wishing to cause her any concern.

'Of course it is, dear. Why wouldn't it be?' She gave Paige a tight little smile and then not waiting for an answer stepped back into the house and closed the door. Paige felt very much as if she had been dismissed. His mother was usually so welcoming, Paige was sure she was covering for Olly for some reason.

The weekend passed slowly and she made several attempts to get her sister to open up, but without success.

'Right, that's it,' she said on the Sunday evening. 'Tonight, you and I are going to sit down and have a chat. Woman to woman.' She caught Clem pulling a face. 'This has gone on long enough. We're all worried about you. I thought you loved Olly and you definitely wanted to be at university, so you need to tell me what's caused all this fuss.' She turned to leave the room. 'I need to fetch some paperwork from the car, but when I get back you're going to tell me everything.'

'It looks like I don't have much choice,' Clem said, pouting.

'None at all. I'm your sister and if you can't confide in me, then I don't know what to suggest.'

Paige was leaning into the footwell in front of the

passenger seat, reaching forward for her briefcase, when she heard her house phone ringing. 'Clem,' she shouted. 'Can you get that for me?' As she picked up her case, she heard footsteps as her sister stamped towards the phone.

'Well, that was embarrassing,' Clem moaned, as soon as Paige came back to the house. 'That was Olly on the phone. He'll be here in ten minutes.'

Paige watched Clem nervously straightening two silver rings on her fingers. Her sister wasn't usually this reticent about sharing information, so it must be something big. 'It'll be fine,' she said, unsure what else to say.

Olly announced his arrival by slamming the front door behind him. He marched into the living room, frowning. 'OK, so what's all this about?' When Clem didn't answer he looked at Paige.

'Don't ask me, I've no idea.'

Clem turned her back on them and stared out of the window. 'I'm going to have a baby.'

'You're what?' Paige dared not look at Olly. 'Are you sure?'

Clem shook her head. 'Of course I'm sure.'

'Am I the father?' Olly said, his voice barely above a whisper.

'You think I'm some sort of slut now, as well as an idiot?' Clem, hands on hips, turned on her ex-boyfriend with a ferociousness that startled Paige.

Paige motioned for her sister to sit down. 'Let's calm down. No one thinks you're either of those things.' She watched Clem glare at Olly. 'Why, if you're pregnant with Olly's baby, do you want to finish with him? I don't get it.' She couldn't believe what was happening. 'And why all the mystery?'

Clem looked utterly miserable and Paige wished she could offer her comfort, but first she needed to know everything.

'Because I was going to have a termination,' she murmured, pointing at Olly. 'And, 'she added, as Olly took a breath to interrupt. 'I knew that if I told him, he'd try to persuade me to keep it.'

'Too right.' Olly's eyes narrowed. 'What's so wrong with keeping my baby anyhow? I thought we loved each other.'

Clem sat down heavily in the armchair. 'I'm twenty years old. I'm too young to start a family. My degree meant so much to me that the thought of giving it up was heartbreaking.'

Paige concentrated on remaining calm. 'I understand how you feel, Clem, but if that's the case, then why didn't you go ahead with the termination?'

'I reached the clinic,' Clem said, her voice barely audible as she focused on the floor in front of her. 'The doctor started questioning me, and I realised I couldn't go through with it.' She looked up at Paige. 'I went back to my room, packed, and booked a flight home. I came straight here.'

Paige crossed the room, sat on the arm of her sister's chair and hugged her tightly. 'You did the right thing.'

'What about the baby?' Olly asked, his face flushed. 'What about me?'

'I'm sorry, Olly,' Clem said, looking guilty. 'I know it was deceitful of me, but this is too important for me to make a decision based on other people's opinions, especially as I'm the one who'll have to live with the consequences.'

'It affects me too, Clemmie,' he said quietly. Paige didn't think she'd ever seen him look so hurt.

'Of course it does,' Paige agreed.

'I know,' Clem said, her voice breaking with emotion. 'But if you don't mind, Ol, I'd like to get things straight in my head for a bit. I still haven't come to terms with everything.'

'I suppose so,' he said, staring at her, his face softening slightly. 'It must have been quite a shock.'

Clem nodded, angrily brushing away a stray tear from her cheek. 'For you too, I should imagine.'

Paige decided to make the most of the confessions going round. 'So, where've you been for the past few days?' she said, changing the focus to Olly.

He shrugged. 'I couldn't think straight, knowing Clemmie was here and avoiding me, so I went to stay at Jake's place for a bit.'

'Jake?' asked Clem and Paige in unison.

'Who's he?' Paige added, trying to recall Olly mentioning anyone by that name.

Olly seemed to brighten up a little. 'He's a good friend. I think you two would get on well.'

Paige shook her head. 'I have more than enough going on right now, thanks, Ol,' she said, not adding that she was too wrapped up in her confusing feelings for Sebastian to want to get involved with anyone else.

Paige had a nervous few days when deliveries from her supplier were delayed due to a postal strike on the mainland. 'It's the worst part of living on this island,' she moaned to Olly. 'They only arrived late yesterday afternoon, just before I locked up for the day.'

Olly slammed down a copy of the *Jersey Society* magazine. 'Page twenty-three,' Olly said, licking his finger and scuffling through the pages until he found what he was looking for. 'Look, it's him.'

Paige sighed. 'I've never known a man so interested in local gossip. What is it now?' Looking down she saw a photo of Sebastian with his arm draped around Sara's shoulders. She was gazing up at him, happiness emanating from her large eyes, and he, in turn, appeared to be very relaxed as he stared directly into the camera lens. The by-line said, 'Mr Sebastian Fielding and friend, enjoying the recent Jersey Business Awards Ceremony'.

She swallowed hard. He was only doing what she had told him to. Well, not the finding a girlfriend bit, but did she, in all seriousness, expect Sebastian never to have another relationship after her? Of course not. It hurt though to see him with someone, however platonic it may have been. 'I suspected as much,' she murmured half to herself.

'What?'

'She runs the restaurant Seb took me to. I could tell she had feelings for him, even though she tried to hide them.'

'They look pally more than anything else,' Olly said, eventually.

'Sara is his business partner.'

'Oh, OK.' Olly narrowed his eyes. 'She doesn't look his type anyway.'

'If you mean she's different from me, then you're probably right.' Paige studied the picture more closely. 'She's very glamorous.'

'If you say so, but I think you're far prettier than she is.'

'That's because you're my friend and trying to cheer me up,' she said, smiling at him.

Olly scanned the other pictures. 'It looks like it must have been great fun. Why don't we ever go to events like these?'

Paige shrugged. 'Probably because no one ever invites us? You usually have to be a member of some club, or at least mix in the right social circles, and we don't do either.'

'True.' Olly flicked through the following pages, commenting on a couple of people he knew. 'She's had work done, that's obvious.'

'How can you tell?' she asked, taking another look at the woman in question. 'She looks perfectly natural to me.'

'Put it this way, she didn't look like that the last time I saw her buying a fortune's worth of make-up a couple of months ago.' He pointed at a painfully thin redhead. 'Wonder what made her think she looked good in that get up?'

Paige shook her head slowly and smiled. 'And you can't understand why no one ever asks you to join their party.'

'You're sulking because Mr Whatshisname isn't pining after you,' he teased, unknowingly stating exactly how she felt.

'You know, Olly, I'm not sure I don't prefer you quiet and miserable, rather than all bitter and twisted like you are today.' Paige turned to go to the storeroom.

Olly was right, although her most pressing problem right now should be what would happen to her shop if she was included in those tenants to be given notice. If only she hadn't taken up the shorter three-year lease, she wouldn't now be in this predicament. She was not going to keep moping around after him. For all she knew, she could soon be looking for new premises. That would be her focus from now on, she determined, not worrying about the social life of a handsome man in a well-cut suit, even if he made her heart hurt more than anyone else had ever managed to.

Having given herself a talking to, Paige started to feel a little more positive. Olly took back the magazine and returned to his office, leaving her to dust her shelves in peace and work on her plans for the future of her shop.

The following day the company's senior secretary visited each tenant, handing them an envelope marked 'Urgent'. Paige opened hers and was interested to read that a meeting had been called on the Friday at six o'clock. Just after closing time. 'Sebastian's giving a presentation of the proposed plans for De Greys,' she murmured as she read. 'This should be interesting.'

137

Maybe she would finally discover the fate of her concession. Not sure if she was ready to deal with Sebastian's decision, she did know that if it wasn't the one she hoped for, then it would definitely mean a big change for her and one that would mean taking her shop in a completely different direction to what she'd expected.

Chapter Sixteen

Sebastian tapped his pen against the notepad on his desk. He could hear Olly's familiar voice coming from the boardroom doorway.

'Hurry up,' Olly said, waiting impatiently by the door. 'I don't want to miss a minute of this.'

Sebastian looked away as Paige entered and made her way to the back of the room to stand next to Olly. He'd known all the tenants would want to hear as soon as possible when any decisions had been made. He didn't blame them, he'd be exactly the same.

She seemed to be trying her best to be less visible to him by standing among the men at the back. Paige pulled a face at Olly as he leant against the wall, his arms folded. He looked ready for battle.

'Thank you all for coming,' Sebastian said, motioning to the screen next to him. He clicked for the first slide. It wasn't going to be easy selling these particular future plans but he never shied from doing his job, even if this time it was proving a little more personal than usual. He took a deep breath and focused his thoughts on the matter in hand, determined not to make eye contact with Paige and her intense questioning gaze.

'Before I begin, I wanted to let you know that the cause of the fire was due to faulty wiring, and an apprentice not being properly supervised while working on repairs in one of the storerooms.' He looked around his audience as they nodded and confirmed this. 'Naturally, we've taken steps to ensure an incident of this nature won't be repeated.'

He indicated the slide. 'This is De Greys as it stands now.' He clicked for the second and third slides. 'This is how we predict it will look.' He waited silently as they studied the clean lines of the newly arranged concessions. 'As you can see we've kept the original architectural detail, such as the plaster mouldings on the ceilings, as well as the ornate balustrading, but at the same time giving the space a more contemporary feel that we believe will work well.' The mutterings displayed a little surprise, but they seemed favourable.

'I can confirm that the final due diligence has been completed and all necessary paperwork signed, and as some of you have probably guessed, the handover phase has now been completed. Letters will be forwarded in the next week to those whose concessions at De Greys are to be given notice.' He waited for the murmurs to calm down before continuing. 'I'm sure you're all aware that quite a few of the commercial tenancy leases are shortly up for renewal, and the board are hoping that most of those contacted will see this as a positive progression for both De Greys and themselves.'

'That's a matter of opinion,' shouted a voice from the middle of the room.

Sebastian waited for the person to make themselves known, but when no further comment was made, he continued. 'The board of directors have also taken into account those tenants who had already used the break clause in their contracts last year, and who had therefore already given twelve months' notice. Most of you will carry on as you have been doing, but in order to make the changes we feel are necessary, we will be giving notice to those whose leases are soon up for renewal, or who have break clauses in their contracts and maybe come to a mutual agreement to terminate these leases, sooner rather than later. There are those leaseholders who have expressed their intention not to renew their lease, and in certain cases compensation will be discussed. Some of you have, I gather, already located alternative premises, others have decided to close down, but I'm fully aware that not everyone will feel this change to be a favourable outcome.'

Someone cleared their throat. 'I think you're referring to those of us who are unable to afford to relocate our businesses.' Paige said, staring at him.

He could see Olly nudge her before mouthing, 'Go, girl.'

Sebastian clenched his jaw and took a moment to consider his reply. 'I appreciate your concerns, Miss Bingham, but unfortunately, in the present economic climate, it falls to me to provide a solution that will ensure this one-hundred-and-fifty-year-old company remains viable. I want to assure you that these decisions haven't been taken lightly.' He looked around the room at the unsmiling faces gazing back at him. 'As chairman of the board, I can assure you that without immediate reorganization, there is little, if any, chance for De Greys to survive as it is beyond the next twelve to eighteen months.'

Groans and whispers filled the room. Sebastian waited for them to finish. He'd done this sort of thing many times and it was always difficult, but somehow this time it seemed far harder to put the process in to action. 'We have also appointed a steering committee who have spent months deciphering legal reports and working out the best way to put these plans into action. My team and I are nearing the end of this stage of the project. Whether we like it, or not, some businesses will work better as a concession in the new version of the store.'

Sebastian waited for the uproar to calm down. 'I do understand how you must be feeling, and I'm aware how difficult this is for the people involved. My aim and that of the board is to assist each of you in any way we can, either by helping you relocate, or finding other avenues to explore.' He glanced at his assistant who was watching everyone in silence. 'Should you wish to discuss anything with me, please contact Miss Spencer, my personal assistant, and she will set up a mutually convenient meeting for us. Any questions?' he asked, taking a deep breath and looking around the room at his audience.

Most of the tenants shouted at once. Sebastian pointed to someone sitting at the front, recognizing him as an older man who had been selling millinery since the end of the occupation. 'Mr Jarvis,' he greeted him, hating that the dignified man must be going through so much anxiety. 'I appreciate that your shop is one of the stalwarts of De Greys and that you have recently retired and handed the running of your shop over to your son.'

Mr Jarvis cleared his throat. 'Yes, and he feels unable to start again elsewhere. I want to know how you intend helping him, if he is to leave De Greys.'

Sebastian listened as the ensuing uproar caused by the valid and emotive question died down. 'Mr Jarvis, I can assure you that each case will be looked at independently, and we will certainly aim to help your son as much as possible.'

He could see Paige whispering to Olly and then she put up her hand. Out of all the delegates in the room, he'd been dreading her asking him a question, but knew instinctively that she would. Paige was a fighter, and not someone who would take on a challenge without doing her best to find a way to win it.

'Miss Bingham?' He was determined to keep his expression neutral. He could see she was looking for something in his gaze, but wasn't sure exactly what.

She stared at him for a second, the challenge in her face unmistakeable. 'What I want to know, is how you can be so certain that by making all these drastic changes you'll manage to save De Greys? What if you end up putting several small companies out of business and wiping out

142

years, in some cases decades, of hard work for the people here this evening?'

Sebastian couldn't help feeling impressed by her force.

'Hear, hear,' shouted Olly.

Sebastian looked from Paige to Olly, and back to her again.

She held up her hand. 'Sorry,' she said. 'I haven't finished.'

He had to concentrate on not smiling. She looked as if she could slap him, and the last thing he needed was to infuriate her further. If only she knew how much he admired her fire.

'Can you be sure this is the best way forward, and the only way to save this company?' She jutted her chin out slightly, obviously waiting for him to find a way to answer her question.

Sebastian liked a challenge and whether these people trusted him or not, he had to do something to make this floundering store a success. He shrugged. 'I assure you that no decisions have been made lightly. We've looked into this in depth, and I promise you I'll do my best to ensure everyone is treated as fairly as possible.'

'That doesn't answer my question,' she snapped.

'Bloody scandal,' said someone he couldn't see. 'You wealthy entrepreneurs come over here to our island, buy everything, make changes, and once you've made more money, you bugger off back to England.'

'Not quite,' Sebastian argued. 'I have family who've lived on this island for decades and a great affection for Jersey.' He looked round the room at the expectant faces waiting for him to reassure them. 'I want this to work as much as you all do. Whatever you may think, I will be working to find a way to make sure that this is as painless as possible for everyone involved.'

He peered through the crowd, locking eyes with her for a moment. 'I do bear in mind the effect this is going to have on everyone involved, but what would you rather me do? If I left matters running as they are, I can assure you De Greys would be forced to close in its entirety, putting you all out of business.' He paused. 'My only choice is to take all the financial aspects into consideration, determining which of the concessions here do not contribute in any way to the board's future plans, and try to help them come to a mutually acceptable solution.' He waited for the muffled response to subside once more. 'If I don't make these changes, someone else will be brought in to do so. There is no question, these changes will be put in place, and soon.'

There were gasps of rage and anger, and Sebastian had to raise his voice slightly to be heard. 'It's not a perfect solution, I agree, but it's the only sensible one open to us.'

Chapter Seventeen

At the end of the meeting, Paige watched as everyone filed out of the room, looking sombre, but sounding less antagonised.

'It's typical. They only tell us what they want us to hear,' Olly said, standing back to let Paige go in front of him. 'While we're fretting about our work, the board will be making decisions, and you can guarantee they'll only tell us information when they're ready, not before.'

'I just hope I'm not one of those who'll have to move like some sort of sacrificial lamb,' she said. 'At least your job should be safe.'

'Thankfully they'll always need an IT Department.' He bent down and lowered his voice. 'His assistant has already told me not to worry.' Olly tilted his head to indicate Sebastian. 'In fact, the three of us in the department were spoken to earlier, but I didn't have a chance to let you know before now.'

'Good. I'm relieved,' she said honestly.

She was about to step out of the room, when a hand took hold of her arm and gently eased her back through the crowd.

Olly frowned. 'Hey,' he said, turning to see who was pulling her back.

'It's OK, Ol,' Paige waved him away, trying to bring as little attention to herself as possible. 'You go ahead. I'll meet you later.'

Olly looked across at Sebastian and raised his eyebrows. 'Whatever you say.'

Paige sidestepped away from the others and looked up, knowing as soon as she'd felt the pressure on her arm that it had been Sebastian. She let him guide her, unwilling to pull away from his grasp, irritated with herself for enjoying the pressure of his hand on hers.

He waited until everyone left, motioning for his assistant to follow. She gave Paige a pointed look before closing the door and leaving them alone in the now-silent room. Sebastian looked down into Paige's eyes, but said nothing.

Paige was unable to keep silent for any longer. 'How can you do this to these people?'

He sighed loudly without looking away from her. 'I thought I'd just explained everything.'

She shook her head. 'I don't see how you can't find a solution that'll be fair for everyone though.'

He stroked her cheek lightly with his right hand. 'I can't. I honestly wish I could.'

'What if you give me notice?' She didn't miss the look of discomfort that crossed his face for a split second.

'If that's the case, I'm sure you'll find somewhere more suitable to relocate.' He smiled, his eyes gentle, unlike his words. 'Paige, it could be the best thing for you, have you considered that?'

Paige jerked her head back in amazement. She was going to have to move. She should have guessed. She couldn't believe he would do such a thing to her. Did she not mean anything to him at all? 'How?' She concentrated on keeping her voice as unemotional as possible.

'We've discussed this. We could become partners. With my backing you could afford larger premises. You could then show your designs off to their full potential.'

'I don't want you backing me. Who the hell do you think you are?' she asked, stunned by his arrogance.

Sebastian leant forward. She could smell the hint of patchouli in his aftershave and wished she could control

146

how she felt towards him.

'I only want to help you become the success you deserve to be. Why is that such a shocking offer?'

'Because I want to do this for myself, and I don't want to be beholden to you.' Paige almost spat the words in her temper.

Sebastian looked as if she'd slapped him. 'I didn't realize I was so contemptible to you.'

'You don't realize a lot of things, Sebastian.'

'For example?'

'Pride. You're not the only one who has it, you know.'

He narrowed his eyes. 'You really don't like me very much, do you?'

No, she thought, staring at his incredible face so close to hers she could feel his breath on her face. She didn't reply.

'This is business, Paige. I have to do my job and I do it with as much compassion as possible.' She tried to steady her breathing. 'If you want to do this by yourself, fine, but the rent here is high, because it's on the main thoroughfare,' he said, taking her hands in his, his voice less tense. 'De Greys is a prominent, well-known store, but that doesn't mean you couldn't find something more suitable, or affordable. If you don't want me as a partner, why not let me help you find a suitable shop where you can set up your company?'

She stepped back, mainly to distance herself from his strong presence and regain a semblance of self-control she could feel slipping away. 'If you're so sure, then why don't you use your limitless contacts and find me somewhere?' She challenged, placing her hands on her hips while she waited for him to answer. 'Go on then, prove to me that you can solve my problem. I don't see how you can do it.'

His mouth drew back in a wide smile. 'You think you know me so well. Why do you always find me so lacking?' He didn't take his eyes off her. 'You don't even know if you're on the list yet.'

'I have a horrible feeling I am though. I want you to prove to me that I'd have options. Show me you can find somewhere equally as viable, and for the same rent. Then, I'll believe you're as brilliant as you seem to think you are.' She was enjoying testing him and couldn't wait to see if he would stand up to her.

He replied by kissing her. The pressure of his soft lips on her own made her forget for an instant what she'd been fighting about. Paige pushed Sebastian away and noticed his assistant's blonde head poked around the door.

'Sorry for the interruption, sir,' she said, looking stunned and giving Paige a disapproving glance. 'There's an urgent message for you' she said handing him a note. 'It's Sir Edmund. He insists you speak to him immediately.'

Paige made pretence of staring out of the window, as if the view of the directors' parking spaces and bin area held some sort of fascination for her. She touched her lips thoughtfully, trying to take in what had just happened between them. As soon as the woman had gone, Paige turned to leave the room.

'I'm going to have to deal with this,' Seb said reading the piece of paper in his hands. 'Could you wait for a few minutes, there's something I need to speak to you about.'

'Sorry, I have to get on,' she said needing time to think things through. Paige walked out of the room without saying another word, determinedly ignoring the concern on his face.

Clem was waiting on Paige's front doorstep as far into the doorway as she could manage. 'Where have you been?' she asked, without bothering to greet Paige first, stepping aside to let her unlock the door.

'Sorry, Sebastian Fielding called a meeting for the

148

tenants. Anyway, where's your key?'

'Forgot it,' said Clem with uncharacteristic rudeness. 'And I wanted to speak to you about something.'

Not more dramas, thought Paige. She was exhausted and hoping for an early night. Paige hung her coat on the hook in the small hallway. 'Are you OK? There's nothing wrong with the baby, is there? What are you now, three months?'

Clem shook her head. 'Yes, just over, and you can stop fretting, everything's fine as far as I'm aware. You tell me about the meeting first.'

Paige, too tired to argue, relayed everything that was discussed, naturally leaving out any details about what had happened between her and Sebastian after the others had left.

Clem listened patiently. 'It would be awesome to have a meeting with such a gorgeous bloke. That Sebastian Fielding is one hell of a catch, if you ask me.'

I didn't, thought Paige flicking the kettle on and taking two china mugs from the cupboard above her. She glanced at Clem and wished she could tell her what was making her so angry. 'We were all invited,' she added. 'It wasn't just me.'

'Yeah, but I can't think of many women who'd turn him down, can you?' she giggled, sitting her bottom on the high stool at the breakfast bar and wriggling to get comfortable. 'I won't be able to perch up here much longer,' she added frowning.

Paige could see Clem was struggling with her emotions. 'You'll be fine.'

'I can't help thinking how much things have changed in the last few months,' Clem said nibbling the side of her fingernail. 'Now I'm pregnant, single, and living with my sister, and you're single and don't know what's going to happen next with the shop, or anything else for that matter.'

149

Paige nodded and passed her a cup, before taking a sip of her drink. 'It's all a bit unnerving,' she said. 'Come on then, what was it you wanted to tell me?'

'You'll never guess what I heard today.'

'Go on,' Paige stifled a yawn behind her hand, thinking she would give almost anything to be able to go to bed and sleep for the next twenty-four hours.

'That other shoe business in De Greys, the large franchise?'

'Yes,' Paige nodded. 'What about it?'

'The guy who has it reckons he's about to be given permission to move from his area over at the far side of the arcade, replace your concession and the one to your right and knock through to open both up..'

Paige nearly choked on her drink. Patting herself on the chest to help clear her throat and let air into her lungs, she had to think. 'If they're doubling in size, there's going to be no room for me.'

'Hah,' Clem shouted triumphantly. 'That's exactly what I thought.'

Paige stared at her sister open-mouthed. How could they have spoken so recently without Seb not telling her about this? Her breath became shallow. So this was to be her fate. 'But I've just seen him. Why didn't he at least hint that this could happen?'

'Maybe he couldn't say because it's not common knowledge yet? The bloke who owns the franchise for those cheaper shoes was flirting with Sebastian Fielding's assistant. I heard him boasting to one of the Clarins girls that this assistant had seen his name when she was typing up some notes the other day. I don't think anything has been formalised yet, but it does sound as if it's true.'

Paige couldn't believe what she was hearing. Sebastian might not have announced this yet, but he had obviously already made the decision to get rid of her shop. She would have hoped that De Greys would want to keep her designer shoes, but they'd obviously decided that they preferred more custom over quality. It was the sensible option, she supposed. She sat down heavily on the couch, trying not to panic. 'This is unbearable.'

Clem stepped down from the stool and gave her sister a hug. 'I'm so sorry, Sis. I should never have told you in such an insensitive way. I'm an idiot.'

'No, it's fine,' she fibbed. 'Don't worry. At least you've had the decency to tell me as soon as you knew. I just can't understand why Sebastian hadn't thought to do the same,' she said immediately realizing what he'd been trying to tell her when she'd stormed out of his office.

Chapter Eighteen

Paige was surprised to find a letter pushed through the letterbox later that evening. It was from Sebastian, and enclosed were details of two properties with what looked like affordable leases. Paige studied them, unsure why he had not bothered to knock and give them to her personally. Recognizing both premises vaguely, she couldn't help thinking it was a strange way to break the news to her.

She was confused. Both shops appeared suitable at first glance, and as upset as she was with him, his speed at finding the vacant shops went some way to lessening her panic at the thought of having to move her concession from De Greys.

The phone rang a little later. Paige reached to pick up the phone. 'Well? How did I do?' he asked an amused tone in his deep voice.

Distracted at hearing his voice, she sat back in her chair more heavily than she'd intended, accidentally kicking the small table next to her and spilling red wine from the glass on top. 'Bugger,' she said noticing the splotch of crimson on her immaculate cream carpet.

'Am I to take it from your reply that I didn't do as well as you'd hoped?' Sebastian laughed.

She stood up and taking the phone with her hurried to the kitchen to find a tea towel to dab at the offending liquid before it could stain. 'I wasn't calling you a bugger, Sebastian,' she said, cross with him for sounding so jovial. 'I've just spilt some of my bloody drink. Hang on a sec?'

After a minute or so dabbing and then scrubbing the

mark on her floor, Paige placed her glass on the mantelpiece out of harm's way, picked up the phone, and sat back down to continue her conversation with him. 'Sorry about that. What were we saying?' She thought for a second. 'Oh yes, you know you did well, so don't act coy, it doesn't suit you.'

She could hear him laughing and despite her annoyance with him the deep chuckle made her smile. 'Good. So you'll meet the agents then?'

'I don't really have much choice.' She knew she had to tell him she had found out about his plans. 'I gather from my sister I'm to be given notice.'

There was a momentary silence. 'Who told you?' he asked his tone serious.

'Not, what a load of crap, or even, sorry for failing to be honest with you when I had the chance earlier in your office?'

'If you recall, I did tell you I wanted to speak to you about something.'

She couldn't argue with that. 'I suppose dropping off these property details were a bit of a giveaway too, weren't they?' she said picking up the property specifications and studying them.

'I knew that if you wouldn't listen to me, this would speak volumes.'

'You didn't tell me, but you managed to kiss me. Funny that?' she said, not wishing to remember how delicious it had been.

'Ah, I wanted to explain about that.'

'What, kissing me or the proposed new properties?'

After a moment's silence, he said, 'Both, really.'

'I expected more of you than that.'

'I assume we're now talking about the properties?'

Paige clenched her teeth. She'd actually meant the kiss, but wasn't going to give him the satisfaction of knowing it.

'I can't understand how your sister found this out,' he

said before she managed to reply. 'No one else has been spoken to yet. When you left I assumed I'd have enough time to tell you privately before word spread. This is supposed to be strictly confidential. Do you know who told your sister?'

Paige told him, instantly feeling mean for snitching on his assistant.

'Ah, I should have thought of that. I'd suspected there was something going on between those two, but I wasn't sure.' He sighed. 'I'm going to have to make sure she understands that this information is confidential and should not be discussed to anyone.' He narrowed his eyes. 'So you'll also know the other shoe franchise will be getting the go ahead,' he said almost to himself. 'Will you go and see the premises I've given you?'

'I may be upset, but I'm not stupid,' she said knowing she was hardly in a position to ignore an opportunity and unable to hide her hurt any longer.

'I'm so sorry it has to be this way,' he said. She could hear him breathe wishing again that things could be different between them. 'Paige? Are you still there?'

She swallowed the lump in her throat. 'Yes.'

'Your designs are startlingly good and understandably expensive. We have to go with products that will bring in the most customers and, as much as I'd prefer seeing your designs displayed in De Greys, economically it isn't the best option for the future of the store.'

'I get it.' She hated feeling so defenceless, especially when she knew he was right.

'Sometimes we have to make crappy choices, and I'm sorry that this is one that I have to abide by.'

He sounded as miserable as she was feeling. The notion cheered her up a little.

'Don't forget to let me know what you think of these properties.'

'OK,' Paige replied, her voice distant even to her own

155

ears.

'This isn't as bad as it looks, you know,' he said, his voice barely above a whisper.

'Isn't it?' She grabbed her glass and took a sip of her drink, staring at the details in her hand yet again.

'It could be the best thing to ever happen to your business. Have you considered that possibility?'

She could sense the tension in his voice. 'Not if I can't afford to make this move.'

'Your lease still has another year to go on it, and the company will pay you compensation if you agree to move as soon as possible. You should be able to fund the new shop and any small improvements you may need to carry out with that money.'

'Do you have an answer for everything?' she asked, disliking the sarcasm in her voice.

'Your insurance money will cover the smoke-damaged stock you had to replenish, so hopefully you should have everything you need to carry on.'

'You've thought it all through, haven't you?' She felt as if all her energy had seeped out of her.

'You do know I'd never hurt you.' He cleared his throat.

'Why did you just post these through the letterbox? We could have spoken about them then.'

'I didn't drop them off,' he admitted. 'I had to go to a meeting, so asked someone else to do it. Did you hear what I said? I don't want you to think I'm trying to hurt you in any way.'

She pictured his secretary with her usual sneer being asked to deliver letters to someone of whom she obviously disapproved. 'I don't really know what else to say.'

She waited for his reply, but was greeted only by silence. Paige listened to his breathing, so steady and light.

'Best of luck then,' he said, his voice back to its usual tone. 'I'll see you at De Greys.'

Paige went to reply, but he cut her off. She listened to the dial tone on her phone for a moment before clicking it off. Not sure quite what to think, she took a large drink from her glass. How did he always manage to cause her emotions to free-fall without any effort at all? It occurred to her that Jeremy had never affected her in that way. She leant back into her sofa staring blindly at the screen. Bugger Sebastian Fielding and her decision to go alone to Sorrento.

Chapter Nineteen

Despite her initial misgivings, Paige viewed both properties later that week. 'It's been more fun than I'd anticipated,' she told Clem as they walked down by the harbour on their way to buy an ice cream. 'The first one had been run as a shoe shop until recently. Apart from painting the walls to freshen the place up, I could move in fairly quickly with little outlay and fuss.'

'Sounds promising, so far.' Clem waved away a determined seagull.

'The small two-bedroomed flat above could be useful for storage, or if the lease allows, I can sublet to bring in an additional income. Sebastian tipped me off in his letter that the landlord was willing to be reasonable when discussing the rent. Apparently, he was losing money since the previous tenant had moved out. The building has been empty for months.'

'So, far from this move having to be the end of the world, you already have two options open to you,' Clem smiled.

'True.' Paige wasn't ready to admit to her sister how much more positive she was already feeling about the change in her circumstances. 'I prefer the second place. It's closer to Sand Street car park, as well as offering one parking space, but it's also more expensive and has less storage. It's being used as an accessory shop at the moment,' she told Clem. 'It'll cost more to adapt, and I'll have to wait two months before I can move in. I'll also have to arrange for the display shelves to be made, so it's just too expensive and inconvenient.'

'It sounds pretty perfect other than that,' Clem said. 'It's such a shame.'

'It's a shame I have to move at all.' Paige said forgetting she'd promised not to dwell on her misfortune. 'I already have a bank loan to consider, and I'll have to hope I can keep the clientele I've built up when I do move. I really don't need this right now.'

'Olly will help, and don't forget he wants to get your updated site up and running as soon as possible. I'm here now, so you can leave the running of the shop to me when you need to. You must stop fretting, Sis,' Clem insisted. 'It won't help in any way.'

'You're a fine one to talk.' Paige nudged her sister and thought about the crumpled up pieces of paper with all her calculations written down in columns that she'd left behind in the cottage. It wouldn't take much to ruin everything she had worked so hard for.

'Have you thought you could be playing right into his grasping hands?' Olly asked, when she told him about the viewings and Sebastian's part in it all the following morning.

'No, I hadn't,' Paige couldn't help feeling a little sick at the suggestion. 'Thanks for making me feel even more miserable.'

'Let's face it, Paige, with you gone from De Greys, that's one less tenant to worry about. It could suit him very well.'

'It wasn't quite like that. He's not as callous as you think, Ol,' she insisted, though not quite sure she was right. 'He did say that I would still get the compensation, if I agreed to leave.'

'And you believed him, of course.'

Despite what she was telling Olly, she did wonder at her judgment in men, which she knew fell very short of

160

being on the clever side.

'Hey, don't listen to me,' Olly said, taking several biscuits from Paige's cream enamelled tin. 'I'm being selfish.'

'How?'

'Because if you move elsewhere I wouldn't be upstairs from you, and couldn't keep popping down to see you, could I?' He raised his eyebrows.

'True, I hadn't thought of that,' she said, taking a moment from counting her takings to watch him, wondering if his bad mood might have something to do with what had happened between him and Clem.

'You also need me to help with the new website,' Olly added. 'especially if you want to establish your brand properly. Eventually you might even be able to forget about having to run a shop at all, then you wouldn't have to think about forking out for rent.'

She rubbed her temples wearily. 'I know, you're right and I can't wait to re-launch the site.'

'Great. I wish you'd listen to me more often, instead of some jumped-up bloke with a smart haircut who you've barely known for five minutes. You're wasting valuable time by not getting on with it.'

Paige puffed up a cushion to get more comfortable, not bothering to argue. 'Fine, put a few ideas together and we'll go through them.'

'Shit!' shouted Olly, grabbing the remote control. He turned the volume up to eardrum bursting level.

'What's the matter now?' She stopped sorting the bank notes to see what was so interesting.

'Look,' he shouted his face the picture of shock. 'There's a picture of Sir Edmund Blake on the news.'

She looked up as the picture disappeared, to be replaced by Sebastian surrounded by journalists and camera crews as he tried to walk along the road, his expression set hard. She strained her ears to try and find out what was going on.

'What's happened? Did you see?' She couldn't make out what the news alert was actually about, but there seemed to be much jostling and shouting going on, and whatever it was, it must be important to warrant so much press attention.

He shook his head. 'It's on the main BBC news, so it must be something big.'

'I wonder what he's involved with now?' she said thoughtfully.

'Balls, they've gone on to something else. Let's look at Sky News.' Olly hurriedly changed the channel once more, before Paige had a chance to disagree. 'Yes. Look, it says on the breaking news ticker tape thing under the presenter. Oh my God, Paige, Sir Edmund Blake is dead.'

They looked at each other in stunned silence for a second, before turning their attention back to the news. 'Do you think we won't have to worry about a takeover now?' Olly asked, in hushed tones.

Paige shrugged. 'No idea,' she said. Catching a glimpse of a picture of Sebastian on the screen, she went cold. 'Olly, look,' she whispered.

He followed her gaze, reading the caption under Sebastian's photo. 'Well, none of us saw that one coming did we? He wasn't just Sir Edmund's hatchet man at all,' he laughed, clapping his hands together with glee.

No,' said Paige, sickened with shock. 'I did think he could be the uncle Sebastian talked about, but he always referred to Sir Edmund Blake in quite a formal way so I wasn't sure. And he is his nephew. Blimey, Ol, I thought Sebastian worked for him, I didn't realise the uncle he talked about in Sorrento was Sir Edmund Blake.'

'How the hell did we miss this nugget of information?'

Paige shook her head. 'I've no idea,' she said wondering why she'd never connected the two men before.

'Then again,' said Olly, the excitement in his voice

obvious. 'Why would we connect Sebastian Fielding to Sir Edmund Blake? They have different last names and it's not as if any of us mix in the same circles.'

Paige shook her head, only half listening to what he was saying. She stared at the composed, but grief-stricken face displayed in all its glory on her 32-inch television screen. Her recent disappointment in him seemed ridiculous now. Gazing at his image, she wanted more than anything to protect him from the bellowing crowds of cameramen and television crews, as they shouted a constant flow of unintelligible questions at him. Only he wasn't hers to comfort, was he?

Chapter Twenty

'Sebastian. Over here.' Click. 'Oi, Fielding.'

'Sebastian.' A microphone was thrust in front of his face, narrowly missing his mouth. Sebastian pushed it and another three like it away. 'Sebastian, I'm Jeff Spires from Channel 104. Can you tell us if your uncle had suffered from a heart condition before this fatal attack?'

'What's going to happen to his empire now? You're the obvious one to take over from him. Sebastian.'

He held a hand up in a vain effort to stem the flow of questions being shouted at him as he resolutely made his way from the car to his London office. Someone pushed into his back. He ignored them, thankful for his strength which prevented him from being dragged forward with the baying crowd.

He reached the steps of the glass-fronted building and turned round to face the horde. 'I'll be giving an official statement shortly. I'm sure you can understand that my uncle's death has come as a terrible shock to everyone close to him and we need a little time to gather our thoughts.'

'Sebastian!'

He heard his name being shouted out; he was unsurprised that no one was giving him the time to come to terms with what had happened the previous night. Well they'd just have to wait. He turned and waited as his driver opened the front door, closing it quickly behind them.

'Thanks, Joseph,' he said. 'I don't know if you want to wait in here, and maybe have a coffee while I go to my office for a bit?'

'No, sir, I'll return to the car. I think I should go and take it round the back away from those bloody vultures out there.' He opened eyes wide. 'Um, I'm sorry, sir, I shouldn't have sworn.'

Sebastian patted the older man on his shoulder. 'Don't worry, Joseph. We've both been through a bit of a rough time this morning. Once you've parked the car, come to Reception and I'm sure they'll make you a coffee. I shouldn't be too long.'

He forced a smile at his secretary and nodded when she offered him a coffee, then closed his office door with relief and sat down. Mrs Hutton had left a message an hour earlier.

'Mrs H, how are you?' he asked, when she answered his house phone.

'I'm fine, Sebastian. It's you I'm worried about.'

'Any reporters at the house yet?'

'A few, but I've told them you're not going to be back here for the foreseeable future. I don't think they believed me though, because they're still camped outside. Poor Harley has had to make do with the garden today. I thought about taking him for a walk, but couldn't get as far as the front gate without them shouting at me.'

'I'll be back as soon as I can and I'll take him out somewhere by car. Are you OK apart from that though?' He hated to think of the paps shouting at Mrs Hutton.

'Yes, don't worry yourself about us. Harley growls at the door and goes mad every time one of them dares to call through the letterbox. I think they've decided to watch us from a distance.' He heard her patting the dog's head. 'You're a good boy for Mrs H, aren't you, Harley?'

'He is. Now remember the list I pinned up for you in the kitchen, Mrs H, the one with the names and emergency numbers on? If you have any problem at all and can't get hold of me, you must call these. I've listed them in order of importance, so start at the top.'

'You've told me this before. Now stop fretting about us, we're fine. Your lawyer chap told me that they're sending a policeman to stand outside the front door.'

'Good. I'm relieved. I don't want you being pestered.'

'The only person I'm worrying about is you. Now, you get along and speak to those paparazzi stalking your office. They made me mad watching them pushing and shoving you like they did. No manners, some of those journalists.'

'Thanks, Mrs H. I'll call you later.'

Sebastian turned off his phone, relieved to have been reassured that his housekeeper and dog were fine. There was a knock on the door. 'Come in, Caroline.' He watched as his secretary placed his cup of coffee on his desk. 'Has Linda called from the Jersey office yet?'

'Yes, Sebastian. She said she'd emailed you the public statement from the PR company. They're waiting for you to approve it and then they can send it out to the newspapers.'

'Give them a call. I'll go through their draft now, but I don't want them to release any statements until I've spoken to the reporters waiting outside here. They'll pretty much say the same thing anyway, but I want to give the statement first, so it can be televised.'

'Of course.' She smiled at him, before turning and leaving his office.

Her gentle smile reminded him of Paige. Had she heard the news, he wondered. There was already too much emotional distance between them. Would discovering his connection with Sir Edmund make matters worse? Probably. She already thought they were too unalike to stand a chance of making any relationship work. Sebastian dropped two lumps of sugar into his drink and stirred. Who was he trying to kid? It was their professional differences that were causing them such insurmountable

167

differences, not their social circles.

'Olly, hurry up. Sebastian's come back out to speak to the reporters.' Paige's heart contracted to see Sebastian looking so alone, as the reporters screamed questions at him. Each trying to shout louder than the next and not caring how much pain he was going through.

Olly came back in and handed her a mug of coffee, holding out an open packet of chocolate Hobnobs. 'Here, take one of these.'

'No thanks,' she said, waving them away. 'Doesn't life really stink sometimes?'

'You're not wrong there. That lucky bastard has it all. I thought I disliked him before, now I loathe him.'

'Olly.' Paige was horrified to hear him say something so callous. 'How can you say that, his uncle has just died and he's being hounded whenever he steps outside, he's obviously going through hell.'

'Well, I'm bloody jealous of him. I don't mind admitting it, and I hope this means he doesn't come back to Jersey. We'll all be well rid of him and his board of directors.'

Paige tried to think of Sebastian from Olly's point of view. 'I doubt Sir Edmund's death will make any difference with the reorganisation plans. I think Sebastian will simply carry on with the takeover and the rest of businesses now.'

'You're probably right.' He took another biscuit from the packet, dunking it in his drink before popping it into his mouth, dropping some of it onto his lap. 'Bollocks.'

'He'll have funeral arrangements to make too, no doubt,' she said thoughtfully. 'Surely we should show just a little generosity of spirit, don't you think? Just this once,' she added as Olly raised his eyebrows in defiance.

'I bet you wouldn't be so forgiving if you didn't fancy him,' he said, after a little contemplation. 'After all, Paige, my job is safe, you're the one who should be finding him a threat, not me.'

'True,' she said, not bothering to deny her feelings and wondering when Sebastian would return to the island.

'Maybe he might not come back to Jersey at all.'

Paige chewed her lower lip. Watching as Sebastian waited for the crowds to become silent before speaking and knew that however much he had hurt her, she still couldn't bear the thought of never seeing him again.

'Shush, he's going to speak,' she said leaning towards the television.

'As you're already aware, my uncle, Sir Edmund Blake, died sometime during last night. He was a well-respected man and loved by those close to him. Although this death comes as a shock to his family, it is also something that he had prepared for and, as such, I will be carrying on in his place with immediate effect. I would hope that you can allow us, as a family and workforce, the dignity of mourning this enterprising, spirited man in peace. Thank you.'

Paige watched, choked, as he held up his hand to signify that he wouldn't be adding anything further to his statement, and then walking towards his waiting car and being driven off.

'That was Sebastian Fielding, godson and assumed heir to Sir Edmund Blake's impressive empire, Gloucestershire estate, and business dealings in Jersey. We understand that Mr Fielding is single and has a home in London as well as his apartment in Jersey where he's patron of a children's charity that he set up some years ago.'

Paige listened in silence unable to come to terms with the fact that this person on the news was Sebastian. 'He lives in another world to us, doesn't he?' she said, half to herself.

'Blimey, you're not kidding,' said Olly. 'Who knew he had all this? What the hell did you two find to talk about?

169

Or are you some secret finance wizard?'

'Stop teasing me. I had no idea when I met him that he was so well-known,' she said, emotionally exhausted. 'I can't watch this any more, I'm going to bed.' Paige turned off the television. 'Why don't you do the same, and go home?'

Olly ignored her and stared at the set in the corner.

'Now, Ol,' she said, straightening cushions, picking up their mugs, but unable to banish the picture of Sebastian's calm expression from her mind.

Olly raked his hands through his unruly blond hair. 'This is so bloody exciting. I can't wait to go to work tomorrow and find out more info on him.'

Paige sighed. 'I'm sure it'll be the main topic of conversation for some time.'

Chapter Twenty-one

It had been several weeks since Sir Edmund's death and despite promising that she wouldn't, Paige couldn't help picking up and reading through the newspapers scattered around the staff room at De Greys. She couldn't believe that the papers were still printing gossip about Sebastian's private life in July.

'If I read any more intimate exposés from impossibly glamorous ex-girlfriends, I think I'll scream,' Paige said fanning herself with one of them and resolving to stop torturing herself. 'There are so many sensational stories about him wherever you look at the moment,' she said. 'Even I'm getting bored of seeing him in the gossip mags.'

'You're not the only one,' Olly groaned when yet another story came on the television. 'When are they going to stop all this speculation? It's been weeks now.'

'I know,' Paige agreed. 'I change the channel whenever the news comes on, and rarely bother to go to the staff room any more.'

'How's the packing going?' Olly asked. 'I've hired a van for you for Sunday, to help move all the stock, but by the sounds of it your sale is going so well you shouldn't have too much to move.'

Paige smiled, relieved that in the heat she would have fewer boxes to lift. Sebastian being kept away in England, while she signed the necessary paperwork for the new premises, had been a blessing in disguise. 'The sale has been brilliant,' she said looking around at the half-empty space.

Olly put his arm around her shoulders. 'Any regrets about leaving here?'

'No, I'm used to the idea now. In fact, it'll be a new beginning for me. It's going to be exciting to walk down the street and see "Heaven in Heels" above a shop for the first time.' She realized he was waiting for her to add something. 'I'll miss having you working upstairs like you do here, but I'm sure I'll see you most lunch times. My new shop is only a few minutes' walk away.'

'Thankfully. I'm glad we can still meet up for lunch.' He stared at his feet briefly. 'Clem still won't speak to me, Paige, not properly anyway.'

Paige touched the side of his face. 'She will, Ol, I promise. Give her time.'

Sebastian watched the intimate exchange between Paige and Olly wishing she felt as relaxed and close to him as she did with that guy. He'd missed her and although he'd kept up to date on her move, he'd been too caught up with executors, business, and family demands to be able to visit her before now. He cleared his throat to let them know he was there.

Paige looked across at the doorway and instantly dropped her hand from Olly's face. 'Sebastian?' She looked astonished to see him. 'I didn't realise you were back in Jersey.'

'Er, I'd better be getting on then,' Olly grimaced behind Sebastian's back to Paige unaware that Sebastian had seen him through a large mirror opposite. 'Um, sorry to hear your news, sir, I mean, um.'

'Thank you,' Sebastian said holding back his amusement as he interrupted Olly's awkwardness.

Paige stepped forward. 'Yes, I also wanted to say ...' she began.

Sebastian shook his head. 'Please don't. I'm starting to think if one more person gives me a pitying look, I might

172

take drastic action.'

Paige narrowed her eyes, and smiled. 'Nice to see you?'

She visibly relaxed when he smiled back at her. It felt good not to be fighting for once. 'It's good to see you, too.' He looked around the bare space. 'Nearly ready to go, I see?'

She nodded. 'Almost there.'

'I was concerned you'd be more resentful with me, but you appear to be fine,' he teased, studying her face.

'What's the point?' Paige shrugged. 'It's done now. No going back.'

He considered her words carefully. Was she referring to leaving De Greys, or to what had once been between them? Whatever it was, it made him feel as if he wasn't the only one to miss what they'd once shared. 'It doesn't have to be this way between us, you know,' he said, the atmosphere turning heavy between them.

She turned away from him, and began dusting one of the glass shelves. 'I think it does. We've both got a lot to deal with at the moment without getting involved with each other's private lives.'

He couldn't mistake the tone of finality in her voice. Maybe he should leave her to get on with her move. After all, he did have a lot to sort out. However, if she thinks this was how it's going to end between us, she doesn't know me at all, he thought. 'I'll leave you to get on. Best of luck, Paige,' he said, not taking his eyes off her and deciding to give her space to deal with her issues. 'And don't forget, if you need anything, don't hesitate to call me.'

She stopped what she was doing and looked at him once more, her mouth moving very slightly up at the corners. 'Thank you.'

'I'm fed up of you acting like a recluse.' Olly said that weekend, interrupting Paige sketching a new idea for next winter's boots. 'Tonight you're coming to a party with me.'

'I don't want to,' she groaned, unable to think of anything she would enjoy less. 'Anyway, I have a mountain of paperwork to get through, and I'm a bit stuck with ideas for a couple of my boot designs. My Spanish supplier has sent a few samples of new materials he's sourced. What do you think?' She held up three swatches for him to consider.

'They're great, but stop trying to distract me. I'm not taking no for an answer. I'll collect you tonight after seven. Be ready.'

'Olly, I'm not in the mood for parties. I still have to finish setting up the new shop.'

He shook his head. 'You're not using that as an excuse, I know it's all in hand. There's someone I think you should meet.'

'I'm not interested, and still have another four designs to work on. This move has come at the worst possible time and I can't afford to miss my deadline.'

Olly waved his hand in front of his face. 'Not listening. You've spent too long thinking about nothing but work.' He pulled a face at her. 'Or people related to it,' he added sarcastically. 'Tonight you'll do as you're told.'

Olly rarely put his foot down. Paige knew he must be determined. Not having the energy for a debate, she relented. 'All right, but I'm not going to enjoy myself.'

'I've heard that one before, I seem to recall,' he raised an eyebrow. 'You'll be going though, so don't think I'll let you change your mind.'

Paige placed her swatches back onto her desk. 'Fine, I'll go and get ready.'

'I'm around the back,' she shouted from her sun lounger when he arrived at the cottage half an hour before they were due to leave. 'To wake you up a bit,' he said holding up a bottle of Merlot and winking at her. 'What a

174

relief to see your legs for a change.'

'It's so hot and this is the coolest dress I could find in my wardrobe.'

'You look great,' he said, giving her a quick hug. 'As soon as you get back here you change into your tracksuit and scrape your hair up into a pigtail.'

She pushed him away, unable to keep a grin from spreading across her face. 'Cheeky bugger, anyway it's a ponytail, not a pigtail.'

'Whatever. All I'm saying is, it's good to see you looking less like you're on a mission and more like the young woman you're supposed to be.'

'Charming,' she laughed, knowing he was right. 'Now, can we please get going, or I'll start to flag and need to go to bed.'

Olly rolled his eyes. 'Don't even think about it.' He grabbed her bag in one hand and took her by the wrist with the other. 'We can stop at The Anchorage first and have a drink there, then go on to the party. You'll have a ball, whether you like it or not,' he assured her. 'You know something? You really do look pretty cute in that little cotton dress.'

Paige smiled, enjoying his compliments. 'Thanks.'

They arrived at the pub and Olly held the door open for her. 'Come along, let's go and mingle.'

'Who's he?' asked Paige, indicating a tall, sandy-haired man watching her from across the main room.

Olly spotted him immediately and tapped the side of his nose at Paige. She looked up, and much to her surprise saw him striding purposefully towards them.

'Jake, hi,' Olly said. 'I wondered where you'd be hiding.'

So, this was Jake. Paige agreed with Olly, he certainly looked as if he would be most at home on a surfboard. Jake took her hand in his, raising it to his lips. His casual, confident air put her immediately at ease. Paige smiled, liking him instantly.

'Hi, so you two had the same idea to have a couple here first?' He bowed his head slightly. 'This is the famous Paige. Olly's told me all about you.'

Paige raised her eyebrows at his unexpected comment. She looked at Olly out of the corner of her eye.

'This chap never stops talking about you. It's always "Paige this and Paige that", so I thought I must come and meet this gorgeous vision, find out what exactly it is that fascinates him so much about you.'

She narrowed her eyes at Olly. 'I daren't ask what you've been saying,' she teased.

'What's wrong with me talking about you?' he said, looking as innocent as possible. 'I didn't say anything I shouldn't have.'

'It's what you did say that worries me.' She glanced back at Jake, who was grinning lop-sidedly at them.

'Hah,' he patted Olly on the back. 'Don't worry, I'm sure he hasn't said anything you'd disapprove of. No indiscretions divulged, unfortunately. How do you fancy coming surfing with me one of these days?'

Paige grimaced; she hadn't expected such an invitation. 'I doubt I'd be any good,' she said. Then unable to ignore Jake's infectious humour immediately rethought her decision and added, 'I'd love to tell you I need to consult my diary first, but I know there's very little in it.'

'I'm here, remember.' Olly nudged her. 'You could do with having some fun, otherwise all you'll be doing this summer will be working on spreadsheets and your sketches.'

'Maybe in a few weeks,' Paige relented. 'Olly, you know how much work I have to contend with right now.' She turned her attention back to Jake. 'I can't take time off to go surfing at the moment.'

'No worries,' Jake said. 'If you change your mind let me know.'

Paige watched him walk away and join his friends.

'At least you have your own projects and do what you love best,' Olly said.

'You enjoy what you do, too.' She knew Olly's change of mood was down to Clem not opening up to him about the baby.

'I know, but I've never had the guts to start up on my own yet, have I?'

'I'm sure you will when the time is right. Anyway, you're going to set up a site for me, so I can be your first client.'

'Hey, you two,' Jake said, striding over towards them. 'We're going on to the party now. Do you want to join us?'

'We'll follow you,' Olly said.

Olly drove up Gorey Hill, turning left and following for a short distance, until Jake's car disappeared through two enormous granite pillars. Driving slowly up the curved driveway lined with pink hydrangeas in full bloom, they rounded the bend and were confronted by a vast white marquee erected in the front garden.

'This is going to be a bit more extravagant than we were expecting,' Paige said, unable to get over the magnificence of the setting. 'Jake never told us his friend's party was going to be this huge.'

'He probably didn't realise,' Olly said. 'I think the birthday girl is someone he met surfing a while ago.' He laughed. 'My twenty-first was never like this.'

'Nor mine,' Paige said, recalling the beach party Jeremy had arranged for her after his mother had refused to allow him to hold Paige's twenty-first celebrations at their family home. 'This place must be fairly near to Jeremy's parents' place,' he said, as if he could read her thoughts.

'Probably,' Paige said. 'It's bigger though,' Paige said, trying to keep her voice level. She gazed at the expanse of greenery all around them as Olly parked the car. Then stepping out, unable to resist, she walked as quickly as she could manage in her heels along a gravel pathway to the edge of the garden. 'Look at that,' she shouted, staring down at the imposing medieval fortification of Mont Orgeuil Castle looming majestically above Gorey village and the small harbour below. 'Now that's a view.'

Olly came and stood next to her. 'It's awesome, isn't it? I wouldn't mind owning a place like this.'

They stared at the granite bastion to the left. 'Wow,' Paige said, unable to contain her excitement as she pointed to the rolling waves breaking on the golden sand of the wide arc-shaped beach to the right. 'I've never seen Grouville Bay from this angle before, it's incredible.'

'We'd better make the most of this, I can't imagine we'll ever be lucky enough to come here again.'

'That's right,' she teased. 'Spoil the mood.'

'Come on, we'd better go and find Jake or he'll be wondering where we are.'

Paige nodded, pleased she'd made the effort to go out for the first time in weeks.

'I think this is going to be fun.' Olly grabbed her hand and quickened his pace as they reached the entrance. 'Hi Jake,' he said waving to attract his friend's attention.

'Come along you two, stop dawdling.' Jake linked arms with Paige and laughed. 'Let's get some drinks.'

'Crikey,' Paige gasped, as she entered the marquee. 'I wonder what her favourite colour can be?' She gazed around the garishly pink interior.

Jake raised his bushy eyebrows. 'You're not kidding. Bit overkill, but whatever floats your boat, I guess. Where's the bar?'

The three barmen filled, shook, and juggled silver cocktail shakers as they prepared a continuous array of pink cocktails.

'I wonder what they're having?' Paige asked, noticing

two girls watching as one of the barmen poured them a drink each.

'This one is a French Knickers,' the barman said, giving her a cheeky wink. 'And this is a Raspberry Cosmopolitan. Fancy one?'

Jake picked a flute of pink champagne from a passing waitress and handed it to Paige. 'Thought this might be more your tipple.' He took a pint of lager from the bar for himself. 'I think I'd leave those fancy drinks for later on,' he grimaced.

Paige took a sip of the cool liquid; unable to shake off the feeling she was being watched. As she looked around at the other guests, she stopped abruptly, coming eye to eye with Sebastian. Her heart lurched instantly, only for her to realise almost immediately that Sara was right next to him. She had her back to Paige and hadn't yet noticed her.

Paige felt her breath disappear like it had been sucked away by a powerful vortex. She looked away, willing the banging in her chest to calm down. Then unable to resist glancing up from under her lashes to take a peek at him, she caught him watching her. Sebastian nodded his acknowledgement that he had seen her. Paige attempted a smile in return, desperate to hide her embarrassment to have been caught out.

'Excuse me,' someone said, interrupting her thoughts.

Paige turned her focus to the woman standing next to her. She thought she recognized her as a customer from the shop. 'Hello. How are you?'

'Oh, you do remember me. I'm so glad. I'm Maddy Jackson. I hope you don't mind me asking you something?'

'Not at all,' Paige answered, glad to have something to take her mind off Sebastian's presence.

'I'm getting married in a few months, and I was wondering if you'd consider designing my wedding

179

shoes?'

Paige tried to contain her excitement. 'I'd be delighted to, Maddy. Do you have any ideas you want to go through with me?'

'A few, yes.'

'OK, why don't I take your number and then we can arrange for me to come to your house and talk through some designs.'

'That would be brilliant,' Maddy said. 'I want a contemporary theme with a hint of Edwardian in it, so I'm not sure how difficult they're going to be put together.'

'It won't be a problem at all,' Paige said, excited by the prospect of having to fit in with someone else's vision.

'I wasn't sure you'd agree to do this.'

'You try and stop me.' Paige noted Maddy's number in her Blackberry and immediately began picturing patterns for the design in her head. She was finding it hard to think inside the noisy marquee, and decided to get some fresh air, away from the chatter and music.

Chapter Twenty-two

Sebastian watched Paige leave the marquee. Sara was deep in conversation with a friend and he needed a break from all the pink. He walked past the groups of noisy people out to the cool pine scented air outside. It was a magnificent garden and even in the duskiness he could see the shapes of the towering trees as they stood majestically along the edge of the garden.

He looked around trying to decide which way Paige must have gone. He walked towards the rose garden, remembering fondly the times he'd been sat there with his father and sister during family barbeques in summers as he was growing up. Seb spotted Paige standing silently, staring out towards the sea and watched as she gazed at the magnificent silvery reflection of the moon across the bay, as the tide rolled back and forth.

'I hope you don't mind me invading your thoughts?' he asked, not sure if she was aware of his presence.

She shivered.

'You're cold?' he said starting to take off his linen jacket.

Paige shook her head and turned to face him. 'No, I'm fine. I was remembering something, that's all.'

He wondered if she'd been thinking about being with Jeremy, they must have spent many evenings enjoying scenes like this one on this pretty island.

'I didn't expect to see you here tonight,' she said looking up at him, her green eyes appearing black in the darkness. I thought you were away somewhere.'

'I'm here for a few days this time.' He took her hand in his. 'Paige, I wanted to say something to you.'

She pulled away from him, surprising him with her force, and making him feel like she'd just slapped him. 'No, please don't.'

'Don't what? You don't even know what I was going to say.' Why does everything have to be so difficult between us, he wondered miserably.

'OK, say it then,' she said, looking as if she was trying to take control of her emotions, but failing.

He knew it would be selfish to ask. 'I just wanted to make sure you were all right,' he lied, unable to make things even harder for her than they already seemed to be. It was clear to him now that she was moving on, if she hadn't already done so. Hadn't he already been the cause of enough upset to this enticing woman?

She raised her eyebrows in disbelief. 'You could have said that when we were both in the marquee. You didn't have to follow me down to the end of the garden.'

'You're not the only one who needed a little peace, you know,' he joked, unable to tell her that he couldn't have kissed her in the marquee. It was foolish of him to hope he could do so here, he now realised. It wasn't just that she was beautiful, he mused, there was something else that he found irresistible and made him yearn to be with her. He stared down at Paige in silence.

'I was sorry to hear about Sir Edmund's death, especially when I found out who he was to you,' she said. 'It must have been a dreadful shock.'

Sebastian was used to being the strong one and found it hard to take when people pitied him. 'Not really, the family were aware of his heart condition,' he said, aware his voice was clipped and unemotional. 'Unfortunately, it was only a matter of time. Those of us who loved him tried hard to take the pressure away from him, but he was incapable of slowing down, never even attempting to take

182

things easy.' He stood silently for a moment, not sure whether to go on with what he was saying. Then, knowing he had to open up to her a little more, added. 'It was the reason I ended up working with him. I needed to make sure someone took the brunt of everything, to keep him from overdoing it.' He looked away from her for the first time since beginning their conversation and sighed. 'I didn't succeed, obviously.'

'You did help me find my new shop and, I have to admit, I am happy there.'

Sebastian was stunned into silence at her unexpected admission. He soon recovered and grabbing her, pulled her into his arms. As his lips touched hers, he watched her close her eyes, then closing his own forgot everything as the sensation of their bodies finally being close again took over. He kissed her with such force he hoped he hadn't bruised her lips. 'I've missed you,' he breathed, his voice muffled as he kissed her neck, then her mouth once more. 'I'd love to take you out again sometime, Paige,' he said, hoping that her kiss had meant something. He felt her tense. 'What's the matter?'

'I can't go out with you, Sebastian,' she said, stepping back from him.

'Why not?'

'Because unlike you, I'm not used to having my private life splashed across the national papers. I couldn't bear to have to be on my guard whenever I went out.'

She had a point. 'I can understand that, but couldn't we at least try to spend some time together?'

She shook her head, without even considering his suggestion, he noted miserably. She'd obviously made up her mind and wasn't going to change it any time soon. 'Fine, I understand. I'm sorry though, I wish I could change your mind,' he admitted.

'I know,' she said reaching up to touch his cheek.

The action, strangely intimate, made him want her even

more than he already did. 'Paige, I ...'

'There you are.' Sara's voice came from the shadows, before Sebastian could say anything further. She peered at Paige through the darkness trying to make her out. 'Oh, hi, Paige,' she said, seeing who Sebastian was with. 'I'm sorry, have I interrupted something?'

Sebastian assumed that Sara must have seen them embracing only seconds before.

'No, nothing,' Paige said, before he had a chance to reply.

Sebastian held back a retort. He knew how she liked to be in control and let her walk away.

'I'll leave you both to it,' she said. 'I've enjoyed catching up with you, Sebastian.'

'Paige,' Sebastian went to follow her.

'Must go, and find Olly and Jake,' she shouted over her shoulder. 'They'll be wondering where I've gone.'

'Is everything OK?' Sara asked. He didn't reply. Seconds later, she added. 'Go and stop her, before she goes back inside.'

'She's already gone,' he murmured, walking along the lawn towards the marquee.

Chapter Twenty-three

Paige hurried towards the light of the marquee, arriving breathless, mostly due to the mixed feelings she was trying to suppress. She found Olly entertaining a group of giggling females surrounding him. He noticed her straight away and held his hand out to her, drawing her next to him. 'Lovely ladies, this is Paige,' he said, a naughty twinkle in his eye. 'Say hello, Paige.'

'Hello,' she said obediently, enjoying his easy way as she forced any thoughts of Sebastian to the back of her mind, determined to deal with them later.

'Come on, drink time,' he said, taking Paige's hand and leading her towards the bar.

'You're such a tease,' she said, seeing the disappointment in his admirers' faces as Olly turned his attention away from them. 'You love all this, don't you?'

He smiled his cheeky grin. 'What man wouldn't?' He leaned in closer to her and lowered his voice. 'Also, a little PR never hurts the coffers, so I take my chances where I see them. I'm going to have to make the most of these parties if I want to build up a following for your new website.'

He's not as switched off as he likes people to believe, Paige realised, grinning at him, and just managing not to laugh out loud at his blatant admission.

'Come on,' he said, taking her glass from her hand and placing it along with his own on a nearby table. 'Boogie time.'

'Oh, please no, I don't want to,' she protested, as he led

her past dancing guests into the middle of the temporary wooden floor.

'I love this,' he said, in between singing along to The Beach Boys' 'Good Vibrations'.

Paige giggled, unable to stop her mood lifting with his infectious high spirits.

'Sing along, then,' he said, taking her hands and waving them in the air.

I must look like a complete fool, she thought, not minding at all and enjoying the feeling of liberation she had from his devil-may-care attitude. 'I don't know all the words.'

'Who cares,' he laughed. 'Make some up.'

Olly spun Paige round, catching her and lowering her backwards when she tripped over her own feet. He pulled her up to stand once more and then spun her around the other way.

'No more,' she giggled. 'Enough. Stop.'

'Hey, watch out,' a woman shouted. 'You almost stood on my toe.'

'Have to make sure we don't miss next time,' shouted Jake, coming up to dance next to them, causing her to bite her lower lip to stop laughing.

'Sorry', she mouthed to the woman, who looked down her nose and turned her back to them.

'Hooligans.'

Jake mimicked her from behind, until Paige motioned him to stop. 'Let's get a drink,' she suggested, her hand at her throat. 'I'm parched.'

'You just want an excuse to stop dancing with me,' he said, leading the way.

Paige giggled. He was right. She tried to catch her breath as she followed him in the general direction of the bar, passing a striking woman about her own age with long platinum blonde hair like a cascade of gold down her tanned back. She was in deep conversation with a friend, neither of them bothering to try and hide the fact they were watching and discussing Paige. In fact, realised Paige, they wanted her to notice. She wondered why the woman seemed so interested in her, and feigning an air of confidence, followed Jake and Olly to the bar.

'Who's she?' she asked Olly, discretely pointing out the two women to him, as Jake ordered their drinks.

Olly raised his eyebrows. 'Don't know, but she's gorgeous,' he said breathlessly. 'Hang on a sec, I do recognize her from somewhere.' He rubbed his chin as he concentrated. 'I think she could be Sebastian Fielding's ex-fiancé. Don't think they were ever actually married though.'

'Are you sure?' Paige asked, her whole body tingling with shock.

'About which bit?' Olly peered surreptitiously over Paige's head.

'Any of it,' she said desperate to know more.

'Didn't you read about it?'

She shook her head, wishing she had done.

'I'm trying to think. I remember her picture from a couple of those articles in the papers recently, but can't remember what they were saying about her.'

'Who were?' she asked, taking a pink cocktail from Jake.

'Who, what?' Jake asked.

'Paige was wondering who that beauty is over there.' Olly motioned in the woman's direction.

Jake looked over. 'No idea, but she's pretty incredible.'

'OK, you two.' Paige wished she had never started the conversation in the first place. 'Stop gawping like a couple of teenage boys, I was trying to be discreet.'

'I never said she was as lovely as you, though did I?' Jake said, winking suggestively.

'It goes without saying,' Paige teased, wondering how Sebastian could ever waste time with her when he was used to a woman who was so much more impressive in every conceivable way. I'll bet she could cope with the paparazzi, she mused.

'Of course it does.' Jake squeezed her to him and tickled her side.

Paige squealed, wriggling out of his grasp, instantly forgetting her insecurities. 'Stop it. I'm going to spill my drink.'

'She will,' Olly said. 'She's incredibly clumsy.'

'Come on,' Jake shouted, putting their glasses on the bar. 'I want to dance some more.'

'Let's not,' Paige tried to argue, but he took no notice and continued waving his arms in the air as he meandered towards the dance floor. 'Oh my God, you look like a regular from the club they made that documentary about, from the seventies,' she said. 'Where was that place again? I remember now, it was Studio 54.'

'What are you waiting for?' he shouted, shimmying in front of her, making her giggle.

Unable to think of a reason not to, Paige determined to forget she was being watched, and joined in with him, punching the air and moving her hips as best she could along with him.

'You sure can move,' he said, as other guests seemed to pick up on his mood and joined them on the dance floor.

The DJ started clapping to the rhythm. 'This is for my very good friend Jake. As we can see, he knows how to get down and dirty on the dance floor. Go for it, Jakey,' he shouted, as the first bars of, 'Boogie Nights' began to filter through the loud speakers at each corner of the room.

'Jakey,' called a young girl, dressed head to toe in candy pink, as she launched herself towards him. Paige assumed she must be the birthday girl. 'Baby, you came. I knew you wouldn't let me down.' She elbowed her way passed Paige to get to him.

'Hey, careful,' he said, peering over her pink angel

wings to Paige.

She smiled. 'Don't worry,' she mouthed. She watched as the birthday girl draped her arms around Jake's neck, half-heartedly glancing in Paige's direction, before focusing her attention back to him.

'Don't you think she looks rather like an overblown strawberry milkshake?' Olly asked from over her shoulder.

Paige laughed. 'That's mean, Olly. It's her birthday; she's allowed to wear what she wants.'

'Yeah,' he said, not looking at all convinced. 'But there should be a limit when you reach your twenties, surely?'

They continued dancing nearby, watching as Jake tried to untangle himself, a forced smile on his face. He reached up, taking the girl's wrists in his hands and attempted to untangle them from his neck.

'She's holding on for grim death,' Olly said, one eyebrow raised in amazement.

Jake tried pulling her hands away from him once more. 'No, Jakey,' she shouted. 'Don't do that.'

'Oh, crap,' Olly said. 'I think she's had a bit too much to drink. He looks like he's having a bit of a battle escaping from her clutches.'

She was about to agree, when the girl flung one arm back from Jake's hold and smacked Paige right in the eye.

Chapter Twenty-four

'Ouch,' Paige yelped, covering her smarting eye with one hand. 'Bloody hell, that hurt.' Tears began streaming from her throbbing eye. She could feel it beginning to swell straight away.

Jake wrestled free from the party girl and pushed her away from him. 'Shit, look what you've done,' he shouted. 'Hey, are you OK?' He rushed over to Paige's side.

'Of course she's not,' said a calm voice Paige recognized. 'What the hell were you playing at, messing around like a teenager in the middle of all these people?' Sebastian said, glaring at Jake. It was obvious someone was going to get hurt.'

Paige closed her eyes. She was embarrassed to be caught in this drama and wished they'd both go away and leave her in peace. 'I'm fine,' she said between clenched teeth.

Jake turned from her to face Sebastian, the rage on his face palpable. 'Why don't you mind your own business, big man?' he said, nose to nose with Sebastian.

Paige forgot the stinging in her eye. 'It's OK, please don't make a fuss,' she said, her voice drowned out by the crying birthday girl.

Undeterred by Jake's threatening demeanour, Sebastian gently took Paige's hand in his and held it away from her eye, bending down to have a look. 'That looks painful. You want to get it checked out,' he said, his voice cold. 'You're definitely going to have a black eye after a punch like that one.'

'I'm fine, really,' she assured him, before noticing Jake grab at Sebastian's shoulder and pull him backwards.

'I said to butt out, and leave her alone,' Jake shouted, his eyes narrowed as he focused his attention on Sebastian.

Sebastian shrugged him off easily.

'Hey.' Olly grabbed hold of her, lifting her away from the drama. 'They're not fighting over you, are they?' he asked, looking delighted.

'Shut up, Olly. I think it's time Jake went home. Do something.'

'Er, no.' He looked at her as if she was insane. 'They're both bigger than me, and by the looks on their faces, ready to kill each other. I think this has more to do with jealousy than anything else.'

Paige winced as Jake punched Seb on the jaw. Seb immediately retaliated. Unable to miss Olly's determination not to get involved, Paige decided she would have to do something. 'Stop it,' she screamed, grabbing hold of Sebastian's arm, just in time to distract his attention enough and allow Jake to take full advantage by punching him hard in the face.

Paige winced. 'Jake. What did you do that for?'

'Yes,' echoed Olly. 'That's enough.' He linked his arms through Jake's from behind, holding him back from Sebastian, enabling Paige to step in.

Paige turned to Sebastian. 'What was that all about?' she asked, stunned by what she had just witnessed between the two men.

'Don't have a go at me,' Sebastian snapped. 'It was your boyfriend who started all this.'

'He's not my boyfriend, not that it's anything to do with you if he was.'

'I think we should leave,' Olly said, glancing from one to the other. 'before Jake gets his second wind.'

'You don't have to tell me twice,' Jake moaned, putting an arm around her shoulder and sneering in Sebastian's direction before walking with her towards the door. 'What the hell is his problem anyway?'

Paige glanced over to see Sebastian staring after them, his bruised face sullen. 'I've no idea,' she said, wondering why Sebastian kept involving himself in her life. What did he want from her? It wasn't as if he didn't have enough attention from everyone else.

'Shit,' Olly shouted, catching up with them by the car. 'I didn't know his lordship was there tonight. What the hell was all that about?'

'I think he only stepped in to stop everything kicking off, to be honest,' Paige said suspecting that Sebastian had only become involved as a reaction to her being hit in the face. 'You're the one who acted like a madman in there,' she snapped at Jake, pushing his arm away from her.

'Yeah, sorry.' At least he had the decency to look a little shame-faced.

'Why don't you come in for a bit and let me have a look at your eye?' Jake asked when they arrived at his house at the edge of the sand dunes in St Ouen's Bay.

Paige shook her head. 'It was only a glancing blow. I think you came out of that worse than I did, don't you?' she said, studying his grazed cheek.

'Bloody toffs,' he said getting out of the car. 'Why do they always wear those stupid pinkie rings?'

'Instigate fights with them often, do you?' Paige teased, unable to stop feeling a little guilty for Sebastian's part in the drama.

'Not every week.' He bent down and gazed into the wing mirror for a moment. 'Bloody hell, I made a bit of a fool of myself tonight, didn't I?'

Paige nodded.

'You had a lucky escape,' Olly said. 'Someone was telling me he's involved in some kids' charity. I'm told he does a lot of training for taking part in charity boxing matches to raise money for one of the homes over here, so he's bloody fit.'

Paige could see Jake was taken aback by Olly's comment. She was too. 'Really? Are you sure?' It was news to her.

Olly shrugged. 'So I gather. Apparently, in his spare time he helps a guy who runs an orphanage where the kids live. I think they were friends when they were kids, and he sets up charity evenings to help raise money.'

Jake groaned. 'If he's so bloody wealthy, why doesn't he write out a cheque so they can do the work instead of him?'

'I don't know,' Olly said, turning to Paige. 'I would have suggested you asked him, but I don't think he'll be in any mood to talk to you right now.'

Neither did she, and she was quite sure she didn't want to speak to him either. It was all getting too confusing. Finding out Sebastian had been engaged to that beautiful woman, and now learning this about him only went to confirm how little she knew about the man and how right her father had been when he spoke about Sebastian being unattainable.

Jake leaned into the car window. 'Do you fancy coming surfing tomorrow morning? The tide should be perfect just after six.'

Paige laughed at his determination. 'I think you could probably do with taking it a little easy and getting a decent lie-in,' she said, breathing in the salty air and listening to the waves lapping against the nearby sand. 'I'm going straight home. I need to get an ice pack on this shiner and see if I can get it to go down a little before I have to return to work on Monday. I can't afford to frighten off my customers.'

'I hadn't thought of that,' Olly laughed. 'A black eye doesn't really give the best impression when you're running an up-market business, does it?'

'Not really,' she said, waving at Jake, as Olly began to drive.

'You'll look like a right thug,' he laughed.

'Olly?' she asked, trying not to giggle at his comment.

'Yes?'

'Shut up and drive.'

As Olly wove the car through the leafy country lanes, she mused about how much easier it was to have fun with a man when you didn't have deep feelings for him. She enjoyed Jake's company, rather more than she had expected to, but was still stunned by Seb's reaction towards him, and even more amazed by his apparent involvement in the nearby children's home.

'Why do you think Sebastian stepped in like that tonight, Ol?' she asked, staring out into the darkness, watching the shadowy shapes of the trees as they drove past. 'He's always seemed so cool and together before.'

'Either because he was being protective of you, or simply because he was jealous,' he said, his tone matter of fact.

'Jealous, of what? Jake's your friend, he's nothing to do with me.'

Olly nodded. 'I know that, but he doesn't.'

'You don't think it was because Jake just annoyed him by acting like a big kid on the dance floor like he said?'

Olly looked at her for a moment. 'It probably didn't help, but the look on his face when that stupid girl hit you in the eye was a picture. It was as if something snapped inside him, and he reacted instinctively. I've never seen anyone's expression change so instantaneously. He really cares for you, you know, whether you choose to believe it or not.'

Paige pulled her cotton jacket tighter around her, as if it could possibly ward off any further confusing thoughts. 'You must be wrong. Surely, if I meant anything to him at all, he wouldn't have lied to me when he found out I had a concession in De Greys?'

'I suppose you're right. Maybe he just likes being in control,' he suggested.

'Probably,' she added, feeling hurt at the thought that Olly could be right.

They drove in silence for a while. Paige lowered her head back against the leather headrest and closed her eyes. Breathing in the sweet evening air, she turned her thoughts back to Sebastian. Why couldn't he be an ordinary guy with a standard nine to five job?

'Good,' Olly said, changing gear badly and causing his engine to protest loudly. 'There's no reason for you to sit at home being miserable and wallowing.'

'What do you mean?' She wound the window down a little further, holding her hand out in the cool air.

'Don't act the innocent with me,' he said, looking at her briefly. 'I saw your face when he strutted over and did his lord and master bit.'

'He did not,' Paige said, immediately wishing she would think before speaking.

'See? You're defending him already,' Olly said, raising an eyebrow. 'And after everything you've said, too.'

Paige couldn't miss the determination in his voice, and decided she needed to hurry up and start sorting things out between Olly and her sister. He needed something to keep him from getting involved in her problems. She'd have to come up with something before he drove her mad.

Chapter Twenty-five

'Sebastian, baby, calm down.' Lucinda soothed.

He could feel her cool hands stroking his back and moved away from her. 'That's enough,' he snapped. 'Please leave me alone.'

'Why can't we be friends? I know I hurt you, but I've regretted my stupidity every day since I left you.'

She looked so sincere, he almost suspected she was telling the truth. The Lucinda he'd fallen for was always a little hot-headed and many times had acted without thinking, but she'd been gentle most of the time. 'We can't go back. I've moved on,' he added guiltily, aware that the depths of his feelings for Paige far exceeded those he'd ever held for Lucinda.

Paige's beautiful face, now bruised. What the hell was she doing larking about with that Jake bloke anyway? Lucinda's nasal voice broke his train of thought. 'What is it?' he said brushing her hand away as she attempted to dab at his face with a damp napkin.

'Your lip is swollen,' she said, pouting and trying again.

He gently took hold of her wrist and moved it away. 'It's nothing, don't fuss.'

'You were spectacular over there,' she said, indicating the dance floor where the barmen were sweeping up broken glass.

'There's nothing spectacular about tonight. I should have stopped the fight, not got involved in it. I need to go and apologise to those chaps who are cleaning up my mess.'

'You were only looking out for Paige,' Sara said. 'It's typical of you, to rescue a damsel in distress.'

'Yes, I noticed her flaunting herself over those two men,' Lucinda sneered, flicking her long hair over her shoulder. 'It's not surprising she ended up with a smack in the eye.'

Sebastian rounded on her with a fury that he had to work hard to contain. 'When did you get to be so nasty?' She flinched, her mouth dropping open in shock. 'You have absolutely no idea what you're talking about, so why don't you go and find someone else to irritate?'

'Fine, I'm going.'

He watched with satisfaction as she marched off towards a group of her cronies. 'What happened to her?'

Sara pulled a face and shrugged. 'No idea, but I'll give you a lift home if you like. Protect you from any more female-related dramas.'

Sebastian groaned. 'I think that's the best suggestion I've heard all night.'

'So, any plans for tomorrow, or is it more meetings, as usual?' she asked, as they walked over to her car.

'I have someone I need to see in the morning.'

'Paige?' Sara asked, unlocking her car and getting inside.

'No. I'll call on her at some point, but first I'm going to visit a young chap who's in hospital.'

'Sorry, I didn't mean to be flippant. Who are you helping out this time?'

'He was a promising young boxer until a few weeks ago when some drunk driver smashed into him. They flew him to Southampton and kept in a drug-induced coma until recently.'

'Oh that's horrible. Will he be OK?' she asked.

Sebastian sighed. 'I hope so. They flew him back to the island today, and his mother has asked me to visit him to try and give him some hope that he may fight again.'

'And will he?'

'No.'

Sara gasped. 'What will you tell him then?'

Sebastian wished he knew. 'I haven't come up with anything yet, but I need to find a way to stop him from thinking his life is over. The one he expected to have certainly is, but I must to think of something to engage him that he can put his energies into that will take the place of his boxing.'

'That's so sad. Poor boy,' she said miserably. 'I hope you come up with something.'

'Me, too.' He pressed the button to open the passenger window. 'I think it's time to call in some favours from the amateur boxing fraternity, but first I thought I'd arrange for him and his mum to go on a trip to the Galapagos Islands. It's the only thing she could think of that he might enjoy, and something he's always wanted to do since he was tiny. It's not ideal, but it's a start. It's also something for him to look forward to over the next few months while he heals. It'll give me time to come up with a decent plan to help him move on.'

Chapter Twenty-six

'I never thought my sister would be sporting a black eye,' Clem giggled.

'Don't,' Paige checked her reflection discreetly on a wall mirror. 'I thought I'd covered it well this morning.'

'Sis, all the make-up in the world isn't going to hide the swelling.'

Paige straightened a pair of boots in the window display. 'Stupid party, I was having fun until that happened.'

'Olly told me Sebastian Fielding was very attentive.'

'He wasn't,' she said, wondering when the two of them had spoken.

'Hey, don't feel bad. I'm not saying this to cause a row, but he told me it was pretty hard to miss the vibes between you both.'

Paige forced a laugh. 'Hardly.'

Clem raised her eyebrow, and folded her arms over her slightly rounded stomach. 'Say what you like. You probably haven't even admitted it to yourself, but there's definitely something going on. Even I know that much.' She put her finger up to her lips and winked. 'Or would be, if you'd let it.'

'Clem …'

Clem laughed. 'Don't fret about it. You two have something that needs to be dealt with, before it drives you, or at least him, nuts.' She nudged Paige's side. 'Stop looking so worried. I don't know what it is that is holding you back, apart from all that guff Dad was waffling on about him having to deal with constant press attention. He's only being protective, and I don't care what Sebastian Fielding does, or where he lives, it doesn't make him a crappy person. You should know that.'

'Can we stop going on about him?' Paige asked. 'I think there are more pressing matters to deal with,' she said glancing pointedly at Clem's stomach.

'Forget it. I'm not ready to talk about this baby yet.'

'Too bad, it's time you two sorted things out. Never mind worrying about me and Sebastian, you and Olly need to deal with this and the sooner the better, if you ask me.'

'I'm not asking you.' Clem sat down on the stool behind the counter and sulked.

There was a knock at the door.

'Good morning,' the postman said. She loved that he always seemed to have a beaming smile on his face, regardless of the weather he had to work in.

'Hello,' Paige said, going over to greet him. 'More bills, I suppose?' She took the stash of envelopes and waved to him as he left the shop humming to himself.

'I don't know what he has to be so bloody happy about.' Clem grumbled. 'I hate it when people are so cheerful in the morning.'

Paige ignored her and skimmed through the assortment of brown and white envelopes in her hand until she reached a larger one at the back. 'Interesting,' she said, opening the expensive-looking envelope hurriedly and drawing out the invitation from *Society*. 'This is from that new glossy magazine where I advertised the opening of Heaven in Heels a few weeks ago.' Her thumb grazed across the top of the embossed wording instantly lifting her mood. 'It's an invitation to their annual corporate evening at Les Landes Racecourse. I've always wanted to go to that. It says I can invite a plus one.'

'Don't bother asking me, I hate horse racing.'

As soon as she arrived home after work, Paige sent

Olly a text. He seemed to beam himself up into her kitchen within seconds.

'Well?' he asked, spotting the white card leaning against the windowsill and picking it up. 'Yes,' he said, punching the air. 'You can bring a plus one, brilliant.'

'You're sure it'll be you, I notice,' she shook her head, taking the invitation from his fingers and tapping him on the back of the head with it before replacing it on the sill.

Olly frowned and then sidled up to her. 'Who else were you thinking of inviting?'

She wagged a finger at him. 'You can come if you promise to behave yourself,' she said, taking out her lipstick and applying it quickly.

'Clem not interested?' he asked quietly, trying to look bored.

Paige smiled. She had been rumbled. 'No, doesn't agree with horse-racing apparently.'

'So, where are you going now then? Seeing Jake?' Olly asked, tilting his head to one side studying her through narrowed eyes.

Paige shook her head. 'I'm not interested, Ol, so give up.'

'Well, where then?'

'You're so nosey.' She shook her head and pulled on her coat. 'If you must know, I'm off to meet a bride-to-be. We only met for the first time at the party the other night. It's a relief that after all the drama of the fight that she still wants me to design her and her mother's shoes for her wedding later in the year.' She checked her watch. 'I mustn't keep them waiting.'

'That's brilliant, well done you.' He gave her a hug. 'We could add the designs under a separate tab on the website to indicate that you'll take on bespoke designs for clients.'

Paige nodded, 'Great idea. Why don't you go and work on the site now?' She didn't like to add, that Clem had already gone out, so there was no point in him waiting in the cottage for her.

Olly put his shoulders back and saluted. 'Right, I'll go and do that now.' They both started for the front door. Olly stopped suddenly, turning back to her just as she raced out to the hall. He caught her just before she crashed into him.

'Hey, careful,' she said, wondering what was wrong.

'You've inspired me, you know?' he said, a wide grin on his handsome face.

'I have?' she asked, not knowing how, but relieved to have done so. 'Good, now bugger off and let me get going to this meeting.'

Chapter Twenty-seven

Paige slid her *Society* initiation into her evening bag, closing the crystal covered clasp with a satisfying clunk, and pulled the slim gold chain over her shoulder. She breathed in the rose scented air by her living room French doors, relieved the August weather was warm enough for everyone to be able to make the most of what promised to be a perfect evening.

'I'm glad you settled on the powder blue satin jacket,' Clem said coming into the room behind her. 'It goes far better with that black dress and those gorgeous shoes.'

'Are you sure you didn't want to come along tonight?' Paige asked, concerned that her sister might want to join her after all.

'Of course, anyway knowing Olly he'll be really looking forward to tonight.' Clem popped two pieces of toast into the toaster. 'How is he by the way?'

'Who, Ol?'

Clem nodded, her back to Paige.

Making the most of the opportunity to discuss him, Paige bent to take a plate from the cupboard nearby and passed it to her sister. 'Don't you think you should give some thought to making things up with him?'

Clem groaned, and Paige could feel her defences going up. 'I know you're right,' Clem said, gently stroking her rounded stomach. 'I'm not quite sure what to say though.'

Heartened by her sister's encouraging response, Paige continued. 'I don't know either, but you need to speak to him soon.' She faced her sister. 'He loves you, Clem, and you're having his baby. You at least owe him a chance to figure out a way forward that's mutually agreeable to you both.' She placed a hand on her sister's stomach, flinching when the baby kicked. 'Did you feel that?' Paige asked. 'Wow, does it hurt when he does that?'

'Not yet, but I'm told it does further along in the pregnancy.' Clem smiled. 'I like the way we're both sure it's a boy.' Her rosy cheeks reddening even more. 'He's a brute, don't you think?'

Paige nodded. 'I didn't realise they kicked quite so hard.'

'Ha, you should feel it from where I'm standing.'

'Olly is missing out on all of this excitement, Clem,' she said quietly.

The sisters looked at each other in silence for a moment. Paige suspected both Clem and Olly wanted nothing more than to get back together again, but for some reason her sister was making things as awkward as possible between them and she wished she knew why.

'Are you sure you'll be OK looking after the place while I'm away?' Paige asked, referring to her impending Spanish trip and doing her best to change tactics. She was determined to get her sister and Olly to communicate before leaving, but was rapidly running out of time.

'Yes, of course.'

'Fine, then tomorrow night the two of you can eat here. It'll give you a chance to chat to each other and try to sort everything out.'

'Tomorrow?' Clem grimaced.

'Yes,' Paige said, before her sister could think of another excuse not to. 'I love you both and I won't leave until I know you've resolved your differences.' She watched Clem sulking. 'I'm going to have to work closely with Olly over the next few months to get the site launched, and it would be much easier for everyone involved if the two of you made up.' She had an idea.

'Why don't you become a part of it too?'

'Me? How?'

'You're better with computers than I am.'

'That's not difficult, and it's only because I have more patience than you do.'

Paige ignored her, determined to make the most of Clem's attention. 'I need to focus on these sales, so maybe you could keep an eye on any orders. You could deal with settlement of the payments and keep track of the stock, where to send it, that sort of thing.'

Clem leant back against the worktop in silence only moving when the toast popped up to begin buttering it. 'I'm not sure I want to spend time working from your cottage.'

'It's up to you.' Paige wondered why she hadn't thought of it before. 'You'll soon be too heavily pregnant to want to stand in a shop all day, and when the baby comes, you can't leave it behind. I think working from here will probably really suit you.'

'If you say so yourself?' Clem laughed, taking a bite of toast. 'I think you could be right though.'

'So?' Paige waited for her to reply. 'Is that a "yes"?'

Clem thought for a moment, and smiled. 'It sounds perfect to me.'

'Good.' Paige was relieved that now her sister had even more of an incentive to sort out her differences with Olly. She sighed, and checked her lipstick in the hall mirror.

'Don't think I haven't worked out what you're doing.' Clem poked her head out of the kitchen and shook her head.

'You shouldn't be so suspicious.' It never ceased to amaze Paige how her sister's immaculate auburn bob settled down as soon as she'd shaken her head, looking as if it had been freshly brushed.

'To be honest, I'll be happy to clear things up with Olly. I'll admit I'm a little embarrassed it's taken me so long. It'll be a relief.'

'I'm glad to hear it,' Paige said honestly. 'Now, I'd better go and meet up with him. The magazine has arranged coaches to collect everyone from various car parks around the island to get us to the racecourse. I haven't been on a coach in years, it should be fun.'

'Don't go flirting with strangers on the back seat, will you.' Clem laughed, giving her pouting sister a quick hug, before pushing Paige towards the door.

'I hope you've bought enough money to do some serious betting,' Olly said, as he waited for Paige to show her invitation to the security guard at the entrance to the impressive marquee.

She glanced around the vast space, instantly spotting several clients of hers, mostly sporting, she was delighted to note, her latest collection as they made small talk to other guests.

'Blimey,' Olly said, leading the way to the free bar where a line was already forming. 'This is the life.' He turned to face her, eyebrows raised. 'Have you seen this lot? They're certainly making the most of what's on offer. And,' he moved closer to Paige, lowering his voice. 'There's even a Tote in here, so we don't have to queue with the hoi polloi outside.'

Paige giggled. 'Don't get too used to this treatment, it'll be back to real life later tonight, Cinderella. And I'll have a champagne cocktail, please.'

'Yes, madam,' he said, leaving her to join the other revellers as he walked over to the bar.

Paige was just about to take a seat at one of the circular tables, when she noticed an enclosure through the back of the marquee overlooking the racecourse. She motioned to Olly that she would wait for him there. Stepping out from the laughter and constant chatter to the warm evening air, she breathed in the sweet scent of the freshly mown grass.

Paige made her way to the white post and rails next to the edge of the track, unable to suppress a gasp at the magnificence of the view in front of her.

'Impressive, isn't it?' Sebastian said, stepping out of the marquee and coming to stand next to her. 'I never get tired of coming here.'

Paige daren't turn to look at him, she wanted to gather her thoughts first, so simply continued taking in the picturesque scene.

They stared in silence, passed the curve of the track in front of them to the ruins of Grosnez Castle, where the purple gorse was beginning to flower. The sun lowered imperceptibly, its orange glow glistening on the Channel between where they were standing and the islands of Sark, Herm, and Guernsey as they lined up neatly in the distance.

'It's not much of a castle, but it's one hell of a view. It makes me wonder why we pay to go anywhere else when we live on such a pretty island,' she said, allowing herself to simply enjoy being near him.

'I don't know,' he said. 'There are other places reminiscent of this one,' he added, his soothing voice taking her back to the magical warm evenings in Sorrento, when they looked out from the terrace over the Bay of Naples with Vesuvius as their focal point across the cerulean water.

She nodded, unable to speak.

Chapter Twenty-eight

Paige turned to face him, trying her best to appear relaxed and unflustered, as if his being there had no effect on her at all. 'I didn't realise you'd be here,' she said, in an effort to bring the conversation back to more mundane matters. 'But then again, why wouldn't you be?' She smiled in an attempt to soften her unintentionally sarcastic tone.

Seb frowned briefly. 'No doubt as you've probably done, I've advertised in their glossy pages.'

Not knowing quite what to say next, she leant on the white railings and stared over at the stone, almost heart-shaped archway that made the last focal point of the island before the Channel began.

'Paige?'

She could feel her heart pounding and hoped that he didn't realise how much of an effect his presence had on her. 'I'm not sure who to bet on, though Olly insists I should make the effort,' she said. 'He claims it'll make the evening more fun.'

'He's right, you should.'

She took a deep breath and turned to face him taken aback at the frown on his suntanned face. 'Really?'

'Paige, about the shop.'

She hurriedly changed the subject. 'Do you have any tips for which horse I should bet on?' She opened the booklet they had received with the invitation. 'I'm completely clueless when it comes to horses. I generally choose the jockey with the prettiest colours on his shirt.'

'Listen to me,' he said, ignoring the couple nearby

whom she sensed could be journalists, if their interest in Sebastian was anything to go by. She hoped not, for both their sakes.

'It's fine,' she said. Realising she was louder than she had intended, she lowered her voice. She gave the couple a knowing smile, before returning her focus on Sebastian, who did not seem in the slightest bit concerned about their audience. 'I don't want to talk business with you.' She moved slightly closer to him. 'I know you didn't become the successful man you are by making easy choices, and I do understand that you were only doing your job. Please, let's not talk about it again.'

She was relieved to notice Olly making his way towards her and smiled politely at Sebastian. 'Here's Olly with my drink.'

Sebastian touched her arm lightly. 'I know you'll be successful, Paige,' he said quietly, his mouth close to her ear. 'You're too talented not to be.'

Paige went to reply, but before she could form the words, a tanned hand with perfectly manicured nails landed on Sebastian's shoulder. 'Sebastian, darling, there you are.'

Paige immediately looked up at the owner of the clipped voice, and felt jealousy grip the pit of her stomach.

'Lucinda,' Sebastian said, his tone flat. 'I wasn't aware you were here tonight.'

'Of course I am, darling. How can you even think that I'd miss your big night?'

'Big night?' Olly pulled a face at Paige.

Sebastian turned to Paige and Olly and shook his head. 'It's nothing, really. Now, if you'll excuse me, there's someone I need to speak to.'

Of course you do, thought Paige, watching him walking away, closely followed by the tall woman from the party, her endless legs disappearing into probably the shortest dress Paige had ever seen.

'Don't worry, Sweets,' Olly whispered. 'I'll bet she's a right cow. Men hate spiteful women, and I can't imagine any bloke wanting to give her one.'

Paige cringed. 'That's a revolting thing to say,' she nudged him, and lowered her voice. 'Thanks for trying though.'

'Here, have a swig of this.' Olly handed her a glass. 'Going by the look on your face, I think you may need it. Mind you, having seen the look on his glum face when I arrived, I think you've probably been a little,' he put his index finger up to his lips feigning thought, 'how shall I put this? Oh yes, shitty.'

'Why do you automatically assume it's me who's been horrible?' Paige asked, taking a sip of her drink and wishing Olly was wrong. She had been pretty unfriendly to Seb. Again. He always seems to bring out the worst in me, she thought miserably.

'Because, dearest friend of mine, I know how you can get when you're in a fury. Did you give the poor guy a chance to explain his behaviour?' He held up his hand to stop her from answering the question. 'Don't bother to answer me, I know full well you didn't.'

'Olly?'

'Yes?'

'Shut up.'

'OK.'

'His ex is stunning, isn't she?' she asked, forgetting she had just told him to be quiet.

'Nah,' he lied. 'Forget her. Hey, look over there, they're about to start the first race, and I haven't even put on a bet yet. Wait here.'

'What about mine?' she said, quickly before he stepped back inside.

'Don't worry. I'll choose the prettiest colours for you.'

'Paige, hi,' Maddy shouted, running up to her. 'Great to see you here. Thank you so much for coming round the other night, Mum was beside herself with excitement when you showed us your designs for my wedding shoes.'

'I'm thrilled you were both so pleased with them. Now, don't forget to let me know which one you decide to go with. I'll need to know sometime this week if that's OK.'

'No problem at all,' Maddy leaned a little closer to Paige. 'Mum has been boasting to all her friends about the shoes being made especially for me, so I suspect you'll be getting a few more phone calls over the coming months.'

Paige smiled at her. 'Please tell her I'm very grateful.'

Maddy waved and left to join her friends. 'Here, have another champagne cocktail,' Olly said, handing her a glass. Seen any more of Sebastian Fielding?'

Paige shook her head. 'No, but I've had some great feedback from the bride I was telling you about the other day.'

'I told you everything would be all right, didn't I?'

'You did,' she agreed.

They watched several races. Paige was enjoying herself more than she expected, thrilled by the speed of the horses and watching the beautifully dressed crowds milling around nearby.

'Right, let's take a breather from all this extravagance and check out the horses for the next race in the collecting ring,' Olly suggested, taking her half-empty glass from her hand and placing it down on their table. 'I've lost on every race so far, and I'm determined to change tactics this time.'

'But you don't know anything about racehorses,' Paige teased, following him out.

'It's worth a try. Maybe I'll be inspired or something.' He pointed over to one of the horses who the groom couldn't seem to be able to keep still. 'That grey seems to have a lot of energy.'

'He's white,' Paige said.

'He's correct, dear,' said a ruddy-faced woman

standing next to her. 'They might look white, but they're called greys.'

'See, I told you.' Olly gave her a smug look. 'My grandfather kept a few horses on his farm. Hey, look over there.'

'That's Sir Edmund's nephew,' interrupted their new friend from below her crooked straw hat. 'Dear chap. Bless him, he's presenting his uncle's trophy.' She sniffed. 'Never missed a Meet, did Sir Edmund. I should think that boy misses him dreadfully, not that he'd show it, mind.'

It was strange hearing someone referring to Sebastian with such affection, Paige thought. She watched as he chatted to the stewards, being patted on the back by jockeys and trainers alike.

'Know 'im, do yer, love?' The woman asked, tiny eyes staring at Paige as she waited for an answer.

Paige shook her head thoughtfully, as Sebastian shook hands with the winner of the previous race. 'Not really,' she said in all honesty.

Olly leant towards the woman. 'Any tips on who we should bet on?'

'You won't go far wrong if you put a few quid on 'is uncle's horse. She was his pride and joy; bred her from his favourite mare, Elusive Queen. He has the best jockey riding for him for 'er first season too. Although after the nasty accident the boy had last year everyone apart from young Sebastian there wrote him off. Just like Sir Edmund, he is, giving the underdog a chance.'

Paige looked over at Sebastian, watching with interest as the jockey bent down from his saddle to say something privately to him. Sebastian nodded and patted his leg.

Olly scanned down the page of the programme, 'Do you mean Elusive Goddess?'

'I do indeed,' the woman jerked her head at the nervous horse, her chin somehow disappearing into her neck. 'He only named her recently. We was all wondering what 'e was goin' ter call the mare. I think Elusive Goddess is a grand name, don't you?'

'Yes,' Paige said.

She and Olly glanced at each other and then over to where Sebastian was now chatting to a tiny jockey, dressed in black and green silks. The thin fabric of his shirt matched in the cover of his racing helmet. 'Not quite the racing colours you'd usually choose,' whispered Olly sarcastically.

'Olly?' Paige said, looking at him through narrowed eyes.

'Yes, I know. I'll shut up.'

'No,' she giggled, knowing he had been right. 'Here's ten pounds. Go and place it on Elusive Goddess for me, will you?'

Having manoeuvred their way through the melee inside the marquee and out to the enclosure by the racecourse, Paige stood next to Olly leaning against the railings to watch the excitable horses impatiently waiting for the race to start.

'And they're off,' shouted the commentator unnecessarily, as the pounding of the horses' hooves reverberated through the ground under Paige's feet.

'Look at them go,' she shouted to Olly, almost willing them on. 'Those jumps look a bit high though, don't you think?'

'It's a steeplechase. They're used to it. Stop fretting.'

She nudged Olly in the ribs. 'She's way in the lead. Look, Ol.'

'Ouch, I hope she bloody well stays there too. I need him to win.'

The atmosphere intensified as Elusive Goddess widened the distance between her and the horse behind.

'She's amazing,' Paige shouted over the noise of the cheering crowds, fascinated by the power of the magnificent creature as she galloped towards the final jump. Ooh, I can't look,' she squinted through half-closed eyes, scared to look, but not wanting to miss anything at the same time.

Without slowing down, the horse took off, landing awkwardly and somersaulted over, her hooves spewing clumps of grass and earth into the air. The jockey landed heavily and ended up somewhere underneath the enormous animal. A collective intake of breath silenced the onlookers, as everything seemed to go into slow motion. Paige heard a familiar voice shouting for someone to call for help. Then, dumbstruck with horror, she spotted Sebastian, stepping between the white railings and running across the track, somehow reaching his jockey just before the other horses galloped past.

All Paige could see through the hooves as they thundered by was Sebastian crouching protectively over the unconscious man beneath him.

Chapter Twenty-nine

As if in the distance, Paige became aware of shouting all around her.

'He's going to be trampled on,' screamed one of the partygoers. 'Who is that idiot?'

'Isn't that Sebastian Fielding?'

'He owns Elusive Goddess,' someone replied. 'The horse crushed the jockey.'

Transfixed, Paige stared as Sebastian, oblivious to the chaos around him, waved over the paramedics and took charge of the situation. She realised she was holding her breath, and seeing he was unharmed, loosened her grip on the rails. It occurred to her that this arrogant man in his now ruined bespoke suit meant far more to her than she'd cared to admit. Her hands and feet tingled with fright at the thought that he could have been killed.

The crowds murmured their opinions on the accident, parting as stewards pulled the railings back to allow the ambulance to reverse over the track.

'Stand back, please,' shouted the steward, pushing back the few journalists who were already taking photos.

Paige watched as they examined the jockey, his leg lying at an unnatural angle, and eventually lifted him carefully on to a stretcher. Sebastian seemed to be soothing him and stood back as they lifted the stretcher into the back of the ambulance. He walked behind the vehicle, talking animatedly to one of the stewards, as it slowly made its way across the track. People surrounded him as soon as they could get near him. He seemed unaware of their presence, as he strode over to his car, his phone held against his ear.

Paige waited for the crowd to disperse a little, then not caring if he chose to ignore her, went after him. 'Sebastian,' she called.

He turned immediately, locking eyes with hers, as he continued to speak calmly to whoever was on the receiving end of his call. He held up his hand motioning for her to wait. 'Paige,' he said eventually, turning off his Blackberry, the concern evident on his face. 'I'm going to have to go.'

'How is he?' She knew it was probably a ridiculous question, noticing a small cut above Sebastian's left eye and dirt on his cheek.

'Pretty bad, I think. They can't tell me much until they get him to hospital. I'm off there now. I'd better get going.'

Without thinking, she opened her mouth to speak. 'Would you like some company while you wait?' She was unable to bear the thought of leaving him to deal with this alone.

He looked a little taken aback by her question for a second before nodding and without further hesitation said, 'That would be good, thanks.'

'I just need to text Olly to let him know where I'm going,' she said, tapping away at her Blackberry. 'He can pass a message on to my sister. I don't want her worrying about me.'

He nodded, spoke quickly with a couple of the course stewards through his Mercedes' window, and drove them both to the hospital.

'It was good of you to do this, you know,' Sebastian said later, as they waited in the Relatives' Room at the Accident and Emergency Department. He passed her a cardboard cup of insipid-looking tea.

Paige sipped and grimaced. 'I think I'll leave that, if

you don't mind.'

He smiled. 'It is pretty grim, isn't it?' Paige shifted on her hard plastic chair. He could see she was uncomfortable and wished he could find somewhere better to wait. 'You're going to miss the end of your evening out,'

'Don't be silly. I couldn't let you wait here alone.'

He turned his body to face her, one arm resting on the back of the seat between them. 'Why not?'

'Because, despite our differences, I can't watch someone do something as dangerous as you did tonight and not be impressed by their complete disregard for their own personal safety.'

He raised an eyebrow. 'Are you trying to tell me I was stupid to go out there?'

Paige shrugged. 'Yes, maybe, but you probably saved that boy's life.'

'I hope he's going to be all right,' he said, willing Mickey, the jockey, to pull through. 'I've tried to contact his wife, but her phone went straight to voicemail. I've left a message asking her to call me.'

Sebastian stood up as soon as he spotted the surgeon coming through the large double doors towards them. A fixed half-smile on the man's face told him that Mickey was still alive, but he'd seen for himself how badly injured the boy had been and couldn't help feeling guilty that it was he who'd persuaded Mickey to ride Elusive Goddess in her first race. He'd suspected the boy may not be fully fit after his fall last year. Why the hell couldn't I just leave it and find another jockey to ride her, he wondered.

'Good evening, sir,' said the surgeon, taking Sebastian's hand and pumping it up and down. Seb recognized him from several dinner parties, and smiled. 'I hadn't realised it was your young chap in the theatre.'

'He's my jockey,' Sebastian said, wondering why he was making such an obvious statement. 'How is he? Will he be all right?' Sebastian heard a sob behind him and

221

turned to find Paige moving towards Ali, Mickey's young bride. Her large rounded stomach told him just how close they were to becoming parents, and was the probable reason why Mickey had not been as eager as Sebastian had expected when given the opportunity of racing his prized horse. He felt doubly guilty for urging him to do so.

'Ali, how did you get here?' he asked, looking behind her to see if anyone was with her.

'My uncle bought me. He's parking the car. I came as soon as I could, but I was at my sister's and didn't get your message for nearly two hours.'

'Never mind,' He led her over to the surgeon. 'This is Mr Golding. He's about to tell us how Mickey's getting on.'

The surgeon shook Ali's hand and gave her his half-hearted smile. 'Mr, ah, Mickey is going to be all right. There's no danger to his life.' Ali sobbed again, this time with relief. Paige dug into her handbag instantly retrieving a tissue, which they waited for her to pass to the distraught woman. 'He has a broken tibia and fibula as well as several cracked ribs.'

Ali stifled a cry. 'Poor Mickey. Will he walk again?'

The surgeon nodded. 'Yes, he'll have no problem walking.' He addressed Sebastian. 'He also has a badly broken arm, but we've done our best to rectify that. We had to remove his spleen, I'm afraid. One of his lungs was punctured by a broken rib, too.'

'But he's going to be fine,' reiterated Sebastian, wanting Ali to calm down and not panic too much with this overload of frightening information.

The doctor nodded and Ali blew her nose.

'But he'll never race again, if he's that badly hurt,' she cried. 'He won't be able to work and we'll lose our cottage. The baby's due in four weeks.'

Sebastian could hear Ali's rising panic and was relieved to see Paige put her arm around her shoulders to soothe her.

'When can I see him?' she asked tearfully.

'Not tonight,' Mr Golding said. 'He's heavily sedated and won't know you're here anyway. I suggest you go home and try to get some sleep. Come again in the morning when I've been able to do my rounds, say around eleven.'

Sebastian thanked the surgeon for all he'd done for Mickey, and walked with him away from Paige and Ali towards the theatre doors stopping just in front of them. 'Do you think he'll be able to race again?' he asked quietly. He needed to know exactly what Mickey's chances were for his future. It was his fault the boy was in this predicament and he had to know exactly how things stood before making any decisions.

The doctor lowered his voice. 'It's doubtful. He's been pretty smashed up, and although I'm no expert on riding horses, I can't imagine he'll ever have the strength in that leg to be able to compete at a professional level. I could be wrong, of course, but I doubt it. There was significant damage to the bones.'

'Hell, poor guy,' Sebastian said thoughtfully.

'I've done all I can for now. I'll visit him tomorrow and discuss any follow-up surgery with him should it be necessary.'

Sebastian nodded. 'Of course, thank you for all you've done this evening.'

He turned to watch Paige sitting with Ali, pain and concern etched on the young woman's face. She was barely out of her teens, thought Sebastian. What sort of life was she going to have with Mickey now that he didn't have the release he found whenever he raced?

She looked up at Sebastian, tears rolling down her drawn face. 'What's going to happen to us, Mr Fielding?' She wiped her damp cheeks with the back of her hand. 'Mickey never wanted to do anything but race horses, and if he can't do that, he'll not be needed at the yard. If he has to leave his job, we'll lose our cottage and then we'll have nowhere to go.'

Sebastian sat down next to her and patted her hand. 'Ali, listen to me,' he said, as gently as possible. 'We don't know if Mickey will race again, but whatever happens I promise you he'll always have a job with me, for as long as he wants one.'

'Really?'

'Yes. Mickey is brilliant with the horses, and I'll always need another trainer in the yard. I'm never going to ask you to leave the cottage. It's your home for as long as you want it to be. He was injured riding my horse and I won't turn my back on him if he's unable to race again. Please don't worry about it. Mr Golding told us Mickey will be fine. He's going to walk again, and will recover from his injuries.'

Ali sniffed. 'Thank you, Mr Fielding.'

'Now,' he said. 'Mr Golding said you were to go home and get some sleep, so why don't you let me give you a lift to the cottage. You can come back here to see Mickey in the morning.'

'No, it's all right,' she looked over to the doorway where an older man stood staring at them in silence. 'My uncle.'

Sebastian nodded to him.

'He'll give me a lift home.' She blew her nose and wiped her eyes. 'Thanks, Mr Fielding.'

'It's Sebastian, and please don't worry,' he said. 'I promise you everything will be fine.' He led her over to her uncle.

When Ali had left, Seb turned to Paige. 'You must be exhausted,' he said taking her hand and helping her up from her seat.

'A little tired,' she said, her eyes glistening from unshed tears. 'It's been an emotional evening all round.

224

How are you bearing up?'

Sebastian shrugged. 'I'm still a little shell-shocked to be honest.' He still couldn't believe she'd offered so readily to accompany him to the hospital and then to sit for several hours while the surgeon operated on Mickey. It was comforting to be this close to her again, as if their antagonism had never happened.

'Come on,' he said, putting an arm around her shoulders. 'Let's get out of here.'

'I won't argue with that,' she said sliding her arm around his back.

The warmth of her hand against his back felt good 'To make up for ruining your evening, can I offer you a snack and something to drink back at my home?' He wasn't sure if he should be asking such a question, and hoped she didn't think he was taking advantage of the situation to make a pass at her.

Paige smiled. 'That would be lovely,' she said eventually.

Relieved not to have offended her and ruined the unexpected closeness they'd managed to forge throughout the long evening, Sebastian opened the car door for her. 'Good, I'm glad,' he said, closing it once she was seated inside.

Chapter Thirty

The Mercedes glided down the seemingly endless tree-lined driveway, the only noise in the still night coming from the wheels of the car crunching over the gravel beneath. Paige was relieved to be in the dark, to be able to absorb the magnificence of the imposing, stark white Georgian house without Sebastian seeing her open-mouthed reaction to his home.

Seb parked and walked around to open Paige's door, took her hand in his, and together they walked up the wide, granite front steps. Two swallows dipped and dived to the side of the house while Paige waited for him to open the front door. He led her through the porch and into the vast black and white tiled hallway. Paige gazed at the plain plaster cornicing, so typical of the era, and marvelled at the splendour all around her. A side door opened and a gentleman wearing a smart grey suit appeared.

'Good evening, sir,' he said, before addressing Paige. 'Good evening, madam.'

Paige smiled, trying to understand who he could possibly be, until it dawned on her that he must be Seb's butler. She opened her mouth to speak, closing it again, unable to make any sound.

Sebastian took her jacket from her, passing it to his butler. 'Harwood, I think we'll take coffee in the drawing room.'

She tried not to think of how delighted her mother would be to see her in such magnificence, and wished they were in the private comfort of her small cottage instead.

Harwood nodded. 'Of course, sir,' he said, instantly leaving via the door through which he had so recently arrived.

'This is incredible,' she said, glad to have met him before knowing he lived in such a palatial place. He showed her into the large cream room where the only colour appeared to be in the sumptuous navy and gold velvet curtains closed over the ceiling height windows and matching cushions on the settees. 'I didn't know you had a home on the island. Well, not like this anyway,' she added, trying not to feel too uneasy. 'I thought you'd probably have a flat somewhere.'

He nodded. 'I did until recently. This used to be my uncle's house. When he died it came to me. I couldn't justify having this place as well as a flat nearby, so I sold it.'

'Do you live here alone?' she asked, sitting down.

'Brandy?' he asked, pouring large measures into two glasses and handing one to her. 'Not all the time. My younger sister, Fiona, lives here with me when she's in Jersey. She's at university at the moment.'

'What about your mother?' She blushed as soon as she'd realised how deeply personal her question sounded. 'Sorry, I can't help being nosy sometimes.'

'Not at all. My mother's dead,' he said, without a hint of self-pity.

'Oh.' Paige could have bitten her tongue. 'Sorry, it's typical of me to put my foot in it.'

'Don't worry about it,' he said. His eyes crinkled slightly at the sides as he smiled at her, making her wonder why she had never noticed how gentle he could seem before now. 'She died years ago, nineteen to be exact.'

'Nineteen?' Paige tried to work out how old Fiona must be.

'Giving birth to my sister.'

Paige cringed. 'Was I that obvious?'

'Put it this way, I could almost hear the cogs of your brain turning and doing the maths.'

'Sorry,' she cringed in embarrassment at her thoughtless faux pas.

'Stop apologising, it's fine, really.' Sebastian stood up and walked over to the ornate marble fireplace. Placing his tumbler on the mantelpiece, he leaned one arm against it.

'Your poor father,' she said, touched by the agony of having been given a baby daughter while coping with the loss of his wife. 'How dreadful it must have been for him to be left with a baby and a small boy.' Paige swallowed a lump in her throat.

'Hey, don't get all maudlin on my account. My father did his best and my sister never seemed to have missed out not having our mother around.' He shrugged. 'To be honest with you, she was rather distant anyway, and always away travelling or at parties.'

'But you were so young.' Paige pictured a young boy sobbing into his pillow every night.

Seb laughed. 'Paige, I was fifteen years old, and away at boarding school. It was a shock, of course it was, but to be honest my life didn't feel very different afterwards.'

'What about your father?'

'He died a few years later, which is when my uncle took over.'

'Didn't your uncle ever marry?'

Sebastian laughed and shook his head. 'Practically every female acquaintance, married or single, appeared up that driveway at some time or other, bearing food, offers of picnics, swimming parties in their pools, and that was just for Fiona and me. They tried every trick in the book to get him interested in them, but nothing worked. He always insisted he was a confirmed bachelor, and that having us meant he didn't need to go through the exhaustion of living with small children.'

'So you didn't have any female influence in your life

229

then?'

'No. There was one particular secretary who did last quite a few years. She doted on him, but eventually left and married a local chap. Wanted a life for herself, I imagine, instead of just being on the periphery of his. She was kind, but not really interested in us.'

Paige noticed a black and white photo of an elegant, grey-haired gentleman in a large silver frame on a mahogany table next to the fireplace, and thought how lucky Sebastian and Fiona were to have been looked after by him.

'And before you ask, yes, he was good to us. Always spoilt Fi rotten and I never lacked any love.' He smiled at her.

Paige felt her stomach flip over and wondered how she'd been able to resist his charms all these months. 'I've been really hard on you, haven't I?'

'You've had your reasons.' He leant forward, and, putting the tips of his fingers under her chin, lifted it slightly and kissed her, making her forget why she'd agreed to come back to his house in the first place. She let him take her glass from her hand as he moved to sit closer to her. 'Thank you for being there for me today. I really appreciate it,' he said, taking her in his arms and lowering his mouth onto hers.

She responded instinctively. His lips and tongue tasted of the rich brandy they'd been drinking and she melted into him, relishing the headiness that came with kissing this man. Sebastian drew back. She followed his gaze towards the closed drawing room door and heard Harwood cough discretely outside just before opening and entering the room.

'Your coffee, sir. Would you like me to pour?'

'No thank you, that'll be all for tonight.'

Harwood nodded, 'Goodnight, sir. Madam,' he said, leaving the room as quietly as he had entered it.

'I'm sorry about that,' Sebastian said, reaching out to take her hand in his. 'It's so long since I've had live-in staff that I keep forgetting I'm not alone here.'

'Did he work for your uncle for long?' She felt a little awkward that the butler had felt the need to let them know he was there, and wondered for a moment if bringing women to his home at night was a regular occurrence for Sebastian, or if it was simply the butler's way of announcing himself.

'Yes,' Sebastian said. 'For years, so it must be a little strange for him having me living here after my uncle being the head of the household for so long.' He kissed the side of her mouth. 'To be honest, he runs this place like a dream, and we really can't do without him.'

He nuzzled her neck, immediately making her forget the next question she had been about to ask. 'I just need to remember he lives here too,' he added his lips brushing her throat.

Paige could feel her resolve weakening. 'So your mother grew up here then?'

'She lived here until she met my father in London in the early seventies.'

'You must need someone to help run a place as big as this one,' she mumbled, trying desperately to retain some semblance of self-control.

Sebastian sat back a little. 'I'm away so often, I just let him get on with it. He knows better than me what needs to be done,' he said, without taking his eyes from her, the heat in them obvious.

Paige tried to take in every detail of his face, so tanned despite spending long hours in the office. His deep blue eyes seemed to bore into her very soul. She sighed. 'Sebastian?' She wasn't sure what to say next and was past caring the instant his lips reconnected with hers.

He pulled her to him. 'I want to make love to you.'

Paige wanted him too. She drank in his musky scent

and pushed her hands into his wavy hair.

He pushed her back into the softness of the vast sofa, moving on top of her, his hardness pressed against her stomach. The pressure of his chest muscles against her as he held her tightly in his arms made her gasp.

'Are you OK?' he whispered, moving away from her.

Paige nodded. She smiled up at him and stood up.

'Where are you going?'

'I'm not going anywhere,' she said, gently pulling her hand from his and lifting her arm to unzip her dress. She watched Sebastian, transfixed and silent, as she lowered first one, then the other shoulder strap, pushing the material slowly past her hips, stepping out of it when it reached the floor.

'You're so beautiful,' he murmured, standing up and kissing her neck.

'I think you've got a little catching up to do, don't you?' she teased. 'You're still fully clothed.'

Sebastian hurriedly pulled off his tie, undid his shirt, losing patience and ripping off the last few buttons.

Paige took hold of his belt, smiling to herself as she felt him hold his breath. She undid the buckle, then his trousers, only taking her eyes off him to look down as they fell onto the floor. Sebastian kicked them off and took her in his arms.

'Not yet,' she giggled. 'We haven't finished undressing.'

Sebastian smiled and slid a finger into the straps of her bra, lowering one side, taking her nipple in his mouth. Paige groaned. He sucked gently, flicking his tongue back and forth across the tip. She felt as if her legs were about to give way, but he held her tightly to him. She dropped her head back, when he lowered his free hand down lightly over her belly and into her lace panties.

She sighed, glad he was holding her up, this was so good. 'No, wait.'

Sebastian sighed. 'Really?' he breathed, his mouth returning to her nipple just as he brought her to the peak of ecstasy.

'Oh God,' she cried. Paige felt like she was dying. She didn't care about anything apart from this man and the incredible places he was taking her to. He held her in his arms, kissing her face, her neck, her shoulders.

Her senses recovering slightly, she smiled at him. 'I'm so selfish,' she whispered, aware she'd done nothing at all for him.

'There's nothing selfish about how you make me feel,' he said.

Paige sighed. She moved back slightly. She loved him and wanted to make him feel as good as she felt. 'Your turn now, I think.'

She slipped a finger in either side of his boxers, slowly lowering them, her eyes widening as she saw him completely naked for the first time. Paige gawped at him for a few seconds and then realized Sebastian was watching her, looked up at his face.

He smiled. 'You're going to make me feel self-conscious, if you keep staring at me like that.' He bent slightly, and putting his hands under her arms lifted her gently to her feet. He stepped out of his discarded shorts. 'You are so beautiful.'

Wanting to take control again, she ran her hands up his muscular thighs, Sebastian tensed when her fingers took hold of his hard buttocks. 'I'm really enjoying this,' she said, sighing happily. She kissed his neck, relishing the pressure of his chest against her breasts. He moved to take hold of her, but she shook her head. 'No,' she said, hearing his breath catch in his throat as she took him in her hand.

Sebastian groaned. 'Enough,' he said quietly. 'Come here.'

She happily let him lower her down to the Persian rug and kissed his shoulder, impatient for him to make love to her.

He worked his way down, from her mouth to her neck, nipping lightly at her breasts. Paige wanted to cry out, when he reached her stomach. He moved down to her hips and between her legs. She pushed her fingers into his hair, losing any thoughts of control.

'Oh, this is ...' She groaned louder, as his tongue connected with her in the most delightful way. Then remembering Harwood was somewhere in the house, Paige bit on her lower lip to keep from making so much noise. 'Please,' she sighed. 'Please' what, she wasn't sure. Losing herself to the pleasure of Sebastian was delicious in so many ways.

'I've been waiting so long to do this,' he said, moving back up to face her, his voice husky with lust. 'You're so perfect.' He paused. 'Shall I get some protection?'

Paige shook her head. 'I'm on the pill.'

Sebastian grinned and kissed her, pressing himself against her as she moved under him, driven to near madness. Sebastian smiled as he entered her.

Paige closed her eyes, lifting her legs around his waist and arching up to him. She wrapped her arms around his broad back, lost in a delirious haze as he thrust into her taking her breath away. She clung to him as the compounding exquisiteness of sensations washed through her. Everything obliterated from her senses apart from this man and what he was doing to her. Paige cried out as she felt her body explode into a million shards of pleasure, seconds before Sebastian groaned, reaching his own shuddering climax.

'You are incredible,' he whispered.

She could feel his heart hammering against his chest as she lay enveloped in his arms. Lost in their own thoughts, their breathing slowly returning to normal. Paige shivered.

'You're cold,' he frowned. 'Come with me.' He stood up and helping her to her feet, picked up his jacket and wrapped it over her naked shoulders, smiling as it swamped her much smaller frame.

'Thank you,' Paige said. She bent to grab her clothes.

'Here, let me,' he said, scooping them up.

She let him take her by the hand and lead her up the stairs to his vast blue bedroom. Throwing back the downy duvet covering his bed, Sebastian lifted her into the middle of it, climbing in behind her and immediately covering them both.

'Better?' he asked, holding her against him, his warm breath causing her to shiver once more although this time with pleasure.

'Yes,' she murmured, snuggling closer into him, feeling certain that she would never be this happy, or content, ever again. Paige knew without doubt this was where she wanted to be, always.

He wrapped himself around her. Paige slowly pushed her hand between her bottom and him, giggling when she discovered he was hard already.

'I know. What can I say?' he said. She could hear the amusement in his voice. 'I've missed you,' he said, his voice serious. 'We have a lot of making up to do.'

She missed him too, but wasn't ready to think about anything further than tonight. She took hold of his erection in her hand.

Sebastian nuzzled her neck. 'If you're going to keep doing what you're doing, then I'm not going to be able to just lie here.'

'Good,' she teased, squealing as he flipped her on her back and was on top of her in no time at all.

'I love you, you gorgeous, sexy woman,' he laughed.

Paige's heart contracted as he voiced her own feelings. She dared not believe he might love her, but couldn't imagine hearing anything more perfect. 'I love you too,' she whispered. 'I think I always have.'

Sebastian stilled. Resting his weight on his elbows, he

235

stared down at her for a few moments, adoration in his dark blue eyes. 'We've wasted so much time.'

'I know,' she agreed, pushing her fingers into his hair and pulling his head down until their lips met.

'Again?' he asked, bending down to kiss her stomach.

'Yes please,' she said, wriggling underneath him in anticipation.

They made love again, each unable to get enough of the other. Finally Paige drifted off into a deep, contented sleep, waking slowly the following morning feeling bruised and sore from their lovemaking. She sighed, gazing around the room through half-opened eyes, relishing her memories of their night together.

Seb's leg lay heavily across her own, with an arm draped protectively over her waist. She moved to get more comfortable, instantly feeling him become aroused. Paige stifled a gasp. He couldn't possibly want her again, she thought, certain he was still asleep.

'I'm not,' he whispered, his voice gruff in her ear.

Paige giggled. 'Did I say that out loud?' she asked, confused, but delighted at his response.

'I read your mind,' he kissed the back of her neck, turning her gently over on her back. 'Yes?' he asked.

'Definitely,' she nodded. Lying back, she slid her hands down over his firm buttocks, pulling him into her as hard as she could. Seb thrust into her slowly at first, then when Paige wrapped her long legs around his waist, wanting more, he moved faster and faster until groaning with pleasure he climaxed, moving until she came too.

'You're exquisite,' he breathed, his heart pounding against her breasts.

Paige held him tightly, as they laid back against the warm, creased sheets in sated silence. She couldn't help smiling. Gradually she dragged her mind back into the present. 'It's Saturday,' she said, panicking that she had forgotten to open the shop.

'No work today. It's Sunday,' he said, nuzzling her neck.

Paige sighed. 'Unfortunately, I still have to leave you,' she said miserably, wishing she hadn't promised to cook the meal for Clem and Olly.

'Why? Where do you have go?'

She looked at her wrist, annoyed that she had forgotten to put on a watch the night before. 'What's the time?'

'Don't panic, it's still early.' He leaned over her to peer at his bedside clock. 'Just after ten.'

Paige pushed herself up against the thick, downy pillows. 'I have to go home,' she said.

'Right now?'

Paige did not want this dream world where nothing else mattered to ever end, but she knew she could not escape reality for long. She held the sheet up over her, the daylight making the events of the night before and earlier that morning surreal, as if already belonging to another life.

'I need to shower, and I really do have to get home to my sister.' She chewed her lower lip thoughtfully and smiled at the big, tousle-haired man looking so sexy in his bed. 'And if I don't move now, I'm going to lose any resolve I have left.'

He pulled her back down to him. 'Then I'll have to think of a way to keep you here. Can't you give your sister a call? I'm sure she won't mind if you explain that you'll be a bit late?' He kissed the side of her neck.

Paige tried to concentrate on giving his suggestion some thought. 'I could, but don't you have things you need to do today?'

'I'd like to spend some time with you.' He pulled a mischievous face. 'And there's nothing on today I can't postpone.' He raised a finger in the air. 'In fact, why don't we start by me cooking you a leisurely breakfast. You can

237

take that shower,' he pointed to his en-suite bathroom. 'Give your sister a call, then I can drop you home in a couple of hours?'

Paige couldn't help smiling at him. There was nothing she'd rather do.

'Say yes.' He pushed a strand of hair away from her face. 'Let's make the most of having this time alone together, while we still have the opportunity.'

Not quite sure what Seb meant, Paige moved to sit at the edge of the bed and pondered for a moment.

'Well? Shall I get my apron on, or not?' he asked, his eyes twinkling.

She knew that if she were truly honest, Clem would probably be only too happy to have the cottage to herself for once. 'I'd love to,' she admitted. 'I've always thought there's something sexy about a man who loves to cook.'

'Then I'd better get into the kitchen.' He winked at her as he stepped out of the warm bed.

Paige noticed the scratches she'd inflicted on him during the heat of their passion. 'Your back,' she winced, grimacing.

'It doesn't hurt a bit.' He bent down to kiss her naked shoulder. 'Now don't be long, your chef will be waiting to serve you downstairs.'

Paige knew he must be lying about his back, but waved him away. 'I'll give you a head start, so you can impress me with your culinary skills.' She watched him pull on a pair of boxers and leave the room, then dutifully picked up the phone.

Chapter Thirty-one

Sebastian hated to leave her. He paused at the door, watching her, wishing he could wake up to this exquisite woman every morning. Paige, oblivious to his presence, sat with the duvet held up against her. She held the receiver to her ear and waiting for someone to answer her call. She noticed him standing there and smiled. Seb had never before seen anyone as appealing as this woman, with her ruffled hair and the dimple in one of her cheeks, and wished more than anything that he could go straight back to join her in his bed.

'Hello?' she said, as he forced himself to turn and leave the room.

Once showered and dressed, he crossed the courtyard to his office and telephoned his investment broker. 'Sorry to change plans at the last minute,' he said, 'but I'm going to need to put off that game of golf until this afternoon.' He knew the man was not going to argue, he'd waited too long to get Sebastian to agree to spend this time with him out of the office. 'I'll catch up with you at one o'clock.'

Ordinarily he hated rearranging meetings at the last minute, but the opportunity of having a quiet morning with Paige wasn't something he was willing to give up. Business was business, but Sebastian decided it was about time he took a morning for himself. Sebastian hummed to himself. The smells of the bacon, eggs, and mushrooms as they cooked made him realise how ravenous he actually was.

'Sir,' said Harwood from the doorway. 'Are you sure

you wouldn't prefer me to cook breakfast?'

'No thanks,' Sebastian said, knowing that despite never allowing himself to ask, Harwood would be inquisitive about Paige. As with his uncle, Harwood had uncharacteristically voiced his dislike of Lucinda, and both men had been furious on Seb's behalf when she'd so publicly jilted him. He smiled at the thought of the favour she'd done him by leaving.

Seb heard Harwood close the door behind him and carried on preparing the food. Hearing footsteps, he said, 'I won't need you for anything today, so if you have somewhere else you'd rather be, please feel free to go.'

'If you're sure,' Paige said, amusement in her voice.

Sebastian swung round and dropped a fried egg onto the terracotta floor. 'Shit.' Grabbing a couple of pieces of kitchen roll he bent down to clear up his mess. Looking up at Paige and seeing her trying to stifle a giggle, he pulled a face. 'I thought you were Harwood.'

'I gathered that,' she said. 'Do you need any help over there?'

'No, thanks.' He motioned for her to sit down. 'I'll try again. As you can see I'm a typical man and can't do two things at once.'

'Oh, I don't know about that,' Paige giggled. 'You seemed perfectly capable on concentrating on more than one thing at a time last night.'

He looked over his shoulder at her and smiled. 'Behave yourself, young lady,' he said, cracking another egg against the rim of the pan before dropping it into the oil. 'I'm finding it difficult enough concentrating on this without you reminding me about last night.' He enjoyed the intimacy of her being in his kitchen with him.

'Sorry, I'll let you focus on my breakfast.'

'I think that's probably wise.' He served her food, placing the plate carefully in front of her. 'I didn't know which toast you'd prefer, so I've done white and wholemeal.'

'This looks delicious,' she said. 'I haven't had a fry-up in months. You're a good cook.'

'You haven't tasted anything yet,' he teased. 'Tell me that when you've eaten it, and I'll be happy. Please start. You don't want it to get cold after all the effort I've just put in to cooking it.'

Paige took a forkful of egg and bacon and put it in her mouth.

Sebastian finally joined her at the table. 'So, did you manage to sort things out with your sister?'

'Yes. I'm going to cook for her and Olly later this evening. They have issues that need to be sorted out, and I thought that the best way to make sure they both talk is to sit them down over a meal and see to it that they have no choice but to get everything out in to the open.'

If only sitting down and discussing things over a meal had worked for them. He watched Paige, waiting for her to bring up their scenario, thankful when she didn't. He didn't want anything to mar this time with her. 'What would you like to do this morning?' Seb asked.

Paige dabbed the corners of her mouth with the linen napkin. 'Are you sure you're not busy?' she asked, as he poured her another cup of coffee.

He wondered if she could be persuaded to do this again. She seemed to fit in to his home so naturally. Or maybe, he thought, it was simply that she fitted him so well.

'I don't know what you were thinking of doing.' She placed her hands over her full stomach. 'That was wonderful, thanks.'

'Whatever you like,' he said. 'We could go for a walk through the woods.'

'Where do they lead to?'

He leant forward and pointing through the large kitchen window towards the towering pine trees said, 'We have direct access to the beach through there. It's only a five-minute walk, and very peaceful.'

'I'd love that,' she said. 'I'm not sure I have the right clothes for walking down pathways though.

Seb smiled. 'Not a problem.' He stood up and pulled her up to join him. Holding her slightly away from him he looked her up and down, enjoying being able to have an excuse to do so. 'You're very slim and probably the same size as Fiona. Sebastian took her by the hand. 'Come with me, I'm sure we can set you up with a pair of her jeans and some boots.' He led the way back up the stairs to his sister's room.

'Wow,' she gasped. 'This is so pretty.'

'My uncle had it decorated especially for Fi about a year ago. He thought she'd love all the pink and frills, and was hoping to make it as feminine as possible.'

'And did she?' Paige asked, stroking the plush velvet curtains. 'Love it, I mean?'

Seb shook his head, remembering with amusement how his sister had reacted when arriving home from university to find that her bohemian bedroom she'd taken years to mess up had been transformed into something more suited to a pop princess. 'She loathed it, and didn't hold back when telling him.'

'Poor man.'

'He was tough in the boardroom, but a complete pushover where Fi was concerned.' He squeezed her hand. 'Now, of course, she refuses to have it redecorated because it's the last big thing he did for her. She won't even change that laced canopy over her four-poster bed because she feels that to do so would show some sort of disrespect to his memory.'

'Poor Fiona,' Paige said.

Seb shrugged. 'Yes. Now, how about we find you some clothes?' He walked over to a double door and opened one side.

'My idea of heaven,' she said when he moved back. 'A

walk-in wardrobe.' She stepped inside. 'It's probably the size of the entire first floor of my cottage.'

He laughed. 'I'll leave you to get kitted out and meet you downstairs.'

He waited impatiently for her, not wishing to waste a moment of their morning together, his heart pounding as he watched her come down the curved staircase moments later. 'Perfect.'

'Not quite,' Paige giggled. 'I had to turn up the bottoms of the jeans a couple of times, and roll up the sleeves in this hoodie. How tall is your sister?'

'Well, I'm 6'2, so let me see.' He tried to picture how tall she was now. His sister never seemed to stop growing. 'I suppose she must be about 5'10.' Seb studied Paige once more. 'I suppose she has a good five inches on you when it comes to height. You look gorgeous though.'

'Thank you, but I feel like a kid playing dressing up in these clothes.' Paige grimaced.

Seb found an old pair of wellington boots for her to wear, and led her across the manicured lawn towards the woods. 'I used to build camps all over this wood with my friends during the school holidays. We thought we were Robin Hood.'

'What a perfect place for children to grow up,' Paige said, stumbling over a camouflaged log.

Seb grabbed hold of her and managed to save her from falling over. 'It's like a minefield in places,' he said pulling her to him. He breathed in her fresh soapy scent and had to hold back from losing what little self-control he still possessed whenever he was around her. 'I'm pleased you agreed to spend some time here this morning.'

'Me, too, Thanks for the invitation.'

'Any time,' he said, glancing over his shoulder and catching the questioning look on her face. He waited for her to get level with him. 'Come along, I have something to show you.'

He held on tightly to her hand and led her through the woods trying not to dwell on her words about this being the perfect place for children to grow up. He glanced up at the powder blue sky over the wood in front of them; it was like something out of a Victorian painting. He'd never considered this place as a family home before, especially not one where he was the father. Her throwaway remark sparked something inside him.

'Why so serious?' Paige asked, stepping carefully over a rotting log.

Sebastian shook his head. 'It's nothing,' he fibbed. 'I'm concentrating on getting you down in one piece.'

Paige laughed. 'I'm not as clumsy as Olly likes to make out, you know.'

'I'll be the judge of that.' He squeezed her hand and pulled her forward. 'It's this way.' As they neared the clearing in the woodland, Sebastian heard Paige sigh.

'It's beautiful,' she whispered.

'You haven't seen anything yet.' He led her through to the edge of a small clump of mossy rocks, stepping over a narrow waterfall and stopped. 'Down there,' he pointed to their private beach, where he vaguely remembered his mother tanning herself when she was pregnant with Fi. How she ever got down here without hurting herself was a mystery, he wondered.

'Is this your own beach?' Paige asked.

'It is. Wait there.' He jumped down and put his arms up to take hold of her. 'It's OK, I won't drop you.'

Paige grimaced. 'You'd better not,' she said stepping forward and allowing him to catch her. He placed her down on the pale golden sand next to him. 'Seb, it's heavenly here.'

He was glad he'd thought to share this special place with her. 'I'm glad you like it.'

'How could I not?' They walked towards where the waves lapped gently against the shoreline, a couple of seagulls swooping around overhead.

'Is that a cave over there?'

Seb couldn't help smiling at her childlike excitement.
'It is. I thought you'd like to have a look inside.'

'I'd love to. Come along.' She kicked off the boots.
'I'll race you.' She laughed and ran along the soft sand
towards the opening of the small cave.

'You cheat,' Seb shouted, chasing after her but letting
her stay a few steps ahead of him until they reached the
ragged mouth of the rocks. He grabbed hold of her round
her waist.

'Hey, that's not fair,' she giggled, trying to wriggle out
of his grasp.

'Too bad.' He placed her down so that her feet touched
the sand and turned her to face him. Paige lifted her chin to
try and kiss him, but Seb smiled. 'Not yet, I want to show
you inside first.' He took her hand. 'Careful now, it can be
slippery.'

He bent so that he didn't hit his head and led her into
the damp, shadowy darkness marvelling at the reflections
of light bouncing off the wet sides of the granite.

'The water's cool in these rock pools,' she whispered.

'They can't get warmed by the sun in here. Watch your
step.'

'How far are we going in?' Her voice wavered a little
when she slipped.

Sebastian put an arm round her waist until she regained
her balance. 'It's not quite the same as the grotto in Capri,
is it?'

'No, but it's very lovely, and it's at the bottom of your
garden.'

They rounded a bend. 'Wow,' Paige sighed as a shaft
of light piercing through a crack in the rocks above
enveloped them.

'Did you ever camp here when you were small?'

Seb thought back to the many times he'd asked his

uncle if he could do just that. 'No, it was too dangerous. The tide rises up to the edge of the rocks twice a day, but occasionally we were allowed to camp at the edge of the woods.'

'So, what do you think?'

Paige sighed and hugged him tightly. 'I love it. I can't believe you're lucky enough to have had this beach all to yourselves when you were growing up. Most of us have to find a free spot on St Brelades Beach, if we're lucky.'

'It was only when we stayed with my uncle in the holidays,' he explained. 'And when the tide is very low you can get here from one of the nearby beaches, but most of the time it's cut off from everywhere else.'

'Thank you for bringing me down to see this slice of heaven.'

'I'm glad you've enjoyed it,' he said delighted that she'd love this place so much. Hopefully we'll have more mornings like these.'

'I hope so,' she said.

As Paige waved goodbye to Seb from her doorstep, she couldn't help thinking how different he looked dressed in a faded AC/DC T-shirt and ancient jeans.

'He looks almost like an ordinary person, younger and not so fierce,' Clem said, from behind her.

Paige agreed with her, but said nothing, following her sister into the cottage.

'So, what did you do this morning?' Clem asked, stroking her bump and flinching. 'Kicks like a ruddy mule.'

'Maybe it is a boy then?'

'Don't change the subject. In fact, I'm still a little stunned at how tasty Sebastian looked in his chill-out gear.'

Paige rolled her eyes, secretly thinking the same thing.

'Tell me everything. Come on, spill.'

246

'He made me a fantastic fry-up and then we went for a long walk through his woods and down to the beach. Then he brought me home.'

'And?'

'And, nothing, so stop bugging me.'

'Stop being so defensive,' Clem giggled. 'You're always like that when you're feeling guilty.' She raised an eyebrow and leant closer to her sister. 'So, how was it?'

Paige groaned. 'How was what?'

Clem ruffled Paige's hair. 'I'm talking about your night with that impossibly gorgeous man, what else?'

'None of your business.' Paige never understood her sister's penchant for discussing all aspects of her relationships with others.

'I know you were speaking about me just then, so don't stop,' Olly said from the hallway.

'Strange as it may seem,' Clem laughed, her face turning a delicate shade of pink. 'We were discussing Sebastian.'

Paige couldn't miss the subtle change in the atmosphere between her sister and Olly, and watched in silence as he stepped up behind Clem, wrapping his arms around her waist. He winked at her over Clemmie's shoulder at her.

'Hello, sweet thing, and before you start with your denials, we both know where you've been all night. So don't bother denying it.'

'Hang on a sec,' Paige said, frowning in confusion. 'Did I just miss something?' She looked from one to the other. 'I don't suppose I need to cook a special supper for you now, do I?' she asked, smiling as she went upstairs to her bedroom to change.

'Not for the reasons you were originally going to,' Olly shouted after her. 'But you did invite us, so we're still expecting to be fed.'

'We'll tell you everything then,' Clem said.

Paige turned to look down at them, smiling.

'Not everything,' Olly argued, before Clem silenced him with a pinch on his waist.

They finished eating and Paige put her fork down. 'Right, what happened between you last night?'

Clem nodded. 'Dad phoned just after I arrived at home. He'd seen the accident at the racetrack on the news and spotted you in the crowd being filmed getting into Sebastian's car. He was furious and wanted to know what the hell was going on.'

Paige sighed. 'I'll bet he did. Go on.'

'He must have been in a particularly grumpy mood because when Olly arrived, I let him in and Dad demanded to talk to him.'

Paige pulled a face at Olly. 'He gave you the third degree, I suppose?'

'Could say that. He told me how unimpressed he was that his daughter had seen fit to give up university to have a baby. He told me she was far too young to become a mother, and said how he could throttle me for being so irresponsible.' Olly waved his fork in the air. 'It's not as if there was only one of us there at the time of conception.'

'Carry on,' Paige said.

'He told me that he expects me to step up and do the right thing. I tried to explain that I'd be only too happy to do so, but he interrupted me and said that I should be a man and not let Clem brush me off so easily.'

'Bloody hell.' Paige glanced at Clem, who was making a point of concentrating on her supper. 'So what did you say next?'

'I told him I'd speak with her and we'd sort it out somehow.'

'Was he happy with that?' Paige knew the answer before he had time to tell her.

Olly rolled his eyes. 'He told us, we had one hour to

talk things through and if we hadn't come to any satisfactory conclusion in that time, he would come round here and make the decision for us.'

Clem slammed down her fork. 'Honestly, Paige, who does he think he is? We're two grown people, not a couple of kids.'

Paige shrugged. She understood how indignant her sister must feel, but knew it was only her father's way of looking out for her. 'Maybe, but you're still his daughter, still a student in fact, and he feels it's up to him to make sure Olly does the right thing.'

'I've been trying to do that all along,' argued Olly.

'I know, babe,' Clem smiled at him, then turning her attention back to Paige, she added. 'So we've decided that I'll stay in Jersey and have the baby, then in a few years, if I still want to carry on with my degree, I can go back as a mature student.'

'Sounds OK to me,' Paige narrowed her eyes. 'I can hear a "but" in there somewhere.'

Clem pursed her lips. 'We were hoping you'd let me stay here.'

'With a baby?'

'Er, yes, of course with a baby.'

Paige groaned. 'Can I think about it for a bit?' She hated the thought of sharing her cottage for any longer than was necessary, but didn't have the heart to cause them any additional problems until she could think of some way round their living arrangements.

'Please, Paige,' Clem pursed her lips theatrically.

'I said I'll think about it, and I will,' she said, wondering why her life seemed to be one dilemma after another.

Chapter Thirty-two

'I know her from somewhere,' whispered Clem out of the corner of her mouth, as she edged closer to Paige a few days later.

Paige stopped sketching to look up. 'Me too,' Paige said, inwardly cringing as Lucinda strode purposefully down the narrow pavement towards the shop.

'Blimey, she looks like she's on some sort of mission.' Clem went forward to greet the customer.

Paige wasn't surprised. She put down her pencil.

'Good morning,' Lucinda said a false smile on her face as she looked down her nose at Paige. 'We've met before.' It was a statement, rather than a question.

'May I help you?' offered Clem.

'I want a pair of knee-high, black patent leather boots,' Lucinda said, her vowels clipped and tone icy.

'Have we met?' Paige asked, not giving Lucinda the satisfaction of thinking she remembered her. She turned to address Clem. 'Why don't you fetch the new designs? Most of them arrived this morning. I think we could have exactly what this lady is looking for.'

'Of course,' Clem said, unable to take her eyes off the vision in front of her. 'I won't be a moment.' She raised her eyebrows as she disappeared into the back room.

Paige turned to face Lucinda with a fixed smile on her face.

'So, you do remember me,' she said, a smug look on her face. 'I wondered if you would.'

Paige shrugged. 'You were at the races the other

evening.'

'Yes, with Sebastian,' she said territorially. 'It turned out to be a bit of a drama in the end, of course. Stupid bloody jockey could have had Sebastian killed pulling a stunt like that.'

Paige tried to live by the premise that the customer was always right, but in this instance, she couldn't stop from disagreeing with what she'd just heard. 'I doubt he fell off his horse on purpose.' Paige stifled a further retort, when Lucinda waved a manicured hand in front of her face.

'Maybe not, but still, if he can't ride properly, he shouldn't take part in something so dangerous.' She stepped forward, extending her hand to Paige. 'Anyway, enough of that nonsense, I'm Lucinda Barrow-Hughes,' she said not taking her eyes of Paige for a second.

Paige took the proffered hand and shook it briefly. 'Paige Bingham,' she said, not quite sure why they were being so formal.

'I thought I'd come and introduce myself to you, especially since Sebastian seemed so reluctant to be the gentleman and do it himself the other night.'

'OK,' Paige said, still a little baffled. Lucinda obviously wasn't aware that she and Sebastian had spent the night together. Paige was unsure where the conversation was leading and waited for her to continue.

'I thought it only right that we meet properly.'

'You do?' Paige didn't care how she went about it, but hoped Lucinda didn't end up buying any of her designs before leaving. She knew that seeing them being worn by that spiteful woman would leave a sour taste in her mouth.

'Yes.' She put her hand down into her large handbag and pulled out a newspaper. 'I don't usually buy this tat, but had to make an exception when I saw this earlier today. She held up the paper, so that Paige could get a clear view of the headlines. 'Now, I don't know what you're thinking when you read this, but I have a feeling you're under the misapprehension that you're a little more important to Sebastian than you actually are.'

Paige stared at the letters emblazoned across the page. 'A Jersey Affair?' For a few seconds Lucinda's voice seemed muted. Paige stared at the picture of Sebastian's mouth close to hers. It had been by the enclosure when he'd lowered his voice to whisper something to her. Her heart pounded at the realisation that she was now public news. She covered her open mouth with one hand, and looked across at Lucinda's face, her mouth still moving.

She read the beginning of the article. *Who is the mysterious woman seen here kissing Sebastian Fielding, and what family secrets is she hiding? We've discovered some of them, but if there's anything you can share about this Jersey Affair please email ...'*

'And I'm sure you're aware, that as his fiancée, this is a little humiliating for both of us.'

Stunned at her words, Paige stared blankly at her. 'I'm sorry, what did you just say?'

'You heard.' She drew back her full red lips to display two rows of blindingly white teeth. Then, as if bored with the effect she had on Paige, threw her head back and laughed. 'Well, ex-fiancée, if you want to quibble about details,' she corrected herself with a slight shrug of her shoulders, as if her blatant lie was a mere trifle. 'If I'm being perfectly honest, that is, but I think it's only fair to let you know that I intend rectifying that tiny discrepancy in the very near future.' She folded the paper and slotted it back into her bag.

Lucinda examined her immaculate manicure briefly, looking thoroughly satisfied with the reaction she'd caused. 'Now, you want to take advice from someone who knows Sebastian better than you could ever hope to, do yourself a favour and prepare to walk away from any thoughts of a relationship you may expect to have with him.'

Paige wished she possessed half the self-confidence Lucinda seemed to enjoy. 'You're right, I didn't know of your connection to him, and as far as my relationship with Sebastian is concerned, it's nothing to do with you.' She could feel her face reddening.

Lucinda laughed. 'Whatever. I just think you should prepare yourself. After all, he now knows I'm back and for good this time,' she said, with emphasis. 'It's only a matter of time before we carry on from where we left off. Seb has never been able to resist my charms.' Paige wasn't sure but she thought she heard a slight waver in Lucinda's voice. 'It's only fair I should warn you. Although they do say all's fair in love and war, and all that rubbish.'

Paige was astounded by the woman's ego, but sensed that for all her protestations, she had probably been as shocked by the headlines as Paige had been. 'You seriously think you can come here and warn me off a man?' Paige shook her head and smiled. 'What are we, teenagers?'

Lucinda thought for a second. 'Sebastian is simply suffering from a case of hurt pride. After all, men do tend to take it badly when you leave them. It's as if you've insulted their masculinity, don't you think?'

'I wouldn't know.' Paige wasn't sure if she should feel sympathy for this woman or loathe her. 'I can't imagine Sebastian having any problem at all with his masculinity.'

Lucinda threw her head back and laughed loudly. 'Good point.' She gave Paige a withering look. 'You can't seriously tell me you see yourself as having a future with him, do you?' Then, when Paige didn't reply straight away, she continued. 'Oh for heaven's sake, be realistic. I dare say he's more than happy to spend the occasional night with you.' She studied Paige intently for a moment, and then seemingly satisfied with what she saw, continued. 'Yes, I thought so.'

Paige, hating that this venomous woman seemed to

254

know she had slept with Sebastian, swallowed back the tears of humiliation and fury that were threatening to flow. 'Now you listen to me,' she said, determined to keep her voice down so as not to alert her sister. 'You seem to have a very high opinion of yourself, but that doesn't give you the right to come marching in here and insult me.' She took a breath, in an attempt to regain some control of her voice. 'It's none of your business what Sebastian and I have between us.'

Lucinda slowly pulled the thick strap of her black Dior crocodile handbag up onto her blade-thin shoulder. 'All I'm saying is that it's obvious by the look of horror on your face when I showed you the newspaper that you couldn't cope with the attention you'd inevitably receive should you end up with him. And, whatever Sebastian professes, both you and I know he will at some point find you lacking, at least in that department.'

Paige wished she could argue with her, but doubted she'd have the first clue how to deal with determined paparazzi.

'I suggest that if you want to protect yourself from being disappointed,' Lucinda added, 'you should take the only option open to you, and finish it, sooner rather than later.'

'Here we are,' Clem said, cheerfully, carrying three large boxes containing Paige's latest designs. 'What's the matter?' She looked from one to the other, confused by the obvious tension in the room.

'Nothing. Miss Barrow-Hughes has changed her mind about the boots. She was just leaving,' Paige said, as calmly as she could, walking over to the doorway. 'Weren't you?'

Lucinda ignored her, giving Clemmie the benefit of her perfect smile. 'I think I'll leave the boots for now. This lady has had a bit of a shock.'

Paige closed the door behind her and leant heavily

255

against it.

'What happened?' Clem lowered the boxes carefully onto the floor.

Paige took a deep breath, and told her sister all about the headlines and picture in the paper.

'Bloody hell, that's so exciting.' Clem squealed. 'Imagine you, a mystery woman.'

Paige frowned. 'There's nothing good about this, Clem. I didn't see the entire story, but I did spot them asking people to email with any information they might have about me. Do you really think our family would welcome that sort of intrusion into our private lives?'

Clem's expression changed. 'Shit, what about Luke's court case last year? The poor guy had to cope with living on a small island and being accused of money laundering.' Clem shook her head. 'We know he was found not guilty, but it still didn't stop people from gossiping and imagining the worst about him.'

'Exactly,' Paige bit the side of her thumb nail. 'I'm going to have to stop this thing with Sebastian before I hurt anyone.'

'Oh, no,' Clem strode over to her and hugged Paige tightly. 'I'm so sorry. I know you haven't said much, but I could tell you really liked him. You would never have spent the night with him if you didn't.'

'That picture was only taken last night,' she said miserably. 'The paps didn't waste any time using it for a story about me. How do people cope with this sort of thing every day of their lives?'

'Who knows? Some of those celebs tip off the papers when they're going out so that they take pictures of them. It's a completely different way of living when you think about it, isn't it?'

Paige nodded. That's what she'd thought and it wasn't a way of life she had ever wanted for herself. She sat down on a nearby chair, upset that her brief relationship to

256

Sebastian would have to end so soon.

She arrived back at her cottage at the end of the day and spotting a stranger at the entrance of her shared driveway wondered if he could be from the newspapers. She stared at him for a moment, but he turned and walked away. Certain she was becoming paranoid Paige unlocked the house and walked inside.

'Did you see him?' she asked Clem, when her sister followed her inside the house.

'Who?'

'There was a man, just by Olly's mum's house. He seemed to be watching the cottage.'

Clem widened her eyes. 'Oh my God, do you think he was a pap?' Without waiting for an answer, Clem raced outside.

'Get back in here,' Paige said following her, blinking when a camera went off in her face as soon as she stepped through the doorway. 'Shit.'

'Bugger off,' Clem shouted. 'We'll call the bloody police if you don't leave us alone. This is private property.'

Paige grabbed her sister by the wrist and pulled her back into the house. 'This is ridiculous; I'm not going to have people coming here and taking photos of us.'

Her mobile rang a couple of hours later. Paige, checked, and seeing it was Sebastian, immediately switched it off. She needed time to think, and was still trying to absorb what had happened earlier in the day. Mulling over Lucinda's words, only helped instil them into Paige's tired brain and made her realise she couldn't ignore what had happened.

She had seen for herself how he lived, his home and everything that went with it. It should have dawned on her when she'd seen him on all the news channels just after his uncle's death. Sebastian's life was interesting to the journalists, whether she liked it or not, and if she was involved with him in anyway, then it went without saying that hers was too.

He needed a partner who could cope with all the attention and probably enjoy it for the most part. Paige swallowed the lump constricting her throat. As nasty as Lucinda might be, Paige realised that it could never possibly work between her and Sebastian and that he and Lucinda were probably much better suited as a couple.

The following day Olly arrived at the cottage to take Clem out for a meal. He held out the *Jersey Gazette* in his hand. 'Have you seen this?' he announced, before closing the front door.

'What is it?' asked Paige not wishing to see a continuation of the previous day's news. She peered over the paperwork she had been working on.

'Look.' He flicked through the pages, folded them back on each other, and slapped it down noisily in front of Paige on the table. 'There,' he pointed. 'It says, "Sebastian Fielding with Miss Lucinda Barrow-Hughes turning heads at the Annual Charity Ball." I know you and he sort of got it together, but you would let me know if you had feelings for him, wouldn't you?'

'Of course.' Paige stared at the paper, tears blurring the picture in front of her. 'She's his ex-fiancée, I already knew that.'

'You knew? I didn't think you bought the papers.'

'She told me,' said Paige quietly, refusing to volunteer anything more and not wishing to worry him by telling him about the photographer on her doorstep the previous day.

His eyebrows shot up and he leaned back to check Clem wasn't waiting for him. 'Well?'

Paige told him about Lucinda's visit to the shop.

'How weird,' Olly said. 'Why would she bother to go

to all that effort, if she was so sure you meant so little to him?'

Paige willed her sister to hurry up and get ready. 'I've no idea.'

'Then you're being bloody dim.' He shook his head. 'She went out of her way to warn you off. Surely you can see that she considers you a threat?'

'Do you really think so?'

Olly covered his face with his hands. 'It's bloody obvious to anyone with half a brain cell.'

He pushed her shoulder lightly. 'I don't know what Jeremy said to you, but you seem to have a lack of awareness when it comes to how fabulous you are. He glared at her. 'That jilting bastard has a lot to answer for. Not every man is a selfish, conceited arse, Paige. Just because Sebastian Fielding didn't make the choice you hoped for with your concession, it doesn't mean he's a shit.'

Paige shrugged him off. 'Fine, but it doesn't take away the fact that I don't want to have my life to be dragged through the papers. When I saw Sebastian in Sorrento it was completely different from how it would be over here.'

'Talk to him,' he said. 'Maybe he knows ways to protect you from all this nonsense?' Olly smiled.

'What?' She couldn't imagine how he'd be able to sort this out.

Olly winked at her. 'I hope Lucinda Barrow-whatsit bought something while she was giving you the low-down?'

'No,' Paige said. 'Arrived, let me have it, and buggered off without parting with a penny.'

'Miserable cow.'

'To be fair I did pretty much ask her to leave, but I'm surprised she didn't mention being with him at the ball when she had the ideal opportunity to do so.'

Olly held out a bag she knew would contain her

favourite chocolate croissants. 'Enough of her. Look, I came prepared,' he said.

'And this is why you're my best friend.' Paige winked at him, taking the bag from him without speaking. It was good having someone around who always knew exactly how to cheer her up. She stood up and went to the kitchen to share them out onto three plates.

'Are you sure this is a good idea before you to go out to eat?' She handed him a plate and tried hard not to dwell on the photo, now engraved in her mind, of Sebastian enjoying the ball with her nemesis.

'Your sister seems permanently hungry,' he said changing the subject. 'She loves these like you do, more so now.'

It must run in the family, thought Paige, sinking her teeth relishing the sticky warm chocolate oozing into her mouth. 'Thanks, Ol,' she said. 'Clem won't be long.' She nudged him. 'So? How are you two getting along?'

Olly beamed at her. 'I think we're going to be OK. I just need to let her get on with things and not try to take over. I think she's secretly worried I might start making plans for the baby that don't coincide with her own,' he widened his eyes. 'So I'm keeping quiet as much as possible.'

'Good thinking.' Paige glanced down at the photo once more, noticing Lucinda's smile. 'Help yourself,' she murmured indicating the kettle.

Pouring a mug of hot black coffee, he followed her into the warm lounge, sitting down opposite her.

'Well,' Olly said. 'As you don't appear to want to discuss the article, shall I tell you about my plans for this evening?'

Paige nodded, biting once more into the warm pastry. 'Don't forget that you're telling me about my baby sister, so no gory details, please.'

His eyebrows knitted together. 'I'm not a complete

idiot. I do love her though, and I'm going to ask her to marry me.'

Paige nearly choked. Olly slapped her several times on the back, as she struggled to regain her self-control and start breathing properly again.

'Shit, don't frighten me like that,' he said. 'Surely it wasn't that much of a surprise?'

She gave him an apologetic look. 'Sorry, I didn't mean to do that. But don't rush things, Olly. You're only just back together. The last thing she needs on top of dealing with a baby is for you to give her a fright. You could end up scaring her, and ruining everything.

'But your dad said I had to do the right thing,' he said, looking hurt by her lack of enthusiasm.

Paige lowered her voice, so Clem could not overhear them. 'Olly, by all means ask my sister to marry you, but it's probably better if you wait a little while. I think the main thing he wants to know is that you'll be there for her and the baby. Give her a chance to get used to being with you again first, before you make any grand gestures. Honestly, you're such a romantic,' she said in an effort to try and lighten the atmosphere between them.

'That's a joke. Don't tell me you spent the night with Himself without feeling anything for him? I know you far too well to believe that. You're not a screw 'em and move on sort of girl.'

He was right, of course, but she was not going to admit it. 'Subtle terminology, Ol, thanks.'

'You know what I mean, and don't try and change the subject. Didn't it occur to you how it looked when you left the event the other night to race off after Sebastian?'

How had it looked, she wondered. She hadn't thought of anyone else at the time, only wishing to comfort Sebastian at the hospital. Was it naive of her to assume none of the other people at the races would think her sudden departure strange in any way?

'I hadn't given it a thought to be honest,' she admitted. 'Well, not until Clem mentioned that Dad had raged about seeing me with Sebastian at the races. I think he's hoping to keep the papers away from Mum. He hasn't phoned me about it though, thankfully.'

'I think Clem explained about the jockey being taken to hospital, so he just thought you were being your usual thoughtful self.' Olly whistled through his teeth. 'Blimey, it all happens to you doesn't it?'

'Hardly,' she argued. 'Apart from going out to a few parties this summer, I've barely left the house except to go to work. Everything else I've done has been pretty dull.'

'You've been away to Spain, don't forget.'

'Yes, for work purposes, and you know as well as I do that my time there is pretty much taken up with meetings and shopping. Again, all to do with work, I have no social life and certainly no love life to speak off, especially now.'

His eyes lit up at her slip of the tongue. 'Why, especially now?'

Paige chewed her lower lip, irritated at her stupidity. 'I didn't mean anything by it. Anyway why do you think my life is so exciting?'

'That wasn't what I meant, and you know it.' Olly pulled a sympathetic face. 'I'm sorry it's all gone tits up with Sir Whathisname.'

She laughed at his turn of phrase, despite feeling utterly miserable. Hearing her sister's footsteps on the stairs, she sighed with relief. 'Go on, bugger off. Be kind, for once, and leave me to sulk in peace.'

'You can join us if you want,' he said, getting up and going to the doorway. 'We're only going to grab a bite in St Aubin.'

Paige shook her head. She wasn't willing to chance having her picture taken again. 'No, thanks, anyway, *Sense and Sensibility* is on again this evening. All I want to do is stuff my face with more chocolate, and settle down to lose myself in it.'

'What, the chocolate?' He looked as if she had just told him she was going to the garden to eat worms.

'No, fool, *Sense and Sensibility*,' she giggled, waving him away.

'Again? You must know the script better than Emma Thompson by now.' He came back to give her a hug before handing over his plate. 'Don't worry, I'm going to leave now. Let you wallow.' He hugged her, leaving immediately afterwards.

Later, just after Emma asked Edward Ferris if he would like to take up the offer of a parish, she heard the front door open.

'Knickers,' grumbled Paige. It didn't matter how many times she sat through the film, she still hated to be interrupted whilst watching it.

She blew her nose on one of the many crumpled tissues lying all around her, before looking over at the doorway. Expecting to see Olly and Clem, she was taken aback to find Clem by herself. Paige looked behind her to see where Olly was.

'Where is he?' she frowned. 'Oh, don't tell me you've fallen out already?'

'No, we haven't.' Clem took the remote control and switched off the television.

'What did you do that for?' she asked, not bothering to hide her irritation.

'You and I need to talk.'

Paige couldn't imagine what must be so urgent her sister would interrupt her film.

'What's the matter?' She felt sick with worry at the seriousness of her sister's tone.

Clem bent down to pick up the newspaper Olly had delivered so annoyingly earlier that evening, and thumbed through the pages impatiently, her tongue poking out of her full lips in concentration until she found what she was looking for. Folding the paper back on itself she passed it to Paige. 'There,' she said. 'I have a feeling you haven't read that bit yet.'

'What bit?' She wondered what could possibly be so important. Tempted to eat the last bit of her Dairy Milk chocolate, Paige went to pick it up.

'Paige, you must listen to me.' Clem grabbed Paige's arm and sat down opposite her. 'When Ol told me about this being in the paper tonight, we chatted and I remembered where I'd seen her before.' Clem picked up the discarded chocolate and popped it into her mouth.

Paige feigned disinterest as best she could. 'And where would that be?'

'Gossip magazines,' Clem said swallowing the chocolate and looking very pleased.

Paige had no idea what Clem was going on about. 'So?'

'Don't you remember all the kerfuffle a couple of years ago?'

'Nope,' Paige shook her head wracking her memory to try and recall anything about Lucinda. 'Tell me.'

Clem clasped her hands together gleefully. 'Lucinda used to be engaged to Sebastian.'

'I know, she told me that, remember?' Paige said, unable to keep the weary tone out of her voice.

'OK, but did you know why she dumped him?'

Paige sat up straighter in her chair, tucking her legs beneath her. 'She mentioned something about it in the shop. I didn't take much notice.'

Why, she wondered, would someone so keen to keep Sebastian for herself, break up an engagement with him. Now she was intrigued, *Sense and Sensibility* forgotten for the time being.

'I knew you'd want to hear more, knowing that juicy little titbit.'

'Go on,' Paige said, not bothering to hide her intrigue.

'I knew I recognized him from somewhere, the first

264

time I met him,' Clem said. 'I remember reading in the gossip magazines about their wedding preparations, flowers booked, bridesmaid dresses created in a haze of silks, that sort of thing, when she went and dumped him completely out of the blue.' She paused for effect.

'She jilted him? But why would she do something like that if she's so into him?' Paige asked impatiently.

'I can't believe you didn't read about this at the time,' Clem said, her eyes sparking with excitement.

'Nor can I,' she sighed heavily. 'Hurry up.'

Clem sat back and folded her arms. 'She only went and ran off with his gardener.'

Paige thought she must have misheard. 'Sorry?'

'You heard.'

Paige frowned thoughtfully. 'From what I've seen of Lucinda and her class snobbery, she doesn't seem the type to choose a gardener over a wealthy businessman. It doesn't sound like her at all.' Something didn't add up, Paige was sure of it.

'I doubt it was his relentless charm or anything, although I gather he was rather hot,' Clem added, shaking her head. 'No, this bloke won the lottery. Scooped over four and a half million, only to then go on to win Lucinda's fickle heart. Surely you remember reading about it in the papers?'

Paige tried to absorb this news. 'Sorry, I don't remember it at all.'

Clem shook her head and laughed. 'I can't believe you missed this story. It was all over the papers for a few days, then in the usual rags for weeks. One minute Lucinda and Sebastian were being photographed arm in arm, showing off all over the place, then just like that,' she clicked her fingers. 'She drops him like the proverbial hot potato and buggers off with Jeeves.'

Paige's opened her eyes wide in disbelief. 'The gardener wasn't called Jeeves, surely?'

Clem groaned. 'No, of course he bloody wasn't, and that isn't the point I'm trying to make here. What I'm nearly killing myself to spell out to you is that your beloved Sebastian used to be engaged to Lucinda sodding Barrow-Hughes, stupid bloody name. Now, if what she told you is right, she's come back to reclaim him. And she has a bloody cheek thinking she can do that, if you ask me.'

'I doubt anyone would ask you,' Paige teased, despite not feeling at all jovial. 'But you're right. She has a lot of nerve.'

'I told you.'

'Yes, but it's not any of our business is it?' Paige said, the reality of what her sister had told her starting to sink in.

Clem sighed. 'It is if you're seeing him.'

'I'm not though, am I?'

'Oh.' Clem looked disappointed by this revelation. 'That was far harder work than I'd expected though. Don't you ever read anything other than *Vogue*?'

Paige shook her head absent-mindedly. 'I must have been so involved with setting up the shop, I didn't really bother with anything not connected to it. Now she wants him back,' she said, almost to herself.

'Well, wouldn't you? He obviously loved her once, they were engaged after all, and now he's inherited his uncle's estate and worth a small fortune. Lucinda obviously realises she's made a boob by buggering off in the first place.' She patted Paige's knee. 'I love you, Sis, but somehow I don't fancy your chances against a devious cow like her.'

Neither did Paige, and she would have preferred it if her sister didn't say so.

'And if they're at that ball together then they obviously still have something going on even if he isn't admitting it to himself, or anyone else.'

Paige noticed Clem fidgeting. 'Do you want to be

somewhere else?'

'No,' she said. 'It's just that I asked Ol to give me a few minutes while I spoke to you about this.' Clem hesitated.

'There's more?' Paige didn't like the look on Clem's face. She looked troubled. 'What?'

Clem closed the paper and pointed to the headlines. 'Mystery Woman Jilts Fiancé to be with Entrepreneur.'

'Bloody liars,' Paige shouted, picking up the paper and reading the false story below. 'They're making me out to be some sort of heartless gold-digger, who literally left Jeremy weeping at the altar.'

'I know,' Clem winced. 'I wasn't sure what to show you first.'

'Bloody hell, how do people live like this?' Paige threw the paper on the floor. 'This story is complete fiction.'

'Paige …'

Paige took a deep breath. 'Surely there's nothing else,' she said, willing her sister to agree.

Clem looked visibly upset. 'Bea phoned earlier, she's distraught. She's our cousin, Paige, and I hate to think of her being upset, especially after everything she and Luke went through last year with his court case.'

'Why? What's happened?' She hoped Bea's new husband Luke hadn't suffered some sort of building accident. They were so happy together, she couldn't bear it if something had gone wrong for them. 'Is Luke OK?'

Clem nodded. 'Physically, yes.'

She wasn't sure whether she should be relieved by Clem's answer, or not. 'What's that supposed to mean?'

'A journalist has been hounding him for comments.'

'About what?' she asked nervously, dreading what was coming next.

'All that stuff about the money laundering.'

Paige groaned. She hated to think how the call from journalists must have affected Luke and Bea, especially after all they had been through the year before. 'But the charges were dropped.'

'I know, but it still makes interesting reading, doesn't it?'

This was disastrous. 'He's only just managing to build up his company again. Poor Luke.'

'And Bea's devastated. She'd only just discovered she was pregnant two days before the phone call, so having all that nastiness dragged back up again is the last thing they need to deal with.'

She clenched her teeth. She'd seen what the previous year's legal fight had done to both of them. There wasn't any way Paige wanted to be a part of them suffering the loss of this much-wanted baby. 'Bloody paparazzi.'

Clem looked as if she was about to cry. 'I'm so sorry, Paige, I didn't want to tell you, but Olly thought you needed to know as soon as possible. I phoned Luke and he said to tell you you're not to worry, but I could tell he'd had a shock. He said they'll deal with the repercussions of the article when it comes out, and you're not to stress about it. After all, it's not as if you can do anything to stop it.'

'It's my fault.' Paige closed her eyes. Opening them, she forced a smile at Clem. 'You were right to tell me. I'll phone Bea and Luke to apologize, and then I'll speak to Sebastian.'

'It's not your fault,' Clem argued. 'They must really want to get at Sebastian if they're going after your cousin. How the hell could you foresee this happening?'

Paige swallowed the rising nausea in her throat and rubbed her pounding temples. Poor Clem, she was just as scared as her for Bea's pregnancy. She had to try and stop this hideous story. This couple had been good to her and deserved to be happy. 'Go on. You get back to Olly, I'll have a think. I'll catch up with you tomorrow.'

'You're sure you're OK?'

268

Paige nodded. 'Yes, I'm fine. Now you go and leave me to digest this mind-blowing information.'

'You're still going to watch that film?' Clem looked stunned.

'If you'll let me, yes.' She picked up the remote control from the coffee table, willing her sister to leave her in peace.

'But it's *Sense and Sensibility*, again.'

Paige winked at her. 'Yes, and I know I've seen it a hundred times, but I want to watch it again.'

'OK,' Clem said, confused. She leant over Paige and gave her a quick hug. 'If you're sure you're all right?'

Paige gave her sister what she hoped was a convincing smile. 'Positive. Now go and meet Ol. I'll give this some thought for a bit. Please tell him everything's fine.' She waited until she heard the door close behind her sister and pulled the chenille rug over her legs.

So, now Luke was involved. This was disastrous. How could those journalists print such lies about her life? If they printed that story about her, how far could they twist the ones about Luke's court case? Paige rubbed her eyes, exhaustion seeping through her. Why was this happening? She was so ordinary it never occurred to her that anyone could make a dramatic story out of her lifestyle.

She drew her knees up to her chest and wrapped her arms around them, thinking back over Clem's words. Seb had been jilted too. It made it doubly difficult for her to understand why he would give someone who had let him down so callously a second chance. It didn't make any sense. Then it dawned on her like a shard of glass in her chest, causing such physical pain she gasped. For Sebastian to forgive Lucinda such a public betrayal, he must love her very deeply. The realisation stunned Paige. Their night together, however memorable it was for her, must have meant very little to him.

'Bloody hell,' she shouted, sitting up and turning off

the television. Paige picked up her mobile and located Sebastian's number. She needed him to help sort this mess out for Luke and Bea's sake. And just because Lucinda had told her she was going to have Sebastian didn't mean that Paige had to stand back and let it happen without a fight. She clicked on his number and waited as it rang.

'I was hoping you'd ring. You must have a few missed calls from me.'

'Hi, Sebastian,' she said. 'I was wondering what you're doing this evening. I think we need to have a bit of a chat.'

'Sounds interesting, I'll come right over.'

Chapter Thirty-three

Sebastian knocked on her front door and smiled when she opened it to greet him. 'You don't look very happy,' he said. 'I'm assuming this has something to do with the picture of you with me in the papers? I did try to call you a few times, but you didn't pick up.'

She followed him into the living room and motioned for him to sit. 'Yes, there was a story yesterday, and an even more ludicrous one today. Oh, and there was also that picture of you and Lucinda at the ball.'

He sat down opposite her. He could tell she was not in the mood to let this one go. 'She can be so infuriating. To be honest I didn't give it too much thought at the time, it was only afterwards that I realized she'd probably set the whole thing up.'

'Go on.' Paige crossed one leg over the other and leant back into her chair.

She looked so tiny sitting there with a scowl on her pretty, make-up-free face. Sebastian forced his mind back to the evening of the photo. 'I wasn't even talking to her at the time. One minute I was speaking with one of my uncle's friends, the next there was a tap on my shoulder; I turned round, saw a camera, and smiled.'

'I see?'

'Yes. You know how it is at these events.'

'Not really.'

Sebastian was beginning to get annoyed. 'Bloody cameras in your face constantly, I just smile and let them get on with it and then carry on with whatever

271

conversation I was having before.'

'You don't care that people might get the wrong idea about you two?'

Sebastian stood up and crouched down in front of her, resting each hand on one of the arms of the chair. 'I don't care what people think, or say, about me. I've had enough experience in the public eye to know they're going to make whatever decisions they choose, whether I like it or not. The only person whose opinion does matter, apart from my sister, of course, is yours.' Their eyes locked and he could tell she wanted to believe him.

'Lucinda's horrible,' Paige said eventually.

Sebastian smiled. 'My sister would agree with you.'

'She wasn't wrong though when she said that you and I weren't suited.'

Sebastian stood up, furious at the thought that Lucinda had been working on both of them. 'When did she say that?'

Paige stood up. 'She came to the shop yesterday.'

'And you didn't tell me?' He'd suspected Lucinda was going to be trouble, but stupidly hadn't expected her to go direct to Paige. He should have known better.

'No, because whether I liked it or not, what she said was true.'

Sebastian raked his hands through his hair. Just when he could believe Paige was beginning to trust him again, Lucinda was plying her with lies. 'Go on.'

Paige crossed her arms in front of her. 'She showed me the picture of us at the races and explained about all the attention I would receive if I was with you.'

'We'll have to be more careful in future.' Sebastian narrowed his eyes. What wasn't she telling him? 'What else did she say?'

'I thought it wouldn't worry me so much, but it's escalated from there. A journalist contacted my cousin, Bea, asking for a comment to go with a piece they're publishing about her husband this weekend.'

'Go on,' he said, imagining only too well what was coming next.

'A year or so ago, Luke was accused of being involved with money laundering, and you know how fascinated the press seems to be about that subject, especially when it's connected to Jersey. He was innocent, and the charges were dropped, but it nearly ruined everything he'd worked for, as well as causing massive problems between him and Bea. The last thing they need is for this to be brought up again.'

Sebastian waited for her to finish.

'It's one thing opening myself up for inspection, but it's a different matter entirely when members of my family are dragged into it.'

And there it was, he thought. Sebastian was only just holding back his temper. 'Leave this with me. I have contacts. It might not be too late to stop this story.'

Paige frowned. 'How do you propose to do that?'

He shrugged. 'By giving them something else to write about instead.'

She looked stunned, 'You can do that, so easily?'

Sebastian wished it was the case. 'I'm not promising anything, but I'll give it a try.' He didn't relish giving them information about himself he'd rather withhold, but he had no intention of letting Paige's family suffer unnecessarily because of her connection with him.

'Thank you,' she said, reaching out and touching the back of his hand. 'Bea will be incredibly relieved.'

'As far as Lucinda's concerned, she's vindictive and extremely cunning. She also knows exactly what to say to get the effect she's after. If she says anything more to you, promise me you'll tell me. Or at least give me the chance to resolve any lies she feeds to you. Will you do that?'

`Paige nodded.

'Good. Because I don't want you taking her lies to

heart and distancing yourself from me again. It's been hard enough trying to work things through as it is.'

'Yes,' she said thoughtfully.

He pulled her tightly against him, breathing in the smell of her perfume. 'I don't want to lose you again.'

When she didn't reply, he bent to kiss her, relieved when she responded instantly. 'I'll do my best to sort this mess out, Paige.'

She turned to go from him. 'We both know that this won't be the last time the papers want to print something about my family. Did you see the story today about me leaving Jeremy sobbing at the altar before racing off to chase you?'

His stomach tightened. 'Don't say it.'

'Whatever I feel for you, we both know that Lucinda isn't the real problem here. I've never been in the public eye before, and I must put my loyalty to my family first.'

He willed himself to remain calm. 'Paige, please.'

She shook her head. 'I can't do this to them. My father will be horrified when he reads today's story, and my mother will want to track down the journalists who wrote those lies about me and batter them. Who knows, it could be something to do with my father's past that they'll print about next time.'

He could tell that she had made up her mind and for now, at least, he had no choice but to walk away. He was going to have to find a way to resolve this problem, if they were ever to have any sort of future together.

Chapter Thirty-four

Paige needed time away before the build-up to Christmas, so decided that taking a break in September was perfect timing. 'There's nothing else for it,' she explained to Clem the following morning over the phone.

'But if you're attracted to him, which is what Olly insinuated the other day when we were chatting, then why do you want to leave him?'

Paige wound the telephone cord absent-mindedly around her thumb. 'I've explained everything to you. I have to be sensible.'

'And running away is sensible, is it?'

Paige groaned. 'I'm not running away.'

'Then what do you call it?'

She could hear the rustle of paper and could imagine her sister throwing down a magazine in temper. 'It could never work between us, Clem. I'm not willing to have my family's private life splashed across the tabloids. I'm not just thinking of myself here.' She sighed miserably. 'Whether I like it, or not, if I was to become a part of Sebastian's life then I would have to accept that anything he did, maybe me too, would become fodder for the papers.'

'There must be a way around all this though.'

'You don't think I haven't thought endlessly about it? It won't work. So, will you run the shop while I'm away?' Paige had known Clem would want to argue with her, but she had made up her mind and no one was going to change it for her.

Clem sighed. 'What choice do I have? It's my job. What are you expecting to get out of this sabbatical?'

'It's hardly a sabbatical. I'm only going away for a couple of weeks. I want to take the next few days off, make a few plans, and book flights.'

'Yes, but I think you're making a mistake. Sebastian might be different from you, Paige, but he's not Jeremy. I think you need to remember that fact and learn to trust him a little.'

'Let me deal with this my way, please,' Paige said, wishing Clem would stop being so annoying.

'If you're sure you can.'

Paige switched off the phone, determined to have as much uninterrupted thinking time as possible. She was in love with Sebastian, but that only made walking away from him even more painful. 'Not really,' she said to herself, sitting down in front of her laptop and clicking on the airline website to check the availability of flights.

Paige booked a return ticket. She then made a list of everything Clem might need to know in case of an emergency. The most important thing was to take her notepads and pencils. After all, she smiled; she could design anywhere in the world.

'You're what? Why?' Olly groaned the next morning in her kitchen, waving his arms about him in frustration. 'I don't get it. It's not like you to go off so suddenly.'

Paige leant against the granite worktop. 'I'm not.'

He marched around to where she was standing, 'You bloody well are.' He stood in front of her, his arms crossed and feet wide apart as if blocking her way. 'What I want to know is, why? Is it this paper thing?'

Paige stared from her best friend to her sister, and back again. 'I just need to get away. It's been a traumatic few months, and I can't think straight here any more.' She passed him a can of beer. 'I was hoping you two could look after everything for me.'

Clem nodded. 'You know I will.'

Olly stared at her, his eyes narrowed. 'What utter bollocks. It's that bloody Sebastian, isn't it?' He slammed his palms down on the worktop, making both women jump.

'It's not just that. There's the issue with Luke being in the papers, and all the lies they keep printing about me.' She repeated everything she had told Clem about her conversation with Sebastian. 'I thought that if I went away for a bit, maybe they would get bored and find something else to write about. I can keep in contact with my suppliers via email. Clem is happy to run Heaven in Heels and you can look after the website, if that's OK with you?'

'Poor Luke,' he said, looking stunned. 'At least Sebastian is going to try and sort that situation out.'

'For now, although who knows what they'll find next time those journalists go looking for another story to print about our family.' Paige didn't dare contemplate what secrets her father could have hidden away in his filing cabinets.

'Stop nagging her now, Ol,' Clem said, taking him by the elbow and pulling him away. 'She's a big girl. She's more than capable of making her own decisions.'

'What will you do when you get there?' he asked.

'I'm not too sure,' she answered honestly. 'Maybe I'll just spend a couple of weeks in the sun doing very little.'

Sebastian left several messages on her house phone. Paige returned his call later the following day.

'Good to hear from you. How is everything?' he asked, sounding as if his cheerfulness were a little forced.

His deep voice resonated through her body, making her wish for the hundredth time things between them could be different. 'Fine thanks. Busy. Takings are up and the new batch of designs has taken off really well.'

'Good, I'm thrilled for you. I'm going to have to go

277

home to London for a few days,' he said. She could tell he was smiling. 'I wondered if you wanted to join me.'

'I'd love to,' she said. 'But I have too much to do here at the moment. Is everything all right?'

'Fine. In fact I'm going back to close up my house and collect Harley. It's time he came to live with me in Jersey. It'll mean losing Mrs Hutton, unfortunately.'

'Couldn't she come and work for you over here?'

He sighed. 'I did offer her one of the cottages, several times, but she seems determined to stay where she is. I can't blame her for that. I did tell her she can change her mind any time though.'

Just like Olly said to me, she thought.

'I should be back by next weekend,' he said. 'I'll give you a call then and maybe we can arrange to spend some time together.'

Paige hesitated, hating having to lie to him. 'I've got a few things on, so I'll give you a call.' She ended the call before he had time to argue.

'Come along, Paige. You're going to miss your flight if you don't get a move on.' Olly shouted impatiently from his car.

Paige gave Clem a quick hug, 'I'll be fine,' she said, touched to think they would miss her so much. 'I know we've gone through everything, but I've left you a spreadsheet, and a list for contacts, that sort of thing. It's on the computer, and I've printed out a copy too. You'll find it on the side in the kitchen.'

'Stop fretting.' Clem sniffed. The car horn sounded once again. 'You'd better go. Have a good break, and don't worry about anything here.'

'Thanks,' Paige said. 'I'll call you soon, and remember, if Sebastian asks where I am, tell him I'm on a buying trip.'

'Will do, now go.'

278

Olly carried her rucksack into the airport and waited while she checked in. 'You'll be fine,' she said, patting him on the shoulder. 'Now, get back to Clem and make the most of having the cottage to yourself.' She forced a smile.

'We'll try,' he laughed.

'Right,' she said, as the attendant handed her the boarding card, and returned her passport. 'That's me sorted. I'd better go. They're already calling my flight.'

He hugged her tightly. 'I love the thought of living at the cottage with your sister,' he added, a dreamy expression spreading across his face. 'I still think it's odd you going back to Sorrento though. I'd have thought that would be the last place you'd want to visit.'

Paige bit her bottom lip. 'It wasn't the first place I thought of going, but I did love it there and I think that as illogical as it may sound to you, if I can go back and have fun without Sebastian, then I think I'll have more chance of doing the same thing when I get home to Jersey.'

Olly scratched his head. 'That sounds odd, but typical of your logic.'

'You're a good friend,' she said. 'Now, go. Clem will be waiting for you.' Paige waved after him. 'Don't forget to look after her for me,' she said before turning and heading for Security, not daring to look back.

Paige was pleased the hotel she'd booked was comfortable. It wasn't as luxurious as the one where she and Sebastian had stayed during her previous trip, but although her room was smaller her bedroom shutters opened out to a perfect unfettered view of the Bay of Vesuvius.

'The hotel is literally built into the side of the cliff,' she told Clem a few days later over the phone. 'I can never moan about being scared of heights again after this.'

'I loved the photo you emailed to us of the scene you wake up to each morning.'

'It sounds blissful. I'm pleased you decided to go.'

So was she. 'Anything new in the papers I should know about?' When Clem didn't answer immediately, she sensed there might be something she wasn't telling her. 'Clem? Nothing's wrong, is it?'

'No,' Clem said, a little too cheerily.

'Hmm, I'm not sure I believe you.'

'It's only a bit more speculation about you and Sebastian, but no more stories about our family, thankfully. The shop is fine, so there's no need to worry about that. Go and visit ruins, or something.'

It was a little bittersweet returning to the same place where she'd experienced so many memorably romantic evenings with Sebastian. Although it was out of season and the sun had lost some of its strength, Paige still walked around wearing a thin cardigan over her cotton dress. Memories of Sebastian were around every corner, and the familiar smells of spices filled the air as she wandered on her own through the narrow back streets enjoying the fewer crowds, stopping every so often to look in to a shop.

Towards the end of her second week, Paige put down the novel she was struggling to read and walked out on to her balcony overlooking Marina Grande. She gazed down at the shabby little marina with the houses crammed into the small bay, some with faded and peeling paint next to others brightly redecorated, and felt an urge to take a stroll down to the water's edge.

She turned the last corner taking her down to the beach and conjured up pictures of 1950s movie stars frolicking in the shallow surf, or chatting over espressos with their photographer boyfriends. It was exactly how she imagined her grandparents had behaved in those far-off heady days when they toured the continent on a honeymoon filled with romance, and a belief that they could change the world for the better.

Breathing in the warm, salty air, Paige felt any

remaining tensions seep away as she took a seat at a weather-beaten table near the edge of the café terrace. She ordered a large mug of hot chocolate and leant back in her chair to stare out across the small wooden fishing boats, the fishermen adeptly checking nets, as the sea lapped gently near their feet.

'Did you seriously think I wouldn't come looking for you?'

Paige caught her breath at the sound of the familiar, deep voice. Her stomach flipped and for a second she thought she must have imagined him being there. She turned to face his broad-shouldered outline, shielding her eyes from the glare of the morning sun.

He watched her silently.

'Sebastian.'

He motioned to the waiter, ordering an espresso before sitting down opposite her. It was hard for her to read his expressionless face as he leant back.

She didn't know quite what to say. This hadn't been in her plans and she could feel her resolve weakening as she gazed at his handsome, although angry face.

'What are you doing here?' she asked eventually, trying to fill the heavy silence.

Seb raised his eyebrows. 'I've tried phoning you, and calling at your home not realising you weren't there to answer. I decided I might have a little more success if I spoke to you face to face,' he said not taking his eyes off her. 'So, here I am.'

She noticed the small muscle working in his jaw, as he clenched his teeth together. She understood his reaction, but didn't know what to say. 'What are you doing here?'

'I've just told you,' he said, his blue eyes piercing into her making her wish that the press weren't so interested in everything he did and he'd never met anyone called Lucinda, or at least that she was still harassing her lottery-winning boyfriend.

When he didn't elaborate, she continued. 'I needed to get away,' she said simply, looking out at the sea, not wishing to see the accusatory look in his eyes for a second longer than she had to, and definitely not wanting to let him see how much his presence had affected her.

Seb thanked the waiter and drank his espresso in one gulp. 'From me, I suppose.'

She chewed her lip thoughtfully. 'Not only you.'

He watched her for a moment. 'Well, if not me, then what? Come on, Paige. The last time we spoke you were too busy to go away with me.'

She picked up her mug, still bemused at him sitting opposite her, 'I suppose Clem gave in, and told you where I was,' she said, knowing she was avoiding his question.

'No, your sister's very loyal.'

Unlike me, thought Paige feeling bad for putting Clem in such an awkward situation, and having to deal with what she should have sorted out before leaving Jersey.

'There was no way she was going to tell me anything. She wouldn't even admit you'd left the island.'

Paige watched his mouth, trying not to remember how good those lips had felt against her own. She owed him an explanation, she knew she did, but felt foolish and unable to decide how best to explain her actions. 'Then how?'

'I said she was loyal. What I didn't say was how easy she is to read. Don't blame her though, she did try to cover for you. I still don't know why you left without mentioning you were going away. I told you I'd speak to the senior editor at the newspapers and work something out with them. I don't want your family brought into the spotlight any more than you do.'

'You did, but we both know that there'll be other occasions when they might have a quiet news day and go looking for scandal elsewhere in my family.' If only the papers didn't find his life so fascinating. 'I suppose I should have said something to you before leaving,' she said wondering if the slight raising of his eyebrows indicated anger, or surprise.

He leant forward, his face inches from hers, his voice quiet. 'Why do you keep running away from me?'

She glanced away, hoping for some relief from the intensity of his stare. It didn't work. 'I didn't,' she lied. 'I just needed to get away. A lot has happened over the past year, and I thought the best way to stop all this and work out what I want out of my life would be to get away from Jersey and everyone there.' She waited to see if he believed a word she said.

He frowned by way of a response and then stared at her for a moment. 'I was under the misapprehension that maybe I'd figure somewhere in that future.' His elbows on the table, he threaded his fingers together and rested his unshaven chin on them. 'What's wrong? Why do I always seem to be chasing you? I'm not going to do it forever, you know. I do have some pride, though not as much as I thought, obviously.' He leant back in his chair, as if his words had been a revelation to him too. 'I wish you'd trust me.'

Paige winced, not daring to repeat how she couldn't help thinking Lucinda had made a valid point about their lifestyles being so mismatched.

'In fact I can't believe I'm here.' He gave a bitter laugh. 'You're making me soft, Paige. Soon I won't recognize myself at all.' He sat upright, more agitated than she had ever seen him.

Unable to bear the look of confusion on his face, and aware she was the cause of him acting so out of character, Paige stretched her hand over the table, to stroke the side of his cheek. He did not move away from her touch, and the coolness of his skin on such a warm day surprised her.

'I'm sorry,' she said, aware she was making the most of what would probably be the last time she would be close enough to touch him so intimately. 'I've thought about it constantly, and I can't see how we can ever make it work between us.'

'No?' he asked, frowning. 'You're certain of that?'

She nodded. 'Our lives are poles apart. I might be able to push aside my need for privacy to be with you, but how long would it be until I resented the invasion into our lives?' She swallowed the lump in her throat.

'I told you, I'd find a way around this.'

'We both know that's impossible. I think we need to break things off before either of us gets hurt.' The thought of dragging out the agony of waiting for the moment when she had to walk away from him was too much. She stood up to leave.

'Running away again, Paige?' His eyes narrowed as he looked up at her. 'Aren't you even going to listen to what I have to say?'

'There isn't anything else you can say, is there?' she asked finally, a dull pain in her chest.

Seb stood up and walked up to her. 'Look at me, Paige. I agree there was some truth in what Lucinda said, but there's always a way around every problem, if you look hard enough.'

She shrugged. 'She's not the only one to think this way though; my father said the same thing. Everything about our lives is different, and as much as I feel for you, I can't be with you at the expense of my family's privacy.'

'And you won't give me the chance to come up with a solution?'

She shook her head miserably.

'This is ridiculous.' He raked a hand through his hair.

'I'd be grateful if you wouldn't follow me this time.'

'I won't, if that's what you want. You go,' he raised his voice after her as she turned and walked away. 'But whatever you may think, Paige, I love you and I'm not in the habit of giving up at the first sign of a problem, even if you are.'

Paige didn't look back. She wanted him so badly, but no matter what he said, it wouldn't change who they were.

Chapter Thirty-five

Seb clenched his fists as he watched Paige leave. He had to fight his instinct to follow her and make her listen to what he had to say. He knew though that if there was to be any hope for them at all, he needed to give her the freedom she craved to find out exactly what she did want from him, if anything. He couldn't force her to listen, although right now he was so frustrated with her for insisting on being left alone that all he could think about was finding a way to make her change her mind.

He suspected she still didn't trust that he no longer had feelings for Lucinda and wished Paige knew how much Lucinda repelled him. He was hard pushed to remember feeling anything much for her at all. He must have once, otherwise why go through the chaos that had been the preparations for their ridiculously flamboyant wedding that never finally happened.

It occurred to Sebastian that despite their other differences, both he and Paige had been jilted. He shook his head in amusement. It was time for him to get back to his meetings in Jersey and find a solution to this impasse.

Paige advised the hotel receptionist she would be leaving that afternoon. She didn't want to chance Sebastian coming looking for her again. She was going to continue with this trip, however tempting it was to return home. Carrying her bulging rucksack down to the marina later that day, she waited silently for the boat to take her on to the nearby island of Ischia.

As the small craft glided quietly towards the island, Paige sat on the wooden bench and gazed back at the magnificence of the turquoise sea across the Bay of Naples. The tiny terrace where she had so recently seen Sebastian caught her eye and it gave her a jolt to think how easy it would have been to let him take her in his arms. Paige shook the thought from her head. No. To do that would only delay the inevitable pain she was experiencing now. Lucinda had made it perfectly clear how much Paige had been kidding herself about her feelings for Sebastian, and she knew her own limitations.

At least this way, there wouldn't be any chance of her bumping into him again. She even persuaded herself that going to the island would cheer her up, especially as she had managed to find a room with a shopkeeper and his wife through the receptionist, before she left the hotel in Sorrento.

As soon as she stepped off the small wooden boat, Paige walked the ten or so steps to the shop door, and let herself in. The shopkeeper's wife clapped her hands together as she welcomed Paige inside. She called for her husband, who limped through from the back room and shook Paige's hand enthusiastically, the broad smile on his cheeky face confirming how thrilled he was to see her there.

The greetings over with, he led her down a long narrow corridor to a small, white room. Her temporary bedroom was at the back of the whitewashed building, overlooking a tiny, tranquil courtyard scattered with pots of brightly coloured plants and herbs. It was perfect.

Paige breathed in the familiar smell of the warm sand on the old floorboards. Yes, she decided immediately, she had made the right decision to get away.

Sitting down to have a black coffee with her new landlords, Paige made the best of her smattering of Italian and then spent her first day getting her bearings in the local area nearby.

She drifted off to sleep that night feeling more relaxed than she had felt for months, managing to push aside any nagging doubts about telling Sebastian they couldn't be together. If this is what people mean by taking stock of their lives, she decided, I've done the right thing coming to Ischia.

The following days were a calming blur for Paige. She kept in contact with Clem, as promised, and her sister assured her the shop was running smoothly and the stories in the papers were diminishing in size and moving further back, away from the front pages.

'Mind you,' Clemmie said during a quick phone call. 'Olly is driving me nuts with ideas for improvements for your website. It's so boring listening to him going on and on about it.'

'Tell him to do whatever he thinks best,' Paige told her.

She didn't hear from Sebastian, although she hadn't really expected to, and it was fine, or so she kept telling herself. Her skin slowly darkened from long relaxing walks in the sun. For once Paige began to feel as though she was regaining some of the natural zest for life her family had always admired in her.

She got to know a few of the locals when they popped in to the shop for a chat. They, in turn, invited her to join them for a meal at their homes. Best of all she enjoyed beginning and ending each day with a swim in the cool sea at the nearby beach. She enjoyed letting her mind wander as she explored the nooks and crannies of the island, keeping up to date with her suppliers by email at the antiquated internet café in by the marina.

Paige visited the other villages, on one trip picking up a colourful painting of her favourite cove unexpectedly cheaply, so small it could fit into the palm of her hand. Then, one morning, towards the end of her trip, she caught sight of her reflection in the mirror, and barely recognized the face looking back at her. She was surprised how refreshed she appeared, with no visible signs of stress on her face. She liked what she saw for once, and sighed contentedly. It was time to go home.

'Ooh, I can't believe you're actually here, it feels like you've been away for longer than two weeks.' Clemmie hugged her sister tightly, as soon as Paige stepped out into the Arrivals Hall. 'You look amazing. In fact, I don't think I've ever seen you look so gorgeous.'

'Thanks, I feel really well,' she said honestly, choked to note how much she had missed her sister. She raised her eyebrows and pointed at Clem's bump. 'Look at this.' Paige said, touching the loose cotton top resting over her sister's stomach.

'I know, I'm suddenly beginning to look pregnant rather than just fat,' she grimaced.

'Rubbish,' Paige laughed. 'And I'll bet that's not what Olly says either, is it?'

Clem's cheeks reddened. 'No, he always tells me how sexy I look.'

'That's because he adores you.' Paige linked arms with her sister and let her lead her to the car. 'I can't believe you're nearly five months pregnant.'

On the way back to the cottage, she began to fill Paige in on all the local gossip. There was nothing new to tell her about the shop, as thanks to Olly keeping her up to date, Clem had repeated all his news through their intermittent emails. 'Olly told me Sebastian is rarely at De Greys at the moment.'

'Where's he now?' She tried her best to sound as disinterested as possible. She knew her sister well enough to realise that if she did not react to her comment, Clem would instinctively know something had happened since she last saw her.

'They say he spends a lot of time working from his

office at home, and Olly reckons he's in London quite a bit too. As soon as the old tenants moved out and freed up the floor space they immediately filled it with less luxurious franchises. The locals are thrilled because they can shop for things they used to only be able to get online. It's a little weird though.'

'It's sad to think of De Greys changing so much,' Paige mused. 'The little family shops oozed much more character than the larger concessions.'

Clem nodded, changing down a gear to overtake the car in front. 'I know what you mean, but I hate to admit, Sebastian was right you know, despite what we all thought.'

'Olly tells me the takings are up in every department now, so I guess he knew what he was doing.'

Clem smiled at her. 'I know we all resented him for forcing changes at De Greys, but with the new branding, décor, and general all-round facelift, it's a fashionable place to be seen in once again. You can't get a table for lunch at the restaurant there for love nor money,' continued Clem. 'Whereas before we all knew how much they were struggling to fill the place.'

Paige chewed her lower lip. 'That is impressive.'

'And your shop has been doing better than ever, so it's turned out well for you, too.'

'I suppose so.'

'And it's all down to his vision and determination,' Clem added. 'We have a lot to thank him for. I feel quite mean now having been so horrible about him when he first arrived on the scene.'

'Well, don't,' Paige said. 'He'll also be making money out of this venture.'

'I know, but you have to admit he wasn't the evil sod we all assumed him to be.'

'No, he isn't.'

Olly was waiting for them back at the cottage with a pot of stew simmering on the cooker.

'I thought I'd ease you back into the Jersey lifestyle slowly,' he said, giving her a hug. 'A nice stew should do the trick for tonight.' He took a knife from the drawer and began sawing through two baguettes. 'I bought these from the market earlier today. Smell delicious, don't you think?'

Paige smiled instantly glad to be back at home again. She picked up the large glass of Merlot he was pointing to, grateful for his thoughtfulness. 'Well it doesn't look like you've caused too much damage here,' she laughed, glancing around the tidy room.

'None actually.' Olly gave her a smug look to try and cover his nervous manner, which Paige hadn't missed. 'Are you sure you don't mind us staying in your spare room? Only I can't face the thought of moving away from Clem and back to my parents' place next door. I'm kind of used to bunking up with an expanding woman.'

'Cheeky bugger,' Clem said, entering the kitchen and flicking on the kettle. She took a mug from the cupboard and spooned in coffee and sugar.

'I don't think I could sleep nearly as well without her.'

'But you were only living ten yards away from my front door.' Paige couldn't help teasing, but wasn't sure how the three of them were going to manage living in the small cottage on a permanent basis. 'And you know you can come and go as you please.'

He stuck out his lower lip. 'Stop torturing me. Can I stay, or what?'

Paige hung up her cotton jacket. 'Go on then. I can see when I'm outnumbered, but I don't know how we'll all fit in here when the baby's born.'

'Me neither,' Clem said, stroking her stomach.

Paige leant back against the worktop and drank some wine, relishing the cool sweetness of it. 'OK, here's the compromise. You keep the majority of your belongings at your parents' house, Ol, as I just don't have the space for any more clothes, books, and all the other bits of paraphernalia you seem to collect.'

He hugged her. 'That's why you're my closest friend.'

'Hey.' Clem punched him playfully on the shoulder. 'What about me?'

'You're the woman I love.' He rubbed his shoulder better. 'Shit, you pack one hell of a punch for a …'

'For a what?'

Paige stepped between them. 'Hey, let's not have a fight, just when I've agreed for you to stay here together.'

Olly took Clem in his arms. 'Sorry, babes.'

'That's better.' Paige shook her head. 'Right, tell me all the news I've missed since I've been away. There must be something you haven't told me.'

Paige took a couple of days to acclimatizing to being back in Jersey before returning to the shop. She tried to tell herself it didn't matter that she would no longer be seeing Seb, but failed. It was good to open a paper and not see her own face looming back at her from the front page, and Olly's ideas had given her something to focus on. She was extremely impressed with the ideas for the website she had come up with during her stay in Ischia.

At the end of her first day back in the shop, Paige said goodbye to her last client, and sat down behind the counter, slipping off first one of her heels, then the other. 'I can't believe how tired I am,' she said, rubbing her aching feet with her hand. 'But I'm beginning to feel like I'm getting somewhere with this business,' she said over her shoulder as Clem counted the takings. 'Is that a little presumptuous?'

'Not at all,' Clem replied. 'You have a good name for yourself now. Don't you notice how many "ladies who lunch" wear your shoes when they're out and about, because I certainly have. So has Ol.'

'So have I,' said a voice from the doorway.

Paige caught her breath unable to stop from glancing at him. Trying to compose herself, she found it hard to believe that after all her good intentions, three simple words spoken so quietly could have such a profound effect on her.

'I'll get going then.' Clem widened her eyes and grinned at Paige. She hurriedly grabbed the takings pushing them haphazardly into a cloth bag and quickly locked the till. 'I'll see you back at home?'

Paige nodded, and watched in silence as her sister smiled at Seb, mumbling a thank you as he held the door open for her, closing it once she had made her hasty retreat.

He turned and fixed his gaze on Paige. 'So, you're back then?'

Chapter Thirty-six

Paige stood up, and couldn't help noticing the unfamiliar dark circles under Sebastian's eyes. He looked exhausted.

'I am.' She swallowed in an attempt to moisten her dry mouth. 'Hello, Sebastian. How are you?' she asked trying to be friendly, and not wanting him to see the state she was in.

'I'm fine.' He did not elaborate, or attempt to add anything else to his comment, and stared down at her as she fiddled absentmindedly with a large silver and turquoise bangle on her wrist.

After a moment's awkward silence between them, Paige cleared her throat. 'I gather from my sister that you're rarely at De Greys any more. I've also heard great reports regarding your improvements there.' Why didn't he speak, she wondered. She was running out of things to say, and was worried that if she wasn't careful she'd lose her resolve and end up flinging herself back into his arms.

He didn't return her smile. 'I'm only needed there occasionally now, but thanks for the compliment. The feedback has been mainly positive.'

'If their takings are up as much as mine, I don't see how they can possibly disapprove.' She pushed her feet back into her shoes, adding several inches to her height, then, picking up her bag and keys, walked past him out of the door and waited for him to follow. Locking the door behind them, she selected her car key from the bunch in her hand. 'You've done a great job, Sebastian,' she said, unnerved by his silence. 'I was wrong to doubt you.'

He raised his eyebrows imperceptibly. 'Generous words, indeed.'

Paige smiled to soften her words. 'Well, I can't hold it against you forever. After all, if it wasn't for you giving me notice, I wouldn't be building up my own shop as I'm doing now.'

'I always knew your designs were too superior not to become successful.'

'Thank you,' Paige stood still and studied him. His hair seemed longer than she had seen him wear it before, curling over the top of his pristine white collar. She wanted to push back a strand falling over his forehead, but stopped from touching him, just before their skin made contact. For once, he was not the immaculate Sebastian she was used to. She wished he didn't still have the same gut-wrenching effect on her, despite constantly insisting to herself that she was getting over him.

He looked into her eyes, the intensity of his gaze making her heart beat a little faster. He lowered his head slightly. She went to move back from him. 'Sebastian,' she said, becoming aware that they were now in the cobbled street. 'Nothing has changed since we last spoke in Sorrento.'

'Come home with me. We need to talk things through properly.'

She wanted to resolve this with him and was tempted. 'Well, I …' Her phone rang and although she tried to ignore it for a bit, the fact that it kept ringing stopped her from concentrating on what she was trying to say. She sighed heavily, and pulled her phone out of her bag. She saw Olly's name on the screen and answered the call. 'I'd better take this. Hi, Ol.'

'Is everything OK?' Sebastian asked quietly.

Paige shook her head. She listened to Olly for a minute. 'I'll be right there,' she said ending the call. 'Sorry, a bit of an emergency with Clem. I'm going to have to go.'

'Is there anything I can to do help?' he asked. Paige shook her head.

'No, but thank you.'

They soon reached her car. She unlocked the door and he held it open for her, closing it as soon as she was seated. He bent down to the window. 'Call me.'

Paige nodded and turned on the ignition.

She arrived home to find Olly leaning over Clem, soothing her and holding out a half-empty box of tissues as she lay draped across the settee. He looked up, his eyes wide with fright, and gave Paige a pleading look.

'Whatever's the matter?' She dropped her bag and coat to hurry over next to her prone sister. She sat down next to her. 'Clem, look at me. What's the matter?' Her sister rarely cried. Paige could not remember ever seeing her so inconsolable.

'Olly,' sniffed her sister, blowing her pink nose on another Kleenex. 'You tell her. I can't bear to,' She grimaced, pointing at a messy pile of magazines.

Olly shook his head. 'What?'

'Never mind,' Clem said, blowing her nose and sniffing. 'Tell Paige what happened.'

'What's the matter? Are you hurt?' She stared at him waiting for him to answer. 'Olly, is she hurt? Is the baby OK? Tell me.'

He stood up, his legs shaky and walked over to stand in front of the fireplace. 'Now Paige, promise you won't panic,' he said, holding his hand out in front of him.

She felt sick to her stomach. 'I'm already doing that.'

He clenched his fists either side of his legs. 'Clem's had a little bleeding,' he said, his voice quiet.

Clem howled in anguish.

Paige took her hand and squeezed it tightly. 'I'm sure it's OK,' she soothed. 'How badly?' she asked Olly.

'We're not exactly sure,' he said, looking so pale Paige was concerned he was about to pass out. 'The doctor is on his way now.' He seemed to find a little resolve and glanced down at Clem. 'He said you were to remain as calm as possible, babes.'

'How can I?' Clem cried, pushing her tearful face into Paige's chest. 'I'm going to lose my baby.'

'You don't know that,' Paige assured her, having no idea if she was right or not.

'And it will be my own fault.'

Paige held her sister away and placing a finger under Clem's damp chin raised it up. 'Look at me,' she said, forcing her voice to remain steady. 'We don't know anything until the doctor's seen you, but whatever he says, you must remember that this isn't your fault. Do you understand me?'

'But after all the things I've said,' she looked at Olly. 'I was going to have a termination. I was going to get rid of our baby, Ol.'

He crossed the room in one movement and took her in his arms. 'Angel, you mustn't talk like that. You were only trying to figure out what to do, nothing more. And you kept the baby after all, didn't you?'

'But look what's happened,' she sobbed. 'I'm losing my baby, I know it.'

Paige moved back to give Olly space on the sofa. 'You don't know that,' she soothed. 'How long ago did you phone the doctor?'

'Fifteen minutes. He should be here soon.'

Paige checked her watch and hearing a car on the gravel, raced to open the front door. 'She's in here,' she called, her voice choking with emotion.

Paige and Olly left the doctor to examine Clem, and within moments, he was out in the hall trying his best to reassure them. 'She needs to keep her feet up and rest,' he said pushing his round tortoiseshell glasses up his narrow nose. 'Above all, she must try and remain calm. It won't do her or the baby any good for her to carry on being upset in this way.'

'We'll make sure she does,' said Paige. 'And the baby, do you think it will be OK?'

'I don't think it's as bad as she fears, but we can't tell just yet. I'll arrange a scan for her in a couple of days, by then we should be able to get a better prognosis.'

'Is there anything we have to look out for,' asked Paige, feeling Olly's anguish as he listened to the doctor's words.

'The bleeding has stopped for the moment.'

'If the bleeding starts again, call me immediately,' the doctor said, 'but above all, please try and remain as calm and supportive to Clementine as possible. She doesn't need you two fretting. She's doing enough of that for everyone.'

He passed Paige his card. 'These are my emergency numbers. If there's a problem, call me on one of these.' He squeezed her hand. 'Don't worry, my dear, I'm sure everything will be fine. Try and get some rest. I'll pop in again in the morning.'

'Thank you,' Paige said, showing him out.

She followed her sister upstairs, assuring her that if the doctor thought there was any immediate problem, he would have arranged for her to go straight to hospital.

Paige waited until Clem was cleaning her teeth and took Olly to one side. 'Olly, promise you'll wake me straight away if she gets in a state,' she lowered her voice. 'Or if anything else happens.'

Olly nodded. 'Of course.'

'It'll be fine,' she said, rubbing his hunched shoulders. 'Don't you get in a state too, she needs us to stay strong for her, remember?'

She stared at him, waiting for his reply. 'Well?'

'Yes, of course, but it's bloody frightening.'

'I know it is,' she agreed, saddened to see him so anxious. 'But if it's this grim for us, you can only imagine what Clem's going through right now.'

Olly shrugged. 'Shit, I'm a selfish sod.'

'No, you're not. Now stop wallowing, and go and give her a cuddle.'

Clem caught them chatting. 'Hey. What are you two nattering about? Did the doctor tell you something?'

Paige could hear the panic rising in Clem's voice, and crossed the room with what she hoped was a confident smile on her face. She gave her sister a hug. 'Don't be daft,' she said, pulling back the duvet and waiting for her sister to get into bed. 'Now settle down and get some rest. Everything will be fine, you'll see.' She covered her sister and walked to the door. 'I don't know about you two, but I'm exhausted. I'll see you in the morning.'

Paige's smile disappeared as soon as she left the spare room. Sitting down heavily on the edge of her double bed, she thought how loving someone could cause you so much heartache and pain. Then, picturing Olly and her sister comforting each other and so much in love, Paige knew she would give anything to go back to Sebastian. She felt very much alone.

Her feelings of serenity from her holiday had dissipated in the midst of this unexpected drama, and already felt a lifetime ago. Lying in her bedroom later that night, she pictured Sebastian's tense face in the blackness. She could see him as clearly as if he were standing in front of her. She missed him and for a moment she envied her sister and Olly's relationship. How could she be selfish enough to feel jealous of her younger sister being with the man she loved, and expecting his baby, especially with what was happening right now? Why did she torture herself like this? Paige heard her sister and Olly's muted voices from the next room and sighed. The sound made her smile. Maybe everything was going to be fine after all.

Olly phoned Paige as soon as Clem's ultrasound

appointment had finished. 'They found a heartbeat,' he said, his voice tight. 'Thank God, it was just a false alarm. Clem is so relieved we decided not to mention it to your parents for now. Imagine how dreadful it would have been to have worried them too.'

'Doesn't bear thinking about,' Paige said, smiling at the thought and thanking him for letting her know everything was back on track.

'I could sleep for a bloody week right now,' Olly said.

'You're not the only one.' Paige pictured her sister's relief. She stifled a yawn just in time to spot two women entering the shop.

'I've come to try on these,' said one of them dangling a pair of Paige's highest high heels from her fingers. 'In a size seven.'

'So,' said the immaculate blonde to her friend, as Paige returned from the storeroom, shoebox in hand. 'When is the big day? Do you know?' Paige took the shoes carefully from the tissue paper, placing them in front of their stocking feet.

'I only know what the article said in the paper the other day. I think it's sometime later in the year, but you can't help admire Lucinda.' Paige tensed instantly, certain they glanced at each other over her head. 'What nerve, dumping someone as glorious as Sebastian Fielding, then having the nerve to come back two years later when he's inherited God knows how many millions, and setting her sights on him for a second time.'

'And succeeding,' laughed the first woman, standing up and walking across the room to admire her reflection in the full-length mirror. She turned her feet to check them at every angle and then addressed Paige. 'Yes, these are perfect. I'll have them.'

Paige didn't think she recognized either of them, but could not be sure. She decided she was probably being a little paranoid, and it could simply be bad luck to have them gossiping about Seb in her shop. She didn't react, but couldn't help listening.

'Do you know him?' One of them asked, following Paige to the till.

'Sorry?' Paige played for time taking the shoes from her. She busied herself by packing them carefully in their box, then into a large cardboard carrier bag with her logo printed across the middle.

The women looked sideways at each other, and Paige instinctively knew that Lucinda had in some way orchestrated this little scenario. She wasn't surprised, just taken aback that she thought Paige such a threat to still be bothering about her.

'Sebastian Fielding. He's getting back together with Lucinda Barrow-Hughes, I imagine they'll be married in no time at all. I would have thought you knew him. You used to work at De Greys, didn't you?'

Paige forced what she hoped was a convincing smile onto her face. 'My shop used to be there, yes.'

'Until you had to leave?' The blonde tilted her head to one side.

Paige refused to give them the satisfaction of seeing they were having any effect on her at all. 'Something like that.'

'So you do know him then?' asked the other woman, looking very smug.

'Yes.' Paige smiled sweetly to each of them, handing the bag over with the woman's credit card and receipt. 'The shoes look so flattering on you. I hope you enjoy wearing them.' If Lucinda's friends wanted to upset her, buying her stock was the wrong way to go about it. Paige chewed her lip to stop from smiling.

Each looked at the other, then back at Paige. She could tell they were aware they had just been dismissed, however politely. She watched them leave, the cheerful smile fixed to her face, as they made their way down the road laughing loudly.

'What's the story, morning glory?' Olly asked, snapping her out of her reverie.

Paige shook her head.

'What?'

'I've just had a visit from a couple of Lucinda's friends.'

'Did they buy anything?'

Paige nodded. 'Yes. They were so busy trying to put me down that they ended up buying one of my more expensive designs.'

'Hah, good for you.'

She narrowed her eyes. 'It's not lunchtime yet, why aren't you at work?'

'They let me have time off to go to the hospital with Clem, so I thought I'd call in and see how you were doing.' He folded his arms and leant back against the counter.

'I'm fine,' she smiled. 'So you can get back to work before you're fired. You need all the money you can get now you're preparing for parenthood.'

'Not until you make me a tea and tell Uncle Oliver exactly what they said to you.'

'It's not worth repeating.' She could see that the trauma of watching her sister have a threatened miscarriage had unsettled him, and he needed something to keep his mind occupied. 'My online sales,' she said, folding her arms across her chest, delighted to have the perfect solution. 'We still have a few issues that need tightening up. I noticed some of the links to the sizes are a little odd.'

He cheered up instantly. 'Yes, I forgot all about that.'

'Fine, so when can I expect you to sort it out?' she asked, knowing he liked working to deadlines.

'With everything that's happened, I'm a bit behind, but I promise I'll crack on tonight, as soon as I get back to your place,' he said, excitement lighting up his face.

'Great,' she giggled. 'Hopefully it'll start earning us decent some money.'

Olly stopped smiling. 'How am I going to make money out of it? You don't have any spare cash to pay me to set up the site, and I wouldn't accept any if you did.'

'I know, and that's why,' she thought, deciding on an idea that had occurred to her only days before, 'I'm giving you a percentage of the online sales.'

'Seriously?'

Paige laughed at his stunned expression. 'Yes. I'll get something drawn up between us, but I was thinking you two could have twenty per cent of the online net profit.'

'Me and Clem?'

'Who else?'

'Twenty, but that's massive,' he shouted, his eyes lighting up at the unexpected offer.

'Not really,' said Paige, now in official mode. 'The site I had was ridiculously amateurish, and would never have worked in the way I need it to. You've set the new site up for me, and you'll be responsible for sorting out any technical hitches, updates, that sort of thing. I'll need Clem to deal with any orders, invoices and payments.' She winked at him. 'Giving you both an interest in the business will save me paying to do all these things.'

'Clem did mention something about running the site from home when she's had the baby,' he said thoughtfully. 'It sounds good to me.'

'Great,' Paige said, happy to have sorted everything out so easily. 'I'll get a contract drawn up in the next few days and we can all sign it.'

'Contract? Is that necessary?'

'I won't do it without one.' She looked at him and loved that he trusted her so completely. 'This is a business agreement and we each have to protect our interests, whether we're friends, relatives, or whatever. It's the only way to safeguard the finer details and ensure they've been covered.'

He looked happier than she could ever remember seeing him. 'OK, bring it on.'

Chapter Thirty-seven

'So? What's the verdict then?' Olly asked, as Paige reviewed the order spreadsheet for her first day's sales.

Clem tucked her legs under herself and glanced at the bottom line of the figures. 'It's been bloody brilliant.' She pointed at the computer screen. 'I've also been contacted through the site by someone who you met in a shop in Sorrento. She said that you'd swapped shoes with her, or something?'

Paige thought back to the young shop assistant who she'd given her sandals to. 'I wondered if she'd ever get back to me. Did she want to make an order?'

Clem nodded. 'Yes, but it's only a tiny one and I think it's for her personally rather than for the shop.'

'It all helps,' Paige said, delighted the girl still obviously liked her designs. She ran her finger down the columns filled with figures and stock references. 'It's better than I'd ever dared hope.' She sat back, chewing the top of her pen absent-mindedly. 'I can't believe it. The best sellers are the thigh-high boots.'

Olly rolled his eyes heavenward. 'Why does that surprise you so much?' He turned to his girlfriend and winked. 'I wouldn't mind seeing you in a pair of those again, Clem.'

'Don't hold your breath,' she said, lifting up her swollen ankles in his direction. 'I'd be lucky to get sandals on over these things.'

Olly went over to her. 'My poor little puffer fish – ouch!' he said when she elbowed him in the ribs. 'What did you do that for?'

'Bugger off and let me finish this paperwork.'

'Ol,' Paige said, waving him over. 'Let's leave Clem alone for a bit and you can give me a lift to the shop, if that's OK with you?'

'I don't know why she's working on all that so early,' he said to Paige as they drove towards town. 'She could have left it for later.'

Paige shook her head. 'Ol, you saw her feet. Clem's best time of the day is morning, and although she doesn't like to go on about it, I think she's getting uncomfortable now she's heavier, especially as the day goes on.'

'She did say something about having a nap some afternoons.' The idea seemed to worry him. 'Do you think she's all right by herself, or should I go back and check on her?'

'I think the best thing we can do is leave her in peace. Let her make the most of some alone time before the baby arrives. She'll phone if she needs anything.'

'True.'

'Right, now go to work. You don't want to be fired, do you?'

Olly grimaced, 'I'll come and get you at closing time, give you a lift home.'

Paige was relieved that the day went quickly, with several excited phone calls from Clem each time a new order was placed online.

'That's great,' Paige said, relieved their new venture was going so well. 'But you're supposed to be taking it easy. I hope you're checking the orders from the sofa?'

'Of course I am,' Clem groaned.

Paige stopped sketching the designs she was working on. She put down her pencil. 'Good, because I don't want Olly giving me a hard time.'

'No, I suppose not.'

'Brilliant.' She put down the phone and checked her

watch. It would soon be time to close up anyway. She was relieved to have so much to concentrate on. She began altering the angle to the heel on one of the sketches when Olly bounded in, like an over-excited Labrador puppy.

'Hey, slow down a bit. What's the hurry?' she asked when he only just managed to stop before crashing into one of the displays.

He snatched the pencil from her hand and slammed it down on the counter grinning from ear to ear. 'You'll never guess what I've just found out!'

Paige sat up and folded her arms. 'I can see by the look of satisfaction on your face that you have gossip you're dying to pass on.'

'Oh, I do,' he said, the enthusiasm in his voice unmistakable.

'No doubt it's fascinating stuff?' She raised an eyebrow, loving Olly's childlike excitement.

'It is.' He leant forward over the counter towards her. 'I've had to sort out problems with some of the software on Sebastian Fielding's secretary's computer.'

'Not exciting quite yet, Ol.' She teased, pulling a face at him.

'It will be if you just listen and stop interrupting me.' He linked his fingers together and cracked them back. 'I went up to the office to find out what the problem was and she told me a document was frozen. Guess what page it was frozen on?'

'I've no idea.' Paige tried to concentrate, but was having difficulty getting the angle of her heel from her mind. 'Go on.'

'Well,' Olly said, glancing over his shoulder when the shop door opened. 'Shit. I'll wait out here.' He raced out to the storeroom, as if he'd just been caught doing something naughty, which, thought Paige, was probably the case.

She looked up, surprised to see Sebastian standing in

front of her. 'Sebastian? What brings you here?' she asked, thinking how uncomfortable he seemed.

'I thought you were going to give me a call,' he said, his eyes humourless.

'Yes, sorry. I've been tied up with the shop, and the re-launch of the site.'

'You think I'm all talk, like that ex of yours seems to have been.'

Paige was conscious that Olly was listening to everything they were saying, and tried to feign disinterest.

'I was going to call you,' she said.

'You don't trust me to work this out, do you?'

She couldn't lie to him. 'I don't want to put myself through any more heartache than I've already had to deal with this year.'

'So, you expect me to accept that we should end our relationship?' He narrowed his eyes. 'And what if I disagree with you?'

'I'd say that for once, Sebastian, someone else is making a decision about your life. I have to think of my family.'

Sebastian stared at her for a few seconds. 'As do I, Paige.' He turned and walked out of the shop, shutting the door quietly behind him.

Immediately Olly reappeared from the storeroom. 'What the fuck did you do that for?'

'What?' Paige jumped, taken aback by his uncharacteristic anger. Olly never swore at her. 'What have I done?'

Olly rubbed his face roughly with his hands. 'Bloody hell, that's what I came to tell you.'

She shook her head, confused. 'I've no idea what you're going on about, but I wish you'd hurry up and tell me.'

'The files I was telling you about before, the page that was frozen open. Well, it was his.' He motioned towards the door.

Paige stepped up on the stool behind the counter. 'Go on,' she said, intrigued to find out what Olly had discovered.

'I'm not sure how to say this, so I'll just spit it out. He's been subsidising your rent here.'

Paige sat bolt upright. 'What did you say?'

'You heard.'

'Sebastian has? I don't understand,' Surely Olly was mistaken. She chewed her lower lip trying to let this unexpected news sink in. 'No, you must be wrong.'

'It's true. Sebastian's secretary went off to make a cup of tea, but before she left she told me that the information was strictly confidential, and that I couldn't repeat anything I'd seen, blah, blah, blah. I had time to double check the information on the document before she came back to her desk,' he added guiltily.

'He'd fire you if he ever found out.' She couldn't believe Olly had done something to endanger his job. 'What did it say exactly?'

He looked thrilled. 'I knew you'd want to know. Apparently, the company you lease this building from is one of his.'

'Are you sure?' she asked, thinking back to the contract agreement and knowing she didn't recognize the landlord's company on it. 'No, Ol, it can't be. I'd have noticed something like that.'

'What? You checked it out, did you?' he asked. 'Your lease is with a holding company. Sebastian is the sole director of the company that owns 100 per cent shares in the holding company, therefore he owns this property.' Olly watched Paige shake her head. 'He actually owns several holding companies, one of which has Sara's restaurant.' He paused for a moment to let this next piece of information sink in. 'Another owns this place. He is, in effect, your landlord, once removed, or something like that.'

Paige could not believe what she was being told. 'But it doesn't make sense,' she said, her voice barely above a stunned whisper.

'Yes it does. In fact, far from being the mercenary shit we all thought him to be, he's been secretly supporting your shop behind the scenes.'

'By how much?' she murmured, wanting to be angry for this deception, while at the same time knowing he had been instrumental in giving her the chance to strike out on her own and become independent.

'It looks like he charged you enough so you'd assume you had to push yourself to make the payments, but not so much that you couldn't cope.'

'I don't believe it.' She was glad to be sitting down, her legs seemed to have turned to jelly. 'And Sara?'

Olly shrugged. 'Who knows? Maybe she's a friend he wanted to help out. Does it really matter that much?'

'No, it doesn't.' Then a thought occurred to her. 'I think he's gone for good this time.'

Olly nodded. 'I heard. So, what are you going to do about it?'

She stared at Olly trying to work out what to do next. 'What do you mean?'

'Come on, Paige. You heard the man. He's spent months trying to get you to try again with your relationship. Granted, we all thought he was a self-centred posh git, but it seems that he isn't how we thought him to be at all.'

Paige thought about him subsidising her shop. 'He didn't expect me to ever find out about this place either, did he?'

'No. He obviously wasn't trying to score points with you.' Olly sighed. 'And look how he helped that kid, the boxer who had that accident. That jockey, too. Come along, Paige think about it, before it's too late.' Olly leant against the wall and crossed his arms.

'What is it?' she asked.

He started to laugh. 'I have a confession to make.'

Paige pulled a face. 'Another one?'

'You know the other night when Clem was in tears and was trying to get me to tidy up the magazines at your house?'

Paige vaguely recalled something to do with the messy pile. 'What about them?'

'She was trying to hide an article in the Glitz magazine about Lucinda and Sebastian Fielding getting married. I think it was a story sold by "a close confidante of Lucinda's".'

'Ah,' Paige sighed, picturing Lucinda's friends from the shop the day before. 'Really, what is wrong with that woman?'

'What is wrong with you, you mean?'

Paige stood up and glared at him. 'Hey!'

'No, it's true. The man does all this on the quiet, the shop I mean, and you still don't believe he's worth your trust.'

Paige chewed her lower lip. She wanted more than anything to be able to do exactly what Olly suggested. 'It's not that easy, I have to think of Bea and the rest of my family getting caught up in his world.' She blinked back tears. 'Anyway, if I phone him, he'll wonder why I've suddenly changed my mind about him. I can't tell him how I know, can I?'

Olly sighed. 'Bollocks, I hadn't thought of that. I suppose not.' He gave her a hug. 'Maybe I shouldn't have told you, then you'd be none the wiser about what he's done. I wish you could tell him.'

'I'm not getting you fired. You need your job at De Greys, especially now,' she said, wishing there was a way around her dilemma. 'If only I'd known this before he came in here this afternoon maybe I could have handled

313

things differently.'

'Timing has never been my strong point,' Olly murmured, looking downcast.

'Nor mine.' Paige wished she could turn the clock back ten minutes. He was helping me all the time, she mused and I never gave him a chance. He'd left believing she was glad to see the back of him.

Sebastian was proud, and she knew she had turned her back on him for the last time. The realisation stung. Paige dare not admit as much to Olly, but fervently wished he had not found out about Sebastian being her landlord. Somehow it made matters far worse knowing she had underestimated him so badly.

'Sod it, Ol, what have I done?' she asked, stunned by this new development. Paige lowered her face into her hands. 'I've been such a fool.'

'Sweets,' he said, taking her in his arms and cuddling her. 'Don't do this to yourself. It's hardly surprising you didn't believe him, even your father warned you off him, so why would you ever think differently?'

'Because I know him better than Dad does, that's why.' She looked up at Olly. 'And because I love him, and should have at least had the courage to give him the benefit of the doubt.'

'Hey, it's not all your fault. There is some good news.' Olly let her go.

'What?' sniffed Paige unable to imagine what it could possibly be.

'His jockey will be able to compete again and Elusive Goddess is on the mend.'

Paige couldn't help feeling a little better to hear this news. 'I'm so relieved,' she said. 'Thanks for telling me. Now you'd better get back to De Greys before you're missed.'

Chapter Thirty-eight

'Where's Ol?' asked Paige when she walked into the living room. 'He's usually here by now.'

Clem pulled the cushion from behind her back and hit it a few times before replacing it. 'He phoned a while ago, said he had to work a bit later tonight.'

'Strange, he never said anything when he came to the shop earlier.'

'Maybe it was a last-minute thing,' Clem said. 'That Sebastian Fielding is a slave driver when he wants a project finished.'

Paige shrugged. 'I suppose that's why he's so successful.' She took off her coat and hung it on the coat stand by the front door. 'He works far harder than he expects anyone else to.' She returned to see Clem trying to stifle a giggle. 'What's so funny?'

Clem gave in, and laughed loudly, holding her side until she managed to contain herself. 'You're very defensive of him all of a sudden, aren't you?'

'No.'

'You know you are, so don't try to deny it.'

'Coffee?' Paige asked, changing the subject and trying not to smile as she left the room. 'Anyway, he's not all bad.'

'Hello, honey, I'm home,' Olly sang, banging the front door shut loudly and striding along the hallway.

'Where've you been?' Paige asked stepping up behind him and making him jump.

'Shit, don't do that?'

Paige narrowed her eyes. 'You're a little nervy tonight.'

'No, I'm not.' He pulled a face and went through to see Clem. 'How's my poor suffering girlfriend today?'

Paige went back into the kitchen to finish making the drinks. It was a relief that the two of them had finally made up, she mused, taking an extra cup from the overhead cupboard, but it did make her feel a little like she was intruding in their love nest.

Paige sat nursing her cooling mug. 'I'm glad you're feeling much better now,' she said to Clem as she snuggled up to Olly on the sofa. 'Do you think you'll enjoy looking after the online sales?'

'Definitely.'

'You won't get a little bored being stuck here by yourself all day?'

Clem giggled. 'I won't be by myself, though, will I?' She took Olly's hand and stroked her stomach lightly. 'I'll have company that's probably going to keep me extremely busy, especially for the first few months.'

Paige nodded. 'True. How could I forget?' She smiled. 'Who's that?' she groaned, hearing someone knocking heavily on the front door.

Olly and Clem looked at her, but didn't move. 'Fine, I'll get it.' She sighed and walked through to the front door. 'What are you doing here?' she asked when she pulled the door back and revealed Sebastian standing on her doorstep, a determined expression on his face. She stepped back to let him in.

'I've come to collect you,' he said.

'Why? Where are we going?' Paige turned to find Olly and Clem standing behind her. 'What?' she said, noticing a mischievous glint in Olly's eyes.

'Pack a bag. You're coming with me.' Sebastian said, taking her mug from her and passing it to Olly.

'Where to?' Excitement began bubbling deep within

her stomach. 'What do I need?'

'At least she's not arguing,' she heard Olly whisper to her sister.

'There's always a first time for everything,' Clem giggled.

Ignoring them, she studied Sebastian's face. 'What's this all about?'

'Olly came to my office earlier and we had a brief chat.'

Paige's eyes widened and she glanced over her shoulder at Olly.

'It's all right, he's told me everything,' Seb said.

Paige daren't say anything in case Seb wasn't talking about the computer incident, and was referring to something else.

'It's true. He knows about me seeing the spreadsheet on his computer.'

Paige sighed with relief. 'And you're not going to fire him?'

'Thanks for putting the idea into his head,' Ol said. 'For once just shut up and listen.'

Sebastian laughed, taking Paige by her shoulders. 'Stop looking so concerned. I'm not going to fire my best IT man. However, I am taking you away with me for the weekend.'

'But…'

'No "buts".'

Paige shook her head. 'Where are we going?'

'I'm not telling you, you'll have to trust me. Do you?' He stared at her with such intensity she knew he wasn't just referring to the weekend ahead of them.

Paige nodded. 'Yes, I do.'

Sebastian smiled. 'Finally,' he murmured into her ear, so only she could hear.

Paige smiled. 'But what about the shop?'

Sebastian laughed. 'Olly has offered to look after it for

you. He doesn't work for me on Saturdays, so will be free to stand in for you tomorrow.'

Paige smiled, and turned to Olly. 'Your penance?'

He nodded, holding his hands up in surrender. 'I didn't have much choice as you can imagine.' He looked over her head at Sebastian. 'I'll be happy to look after everything if it means you two finally sorting things out.'

'OK,' Paige agreed. 'Give me five minutes.' She ran up to her room and hastily changed into her favourite jeans, a plain white T-shirt, and grey cashmere sweater. 'How smart do I have to be?' she shouted.

'Casual,' Seb answered. 'Now get a move on.'

Pulling the most comfortable boots she possessed on over her jeans, she grabbed her toothbrush, knowing she had other essentials in her handbag. Then pushing in a couple of pairs of pants, she zipped up her case and pulled on a quilted jacket and scarf. 'Ready,' she announced, picking up her Blackberry, weekend bag, and handbag, and running down the stairs to find them all still waiting for her in the hallway.

'You can leave that behind,' Sebastian said taking the Blackberry from her hand and passing it to Clem.'

'But what if there's an emergency?' She glanced at her sister.

Sebastian took her bags from her, opening the front door. 'Olly knows where to find us.'

'Where?' she whispered, as soon as Seb walked out of the house.

Olly shook his head. 'You'll have to wait and see. I've been sworn to secrecy.'

'He won't tell you, so don't bother interrogating him.' Sebastian smiled at her, and held the passenger door open. 'Now, come along.'

Paige watched Olly with his arms around Clem as they waved to her and Seb from the doorstep. 'Have a good time.'

Paige watched Sebastian in silence, wishing he'd say something as they drove down the narrow lanes. 'We're going to the north coast?'

'We are.' He smiled at her briefly.

'I still don't understand what's happening.'

He put one of his hands over hers. 'I've spent too many months chasing you, and listening to you telling me why a relationship between us would never work. This weekend I'm going to show you that all our differences are superficial, and that the ones we do have are unimportant.' He stopped at a yellow line and waited for a tractor to pass. 'I love you, and I want to spend my life with you. I just need to persuade you that we could enjoy an incredible future together, if only you'd give our relationship a chance.'

Paige couldn't help smiling. 'OK.'

'We fit together. There's nothing we can't work through.' He didn't say anything further, but marvelled at the dramatic coastline so different from the gentle slopes down to the golden sandy beaches on the south and east of the island. 'Nearly there.' He indicated, slowing down before an entrance to a long dirt track.

Chapter Thirty-nine

'I'm not camping, if that's what you think,' Paige said.

Sebastian laughed. 'Do you seriously think I'd expect you to?'

Paige shook her head and smiled. 'No, but I never really know what you're going to do.'

Sebastian realised that what she'd just said was part of their problem. She didn't know what he was thinking, or his reasons for doing some of the things he'd done in the past, and now was the time to show her that whatever his choices, she could trust him. He shook his head. 'No, this is far more comfortable than a tent.' He heard her gasp when they reached the end of the track.

'It's a fort.'

Sebastian enjoyed her surprise. At least she hadn't insisted he turn the car round and immediately take her back home. He was hoping for as little argument from her as possible during this weekend. He didn't answer her, but turned off the ignition and watched Paige step out of the car, and walk over to the circular building. She placed her hands against the pink granite of the wall, and leant against it with a look of, what was it, he wondered, exhilaration? He hoped so.

'It's incredible,' she shouted, staring across the headland to the waves crashing against the rugged cliffs nearby. 'I can't believe we're staying in here.'

'It is a little dramatic, but I thought it suited our relationship perfectly.' Paige laughed. He took her case and his own small leather weekend bag to the front door, and unlocked it. 'It's very organized, though don't expect to find a television here, there's no reception,' he said, waiting for her to pass him. Taking their cases through, he put them into one of the bedrooms and then followed her into the airy circular living room where she was surprised to discover a comfortable lounge suite and small dining table and chairs taking up one half of the room with a well-equipped kitchen area over on the other side.

Paige looked up at the vaulted ceiling. 'It's so isolated. I love it.'

'Good. I hoped you would.' He took her hand and led her to some steps. 'Up here is a walled-in garden. It's pretty sheltered from the wind, which is a good thing on this headland.' He pointed to the side of the small peninsular. 'Down there is a bay where we could swim, if you really wanted to.'

'Maybe next summer,' Paige laughed. 'I don't fancy the thought of getting hypothermia just now.'

He stood behind her and wrapped his arms around her, holding her close to him. The wind howled around the fort. Paige snuggled back into him.

'Is that Guernsey over there?'

Seb held her tightly. 'You should be telling me,' he smiled.

'I can never remember which order they're in.'

'The smaller one is Sark. That's Guernsey, and France is over there.'

Paige tilted her head to the side, resting it against his chest. Seb kissed her cheek, and then turning her to face him, he found her lips. As Paige put her arms around his neck he knew he'd made the right decision, bringing her here. 'You're cold,' he said, moving back. He took her hand in his. 'Time to go back inside, I think.'

'It's a remarkable place. Is it yours?'

Seb laughed. 'No, it's owned by Jersey Heritage. They hire this and various other historical places out to the public at certain times. I was tempted by a Martello tower at Archirondel, but thought this was further away from civilisation.'

He watched her walk into the kitchen and open the fridge, and then several of the cupboards. 'It's very well stocked. I'm assuming that's down to you.'

Seb took two glasses out of the cupboard and poured them both a whiskey. 'Shall we?'

She sat down on one of the seats in front of the long picture windows in the living area.

Sebastian sat opposite her, and sighed. 'Peace at last.'

Paige smiled and took a sip of her drink. 'You were determined to get me here, weren't you?'

Sebastian nodded. 'I would have found some way to make sure you came here this weekend.' He thought back to Olly, and how his admission had made things so much easier for Seb to put his weekend plans into action. 'Olly is a very loyal friend to you.'

'I know. He's helped me with the business, and he's always there when I need someone.'

Olly had been taking a chance when he told Seb what he'd seen on his PA's computer, and Seb knew that the man had been surprised and relieved at his unexpected reaction. He smiled. Poor Olly, he'd been only too happy to help Seb persuade Paige to come away with him this weekend. 'He seems very happy with Clem and the idea of his impending fatherhood,' he said.

'I'm so happy they're sorting everything out between them. They're so well-suited.' She narrowed her eyes. 'I hope you didn't make him suffer too much when he told you about his discovery.'

Seb pulled a face. 'Not too much.'

'He must have caught you at a good time.' Paige teased.

'His timing was perfect,' Seb agreed. 'He told me about Lucinda's friends coming into the shop and talking nonsense about a fictional wedding. He didn't think you took too much notice, is that true?'

'It is. I've finally woken up to her antics. I realize that when you said to trust you, you meant it.'

He smiled 'Good.' Seb leant forward in his chair. 'And the lease on the shop? You're not too angry about my deception, I hope?'

Paige thought for a moment. He wasn't sure how she really felt about this recent discovery. She suspected she should be affronted, but had to admit he'd done it for all the right reasons. 'I was stunned,' she said eventually. 'But I know you did it because you wanted to help me.'

Finally, thought Seb. 'Your designs deserve to be shown off to their best advantage and you need your space to display your products to everyone. You're a very talented designer.'

'Thank you, but why weren't you honest with me about the lease?'

Sebastian raised his eyebrows and smiled at her. 'Do you really have to ask that question?'

'Yes.' Paige crossed her legs. He could feel her preparing to raise her defences against him.

'Seriously?'

She nodded and he wondered if she was teasing him.

'I suggested we become partners months ago,' he said, not wishing to take any chances and leaving any questions she may have unanswered. 'You also knocked back the idea of me investing in your company, don't forget.'

Paige chewed her lower lip. 'True.'

'I knew you wouldn't accept anything from me that you considered help and so I didn't feel I had any option but to do it the way I did.'

He watched her consider his words carefully and then shrug. 'You're right. There was no other way.' She smiled at him and he couldn't help returning the gesture. 'You know me pretty well, don't you, Sebastian Fielding.'

'I think I have an idea how your mind works, but I can't say I know you well. That's a pleasure I'm still hoping to experience.' He watched her sipping her drink thoughtfully. 'I'm relieved that you finally feel you can trust me. You're also aware about the shop now and my part as owner of the building. What else?' He sat back waiting for her to speak.

'The difference in our lifestyles?'

'Ah yes, those. What are they again?'

Paige scowled at him. 'You're laughing at me.'

Sebastian shook his head and leant forward taking her hand in his. 'I'm not. Tell me what it is you think we can't overcome, because I can't see any reason why we shouldn't be together. Unless, that is, you don't want us to be?'

Paige frowned and stood up. 'Of course I do.'

He could see she was a little distressed, but if he wanted to sort this matter out then he was going to have to deal with every aspect of her concern about their relationship.

She put her glass down on the table and walked over to the middle window in silence.

'So?' Sebastian remained seated, folding his arms to stop him from reaching out and taking hold of her.

'Everyone you've ever socialised with has come from the same or similar background to you. You've all travelled extensively, you're successful,' she turned to face him. 'The women are calculating and relentless in the fight to get the man they want, even if they don't want him for the right reasons.'

Sebastian raised his eyebrows. 'These things don't matter to us.'

'Maybe not, but my father is suspicious of you. None of my friends would dream of making up stories about someone getting married, simply to warn a woman off the man their friend was interested in.'

'I'm glad you saw through that façade.'

Paige nodded. 'I did.'

'You see?' Sebastian stood up and walked over to her.

'What?'

'We can get past these incidents. The Lucindas of this world won't even register on your radar, once you understand what they're up to, and you've already worked that out. Your father will realise I'm not Jeremy, and will eventually like me,' he laughed. 'I'll make it my mission to ensure that he does. My sister can be a little bit of a drama queen, but having met Clem, I think they're not dissimilar.'

He could see Paige was mulling over his words. She wasn't immediately arguing, which was a first. He began to feel a little more confident that this weekend might not be the battleground he'd expected. 'I've let it be known that should you, or your family, be dragged into any future articles the papers print about me, I'll sue.'

'You think that will work?'

'Hopefully, and Mrs Hutton has agreed to move in over here for part of the year. I've already brought Harley back to Jersey.'

Paige stared wide-eyed at him. 'What about photographers?'

'That's the reason for me selling up in London. Although my move was helped by the fact that now I've inherited my uncle's business and properties, I can only spend up to ninety days in England. There are two entrances at my house here, as well as far more interesting people than me living in Jersey, so I doubt the paparazzi will bother coming to the island to hound me. If they did, we'd soon lose them down these narrow lanes.'

Paige laughed.

'The gardens are totally private, as is the house, so we wouldn't have to worry about any intrusion.'

'What do you mean, "we"?'

326

'I love you,' he said. 'I want you to marry me, and come and live in the mausoleum I call home. It's far too big for one.'

She narrowed her eyes. 'You're hardly alone.'

He shook his head keeping eye contact all the time. 'Stop finding excuses. Anyway, your cottage is going to be far too cramped with Olly, Clem, and their new baby. Do you really see those living arrangements working in your favour for very long?'

Paige laughed. 'No, I can't say that I do.'

A shard of golden light shot in through the window. Paige blinked and put her hand up to shield her eyes, and as she turned away she spotted a colourful painting on the wall. She stared at it, eyes narrowed as if trying to think where she had seen it before. She walked over to study it more closely. 'Don't you think this painting looks like one of Carlo's?' She gasped. 'It is one of his paintings.' She turned to Sebastian her mouth open in surprise.

He smiled at her, delighted she was so overjoyed to see it.

'It's the one I liked so much.' She glanced back at the painting.

Sebastian walked over to stand next to her. 'I thought you should have something from Capri.'

'It's mine?' she asked, after a brief silence.

Sebastian nodded. 'Come along, let's go outside.'

He grabbed a blanket from the back of the sofa, took her hand, and ran with her out of the door into the walled in garden.

Three rabbits bounced away on the outside of the wall before disappearing into the heather. 'It's glorious,' she said, squeezing his hand.

'Here.' He sat down on a large sunbed, pulling her in front of him and covered her body with the blanket. Paige sighed.

Sebastian couldn't help smiling. He put his arms round

327

her and drew her back into him.

Paige rested her arms on his and lay back against his chest. She murmured in agreement. 'Tell me more about us,' she said quietly, as they stared out across the darkening sky.

'We're stubborn, strong-willed, and determined,' he kissed her shoulder. 'We're business-minded and creative.'

'Mmm, don't forget we enjoy good food and drink,' she said quietly. 'What else?'

'We've both been jilted,' he teased, kissing her when she lifted her head and giggled. 'So we both have a lot to be grateful for.'

Paige laughed. 'We do. Anything else you can think of?'

He sensed she was enjoying lying with him as much as he did. He breathed in the faint smell of her perfume, and slowly the heat of her body warmed him as they lay there. 'We're extremely attracted to each other.'

'True,' she agreed.

'And I love you.'

She snuggled back into him. 'I love you, too,' she whispered.

Georgina Troy
The Jersey Scene

A Jersey Kiss
A Jersey Affair
A Jersey Bombshell
A Jersey Dreamboat

For more information about **Georgina Troy**

and other **Accent Press** titles

please visit

www.accentpress.co.uk

Lightning Source UK Ltd.
Milton Keynes UK
UKOW04f0051080815

256556UK00001B/3/P